Germany as Model and Monster

Germany as Model and Monster

Allusions in English Fiction, 1830s–1930s

GISELA ARGYLE

McGill-Queen's University Press
Montreal & Kingston · London · Ithaca

Legal deposit third quarter 2002
Bibliothèque nationale du Québec

Printed in Canada on acid-free paper that is 100%
ancient forest free (100% post-consumer recycled),
processed chlorine free, and printed with vegetable-
based, low VOC inks.

This book has been published with the help of a
grant from the Humanities and Social Sciences
Federation of Canada, using funds provided by the
Social Sciences and Humanities Research Council
of Canada.

McGill-Queen's University Press acknowledges the
financial support of the Government of Canada
through the Book Publishing Industry Development
Program (BPIDP) for its publishing activities. We also
acknowledge the support of the Canada Council for
the Arts for our publishing program.

**National Library of Canada Cataloguing in
Publication Data**

Argyle, Gisela
    Germany as model and monster: allusions in English
    fiction, 1830s–1930s
    Includes bibliographical references and index.
    ISBN 0-7735-2351-0
    1. English fiction – 19th century – History and
    criticism. 2. English fiction – 20th century – History
    and criticism. 3. Germany in literature. 4. English
    fiction – German influence. I. Title.
    PR868.G36A73 2002   823.009′3243   C2001-903668-x

This book was typeset by Dynagram Inc.
in 10/12 Palatino.

For Ferris and Malcolm

Contents

Acknowledgments

For constant intellectual companionship during the writing of this book, I thank Deborah Heller. Other major advisers and supporters of the project to whom I owe special gratitude are Ekbert Faas and Michael Millgate. The final revision was greatly helped by Lisa Wood's diligence and acuity. Hammond Dugan has been my "common reader" through the whole enterprise, and I thank him for his unstinting support and encouragement and especially for his questions. I am also grateful to the publisher's copy editor, Elizabeth Hulse, for her thorough work.

I am grateful to the staff of the Resource Sharing Department of York University's Scott Library for their ready and indispensable help with interlibrary loans. I am also indebted to the Göttingen University Library and the Bayrische Staatsbibliothek in Munich.

For institutional financial help, I thank the Faculty of Arts and the Division of Humanities of York University for research grants at several stages of the project.

Parts of this book have been published in earlier versions. A portion of chapter 2 appeared as "Carlyle's Travels with Goethe" in the *Victorian Studies Association Newsletter* (Ontario) 54 (fall 1994): 14–16; reprinted by permission of the editor. Portions of chapter 5 appeared as "The German Key to Life in *Middlemarch*" in *ARIEL* 7.3 (October 1976): 51–68; reprinted by permission of the University of Calgary, *ARIEL*. A passage from chapter 8 appeared as "Gissing's *Whirlpool* and Schopenhauer" in the *Gissing Newsletter* 17.4 (1981):

3–21; reprinted by permission of the editor. Portions of chapters 5 and 6 derive from my earlier study, *German Elements in the Fiction of George Eliot, Gissing, and Meredith* (Frankfurt: Peter Lang, 1979); the copyright is mine.

Denn daraus nur kann endlich die allgemeine Weltliteratur entspringen, dass die Nationen die Verhältnisse aller gegen alle kennen lernen, und so wird es nicht fehlen, dass jede in der andern etwas Annehmliches und etwas Widerwärtiges, etwas Nachahmenswertes und etwas zu Meidendes antreffen wird.

For universal world literature can only arise when the nations come to know the reciprocal relations of all with all; and then they will each be sure to encounter in the other something pleasing and something disgusting, something worth imitating and something to avoid.

Goethe

Introduction

To invoke two commonplaces framed in hyperbole: G.K. Chesterton suggested that one might well explain the English national soul to a Teuton by saying, "Well, you know Germany – England's the opposite," and Henry James imagined, as a response to the intellectual demands of George Eliot's novel *Daniel Deronda*, that one might "as soon read a German novel outright."[1] As Chesterton observed about his epigram, though fallacious, these judgments are not wholly false; they represent a common habit of English self-definition through contrast with Germany.

The German allusions that this study examines deal with aspects of the two areas introduced in the quotations above, namely, English life as represented by fictional characters and the genre of the novel as practised in England. At their most interesting, the novelists under examination use German allusions as authorization for a critique of both. In doing so, they go beyond the humorous or farcical treatments of German differences, as, for instance, in Thackeray's portrait of the ducal town of Pumpernickel in *Vanity Fair*. Such treatments, whether seriously or ironically, indulge the reader's "Podsnappery" – the belief that "other countries [are] a mistake."[2]

Instead, the novelists in this study adopt a cosmopolitan vantage point from which to contemplate both the question of the good life and the art of fiction. For their fictional experiments with the good life, they allude to examples of German social, cultural, and political life for standards of comparison, either for emulation or as deterrent. The majority of the authors combine their "criticism of life" with an

THE WATER CURE.

experimentation in novel-writing modelled on German practices. These authors expand, in Henry James's words about *Daniel Deronda*, "what one may do in a novel"[3] and, because of the persuasive power of fiction, also what one may do in life. By enlisting the reader's knowingness, the allusions create a sense of exclusive, right thinking, of group identity, which aids their transformative effect.

To stress the strategic, heuristic quality of such German allusions, it is important to note that the principal German figures whom the English novelists recruited as authorities for their criticism of domestic conventions in life and literature – Goethe, Heine, Schopenhauer, and Nietzsche – were themselves avowed cosmopolitans, *Weltbürger* (citizens of the world), aiming at a *Weltliteratur*, in Goethe's terms, and outspoken critics of German life and letters, as well as admirers of aspects of England. Also, to focus here on the German context of comparison is not to to diminish other foreign standards invoked by the authors, such as French, Italian, and Russian, as well as standards of

" SCHLAFEN SIE WOHL."

the English past. Moreover, for nineteenth-century fiction the reverse direction, from England to Germany, was generally more prominent with respect to both popularity and influence.[4]

I use the term "German" here to mean belonging to the German-speaking community, in conformity with the loose usage contemporary with the novels and with modern scholarly practice in comparative studies.[5] Similarly, English usage of the terms "English" and "British" was slippery and variable in this period. More importantly, the use of "nation" and "race" was equally loose, comparisons of the German and English cultural communities being frequently defined as "racial," as between the Teuton and the Saxon, akin to Matthew Arnold's comparison of Celt and Saxon in "On the Study of Celtic Literature" (1866) and to Kingsley's essay on *The Roman and the Teuton* (1864).[6]

The period that is fruitful for this inquiry starts with Thomas Carlyle's "Germanizing" efforts in the 1830s and ends before Hitler's Third Reich and the Holocaust, the latter being unique events that seem to preclude comparisons. Sir Leslie Stephen quips in his essay "The Importation of German," "It is a familiar fact that no Englishman read German literature in the eighteenth century."[7] He then qualifies this commonplace with a fair account of the slow revitalization, in the later part of that century, of German literature and its emancipation from French models, aided by its enthusiasm for English literature, especially Shakespeare's plays and eighteenth-century novels. There followed a first wave of English translation and adaptation of sensationalist and sentimental German works, particularly of the Sturm und Drang (Storm and Stress) movement, notably influential for Walter Scott's historical novels and for Mary Shelley's *Frankenstein* and satirized in several of Jane Austen's novels. But Coleridge's preaching of German idealist metaphysics and aesthetics remained largely unappreciated. Stephen concludes his survey with the appearance of Carlyle. Throughout the period under consideration here, as in the late eighteenth century, the literary traffic was generally heavier in the direction from England to Germany, Richardson, Scott, Dickens, and Thackeray being the most popular both for reading and for imitating and their success equalled only by Goethe's *Werther* and the novellas of E.T.A. Hoffmann in Germany.[8] And anglophilia, or even anglomania, was more widespread than any German influence.[9]

Carlyle set himself the task of remedying the false start of German "imports," the "false change and tawdry ware,"[10] while acknowledging Mme de Staël's pioneering work *De l'Allemagne* (1810–13) as a sympathetic guide to contemporary German literature and philosophy.[11] By 1856 George Eliot could plausibly write in a periodical article: "[Germany] has fought the hardest fight for freedom of thought, has produced the grandest inventions, has made magnificent contributions to science, has given us some of the divinest poetry, and quite the divinest music, in the world."[12]

Over the period of my study, both countries experienced immense social and political changes which in turn effected changes in their relations with each other (see chap. 9 below). For the background, Paul Kennedy's *The Rise of the Anglo-German Antagonism, 1860–1914* (1980) and Norbert Elias's *The Civilizing Process* (1939; trans. 1994) are particularly informative. Roughly speaking, England over this period changed its preoccupations from the domestic problems associated with growing industrialization and the democratizing after-effects of the French Revolution to its international role as a major imperial power. In contrast, Germany started off impoverished and ruralized after decades of war. It consisted of numerous petty feudal principalities, such as Goethe's Duchy of Sachsen-Weimar-Eisenach, portrayed either sympathetically or scornfully by such foreign visitors as Mme de Staël and H.C. Robinson, on the one hand, and Henry Mayhew, on the other.[13] It was transformed first into the industrialized and militarist Kaiserreich and then into the defeated, unstable state of the Weimar Republic. These developments caused changes in the dominant English political attitude from condescension to rivalry to ambivalent support. Political attitudes affected the representation and the reception of both political and non-political German allusions. Benedict Anderson's definition of the new, nineteenth-century nations as artifacts created as "imagined political communities"[14] can be extended to the delimiting "other" nation in order to explain the changing and complex English iconography of Germany.

English theorizing about the novel in terms of both the English tradition and European alternatives such as the *Bildungsroman* and the *Tendenzroman*, or *roman à thèse*, also started and grew in this period. Richard Stang's study *The Theory of the Novel in England, 1850–1870* (1959) and Kenneth Graham's *English Criticism of the Novel, 1865–1900* (1965) are useful surveys. In the latter part of the period the patriotic demand for a "literature for England" arose,[15] a fact that gives special prominence to the enterprise of the authors in this study.

It is partly as a result of the historical Anglo-German antagonism that work in this area is still to be done. Michael Hamburger, a principal translator and critic of German literature, in 1965 deplored the provincial state of affairs concerning the publication and reception in England of critical studies of German literature.[16] Since then there has been some catching up, for instance, through Rosemary Ashton's work, which is also free from the frequent compulsion to read various past German ideas and works uniformly as trends towards Nazism, as in Ronald Gray's *The German Tradition in Literature, 1871–1945* (1965). Although the present study contributes to inquiries about literary influence and about constructions of national character and mentality,[17] it focuses on selected major topics of German allusion that function in the community of author and reader as criticism of English culture, which in many of the novels is combined with genre criticism. Given this interest, I do not survey every important German figure and issue of the period, nor do I generally discuss the reverse reception of the English novels in Germany.

The cultural, social, and political frames of reference that I examine relate to the fifth "cultural" code that Roland Barthes defined for the "readerly text."[18] I am using the term "allusion" in this study as best suited to my focus on the function of the references as criticism of English culture that the authors direct readers to read competently and, ideally, to act on. In the "Cold War" between the parties of "allusion" and "intertextuality," I side with critics who prefer "allusion" for its sense of authorial intention and "allusive interpretability"[19] to "intertextuality," with its ideological baggage since its inception with Julia Kristeva and the Tel Quel group. In classical literary studies, the term "allusion" has been emancipated from traditional positivistic *Quellenforschung* (the study of sources and influence) and approximated to intertextuality as understood in Gérard Genette's sense of "transtextuality." Genette stresses the "socialized," "openly contractual" relationship between a text and its readers, "pertaining to a conscious and organized pragmatics."[20]

As examples closer to my subject, Allan Pasco, in his study of allusion in French literary works, *Allusion: A Literary Graft* (1994), "[insists] upon function" and on the reader's role in allusion: "allusion *must* be perceived" by the reader. It is "the metaphorical relationship created [by the reader] when an alluding text evokes and uses another, independent text."[21] He uses the term "text" to include, as I do, non-verbal facts such as historical events and persons. Michael Wheeler, in *The Art of Allusion in Victorian Fiction* (1979), attends to the "temporal moment" of a work's publication.[22] Like my own, his concern is with "marked quotations, unmarked quotations, and references." However, unlike me, Wheeler limits himself to a "strictly literary" subject, namely, the relationship between Victorian novels and "earlier or contemporary literary works."[23] There happens to be no overlap between the subjects of his inquiry and mine, even when he examines the same novel. Lastly, R.D. McMaster, in *Thackeray's Cultural Frame of Reference: Allusion in* The Newcomes (1991), follows Wheeler, but limits himself to one novel and broadens the repertory of allusions. He considers *The Newcomes* exemplary in its allusive "saturation," the "range and density of allusion," from literature and history to politicians and pugilists. In accordance with the methodology of allusion studies referred to, he examines "the topical and popular cultural reference" of the novel in order to "speculate on the cultural and affective relationship the text bore to its readership, and to discern something like a map of Thackeray's consciousness."[24]

The methodology of allusion, as presented here, fits well with my general approach, which is based on Hans Robert Jauss's reception theory. In his seminal essay "Literary History as a Challenge to Literary Theory" (1970), Jauss makes it the literary historian and critic's task to reconstruct the "triangle of author, work, and public" in terms of the reader's literary and non-literary "horizons of expectations." He stresses the "socially *formative* function of literature," in that, through the juxtaposition of the horizon of expectations of literature with the horizon of expectations of "historical lived praxis," the "experience of reading can liberate one from adaptations, prejudices, and predicaments of a lived praxis." In conjunction with this synchronic concern, Jauss proposes a diachronic one. An aesthetics of reception demands that the reader insert the work under consideration into a "literary series": "the next work can solve formal and moral problems left behind by the last work, and present new problems in turn."

Since authors are readers of their own work in the writing of it, such a series implies a "dialogical and at once process-like relationship" between work, audience/author, and new work.[25]

To establish the status of the allusions in the public conversation, I move, as each case makes advisable, between literary and extra-literary contexts contemporary with the novel under examination. These include biographical material about the authors as their own first readers, contemporary literary works, periodical articles, and other documentation that indicates the understanding which the authors could assume in their readers. I also discuss the fidelity of the English transmission of the German originals since it can indicate the rhetorical use to which they are put.

Several major Victorian periodicals added to English familiarity with German matters, previously derived from personal travel and educational stays and from reading in the original or in translation. In 1848 the *Westminster Review* was renamed the *Westminster and Foreign Quarterly Review*. Its title page carried two epigraphs, one from Shakespeare and the other from Goethe. Half of the publications reviewed were Continental, mostly German and French. The same distribution was true of the *Fortnightly Review* and the *Pall Mall Gazette*. A different type of source was German residents in Britain, from early times a sizable immigrant group, especially in London, where in 1911 they numbered a quarter-million.[26] Of particular interest for this study are two events: Prince Albert's invitation to and patronage of German experts in many fields – according to one contemporary, "[t]he marriage of Queen Victoria gave a fresh impetus to the Germanisation of Britain";[27] and the exile of German radicals after 1848, notably Karl Marx, who, with others, was provided with a forum for his revolutionary arguments by liberal journals, such as G.H. Lewes's *Leader*.

The focus of this study results in a selection of novelists and works which is not altogether canonical and which is uneven in terms of literary criteria.[28] Some authors, such as Edward Bulwer-Lytton and Mrs Humphry Ward, appear because in their day their novels were influential, being both popular successes and read as serious literature. Other authors, such as James Anthony Froude and Mark Rutherford, are included to indicate the range of a topic – in this case, the higher criticism.

While conceived as a cumulative exploration in terms of a Jaussian literary series, my study can also be read as a group of self-contained essays. My main subjects are the following topics, authors, and novels. In chapter 1 I outline the ideal of *Bildung* (self-culture) in its late-eighteenth-century conception by Herder, Schiller, and Wilhelm von Humboldt and in its representation by Goethe in his fiction of *Wilhelm Meister* (1795–96, 1829). Goethe's novel was not only foremost in spreading the concept of *Bildung* but also in modelling the genre of the *Bildungsroman* (apprenticeship novel). The Victorian sages Thomas Carlyle, J.S. Mill, and Matthew Arnold imported the concept of *Bildung* as an antidote to the ills they diagnosed, each somewhat differently, in English society. The genre of the *Bildungsroman* was introduced through Carlyle's criticism and translation of *Wilhelm Meister* and through his own *Sartor Resartus*. I conclude the chapter with a review of German theorizing about the genre and current critical debate on it.

The next three chapters deal with three novelists who each adapted the model of the *Bildungsroman* to his particular diagnosis of English life. Chapter 2 attends in detail to Carlyle's interpretation and adaptation of Goethe's model. The most important changes are Carlyle's omission from *Bildung* of the beautiful as principle and experience and his substitution in his *Bildungsroman* of moral didacticism for Goethe's ambiguity, or Romantic irony. Chapter 3 discusses Edward Bulwer-Lytton as a neglected but important theorizer and popularizer of the *Bildungsroman*, with close reference to *Ernest Maltravers* and *Alice*. In contrast with Carlyle, he integrated Byronism with Goethean *Bildung*. He also modified Goethe's type of realism with an idealism he associated with Schiller. Bulwer's most influential contribution was the *Bildungs* plot in three phases: the protagonist's rebellion, his quest, and his ultimate revaluation of his original point of departure. Chapter 4 examines George Meredith's novels *The Ordeal of Richard Feverel* and *The Adventures of Harry Richmond*. Meredith invokes the German model in order to expose misguided education, with false ideals and by egotistic mentors, as well as to recommend his own fiction, full of "brainstuff," to his English readers.

Chapters 5 and 6 treat George Eliot's *Middlemarch* and *Daniel Deronda*. In *Middlemarch* she evaluates the English social milieu and the chances it permits of an ideal vocation and a true "key to life," or *Lebensanschauung*, against a cosmopolitan, particularly German, background comprised of Goethe, Heine, and German scholarship and science. In *Daniel Deronda* she broadens the inquiry from the provincial milieu to the national and deepens it by interrelating the main themes – gambling, music, the historic organic community, and Judaism – all of which function in German contexts. The figure of Heine stands for a combination of anti-philistinism, music, and Judaism contrasted to degenerate English society.

The last three chapters each deal with several authors whose novels exhibit a typical and interesting range of responses to successive

German phenomena. Chapter 7 examines the role of the Tübingen higher criticism in novels of deconversion, mainly by Mrs Humphry Ward, Anthony Froude, Mark Rutherford, and George Gissing, while chapter 8 treats allusions to Schopenhauer and Nietzsche, usually both, in novels principally by Gissing, E.M. Forster, Joseph Conrad, and D.H. Lawrence. Chapter 9 discusses allusions to the imperialism of the new German Reich, or "Potsdam Germany," and to the radical aesthetics and morality of the Weimar Republic, or "second Weimar Germany"; the first in novels by Benjamin Disraeli, Meredith, Gissing, Conrad, and Forster, the second in novels by Ford Madox Ford, Lawrence, and Christopher Isherwood. In the conclusion I reflect on the prevalent allusions to Nazism and the Holocaust in English post–World War II fiction, anomalous events that preclude the traditional criticism of English life by means of comparison with a kindred Germany. I also relate the general obsolescence, in contemporary English fiction, of German allusions for the sake of cultural criticism to changed, global conceptions of Englishness and of national literatures.

1 *Bildung* and the *Bildungsroman*

Within the tradition of the English novel as "baggy monster," there are novels that ask more or less explicitly to be read as belonging to or participating in the more definite German sub-genre of the *Bildungsroman*, or as it is often anglicized, the apprenticeship novel.[1] Critics of this sub-genre usually differentiate between more or less pure examples, with the result that among English novels only minor ones are judged to come close to the German model. Although the concept of the *Bildungsroman* has proved useful to many critics in English, questions about its fit continue to arise, such as the following. Is every personal development equivalent to the idea of *Bildung*? Was there a Victorian goal of *Bildung*, implied in the idea of apprenticeship, as existed in Weimar classicism? Is the sub-genre merely marginal in English literature? For instance, Jerome Buckley, in *Season of Youth: The Bildungsroman from Dickens to Golding* (1974), defines the *Bildungsroman* in its pure form as a novel of self-culture, consciously sought by the hero, and he then goes on to establish his own criteria for the novels of his choice, none of which qualify as examples of the pure form, but rather, belong to what in German criticism is the more general category of the *Entwicklungsroman* (novel of development).[2] It seems useful to reconsider the characteristics of the original model, "that cultural hitch-hiker," in J.D. Enright's phrase, and its reception in Britain.[3]

The main British mediator of the *Bildungsroman* for both the novelists and their readers was Thomas Carlyle, first, through his translations of Goethe's novel *Wilhelm Meisters Lehrjahre* (1795–96) as

Wilhelm Meister's Apprenticeship (1824) and its sequel, *Wilhelm Meisters Wanderjahre* (in the first, incomplete version of 1821) as *Wilhelm Meister's Travels* (1827); and secondly, through his own novel, *Sartor Resartus* (1833–34), "the handbook of the Victorian *Bildungsroman*."[4] Before examining Carlyle's translations of *Wilhelm Meister* and his *Sartor Resartus*, I shall review the main criteria of the German concepts of *Bildung* and the *Bildungsroman* and the British reception of the idea of *Bildung*.

In Wilhelm Meister, apprentice to life, Goethe added to the responsiveness and reflectiveness of the Wertherian sensitive soul a conscious striving for self-development accompanied by a quest for a suitable vocation and role in the community. In direct contrast to *Die Leiden des jungen Werther* (*The Sufferings of Young Werther* [1774, rev. 1786]), both quests are successful, although experienced by the protagonist with continued ambivalence and presented with sustained authorial irony.[5] The action is set in an unspecified period not long before the French Revolution, when the feudal order is losing legitimacy, and art, or culture, has replaced religion as a source of ideals.[6] A merchant's son, Wilhelm begins by seeing his quest as the choice between commerce and art, in particular the theatre. He associates with what Goethe planned as a spectrum of social milieux, from travelling acrobats to landed nobility; vocational ideals, from the theatre to the secret Society of the Tower's guardianship; personality types, from the skeptical and practical Jarno to the passionately imaginative Mignon; and *Weltanschauungen*, from the "beautiful soul's" pietism to the Society of the Tower's Enlightenment philosophy. Through these encounters, Wilhelm explores what he truly is and how he can serve the community. After many errors and regrets, which in Goethe's conception of *Bildung* are necessary stages, he ends, in the *Lehrjahre*, by receiving his patent of completed apprenticeship from his mentors, the Society of the Tower.[7]

Wilhelm Meisters Lehrjahre employs features of the picaresque novel and romance to portray the *bildbare* (educable) hero in reciprocity with the *bildende* (educating) world. Its sequel, *Wilhelm Meisters Wanderjahre, oder Die Entsagenden* (1821, 1829), is primarily a wisdom book, but from the perspective of an artist rather than a philosopher. Indirectly, through interpolated novellas, it completes Wilhelm's quest for his social place in the framing story and the exploration of the self in private relations. Alluding to topical post-revolutionary socio-economic and pedagogic projects, Goethe makes Wilhelm, now a certified "journeyman" in the enlightened ethos of the Society of the Tower, its emissary in the recruitment for colonial communities in America and Europe.

Goethe's characteristic irony in the presentation of his hero, the "armer Hund" (poor dog), and his equally elusive and understated responses to questions about "the idea" of the *Lehrjahre* contributed to an often baffled or dismissive reception by his contemporaries. Not expecting popularity, he was addressing the work to the initiated, that is, to the reader who pursued his own *Bildung* in the process of creating meaning from the story.[8] All the problems that would puzzle readers and Goethe's rationale for them, as well as Friedrich Schiller's congenial interpretation and enthusiastic praise of the whole, are found in the correspondence between Goethe and Schiller, which accompanied and influenced the work-in-progress.

Another major theoretician of the *Bildungs* ideal, Wilhelm von Humboldt, also praised the book. So did the Romantic authors Christian Gottfried Körner, Jean Paul (Johann Paul Friedrich Richter), and Friedrich Schlegel in extensive reviews. Schlegel defended Goethe's inclusion of low society with reference to Henry Fielding, among other European authors. He famously called the *Lehrjahre*, together with the French Revolution and Fichte's *Wissenschaftslehre*, "die grössten Tendenzen des Zeitalters [the greatest tendencies of the age]." Novalis (Friedrich von Hardenberg), probably anxious about Goethe's influence on his own *Heinrich von Ofterdingen* (posthumous, 1802) changed from praise for the novel's Romantic irony, which, in recognition of the human condition between the finite and the infinite, gives equal weight to the common and the important, to condemnation of the book as "so prätentiös und preziös ... ein 'Candide,' gegen die Poesie gerichtet [so pretentious and precious ... a 'Candide,' directed against poetry]."[9] Only Novalis's negative views were published at the time by his posthumous editors, Ludwig Tieck and Schlegel. The sequel to the *Lehrjahre, Wilhelm Meisters Wanderjahre*, was received coolly in both versions, even by Goethe's friends. A notable positive review, which particularly praised the treatment of social themes, came from Varnhagen von Ense, who would later become the principal source of information on Goethe for G.H. Lewes and George Eliot.

In England both the *Lehrjahre* and the *Wanderjahre* were reviewed in the *Monthly Review* soon after their respective German publications, but then largely neglected until their translation and promotion by Carlyle. The Goethe-Schiller correspondence, with its discussion of the *Lehrjahre* in progress, was reviewed both in the original (1813) and in the English translation (1845).[10] Mme de Staël's influential book of advocacy, *De l'Allemagne* (1813, trans. 1814), which was first published in England, recommended *Wilhelm Meister* as foremost a record of Goethe's philosophy, from which the romance merely distracted, especially since its effect was diminished by the detached authorial tone unhappily derived from Romantic aesthetics, that is, Romantic irony. However, like many other readers, de Staël was fascinated by Mignon, the emblem of Romantic yearning.

Coleridge wrote his own quasi-*Bildungsroman* in *Biographia Literaria* (1817), which also departed from English tradition by attempting to derive, in the German manner, principles of literary criticism from philosophical speculation. His opinions on Goethe were disseminated indirectly, mostly through his conversations. He counted Goethe among the three great modern dramatists, with Shakespeare and Lope de Vega, and had plans to translate *Faust*. On receiving Carlyle's gift of his translation of the *Lehrjahre*, Coleridge said he liked the novel "the best of Goethe's prose works." He himself translated the first stanza of Mignon's famous song "Kennst du das Land" and apparently modelled the title of his *Confessions of an Inquiring Spirit* on Goethe's "Bekenntnisse einer schönen Seele," having corrected Carlyle's translation, "Confessions of a Fair Saint." Coleridge compared Goethe with Wordsworth in that, despite general dissimilarity, "[t]hey are always both ab extra – feeling *for* but never *with* their characters." Schiller, he found, was "a thousand times more hearty than Goethe."[11]

Wordsworth was hostile to German literature in general and Goethe in particular: he found the "profligacy" and "inhuman sensuality" in Goethe's works, which he admittedly did not know intimately, "utterly revolting" and indicted him for "wantonly outraging the sympathies of humanity" in *Wilhelm Meister*, of which he apparently read no further than book 1.[12] So he did not acknowledge a German aesthetic context for the *Prelude*, "the history of a Poet's mind," arguably a typical Romantic *Bildungsgeschichte* (story of *Bildung*) and linked in its origins with the recent publication in Germany of examples of the *Bildungsroman* and the *Künstlerroman* (artist novel), "two portentous innovations in prose fiction," according to M.H. Abrams.[13] Nor did he, like Carlyle, direct his reader to receive his exemplary story of the growth, crisis, and salvation of his mind in the light of a German remedy for English ills.

As in Germany, but in England outraging a more established public taste, as well as being grouped with the earlier "Jacobin" Sturm und Drang imports, the *Lehrjahre* was frequently denounced as frivolous and immoral, most notoriously by Thomas De Quincey, who in his review of Carlyle's translation called the novel "revolting to English good taste."[14] The main early champions of the novel as truly moral were Carlyle, Lewes, and George Eliot, although they differed in the completeness of and the reasons for their approval, as we shall see. All three also demonstrated their admiration by writing *Bildungsromane* of their own.

The ideal of *Bildung* was generally familiar to the German educated public by the time of Goethe's *Wilhelm Meisters Lehrjahre*; the term itself had appeared in a number of book titles at the time.[15] The roots of the word in its figurative meaning are in medieval mysticism: Christians were to *form* God's image *in* themselves in a process of correction – *sich Gott einbilden*. For his general public influence as well as his particular influence on his younger friend Goethe, Herder was especially important in giving the term a secular meaning, substituting for spiritual salvation a reaching up to the highest possible humanity. For instance, in letter 27 of the *Briefe zur Beförderung der Humanität* (Letters for the promotion of humanity [1793–97]) Herder wrote, "Das *Göttliche* in unserm Geschlecht ist also *Bildung zur Humanität* (What is *divine* in our species is therefore the *cultivation of our humanity*]."[16] To the Enlightenment idea of the perfectibility of humankind is here joined the concept of individual development. Herder pursued the idea of the *humane Mensch* (humane individual), an ideal that derived from Christian virtues as well as classical Greek and Roman ones.[17] For Herder as for Lessing and Schiller, the ideal was the same for all humans, which is where Humboldt and, more emphatically, Goethe differed.[18]

Humboldt maintained that the means for the pursuit of personal *Humanität* was "die Verknüpfung unsres Ichs mit der Welt zu der allgemeinsten, regesten und freiesten Wechselwirkung [the connection of our self with the world for the most general, lively, and free interaction]." The individuality implied here is explicit in the lines quoted by J.S. Mill in the chapter "Of Individuality" in *On Liberty*: "The true aim of man – not the one prescribed by changing inclination but the one prescribed by unchanging reason – is the highest and best proportioned cultivation [*Bildung*] of his powers into a whole." These lines are followed in the original by the qualification that human beings must associate with others, "Denn auch durch alle Perioden des Lebens erreicht jeder Mensch dennoch nur Eine der Vollkommenheiten, welche gleichsam den Charakter des ganzen Menschengeschlechts bilden [For even through all periods of his life any man achieves only one of the perfections which form as it were the character of the whole human race]."[19]

Goethe's conception of *Bildung* shared with that of all his contemporary thinkers the secular context and the idea of ethical duty. In a letter to Johann Kaspar Lavater in September 1780, he described *Bildung* as a daily duty: "Diese Begierde, die Pyramide meines

Daseyns, deren Basis mir angegeben und gegründet ist, so hoch als möglich in die Lufft zu spizzen, überwiegt alles andre und lässt kaum Augenblickliches Vergessen zu [This desire to raise the pyramid of my existence, the base of which is given and founded for me, as high as possible into the air, outweighs everything else and hardly permits even momentary forgetfulness]." Goethe's dedication to this ideal in his own life, his account of it in his autobiography, *Dichtung und Wahrheit* (Fiction and truth [1811–33; trans. 1846, 1848]), which can be read as a quasi-*Bildungsroman*, and its presentation in other works, most notably in *Wilhelm Meisters Lehrjahre*, had the effect that "it is to him more than to any other of the German classics that the ideal of the pursuit of 'allgemeine Bildung' owes the strong hold it obtained over the educated class."[20]

Under Schiller's influence, Goethe came to include aesthetic experience and education as a necessary contribution to the ethical character of *Bildung*. Thus the collection of paintings owned by Wilhelm Meister's grandfather sets Wilhelm on the privileged path of *Bildung* in his childhood and confirms his direction in his later visit to the Society of the Tower's Hall of the Past.[21] During the period when Goethe and Schiller discussed the progress of *Wilhelm Meister*, Schiller wrote in the *Aesthetische Briefe*: [22] "Durch die ästhetische Kultur bleibt also der persönliche Wert eines Menschen oder seine Würde, insofern diese nur von ihm selbst abhängen kann, noch völlig unbestimmt, und es ist weiter nichts erreicht, als dass es ihm nunmehr *von Natur wegen* möglich gemacht ist, aus sich selbst zu machen, was er will – dass ihm die Freiheit, zu sein, was er sein soll, vollkommen zurückgegeben ist [Aesthetic culture, then, leaves the personal value of a man or his dignity, as far as this can only depend on himself, completely undefined, and nothing more is achieved than that he is now enabled *on account of nature* to make of himself what he will – that the freedom to be what he ought to be has been returned to him completely]." He summarizes: "Mit einem Wort: es gibt keinen andern Weg, den sinnlichen Menschen vernünftig zu machen, als dass man denselben zuvor ästhetisch macht (In one word: there is no other way of making sensual man rational than to make him first aesthetic)."[23] Schiller's poem "Das Ideal und das Leben" (The ideal and life) expresses the liberating effect of aesthetic contemplation – to the point of likeness with the gods: "Dann erblicket von der Schönheit Hügel / Freudig das erflog'ne Ziel [Then perceive joyfully from the hill of beauty the goal which you have reached through flight]."

With Humboldt in particular, Goethe shared the notions of individuality and action in association with other men and women. The one is more strongly presented in *Wilhelm Meisters Lehrjahre*, the other in

Wilhelm Meisters Wanderjahre. In the *Lehrjahre* Wilhelm pursues the most complete and harmonious development of what he thinks are his particular gifts: "mich selbst, ganz wie ich da bin, auszubilden, das war dunkel von Jugend auf mein Wunsch und meine Absicht ... Ich habe nun einmal gerade zu jener harmonischen Ausbildung meiner Natur, die mir meine Geburt versagt, eine unwiderstehliche Neigung [to cultivate myself, completely as I am has been my desire and my purpose since my childhood ... I happen to have an irresistible inclination towards that harmonious cultivation of my nature which my birth denies me]."[24] This aristocratic ideal, he writes to his philistine friend Werner, is the opposite of the specialization required of the burgher, whose role in society is to be useful.[25] The value of Wilhelm's pursuit, despite his errors about his vocation, is demonstrated in the comparison with Werner when they finally meet again and are surprised to find each other much changed. Werner remarks that his friend is "grösser, stärker, gerader, in seinem Wesen gebildeter und in seinem Betragen angenehmer [taller, stronger, straighter, more cultivated in his character, more agreeable in his manner]," whereas Werner himself – and here the narrator adds his authority to Wilhelm's observation – "schien eher zurück als vorwärts gegangen zu sein [seemed rather to have regressed than progressed]."[26] Goethe believed that in all forms of life there could only be either the one or the other movement.

The idea of individuality in *Bildung* is most pointedly expressed by the Abbé, the pedagogue of the Society of the Tower and one of Wilhelm's secret guardians, of whom Natalie reports to Wilhelm that, in his insistence that education can only follow inclination, he would maintain: "Ein Kind, ein junger Mensch, die auf ihrem eigenen Wege irregehen, sind mir lieber als manche, die auf fremdem Wege recht wandeln [I prefer a child, a young person who gets lost on his own path to some who walk correctly on an alien path]."[27] That the source's (Natalie's) own opinion and practice differ represents Goethe's typical dialectical presentation of the truth, which the readers themselves must produce.

The idea of association is presented in the *Wanderjahre* when Wilhelm, after achieving a greater measure of many-sided culture than his bourgeois background would have provided, joins a group of diversely gifted and cultivated individuals, who under the guidance of the Society of the Tower are going to colonize undeveloped regions in Europe and America. In the revised and expanded final version of 1829, Goethe clarified Wilhelm's particular usefulness: he has meanwhile trained to be a surgeon. Jarno, a member of the Society of the Tower, encourages Wilhelm to act on his vaguely felt wish for this vocation, as usual, "without sparing him" and arguing his case too one-sidedly, in response to the new machine age. "Narrenpossen ... sind eure allgemeine Bildung und alle Anstalten dazu. Dass ein Mensch etwas ganz entschieden verstehe, vorzüglich leiste ... darauf kommt es an, und besonders in unserem Verbande spricht es sich von selbst aus [Your general culture and all efforts towards it are mere folly. What matters is that a person understand something completely, execute it perfectly ... and especially in our association this goes without saying]." Wilhelm concludes the written report of this talk to his betrothed, Natalie, with the following assurance: "bei dem grossen Unternehmen, dem ihr entgegengeht, werd' ich als ein nützliches, als ein nötiges Glied der Gesellschaft erscheinen" [in the great enterprise which you all are approaching I shall appear as a useful, a necessary member of the society]."[28] However, the characteristically human many-sidedness, which for Humboldt was the highest good provided by society and which could only result as a sum of the association of several different individuals, was for Goethe in his own life a possible individual achievement, although only through interaction with the world. That his many-sidedness did not reach the totality of human potential – for instance, he found he could not master painting and musical performance – was cause for *Entsagung* (renunciation) and does not discredit the ideal.

Although in conflict with his stress on the ethical and historical dimensions of human development, for a metaphorical purpose, Goethe also elaborated the organic analogy that Herder and Humboldt associated with the idea of *Bildung* as personal culture. When he began reworking *Wilhelm Meisters Lehrjahre* in 1794, he did so partly in terms of the organic notion of entelechy, which he had formulated four years earlier in *Die Metamorphose der Pflanzen* (Metamorphosis of plants). In his characteristic unifying tendency, he transferred to the *Bildung* of humankind his observations and insights about the physical *Bildung* (both the shape and the dynamic process of taking shape) of a plant through regular and progressive phases to its climax, propagation (*regelmässig, fortschreitend, stufenweise, Ausbildung, gleichsam auf einer geistigen Leiter*).[29] In the poem of the same title, written for his future wife, Christiane, in 1798, he explained the "secret law," "the sacred riddle" of the thousand-folded mixture of flowers in their garden: "Werdend betrachte sie nun, wie nach und nach sich die Pflanze, / Stufenweise geführt, bildet zu Blüten und Frucht. [Growing observe the plant, how progressively, step by step, it transforms itself into flowers and fruit]." Together with the idea of individuality, even originality, this organic connotation gave a Romantic shift to the Enlightenment ideal of *Bildung*. The concept was enthusiastically adopted and promoted by the

German Romantics; however, its corruption, signifying mere intellectual acquisition as a marker of social rank, by 1860 produced the derogatory term *Bildungsphilister*, forerunner of Nietzsche's *Bildungskosak* and *Bildungskamel*. It is from this corrupt meaning, "a smattering of the two dead languages of Greek and Latin," that Arnold dissociated himself in *Culture and Anarchy*.

In "The Critic as Artist," Oscar Wilde paid the following tribute to Goethe: "self-culture is the true ideal of man. Goethe saw it, and the immediate debt that we owe to Goethe is greater than the debt we owe to any man since Greek days."[30] (However, Wilde here appropriated self-culture for his campaign against the British philistine, opposing the "fine intellectual virtues" of self-culture and the contemplative life to the "shallow and emotional virtues" of self-sacrifice and the active life, a dichotomy and evaluation that is alien to Goethe.) The word "self-culture" is first documented in the *Oxford English Dictionary* for 1829, when John Sterling, a disciple of Coleridge and friend of Carlyle, used it in a letter to his brother: "I have no doubt that, by practice and self-culture, [Fanny Kemble] will be a far finer actress."[31] The connection with the theatre points to *Wilhelm Meister*. In the sense of self-culture, Carlyle had used "culture" in the absolute in 1827, in an article on Jean Paul: "For the great law of culture is: Let each man become all that he was created capable of being; expand, if possible, to his full growth."[32]

In the introduction to his book *Culture and Society in Classical Weimar, 1775–1806*, W.H. Bruford explains three principal meanings in English of the word "culture," besides its scientific use: the process of the cultivation of an individual mind, the result of this process (both *Bildung* in German), and civilization, or group culture, (in German, *Kultur*). He comments that the "comparative poverty of our English vocabulary in these matters seems to indicate that an interest in the theory of culture developed later than in Germany." Bruford expresses his indebtedness to Raymond Williams's study of England, *Culture and Society, 1780–1950*, in which Williams focuses on five key words – "industry, democracy, class, art, and culture" – which first came into common use or acquired new and important meanings towards the end of the eighteenth century and in the first half of the nineteenth. He argues that, of these key words, the emergence of "culture" as an abstraction and an absolute indicates most comprehensively the changes in social, economic, and political life in this critical period, "[merging] two general responses – first, the recognition of the practical separation of certain moral and intellectual activities from the driven impetus of a new kind of society; second, the emphasis of these activities, as a court of human appeal, to be set over the processes of practical social judgment and yet to offer itself as a mitigating and rallying alternative."[33] Williams stresses that these were not only responses to industrialism but also to democracy.

Neither industrialism nor democracy was in the Germany of the period under consideration here the force that it was in Britain.[34] The colonizing project of the association that Wilhelm Meister joins in the *Wanderjahre* is partly a response to the new *Maschinenwesen* (machinery) and the resulting unemployment of spinners and weavers in the obsolescent cottage industry, but Goethe only introduced this issue in the final version of 1829 (which was not translated by Carlyle), more than thirty years after the initial German debate on *Bildung* sketched above. However, the ideal of *Bildung* was partly evoked against the perceived threat of the fragmentation of human nature into separate, specialized faculties brought about by new social and economic conditions.[35] Kant had argued in his essay "Beantwortung der Frage: Was ist Aufklärung?" (Answer to the question: What is enlightenment? [1784]) that laziness and cowardice kept a large portion of humanity under the tutelage of others, who set themselves up as its guardians. "Daher giebt es nur Wenige, denen es gelungen ist, durch eigene Bearbeitung ihres Geistes sich aus der Unmündigkeit heraus zu wickeln und dennoch einen sicheren Gang zu thun [Therefore there are only a few who have succeeded by their own exercise of their mind in developing themselves from immaturity and in walking steadily nevertheless]."[36] For men and women who were emancipating themselves from the traditional religious and social prescriptions but wanted to go beyond Enlightenment skepsis, the spirit of negation symbolized by Goethe's Mephisto, *Bildung* was to provide both a path and a goal for "walking steadily."

The British borrowers of the ideal of *Bildung*, most importantly the Victorian sages, Carlyle, J.S. Mill, and Matthew Arnold in particular, invoked it eclectically at some stage of their careers either as an antidote to the results of such emancipation – namely, materialism, skepticism, and democracy – or as compensation for an insufficient ideal, such as "right conduct" in Arnold's case. They all acknowledged their debt to Goethe and often also to Humboldt and other German humanists or "idealists." "For all interested onlookers, German writers composed, in the eighteenth century and under Napoleonic rule, a cultural commonwealth filled with promise for the power of mind and letters over present circumstances."[37] Or, in a hyperbolic declaration from Carlyle's *Sartor Resartus*: "Germany, learned, indefatigable, deep-thinking Germany comes to ... [the] aid" of England, which Teufelsdröckh calls "the wealthiest and worst-instructed of European nations."[38] In addition to the foreign models, there were, of course, native traditions and sources, some of which, such as Shaftesbury, had in fact been sources for the German concept of *Bildung*. Among prominent native tendencies at the time were the ethic of enthusiasm and the ethic of earnestness. Stefan Collini, in *Public Moralists*, refers to the same two dominant values in Victorian culture as "the cultivation of feelings" and "the primacy of morality," describing the first as an instrument of the second.[39] However, morality, epitomized in the ideal of "character," seemed to some social critics, notably Mill and Arnold, too narrow or "philistine"[40] a conception of human potential, especially when compared with the German notion of *Bildung*.

Carlyle, Mill, and Arnold belong to the first, artistic and intellectual phase of the German influence in Britain, in contrast to the second, institutionalized, professional phase.[41] A few examples will show the range of the indebtedness and adaptation. Mill, who had studied in Germany, introduced *On Liberty* (1859) with a passage from Humboldt's essay *Ideen zu einem Versuch, die Gränzen der Wirksamkeit des Staates zu bestimmen* (see above) as an epigraph: "The grand, leading principle, towards which every argument unfolded in these pages directly converges, is the absolute and essential importance of human development in its richest diversity."[42] In chapter 3, "Of Individuality, as One of the Elements of Well-Being," he quotes Humboldt's "doctrine" (quoted above) that man's true aim is "the highest and most harmonious development of his powers to a complete and consistent whole." He refers to this doctrine again in his *Autobiography* (1873) as "the leading thought" of his essay *On Liberty*. In the *Autobiography* he chronicles several periods and modes of "self-cultivation" (this is the first documented use of the term), including the cultivation of the feelings and the imagination neglected by his father and impressed on him especially by Wordsworth as well as German writers. During his mental crisis, "the maintenance of a due balance among the faculties ... seemed to [him] of primary importance," and "Goethe's device, 'many-sidedness,' was one which [he] would most willingly have taken for [his]."[43]

Defending culture and the particular need for it in Britain, where it had "a rough task to achieve," Arnold wrote in *Culture and Anarchy* (1869) that it "places human perfection in an *internal* condition, in the growth and predominance of our humanity proper, as distinguished from our animality. It places it in the ever-increasing efficacy and in the general harmonious expansion of those gifts of thought and feeling, which make the peculiar dignity, wealth, and happiness of human nature."[44] Such personal culture, he argued, must precede any social action for the latter to be truly good. Arnold's ideal here, of gifts of thought and feeling, is close to Herder's "humane individual," and rather narrower than Goethe's "many-sidedness." The modern source of culture for Arnold was poetry, particularly German poetry. For instance, he wrote in the essay "On the Study of Celtic Literature" (1866): "the grand business of modern poetry, – a moral interpretation, from an independent point of view, of man and the world, – it is only German poetry, Goethe's poetry, that has, since the Greeks, made much way with."[45]

For a testimony to the popularization of the ideal of self-culture, we can look at Samuel Smiles's *Self-Help* (1859), which contains a chapter entitled "Self-Culture: Facilities and Difficulties." In the introduction the author refers to culture as "that finishing instruction as members of society, which Schiller designated 'the education of the human race,' consisting in action, conduct, self-culture, self-control." In the chapter "Self-Culture" Smiles warns the budding entrepreneur not to degrade the ideal of self-culture "by regarding it too exclusively as a means of 'getting on,'" but to use it instead "as a power to elevate the character and expand the spiritual nature," character, more than culture, ability, or wealth, being the mark of the true gentleman.[46]

Regretting the lack in England of the German and French concept of the state as a source of authority, "the organ of right reason," Arnold observed in *Culture and Anarchy* that soon (actually seventeen years) after Humboldt had argued, in the essay referred to above on the limits of the state (1792),[47] for the restriction of state interference to matters of security only, for the sake of the freedom necessary for *Bildung*, he became minister of education in Prussia, as a result of the insight that "for his purpose itself, of enabling the individual to stand perfect on his own foundations and to do without the State, the action of the State would for long, long years be necessary."[48] Thus the institutions founded by Humboldt – Berlin University (1810) and the Prussian system of grammar schools, the classical *Gymnasium* – were inspired by the Weimar ideal of *Bildung* formed in close exchange between him, Goethe, Schiller, and Herder.

Another contributor, specifically to the *Bildungs* ideal of the scholar, was Johann Gottlieb Fichte. In his popular and influential lectures on *Wissenschaftslehre* (1794–95) at Jena, which was a magnet for students from all over Europe at the end of the eighteenth century, and, in an expanded version, at Erlangen, Fichte defined the scholar's vocation as "die *oberste Aufsicht über den wirklichen Fortgang des Menschengeschlechts im allgemeinen, und die stete Beförderung dieses Fortgangs* [the supreme supervision of the actual progress of the human race in general and the constant promotion of this progress]." The scholar's knowledge of the truth makes him the teacher (*Lehrer*) of humankind, while his prophetic knowledge of the necessary future steps in pursuit of human progress makes him the educator (*Erzieher*). For the students, the university is not to be "bloss eine Schule der Wissenschaften [merely a school of scientific knowledge]" but also "eine Schule des *Handelns* [a school of *action*]."[49]

Well before Arnold's three visits, as commissioner for English educational reform, to German and French schools and universities between 1865 and 1886,[50] several men, notably Henry Crabb Robinson and Thomas Campbell, who were familiar with and admired the new German universities, Berlin (1810) and Bonn (1818), proposed them as a model for the foundation in 1825 of University College London, which was to be a modern alternative to Oxford and Cambridge.[51] Many scholars on the new faculty at London, such as John Austin (law), George Grote (history), and F.A. Rosen (Oriental studies), had studied at German universities.[52] The guidelines laid down for Berlin University by Friedrich Schleiermacher, whom Humboldt had recommended for the university commission, stipulated the following: connection between disciplines to create organic unity, with philosophy at the centre; freedom of research and teaching from state and church; and the development (*Bildung*) of a harmonious personality. However, in his letter to the *Times* (9 February 1825) entitled "A Proposal of a Metropolitan University in a Letter to Henry Brougham," Campbell appealed to English middle-class sensibility by stressing, not ideal *Bildung*, but the practical education in the liberal arts and sciences "of a British merchant of superior grade."[53] In consequence of these factors, it is not surprising that the new institution was commonly called the "German University" or the "Godless University." Nevertheless, Carlyle's hope of an appointment in moral philosophy in 1827 was ill-founded, since he was seen as "a *sectary* in taste and literature," as Francis Jeffrey explained to him in order to disabuse him.[54]

If Goethe's *Wilhelm Meister* was the main medium for spreading the ideal of *Bildung* among Germans, Carlyle's articles on and translations from Goethe, as well as his own version of the *Bildungsroman*, *Sartor Resartus*, were the most influential in introducing the concept to England. In *The German Idea*, her study of the four British thinkers who "count ... as the most important introducers to the British public of the best examples of German thought" Coleridge, Carlyle, G.H. Lewes, and George Eliot – Rosemary Ashton writes: "Unlike Coleridge's, Carlyle's influence can be perceived directly, since so many of his readers described the effect on them of the most 'German' of English works, *Sartor Resartus* (1833–4). Hardly a young person survived the 1830s without being struck by *Sartor* and by it inspired to read – even if only in Carlyle's English translation – *Wilhelm Meister* in the light of Teufelsdröckh's praise of Goethe as the 'Wisest of our Time.'"[55] In this spirit Lewes dedicated his *Life and Works of Goethe* (1855) to "Thomas Carlyle, who first taught England to appreciate Goethe."

Goethe's titles, *Lehrjahre* and *Wanderjahre*, as well as Wilhelm's family name, Meister (master), connote the obligatory years of resident apprenticeship and travelling journeymanship before he can become a master craftsman. When Wilhelm consciously takes on the task of "the harmonious cultivation of his nature," he adopts a new name instead of "Meister," which is a title he is ashamed to claim for himself at this stage.[56] The term "Bildungsroman" made early isolated appearances, as, for instance, in a lecture in 1819 by Professor Karl Morgenstern called "Über das Wesen des Bildungsromans" (On the nature of the *Bildungsroman*), which defined the genre in terms of both the hero's and the reader's *Bildung*: "erstens ... weil er des Helden Bildung in ihrem Anfang und Fortgang bis zu einer gewissen Stufe der Vollendung darstellt; zweytens aber auch, weil er gerade durch diese Darstellung des Lesers Bildung, in weiterm Umfange als jede andere Art des Romans, fördert [first, ... because it represents the hero's *Bildung* in its inception and progress to a certain stage of completion; secondly, because it promotes the reader's *Bildung* through this very representation, to a greater extent than any other kind of novel]."[57] This definition seems to have been based on a letter written by Körner to Schiller on the *Lehrjahre* in 1796, which Schiller published in *Die Horen*.[58] But the term was only made current by Wilhelm Dilthey, who first used it in *Das Leben Schleiermachers* (1870)[59] and defined the genre and gave its history in the chapter on Hölderlin's novel *Hyperion* in *Erlebnis und die Dichtung* (1906).

Dilthey's affirmative definition has been problematized in postwar German criticism by association with subsequent Wilhelmine and Nazi ideological appropriations of the genre as representative of German national identity. From outside this domestic German debate, his description, drawn from Goethe and the Romantics, is useful here.[60] English use of the term is first documented for 1919 in the *Encyclopaedia Britannica*; it has only become more general in literary criticism since the 1950s.[61]

Dilthey described the genre as having developed in the German classical-Romantic period under the influence of Rousseau and the period's tendency towards inward culture. Goethe and Jean Paul were the first practitioners, followed by Tieck and Novalis. Novels of this genre all portray the following: "wie [der Jüngling] in glücklicher Dämmerung in das Leben eintritt, nach verwandten Seelen sucht, der Freundschaft begegnet und der Liebe, wie er nun aber mit den harten

Realitäten der Welt in Kampf gerät und so unter mannigfachen Lebenserfahrungen heranreift, sich selber findet und seiner Aufgabe in der Welt gewiss wird [how (the youth) enters life at a happy dawn, looks for kindred souls, meets friendship and love, but now has to struggle with the hard realities of the world and thus matures through manifold experiences, finds himself, and reaches certainty about his task in the world]."

Dilthey saw the genre as expressing "den Individualismus einer Kultur ..., die auf die Interessensphäre des Privatlebens eingeschränkt ist. Das Machtwirken des Staates in Beamtentum und Militärwesen stand in den deutschen Mittel- und Kleinstaaten dem jungen Geschlecht der Schriftsteller als eine fremde Gewalt gegenüber [the individualism of a civilization ... which is limited to the sphere of private life. In the medium-sized and small German states the power of the state, operating through the civil service and the military, confronted the young generation of writers as an alien force]." He distinguished the *Bildungsroman* from other fictional biographies, such as *Tom Jones*, by its conscious and artistic presentation of the universally human in a particular life. In complete correspondence with Goethe's organic conception, Dilthey observed a lawful development in the life of the individual, every stage having its own value and forming the basis for a higher stage.[62] "Die Dissonanzen und Konflikte des Lebens erscheinen als die notwendigen Durchgangspunkte des Individuums auf seiner Bahn zur Reife und zur Harmonie [The dissonances and conflicts of life appear as the necessary stages of the individual on his path to maturity and harmony]."[63]

According to Dilthey, the goal is humaneness (*Humanität*), *Bildung* meaning both the achievement and the process towards it; and the novels of the classical-Romantic period are optimistic about the hero's success. What all such novels have in common is the advocacy of a *Weltanschauung*. With its close reference to historical conditions, particularly related to classical Weimar, Dilthey's definition seems to exclude most later so-called *Bildungsromane*, for which also the terms "*Entwicklungsroman*" (novel of development) or "*Erziehungsroman*" (novel of education) have been used. *Bildung* is a special type of development in its stress on the hero's conscious effort and on the manifold aspects of human endeavour; it is distinguished from education in its stress on the hero's interior motivation and goal.

Jeffrey L. Sammons, in "The Mystery of the Missing *Bildungsroman*, or: What Happened to Wilhelm Meister's Legacy?" has gone as far as to argue that the genre is a mere legend, since among the great variety of historical, social, political, and "individual" nineteenth-century

German novels, which resemble those of other Western nations, he can find no more than two and a half examples in addition to *Wilhelm Meister* which can be admitted to the category. He concludes that it is a spurious canon formation of an essentially German tradition, invented to serve the nationalist interests of the Wilhelmine period.[64] While this pragmatic explanation is persuasive as far as the German privileging of the genre in the late nineteenth and early twentieth centuries goes, on the question of the usefulness of the genre for the reader's orientation, I agree with Martin Swales, who, in *The German Bildungsroman from Wieland to Hesse*, rejects Jürgen Jacobs's calling of the *Bildungsroman* "eine unerfüllte Gattung" (an unfulfilled genre)[65] and insists instead that "the genre works *within* individual fictions in that it is a component of the expectation to which the specific novels refer and which they vivify by their creative engagement with it ... Even nonfulfilment of consistently intimated expectation can, paradoxically, represent a validation of the genre by means of its controlled critique."[66] This description serves well for the function of the genre that we shall observe, centrally or in passing, in many of the English novels discussed below.

2 The *Bildungsroman* Retailored: Carlyle and Goethe

To develop and promote his own *Weltanschauung* was the task that Thomas Carlyle set himself as compensation for abandoning the vocation of a minister, which his parents had favoured. Far beyond the expectations raised by Mme de Staël's *De l'Allemagne*, he found inspiration for this task and, if not new principles, then ready-made terms and aphoristic phrases to express his *Weltanschauung*, at least for this early period in his career, in German eighteenth-century and nineteenth-century thought and especially in Goethe's life and work. At twenty-four, guided by the Calvinist ethos of his youth, he resolved that his duty was not merely to think and endure but to act, a conviction that he was to find echoed in Goethe's writings. Goethe, if he had been more widely known in England, would have been Carlyle's "chosen specimen" of the "Hero as Man of Letters."[1] For Carlyle, to act was to write, and he finally found his subject through his German studies, which were revealing to him a "new Heaven and new Earth."[2] As he was to write in his first article for the *Edinburgh Review* as part of his task of "Germanizing the public," "The State of German Literature" (1827), in Goethe, Schiller, Tieck, Herder, and Jean Paul, "[t]he Nineteenth Century stands before us, in all its contradiction and perplexity … yet here no longer mean or barren, but enamelled into beauty in the poet's spirit; for its secret significance is laid open … the Spirit of our Age."[3] The article was widely read.[4]

In 1823, four years after he had begun to study German, Carlyle decided to translate *Wilhelm Meisters Lehrjahre*, in addition to writing a commissioned biographical sketch of Schiller, which grew to book length.[5] *Wilhelm Meister's Apprenticeship* was published a year later and received mixed reviews, but it became "somewhat fashionable" in London.[6] When his growing fame, especially with the appearance of *The French Revolution* (1837), produced interest in his earlier works, he brought out a second, slightly revised edition of the *Apprenticeship* in 1838. *Wilhelm Meister's Travels*, his translation of the first part of Goethe's *Wanderjahre* (1821), which he chose instead of *Werther* for the collection *German Romance*, appeared in 1827.

There is general agreement that Carlyle's translations from Goethe are on the whole accurate,[7] although his versions of the songs are prosaic,[8] but that in his writings on Goethe, which focused on the man rather than the work, he "[refashioned] him in an image more congenial to himself and his English readers";[9] that is, he saw and portrayed Goethe as having travelled the same road as his own, from skepsis to a belief which, although not orthodox, deserved the name "Christian," and as living by the same philosophy as his own of work and struggle. A closer scrutiny of Carlyle's translations and interpretations of *Wilhelm Meister* will help to assess his role as mediator. Of the three kinds, or phases, of translation that Goethe defined, in his notes to the *West-östlicher Divan* – the *schlicht prosaische* (simply prosaic), the *parodistische* (parodistic), and that which is *dem Original identisch* (identical to the original) – a combination of the latter two would best describe Carlyle's translations.[10]

In *Wilhelm Meister's Apprenticeship* (in the revised edition) the effect of the novel's main theme, *Bildung*, is weakened and obscured. First, in the original as the reader experiences it, all the external and internal events, whether in Wilhelm's life or in the lives of the other characters, as well as the general reflections by the characters or the narrator, are verbally subordinated to the theme of *Bildung*. In contrast, as a principal anglicizer of the new usage of *bilden* and its cognates, Carlyle translates, only partly from necessity, *Bildung* and *bilden*, as well as compounds such as *Ausbildung* and *überbildet*, with a whole range of English synonyms. Some examples of his synonyms are "instruction," "cultivation," "to perfect," "to form"; for instance (emphases in the translation added), the unknown clergyman corrects Wilhelm's reliance on natural talent: "[es] dürfte dem Künstler manches fehlen, wenn nicht *Bildung* das erst aus ihm macht, was er sein soll, und zwar frühe *Bildung*" / "many things will still be wanting to an artist, if *instruction*, and early *instruction* too, have not previously made that of him which he was meant to be." Wilhelm reflects on his choice between trade and art: "aber dein innerstes Bedürfnis erzeugt und nährt den Wunsch, die Anlagen, die in dir zum Guten und Schönen ruhen mögen, sie seien körperlich oder geistig, immer

mehr zu entwickeln und *auszubilden*"/"the desire still farther to unfold and *perfect* what endowments soever for the beautiful and good
... may lie within thee." Wilhelm writes to Werner about his intention: "mich selbst, ganz wie ich da bin, *auszubilden*"/"the *cultivation*
of my individual self, here as I am." At their second encounter the
clergyman corrects Wilhelm's sense that he wasted his time in the
theatre: "alles trägt unmerklich zu unserer *Bildung* bei"/"everything
contributes imperceptibly to *form* us."[11]

Secondly, there are important inaccuracies in Carlyle's translation.
His mistaken translation of *schöne Seele* by "fair saint" in the title of
book 6, "Bekenntnisse einer schönen Seele" (Confessions of a beautiful soul) has generally been noted. Deriving originally from Plato, the
term "beautiful soul" signified a person who was naturally inclined
to the good. Transmitted via St Augustine and medieval mysticism, it
came into more general use in the eighteenth century – for instance,
by Rousseau[12] – and in German Pietism, the religious persuasion of
Natalie's aunt, who is the subject of book 6.[13] What has not been
noted is the fact that, having missed this technical meaning, Carlyle
omits the important final verdict, by Lothario at the end of the novel,
on what constitutes a truly beautiful soul. Speaking here for the
author, Lothario says of the aunt: "Unerreichbar wird immer die
Handlungsweise bleiben, welche die Natur dieser *schönen Seele*
vorgeschrieben hat"/"No other need attempt to rival the plan of conduct which has been prescribed by nature for that *pure and noble
soul*."[14] Carlyle omits Lothario's conclusion that Natalie deserves this
honorific title more than many others, more even than their noble
aunt, who was "the most beautiful nature" in their circle at the time
when her manuscript was given its title.

Without the concept of the beautiful soul, Carlyle would not have
been able to make sense of this comparison. But it clarifies Goethe's
belief (the opposite of Carlyle's Calvinist attitude) that a natural inclination to good – as her name indicates, Natalie is good "by birth" – is
superior to an achievement of good through ascetic struggle, as in the
aunt's case. It is evident from the Goethe-Schiller correspondence
that Goethe in fact added this clarification in response to Schiller's
comment on Natalie, whom he described as "heilig und menschlich
zugleich [simultaneously saintly and human]," that he wished that
the title of a *"schöne Seele"* had not been pre-empted by the aunt,
"denn nur Natalie ist eigentlich eine rein ästhetische Natur [for only
Natalie is truly a purely aesthetic nature]." In his answer Goethe
announced appropriate changes in his next draft.[15]

Another error in translation makes nonsense of an important analogy in relation to the central issue of outside guidance (from the

secret Society of the Tower) with respect to *Bildung*. The narrator compares Jarno's advice to Wilhelm, to read Shakespeare's plays in order to correct his admiration for Racine and Corneille, with the rescue of a traveller who on his way to an inn has fallen into a river. Without help he would likely get out on the opposite side (*am jenseitigen Ufer*) and "have to make a wearisome and extended detour." For *am jenseitigen Ufer*, Carlyle has "at the side where he tumbled in."[16]

Carlyle found less to deplore and more to admire in the sequel, *Wilhelm Meisters Wanderjahre*. Of the *Lehrjahre* he wrote in the preface to the first edition of his translation, "[in] many points, both literary and moral, I could have wished devoutly that [Goethe] had not written as he has done; but to alter anything was not in my commission" – Carlyle wrote more strongly in private letters – whereas he described the *Wanderjahre*, in a review article on Goethe in 1828, as "one of the most perfect pieces of composition that Goethe has ever produced."[17] He only translated the first part, that of 1821, *Wilhelm Meisters Wanderjahre oder Die Entsagenden, Erster Theil*, a fact that is sometimes omitted by critics.[18] He mentioned Goethe's final revised and expanded version of 1829 in the preface to the second edition of the *Apprenticeship* and the *Travels* in 1839, vaguely concluding that it "continues a Fragment like the first, significantly pointing on all hands to infinitude; not more complete than the first was, or indeed perhaps less so."[19]

To continue with the examination of the fidelity of Carlyle's translations, here the first problem arises with his title. Unlike "travels," *Wanderjahre* denotes the journeyman's phase, which follows the years of apprenticeship and precedes the final accreditation as master, here not of a craft but of the art of living. Carlyle acknowledged the problem in a footnote to the introductory essay on Goethe, reporting that his search for a more accurate term had remained vain. Most important is his misinterpretation of Goethe's concept of *Entsagung* (renunciation), as in the novel's subtitle, *oder Die Entsagenden* (or The renunciants). Carlyle wrongly assimilates Goethe's *Entsagen* to Novalis's concept of *Selbsttödtung* (literally, self-killing), which he translates as "annihilation of self" in his essay on Novalis and in *Sartor Resartus*.[20] Novalis is arguing, in an epistemological and ontological, not a moral, context, for a transcendence of the lower ego for the sake of the higher self's mystical union with the *Weltseele* (world soul). For instance, "Der Act des sich selbst Überspringens ist überall der höchste – der Urpunct – die *Genesis des Lebens* [The act of transcending (literally, leaping over) oneself is everywhere the highest – the primary point – the *genesis of life*]."[21] Carlyle's ascetic implication is demonstrated in his translation of *Entbehren* (deprivation) as "renounce." During his obligatory journeyings, Wilhelm concludes a letter to Natalie: "bis ich das Glück habe, wieder zu Deinen Füssen zu liegen und auf Deinen Händen mich über alle das Entbehren auszuweinen" / "till I have once more the happiness of lying at thy feet, and weeping over thy hands for all that I renounce."[22]

However, this deprivation of closeness to his betrothed is not the renunciation that the members of the migrating society undertake as a duty; it is merely a side effect of it. Lenardo, one of the leaders, explains renunciation as a means of *Bildung* to Wilhelm with reference to the barber, who, like all associates of the Society of the Tower, for his own *Bildung* "sich von einer gewissen Seite bedingen muss, wenn ihm nach anderen Seiten hin die grössere Freiheit gewährt ist" / "to constrain himself in some particular point if the greater freedom be left him in all other points." That is, the barber "hat nun auf die Sprache Verzicht getan, insofern etwas Gewöhnliches oder Zufälliges durch sie ausgedrückt wird" / "has renounced the use of his tongue" for idle talk and instead has gained "die Gabe des Erzählens" / "the gift of narration."[23] Unlike Carlyle's meaning, such renunciation may be temporary only, as Jarno explains to Wilhelm at their first reunion during their wanderings: "wir mussten uns resignieren, wo nicht für immer, doch für eine gute Zeit" / "we were forced to resign ourselves, if not forever, at least for a long season."[24]

Examples of such renunciation in the *Lehrjahre* are the following. First, Lothario, the noblest member of the society, speaks to Jarno about a "Hauptfehler gebildeter Menschen, dass sie alles an eine Idee, wenig oder nichts an einen Gegenstand wenden mögen" / "the besetting fault of cultivated men, that they wish to spend their whole resources on some idea, scarcely any part of them on tangible existing problems." Thus he pursued dangerous adventures in the American War of Independence until he decided, as he then wrote in a letter to Jarno, "Ich werde zurückkehren und in meinem Hause, in meinem Baumgarten, mitten unter den Meinigen sagen: *Hier oder nirgend ist Amerika!*" / "I will return, and in my house, amid my fields, among my people, I will say: *Here or nowhere is America!*" Secondly, Wilhelm reports to Werner: "Ich verlasse das Theater und verbinde mich mit Männern, deren Umgang mich in jedem Sinne zu einer reinen und sichern Tätigkeit führen muss" / "I am abandoning the stage; I mean to join myself with men whose intercourse, in every sense, must lead to a sure and suitable activity."[25] *Entsagen*, then, is for Goethe the renunciation of some trait or activity that hinders the achievement of a harmonious self. However, a feminine sub-genre of the *Bildungsroman* arose in Goethe's time, the *Entsagungsroman* (novel of renunciation), which denied its heroines this achievement, one example being *Gabriele* (1819), by Goethe's Weimar neighbour and friend and Schopenhauer's mother, Johanna Schopenhauer.[26]

In his letters to Carlyle and his conversations with Eckermann about him, Goethe always expressed satisfaction with Carlyle as a "worthy reader." (The *Conversations*, in John Oxenford's translation [1850], was the most popular of Goethe's works in England.) After reading Carlyle's review article on Goethe in the *Foreign Review* (1828), Eckermann commented to his friend that the spirit in which Carlyle was recommending German literature was admirable; concerned about his nation's culture, rather than looking for "die Künste des Talents" (the skills of talent), Carlyle looked in foreign literary productions for the "Höhe sittlicher Bildung" (level of moral culture) to be gained from them. Goethe agreed and added, "Und wie ist es ihm Ernst! und wie hat er uns Deutsche studirt! Er ist in unserer Literatur fast besser zu Hause als wir selbst; zum wenigsten können wir mit ihm in unsern Bemühungen um das Englische nicht wetteifern [And how seriously he takes it! and how he has studied us Germans! He is nearly more at home in our literature than we are; at least, we cannot compete with him in our efforts on behalf of English literature]."[27] The last point might be moot – if Goethe's "we" is not the genius's plural – especially given Schlegel's influential translations of Shakespeare's plays, which had been published by then.

Goethe's "worthy reader" was by no means a faithful reader, however. As a writer, Carlyle read, like Goethe himself, for his own authorial purposes, and some of his difficulties with *Wilhelm Meister* are nicely foreshadowed in Schiller's reservations. In his letter to Goethe with suggestions for clarification in the *Lehrjahre*, Schiller had concluded, "Ich möchte sagen, die Fabel ist vollkommen wahr, auch die Moral der Fabel ist vollkommen wahr, aber das Verhältnis der einen zu der andern springt noch nicht deutlich genug in die Augen [I would say, the story is completely true, and the moral of the story is completely true, but the relation of the one to the other is not yet obvious enough]." Goethe answered with a corresponding list of changes he was going to make, but he also "confessed" his "flaw" (*Fehler*), which arose from "meiner innersten Natur, aus einem gewissen realistischen Tick, durch den ich meine Existenz, meine Handlungen, meine Schriften den Menschen aus den Augen zu rücken behaglich finde [my inmost nature, from a certain realistic tic, as a result of which I find it agreeable to withdraw my existence, my actions, my writings from people's eyes]." In reply, Schiller urged him not to renounce his "realistic tic," which belonged to his "poetic individuality"; that as long as Goethe had provided for the reader's finding everything in the work necessary for its explanation, the reader needed not be spared the search: "Das Resultat eines solchen Ganzen muss immer die eigene freie, nur nicht willkürliche Produktion des Lesers sein; es muss eine Art von Belohnung bleiben, die nur dem Würdigen zuteil wird, indem sie dem Unwürdigen sich entzieht [The result of such a whole must always be the reader's own free, though not arbitrary, production; it must remain a kind of reward, which is only granted to the worthy reader, while eluding the unworthy one]."[28] Henry James professed himself such a reader in a review of a new edition of Carlyle's translation in 1865: "each reader becomes his own Wilhelm Meister, an apprentice, a traveller, on his own account."[29]

For our consideration of Carlyle's reading of Goethe in general and *Wilhelm Meister* in particular, the following essays are relevant: in addition to the retrospective review of 1828, on the occasion of the publication of the second part of Goethe's collected works in 1827, there is an earlier essay on him, which accompanied *Wilhelm Meister's Travels*, first published as part of *German Romance* (1827), and also his preface to the first edition of *Wilhelm Meister's Apprenticeship* (1824). In the course of these pieces, Carlyle did not revise his judgments; he quoted long passages from the earlier essay in the review article and reprinted the preface in subsequent editions. In his assessment of the *Lehrjahre* in the preface, he proceeds defensively with various rhetorical gambits, claiming the role of the disinterested translator, whose business is not to judge but to prepare others for judging: "The literary and moral persuasions of a man like Goethe are objects of a rational curiosity."[30]

Anticipating the dismay and contempt of readers of "low character," who will expect a novel like *Werther*, Carlyle first exaggerates possible reservations: this novel lacks romance interest; "the characters are samples to judge of, rather than persons to love or hate; the incidents are contrived for other objects than moving or affrighting us"; the hero is a near-despicable "milksop" (Goethe himself had called him a "poor dog"); and the author "wears a face of the most still indifference," even a "slight sardonic grin." Although he implies that the reader of "higher character" will not be dismayed by these features, Carlyle was by no means altogether out of sympathy with these judgments. He counters his warnings with the most positive assessment possible, but brackets this with the admission that even among "readers of far higher character," rhetorically including himself, few "will take the praiseworthy pains of Germans, reverential of their favourite author, and anxious to hunt-out his most elusive charms."[31]

It is only after these two oblique approaches that Carlyle affirms "the beauties in *Meister*, which cannot but secure it some favour at the hands of many." They are "[t]he philosophical discussions ...; its keen glances into life and art; the minute and skilful delineation of men; the lively genuine exhibition of the scenes they move in; the occasional touches of eloquence and tenderness, and even of ... the essence of poetry; the quantity of thought and knowledge embodied in a style so rich in general felicities." For the few "who have penetrated to the limits of their own conceptions, and wrestled with thoughts and feelings too high for them," he recommends this work by "the first of European minds" for a long study.[32] Among these few readers Carlyle himself is to be counted, and the role he ascribed here to Goethe is the one which he stressed in all his evaluations of him and which he himself wished to play, and came to play, for the British, at first through his German work and *Sartor Resartus*.

The first essay on Goethe, introducing the *Travels*, mainly sketches his "spiritual and moral growth" and is based on Goethe's autobiographical *Dichtung und Wahrheit* (excluding part 4, which was published only in 1830). Judging that "Goethe's culture as a writer is perhaps less remarkable than his culture as a man," Carlyle makes only passing general comments on his other works, but emphasizes the enterprise of self-cultivation in Goethe's life. "To cultivate his own spirit, not only as an author, but as a man; to obtain dominion over it, and wield its resources as instruments in the service of what seemed Good and Beautiful, had been his object more or less distinctly from the first, as it is that of all true men in their several spheres." Identifying with his portrait of Goethe, Carlyle quotes Goethe's "deep maxim, that 'Doubt of any sort can only be removed by Action,'"[33] where for Goethe, and himself, action consists in being a "Poet for the World in our own time," or rather, a philosopher, "for he loves and has practiced as a man the wisdom which, as a poet, he inculcates."[34] After this treatment of Goethe, Carlyle introduces *Wilhelm Meister's Travels* in one short paragraph, reserving his judgment even more cautiously than in the preface to the *Apprenticeship*.

The expanded review article on Goethe, besides surveying some of his works, repeats the same stress on his self-cultivation as a man in the service of his nation's culture and, in contrast to Voltaire, as a philosopher for the times, "these hard, unbelieving utilitarian days." As the "Teacher and exemplar of his age," Goethe "has not only suffered and mourned in bitter agony under the spiritual perplexities of his time [as evidenced in *Werther* and like Byron]; but he has also mastered these, he is above them, and has shown others how to rise above them [unlike Byron]. At one time, we found him in darkness, and now he is in light; he was once an Unbeliever, and now he is a Believer; and he believes, moreover, not by denying his unbelief, but by following it out."[35] Here we have not only Carlyle's self-identification but also, in sentiment and style, the prototype for Teufelsdröckh's spiritual history. Here is also the origin of the injunction in *Sartor Resartus*: "Close thy *Byron*; open thy *Goethe!*"[36] with which, of course, Goethe would not have agreed. He commemorated Byron in the character of Euphorion, child of Faust and Helena in *Faust, Part Two*.

In his account of the *Lehrjahre*, from the "second and sounder period of Goethe's life," Carlyle confines himself to "looking at the work chiefly as a document for the writer's history"; the "temper of mind" is of an idealist poet, who "knows that the Universe is *full* of goodness; that whatever has being has beauty." The reader's question must be "How may we, each of us in his several sphere, attain [this temper of mind], or strengthen it, for ourselves?"[37] Given this spiritual search, it is no surprise that Carlyle favoured the *Wanderjahre*. In the preface to the second edition of the *Apprenticeship* and the *Travels*, he recommended Goethe's final version of the *Wanderjahre* with vague generalities to the "trustful student of Goethe," but thought it superfluous for the "mere English reader."[38] Even in 1858, long after the main period of his German enthusiasm, he praised the *Wanderjahre* as "the Book of Books on Education of the young soul in these broken distracted times of ours."[39] In the review article on Goethe, he adds to a comparison with *The Faerie Queene* as a utopia in the earlier essay that Goethe's novel is an allegory of the nineteenth century, "a picture full of expressiveness, of what men are striving for, and ought to strive for, in these actual days."[40]

The only specific examples Carlyle singles out are, predictably, chapters 10 and 11,[41] "where, in poetic and symbolic style, [the readers] will find a sketch of the nature, objects and present ground of Religious Belief."[42] He quotes extensively from Wilhelm's visit to the Pedagogic Province, including the lecture on the four kinds of reverence (*Ehrfurcht*) and the respective religions based on them. The first is reverence for what is below us: ethnic religion; the second, reverence for what is around us: philosophical religion; and the third, reverence for what is below us: the Christian religion. Asked by Wilhelm to which of these three kinds of religion the leaders of the Pedagogic Province belong, they answer: "To all three ... for in their union they produce what may properly be called the true Religion. Out of these three Reverences springs the highest Reverence, Reverence for Oneself, and these again unfold themselves from this; so that man attains the highest elevation of which he is capable, that of being justified in reckoning himself the Best that God and Nature have produced."[43]

This religious cast of the ideal of *Bildung* was the one most congenial and useful to Carlyle, and it is the only one in terms of which Teufelsdröckh can be said to pursue self-cultivation. In a letter to Goethe that refers to *Sartor Resartus* (when Carlyle was about to try to find a publisher for it), he called Goethe "our Prophet" and declared, "[I]t can never be forgotten that to him I owe the all-precious knowledge and experience that Reverence is still possible, nay Reverence for our fellow-man, as a true emblem of the Highest, even in these perturbed, chaotic times."[44]

But far from this single appeal, the *Wanderjahre*, even in its first partial version, presents the reader with a panorama of the greatest diversity in goals and paths of vocation, social relations, religious practice, and love, some experienced by Wilhelm, as on his journey to Italy (chap. 13); some observed by him, as in his stay with St Joseph the Second (chap. 2), his visit to the Pedagogic Province (chaps. 10, 11, 14), and his joining up with the Migration Society (chaps. 15, 17, and the last); some only heard or read by him, such as St Joseph the Second's story (chaps. 2–4) and the novellas "The Man of Fifty," "The New Melusina" (chap. 16), and "Who Can the Traitor Be?" (chap. 18). For the reader, the whole novel serves as an experiment in living humanely in a society in critical transition.[45]

Goethe would, no more than with the *Lehrjahre*, commit himself, either in the work or in comments about it, to a particular moral teaching. In a letter written after the completion of the second version he explained that such a "*kollektiv*" work, which presented a combination of the most disparate details, "erlaubt, ja fordert mehr als eine andre dass jeder sich zueigne was ihm gemäss ist [permits, even demands more than any other that everyone appropriate for himself what is suitable for him]."[46] It is in this manner that Goethe used his own reading.

While he was working on the translations for *German Romance*, including *Wilhelm Meister's Travels*, Carlyle began to plan an original novel. Modelled on *Wilhelm Meister*, "Wotton Reinfred" was to be the strongly autobiographical and didactic story of a young man aspiring to art and spiritual certainty. In writing it, Carlyle, in a letter to his mother, compared himself to a missionary "to the British Heathen, an innumerable class, whom he would gladly do something to convert."[47] Since the novel remained incomplete and unpublished, it need concern us here no further, its intended effect having finally been achieved by *Sartor Resartus* (1833–34).

Carlyle's indebtedness to various German thinkers is part of the message of *Sartor*, and the sources have been researched thoroughly.[48] He introduced the novel with an epigraph from Goethe.[49] The most important borrowings, direct and indirect, are the following: from Kant, the "Thought-forms, Space and Time";[50] from Fichte, the concept of the Me and the Not-Me[51] and the role of the scholar-teacher (*Gelehrter*) as priest and prophet;[52] from Novalis, "Annihilation of Self (*Selbsttödtung*)" as the first moral act,[53] the "Body of Man" as the only temple,[54] and the idea that "Nature is ... but the veil and mysterious Garment of the Unseen,"[55] which Carlyle expressed in *Sartor* with a quotation from the Earth Spirit's speech in *Faust, Part One* ("Nacht"): "'Tis thus at the roaring Loom of Time I ply, / And weave for God the Garment thou seest Him by."[56] Here it is important to distinguish Carlyle's and Faust's contempt for the lesser reality of the garment from Goethe's own respect for material reality and sense experience, what he referred to as his "reine, tiefe, angeborne und geübte Anschauungsweise, die mich Gott in der Natur, die Natur in Gott zu sehen unverbrüchlich gelehrt hatte [pure, deep, innate, and practised manner of observation, which had taught [him] to see God in nature, nature in God]."[57]

The style, tone, and structure of *Sartor Resartus* resemble Jean Paul's novels, such as *Flegeljahre* (1804) and *Leben des Quintus Fixlein* (1796), more than *Wilhelm Meister*. In his article on Jean Paul for the *Edinburgh Review* in 1827, Carlyle noted Jean Paul's "fantastic, many-coloured, far-grasping, every way perplexed and extraordinary ... mode of writing,"[58] which would have confirmed his own natural style more than what he justly described as Goethe's inimitable, simple, even common style, free from all mannerisms.[59] Carlyle's fictive role as editor in *Sartor* resembles Jean Paul's in "endeavouring to evolve printed Creation out of a German printed and written Chaos"[60] made up of Teufelsdröckh's book on the philosophy of clothes and six paper bags filled with "miscellaneous masses of Sheets, and oftener Shreds and Snips," including scholarly disquisitions, autobiographical notes, wash bills, and so on. Although on several occasions in the *Wanderjahre*, Goethe assumes the role of the editor commenting on his "uncertain problem of selecting from those most multifarious papers, what is worthiest and most important,"[61] it is a sober business compared with Jean Paul's extravagant humour. According to Carlyle, "[every] work, be it fiction or serious treatise, is embaled in some fantastic wrappage, some mad narrative accounting for its appearance, and connecting it with the author, who generally becomes a person in the drama himself, before all is over."[62] Carlyle added another link to this connection by having Teufelsdröckh quote "[his] friend Richter."[63] Of the content, the idyllic village life of the hero's childhood and the social milieu of his professorial life, including the names, again recall Jean Paul's novels rather than *Wilhelm Meister* or Goethe's own circumstances, described in *Dichtung und Wahrheit*, although the connection between Weissnichtwo and Weimar would be established not only by the alliteration but also through the well-known indulgent description in Mme de Staël's *De l'Allemagne*.[64]

To return to our main concern, what kind of *Bildungsroman* is *Sartor Resartus*, and what kind of *Bildung* is promoted in it? The biographical book 2 meets Dilthey's definition of the *Bildungsroman* (see chapter 1 above): "the youth enters life at a happy dawn, looks for kindred souls, meets friendship and love, but now has to struggle with the hard realities of the world; through manifold experience he matures, finds himself, and reaches certainty about his task in the world." The inclusion in such a novel of discursive material connected with the characters, such as the excerpts from Teufelsdröckh's book, is common, if not in this proportion. However, a comparison with *Wilhelm Meister* and with Schiller's discussion of the *Lehrjahre* shows important differences in *Sartor*. Here a *Weltanschauung* is not gradually and experimentally produced by the reader through his or her search for meaning in the hero's encounters with the world and reflection on them, but explicitly stated from the start, notwithstanding the authorial irony. Long before the hero makes his appearance as an infant whose maturity seems as uncertain as his origins, the reader knows what his goal ought, and is, to be from the mature scholar's – that is, the master's – philosophical treatise. This approach is the very opposite of *Wilhelm Meister*, which has the reader as uncertain of the outcome as the hero and consequently sharing the process of *Bildung* and the gradually emerging intimation of the possibility "dass alle die falschen Schritte zu einem unschätzbaren Guten hinführen [that all the false steps lead to an incalculable good]," which Goethe noted as the original, darkly felt truth with which he had begun the first version, "Wilhelm Meisters Theatralische Sendung."[65] This optimistic conclusion is clearly expressed by Friedrich to Wilhelm at the end of the *Lehrjahre* (in Carlyle's translation): "thou resemblest Saul the son of Kish, who went out to seek his father's asses, and found a kingdom."[66]

Further, instead of the hero's receptivity to cultivation, his plasticity (*Bildsamkeit*), on the one hand, and the world's power of cultivation, on the other, which Schiller and Körner had noted in *Wilhelm Meister*, Carlyle, who could not "write anything but disguised autobiography,"[67] created a heroic protagonist – no "milksop" or *"armer Hund"* – and a world that remains, in characters, settings, and events, a general, abstract, and schematic backdrop, except for the childhood environment, whose concreteness derived from Carlyle's sentimental attachment to his own childhood village. The "sybilline" hints and comments from Teufelsdröckh's notes and the author-editor's generalizing glosses are more compatible with the moral sublime, which Carlyle in his role as "Priest and Prophet"[68] was aiming at, than with the irreducible particularity and concreteness of true life, which he often found objectionable in Goethe's original. For instance, instead of Wilhelm's diverse entanglements with women, to show both what furthers and what hinders the hero's cultivation and what he assimilates or rejects, Teufelsdröckh experiences a single, idealized example of unrequited love, since "each human heart can properly exhibit but one Love, if even one."[69]

The *Bildung* that Carlyle promotes in *Sartor* is not Goethe's organic concept of a gradual, manifold, and harmonious cultivation of an individual's own nature. In this context, Carlyle's repeated misquotation of Goethe's triad in the poem "Generalbeichte" (General confession) is telling: he substitutes "the True" for "the Beautiful" when referring, even in a letter to Goethe himself, to Goethe's "Precept, *Im Ganzen, Guten, Wahren resolut zu leben* [to live resolutely a whole, good and true life]."[70] The implicit reservation of Carlyle's about the aesthetic component of *Bildung* would in later years turn into outright denunciation of culture conceived as the worship of art.[71]

Instead of "the development of man in all his endowments and faculties," in Carlyle's own description of the *Lehrjahre*, Teufelsdröckh undergoes a training of reason and will for a test in the moral and spiritual spheres alone, as is exemplified by the contrasting chapter headings "The Everlasting No" and "The Everlasting Yea" and by his own comparisons of himself with Faust. But unlike the productive conflict of Faust's two souls, which ends only with his death, Teufelsdröckh's struggle results in conquest and peace. It is true that Wilhelm Meister also passes through a phase of nihilism, but it is not presented in stark contrast and as the critical turning point, as in *Sartor*. Frustrated in his love of the theatre and Natalie and impatient with the interventions of the Society of the Tower, he decides to leave with his son: "er übersah den ganzen Ring seines Lebens, nur lag er leider zerbrochen vor ihm und schien sich auf ewig nicht schliessen zu wollen"/"the whole ring of his existence lay before him; but it was broken into fragments, and seemed as if it would never unite again."[72]

Nevertheless, the principles of Teufelsdröckh's "sorrows" and conversion are linked with Goethe by many allusions. Even from childhood, Teufelsdröckh's life is encircled with "a dark ring of Care … It was the ring of Necessity whereby we are all be-girt."[73] Goethe had shown in *Wilhelm Meister* and written in *Dichtung und Wahrheit*:

"Unser Leben ist, wie das Ganze, in dem wir enthalten sind, auf eine unbegreifliche Weise aus Freiheit und Notwendigkeit zusammen-gesetzt [Our life, like the whole in which we are contained, is com-posed of freedom and necessity in an incomprehensible manner]."[74] In *Faust, Part One* the contemplation of care (*Sorge*) contributes to Faust's decision to seek his death.[75] Like Goethe and Werther (and like Carlyle in one of his plans for himself), Teufelsdröckh trains to be a lawyer. Like Wilhelm in the *Lehrjahre* with mixed success and in the *Wanderjahre* profitably, and like Goethe with respect to Weimar, Teufelsdröckh decides that to make your way in life you have "to unite yourself with some one and with somewhat [*sich anzuschlies-sen*]."[76] As Goethe had to pass through the stage of writing the "*Sor-rows of Werter* [*sic*], before ... he could become a Man," so Teufelsdröckh must, through his wanderings "(by footprints), write his *Sorrows of Teufelsdröckh*."[77] He cannot thrive until he sees "the folly of that impossible Precept, *Know thyself*; till it be translated into this partially possible one, *Know what thou canst work at*."[78] This precept echoes the second of the "Betrachtungen im Sinne der Wanderer" (Reflections in the spirit of the wanderers) in the final version of the *Wanderjahre*: "Wie kann man sich selbst kennen lernen? Durch Be-trachten niemals, wohl aber durch Handeln. Versuche deine Pflicht zu tun, und du weisst gleich, was an dir ist [How can one get to know oneself? Never through contemplation, but certainly through action. Try to do your duty and you will know immediately what stuff you are made of]."[79] And this work is to be in the nearest duty, as advised by "the Lothario in *Wilhelm Meister*, that your 'America is here or nowhere.'"[80]

The metaphysical concepts connected with Goethe are, as we have seen, the ideal of wonder and reverence and the idea that nature is "the living visible Garment of God." In addition, Carlyle owed the concept of alternating periods of belief and unbelief, as well as the bi-ological terms "systole" and "diastole," to Goethe's dynamic concep-tion of history. One of Teufelsdröckh's notes reads: "If our era is the Era of Unbelief, why murmur under it; is there not a better coming, nay come? As in long-drawn systole and diastole, must the period of Faith alternate with the period of Denial."[81] The source is in Goethe's notes to the *West-östlicher Divan*.[82]

While trying to find a publisher for *Sartor Resartus*, Carlyle noted in his journal: "Canst thou in any measure spread abroad Reverence over the hearts of men? ... Is it to be done by Art; or are men's minds as yet shut to Art, and open only at best to oratory; not fit for a Meister, but only for a better and better *Teufelsdreck* [*sic*]; *Denk und schweig!* [Think and be silent]."[83] Even in 1858, in the letter quoted above recommending the *Wanderjahre* as *the* book on education, he concluded that he did not find "that almost any English person yet reads it with understanding."[84] So it is explicit didacticism, although presented ironically, which the reader of *Sartor Resartus* encounters, instead of Goethe's "realistic tic," which compelled him to be equivocal in the *Lehrjahre*, and the conviction of his old age, which shaped the *Wanderjahre*, that no single doctrine could do justice to life, as well as his general rejection of moral didaxis in art.[85] Carlyle preached that skepticism is wrong and evil, belief is right and good, the moral imperative is self-denial, and the right metaphysical dogma is natural supernaturalism.

Considered in terms of a Jaussian series, Carlyle's response to Goethe's *Wilhelm Meister* in his criticism, translation, and appropriation strongly reveals his own *Weltanschauung* and literary purposes, as well as his diagnosis of and prescription for the condition of England. In turn, his work serves as a standard for assessing the deviations of his contemporaries, especially Edward Bulwer-Lytton, Matthew Arnold, George Eliot, G.H. Lewes, and George Meredith, who, mostly after Carlyle's initial guidance, arrived at an independent judgment and individual use of Goethe and his work.

3 The *Bildungsroman* Assimilated: Edward Bulwer-Lytton's *Ernest Maltravers* and *Alice*

After Carlyle, the author who played the most important role in domesticating the *Bildungsroman* while preserving the notion of its German provenance was Edward Bulwer-Lytton. Although he lacked Carlyle's authority, he exercised a greater influence on the practice of fiction by virtue of the popularity of his novels – next to Dickens, he was possibly the most widely read novelist of his time – and of the importance of his essays and prefaces on the aesthetics of fiction. In the 1820s and 1830s, before the ascendancy of Dickens and Thackeray, Bulwer was the principal experimenter in, as well as theorist on, the craft of fiction.[1] Familiar with Germany through many long stays, knowledgeable about the pre-Romantic and Romantic authors, and a close student and admirer of Goethe and Schiller, Bulwer acted in Britain as one of the chief advocates for German letters, giving Matthew Arnold, for instance, according to Arnold's own testimony, "the sense of a wider horizon, the anticipation of Germany, the opening into the great world."[2]

Carlyle himself came to address Bulwer as a fellow prophet. After having satirized the hero of Bulwer's *Pelham* (1828) – possibly only from second-hand knowledge from a review – as the Mystagogue of the Dandiacal Body in *Sartor*,[3] he wrote to Bulwer about *Zanoni* (1842) that he "confidently gather[ed] … that this Book, like its predecessors, will be read and scanned far and wide; that it will be a liberating *voice* for much that lay dumb imprisoned in many human souls."[4]

Bulwer's novels are generally indebted to what in *The Pilgrims of the Rhine* (1832) he described as the German muse, a combination, resembling the scenes through which the Rhine passes, of "the classic, the romantic, the contemplative, the philosophic, and the superstitious."[5] In Germany in the 1830s and early 1840s – that is, after Byron and Scott and before Dickens and Thackeray – his popularity surpassed that of contemporary German novelists and was rivalled only by George Sand and Balzac.[6] For instance, the famous *Vormärz* (pre-1848) novelist Fanny Lewald cited Bulwer's novels as discouragingly superior, together with those by Goethe, Balzac, Sand, and Scott, and quoted from his novel *Pelham* for the epigraph of her first novel, *Clementine* (1843).[7] The Germans even adopted as a self-definition Bulwer's description of them, in the dedication of *Ernest Maltravers*, as "a race of thinkers and of critics,"[8] changing it to a "Volk der Dichter und Denker [nation of poets and thinkers]."

Most of Bulwer's novels are out of print, none are available in paperback, and there is little scholarly interest in this second-rank novelist, whose popularity did not outlast his lifetime. Yet his innovative theory and practice deserve study for the sake of their direct and indirect influence on many British novelists who still enjoy the interest and respect of readers and scholars. The following self-appraisal is fair: "In thus enlarging the boundaries of the Novelist, ... I have served as a guide to later and abler writers, both in England and abroad."[9] In the terminology of reception theory, Bulwer's *Bildungsromane* changed the "horizon of expectations" of the contemporary British novel reader, including that of other novelists, an effect that is a "criterion for the determination of [a work's] aesthetic value."[10]

In his experimentation with the still new and little theorized genre of the novel, *Wilhelm Meisters Lehrjahre* and *Wanderjahre* served Bulwer as the principal examples of the kind of fiction he was advocating and trying to fashion at his most ambitious. He called it "metaphysical," a term which then generally connoted a German mentality. For instance, in his essay "On the Different Kinds of Prose Fiction, with Some Apologies for the Fiction of the Author," which accompanied the 1835 edition of *The Disowned*, he distinguished between three principal forms, the actual, the satiric, and the metaphysical, planning to cultivate each in turn.[11] In his essay "On Art in Fiction" (1838), which Richard Stang, in *The Theory of the Novel in England, 1850–1870*, calls "one of the most important critical documents of the period,"[12] Bulwer contrasts Scott's "mechanical art" with "metaphysical" or "intellectual art," which appeals to the intellect and the passions through a noble, idealizing "grandeur of conception." As for the characters, "the metaphysical operations of stormy and conflicting feelings," "ground little occupied hitherto by the great masters of English fiction," are to be portrayed instead of mere manners and appearance. The cast of characters represents "views of life" symbolically, or what in the "Note" to *Zanoni* he called "typically."[13] That is, his method resembles Goethe's in the latter's list for the characters in *Wilhelm Meisters Lehrjahre*, such as "Wilhelm: ästetisch-sittlicher Traum – Lothario: heroisch-aktiver Traum [Wilhelm: aesthetic-moral dream – Lothario: heroic-active dream]."[14]

More or less inclusive, depending on the critic's criteria for the genre, the list of Bulwer's apprenticeship novels comprises, in a conservative reckoning, *Pelham* (1828), *The Disowned* (1828), *Godolphin* (1833), *Ernest Maltravers* (1837) and its sequel *Alice* (1838), and *Kenelm Chillingly* (posthumous, 1873). The main traits of the *Bildungsroman* that Bulwer transmitted were as follows. First, the hero shares characteristics of sensibility and "plasticity" (*Bildbarkeit*) with Werther and Wilhelm Meister respectively. Secondly, he is guided in his *Bildung* by both male and female mentors. Most importantly, in the course of these novels, Bulwer elaborated a model of the hero's psychological and moral development through three phases: rebellion, quest, and chastened return to a revaluation of his point of departure.[15]

The moralistic, even punitive, tenor of this plot is of course alien to *Wilhelm Meister*, but it is indebted to Carlyle's meaning of renunciation in *Sartor*, and it proved very influential for Victorian fiction.[16] *Wilhelm Meister* ends, as is typical of Goethe, with progress through alternation (*Systole/Diastole*) to enhancement (*Steigerung*): like Saul, who in search of his father's asses found a kingdom, Wilhelm finds a vocation, social role, and love which are shown to be far superior to what Werner, his stay-at-home opposite, has achieved. Yet Bulwer's model matches a reading of Goethe's novel that stresses the cyclical effect of the ending: Wilhelm's choice of a bourgeois vocation and his rescue of his son. Bulwer differs from Carlyle in giving his heroes in the second phase a wide range of experience; notably included is aesthetic experience, Bulwer restoring the ideal of beauty, which Carlyle had omitted from Goethe's triad of personal culture: the whole, the good, the beautiful (see chap. 2 above). David Masson, in *British Novelists and Their Styles* (1859), called the genre of *Wilhelm Meister* "the Art and Culture Novel" and declared Bulwer its most faithful British practitioner.[17]

Among familiar examples of plots indebted to his transmission is that of Dickens's *Great Expectations* (1861). Lack of structure was what Bulwer had criticized in Dickens's early work, *The Old Curiosity Shop* (1841).[18] Although Dickens rarely commented in writing on the theory of fiction, he participated in the theoretical discussions of his friends, who besides Bulwer included G.H. Lewes, Richard Holt Hutton, Wilkie Collins, and John Forster.[19] The shared interest of Dickens and Bulwer, during their long friendship, in theoretical and technical questions about the art of fiction seems to have been instrumental in Dickens's achievement of a more complex and unified form.[20] With either of the two endings, *Great Expectations* exhibits the three-stage structure. But the revised, "happy" ending, which Bulwer had strongly recommended, is truer to the optimistic meaning of *Bildung*. Disraeli, who read no novelist after Scott except Bulwer,[21] adopted the latter's model for *The Young Duke* (1831), for instance. Thackeray, whose admiration for Bulwer was more mixed[22] and who parodied *Ernest Maltravers* in his novelette *Catherine* (1839–40), adopted his model for *The History of Pendennis* (1848–50). George Eliot's *Mill on the Floss* (1860) is an interesting variant. She adapted the model to a female life and, tellingly, made the final phase wholly pathetic.

Ernest Maltravers and *Alice, or The Mysteries: A Sequel to Ernest Maltravers* are the novels – or "really one novel in two parts"[23] – which most explicitly and consistently establish their indebtedness to *Wilhelm Meister* and most clearly exhibit Bulwer's three-stage development plot. In a retrospective note prefacing the 1851 edition of *Alice*, he judged the two novels in terms of his theory of metaphysical fiction: of all his novels, they best achieved "harmony between premeditated conception and the various incidents and agencies employed in the development of plot," their unifying "interior philosophical design" being that "GENIUS [typified by Ernest] if duly following its vocation, reunites itself to NATURE [typified by Alice] from which life and art had for a while distracted it; but to nature ... [meanwhile] elevated and idealized."[24]

A general German context is established by the dedication of *Ernest Maltravers* to the "great German people, a race of thinkers and critics," and by Ernest's youthful enthusiasm for German idealist philosophy and Sturm und Drang literature and his subsequent adventures in love and anti-philistine rebellion as a student in Germany before the story opens. Despite this foreign influence on his intellect, sensibility, and manners – "full of strange German romance and metaphysical speculations," he has on his return "nothing of the sober Englishman about him"[25] – the critical setting for testing his faculties has to be England, which, in Bulwer's view, ultimately permitted greater scope for genius in action. In his "Life of Schiller" Bulwer argued that practical political liberty and theoretical speculative liberty existed in reverse proportion in England and Germany.[26] In the same spirit he recommended German letters, learning, and education in his historical-sociological essay *England and the English* (1833).[27] Indeed,

Ernest's student activities as a republican ringleader have resulted in danger to his life and in his expulsion from Germany. So there are no German settings or characters in the novel. Not even the old German songs which Ernest teaches Alice at the start and which Evelyn, her stepdaughter, later recalls are quoted, unlike other songs. Of the chapter epigraphs from classical and modern authors, only one is from the German – from Schiller's tragedy *Don Carlos*[28] – in contrast to the many German epigraphs in *Zanoni*.

Wilhelm Meister is established as the point of departure in the preface to the 1840 edition of *Ernest Maltravers*, where Bulwer acknowledges his debt to the German work for the "philosophical design, of a moral education or apprenticeship." However, in contrast to what he calls Goethe's apprenticeship in "theoretical art," his is "rather that of practical life."[29] This absolute distinction matches his own work as little as it does Goethe's, but it does reflect his sense of the difference between "despotic" Germany and liberal England in their respective scope for the praxis of idealism in public life, as evidenced, for instance, in his apostrophe to London on Ernest's return from the Continent: "CITY OF FREEMEN!"[30] Besides the conception, Bulwer's invention of character types and their relations and of motifs, incidents, and settings is indebted to *Wilhelm Meister* to a large degree.[31]

What are the salient features of the *Bildungsroman* that Bulwer in *Ernest Maltravers* and *Alice* contributed to British fiction? The story is of a gifted, handsome, and wealthy young Englishman who seeks a suitable vocation and love, in which quest he is helped by several male and female mentors and shadowed by lesser, partial versions of himself. The conscious and self-conscious quality of his quest, typical of Wilhelm Meister and his German descendants, distinguishes Ernest from many of his British successors. He is "earnest" about his idealism and its application, in contrast to his early companion and later rival, Lumley Ferrers, who in his cynical egotism plays a role reminiscent of both the realistic Jarno, as he functions in the early part of the *Lehrjahre*, and the skeptical sensualist Mephistopheles in Goethe's *Faust*. Just as Mephisto misjudges Faust, so Lumley misjudges Ernest because his "finesse" is only adequate for worldly characters. (In his harmless moments he plays Sancho Panza to Ernest's Don Quixote.)

After first wasting his talents for lack of a goal that would answer to his "over-reaching" aspirations for "the Beautiful, the Virtuous, the Great"[32] – one of Bulwer's variants of Goethe's triad and Carlyle's adaptation, cited above – Ernest turns to authorship as a means of expressing "the Ideal." He is guided in this course by the example and precept of two mentors, his guardian, Cleveland, and De Montaigne, both men of letters themselves. In their personalities and social rank they recall the aristocratic Uncle and Lothario of the Society of the Tower. Cleveland subscribes to the idea of apprenticeship through experience: "action, and adventure, and excitement," resulting in "the fierce emotions and passionate struggles, through which the Wilhelm Meister of real life must work out his apprenticeship, and attain the Master Rank." But he becomes impatient for Ernest to fulfill his promise as a great author or a great man, warning him against "sink[ing] down into a virtuoso."[33] The term "virtuoso" is Lord Shaftesbury's, denoting the ideal of a full personal development that is pursued like the perfection of a work of art. It was an influential source, through Christoph Martin Wieland, for Goethe's ideal of *Bildung*. Bulwer's dismissal of it, through Cleveland, indicates the sway of Carlyle's "Gospel of Work."

Ernest's second mentor, De Montaigne, who lives up to his name, counteracts the caricaturing effect that the insane ambition of Ernest's rival, Cesarini, for literary fame has worked on Ernest by advocating, "with almost a religious solemnity in his voice," the pursuit of a literary career as a service to the public and posterity, which would "[entail] on the world an heirloom of instruction or delight." Writing essays based on his personal impressions, "form[ing] himself, as a sculptor forms, with a model before his eyes and an ideal in his heart," Ernest "was a silent but intense enthusiast in the priesthood he had entered. From LITERATURE he imagined had come all that makes nations enlightened and men humane."[34] His literary ambition, then, resembles Wilhelm's ambition to promote the sentimental and moral cultivation of the German public through the theatre (an ambition that Goethe shared in his youth but later despaired of).[35]

Bulwer's portrait here is of the apprenticeship of an author, a branch of the *Künstlerroman*, which was a genre favoured by the German Romantics and like it derived from *Wilhelm Meister*. It was preceded in Britain by *Contarini Fleming* (1832),[36] a novel by Bulwer's friend Disraeli, and had among its successors Gissing's *Born in Exile* (1892) and Joyce's *A Portrait of the Artist as a Young Man* (1916). Elizabeth Barrett Browning's verse romance *Aurora Leigh* (1856) is particularly interesting as the apprenticeship of a woman poet, its main conflict being between her career as a poet and the hero's engagement in social reform and his wish to enlist her as wife and helpmate. For Ernest, these two spheres are not mutually exclusive.

His alternative career in political life, which he enters as a member of Parliament at the urging of Florence Lascelles, "the high-souled Idealist" (whose anonymous letters to him recall the messages to Wilhelm

Meister from the Society of the Tower), as well as by the example of De Montaigne, has no parallel in *Wilhelm Meister*; it thus exemplifies the difference that Bulwer, as we have seen, stressed between autocratic Germany and liberal England. The political sphere, in the strict meaning of the word, is not an option in Goethe's novel, its society still being ruled in a feudal fashion. (In the wider sense of the word, Wilhelm's early plan for a national theatre in the *Lehrjahre*, the Migration Society, and the Pedagogic Province in the *Wanderjahre* all represent political activities.) As we have seen, the ideal of *Bildung*, as well as the genre of the *Bildungsroman*, originated and continued to function in Germany largely as compensation for a lack of political power in the middle class, whose members were, according to Heine and the Jungdeutschen (Young Germans), slumbering and dreaming in their *Federbetten* while their neighbours were planning revolution.[37] German *Bildungsroman* heroes are typically not politically active. Hölderlin's Hyperion, in the epistolary novel of the same title (1797–99), is a notable exception in undergoing the *Bildung* of a *citoyen*.[38] In Britain Bulwer's novel of political apprenticeship[39] was preceded by Disraeli's *Vivian Grey* (1826–27)[40] and succeeded, for instance, by Meredith's *Beauchamp's Career* (1875) and George Eliot's *Daniel Deronda* (1876).

Whenever the "Great World" disappoints Ernest in his "mystic pursuit of utility,"[41] he has available a third sphere of useful activity, that of an improving landlord. His management of his estate and peasantry according to the ideal of justice[42] recalls Lothario in the *Lehrjahre*, who, after his adventures in the American Revolution, has returned to declare that he will now find his America on his own estates (see chap. 2 above). However, the sad sobriety of Ernest's renunciation of idealism at these times has more in common with the resigned spirit of Candide's resolution to cultivate his garden than with the sanguine wisdom of Goethe's character. And, indeed, Bulwer always leads Ernest back into the public arena.

Does Ernest's apprenticeship constitute *Bildung*? In proportion to Bulwer's stress on Ernest's Byronic heroism, the theme of self-culture diminishes.[43] Both the narrator and other characters acknowledge and admire Ernest's superiority of rank, beauty, and genius. For an instance of his "many-sided" talents, the typically enthusiastic narrator reports that "he had all the passion of a German for song and music – that wild Maltravers! – and his voice was sweet, his taste consummate, his science profound."[44] The "wanderer's ban" that repeatedly drives Ernest from England is caused, like Childe Harold's and Manfred's as well as Teufelsdröckh's, by the world's pressure on the sensitive hero, instead of resulting, as in Wilhelm's case, from the hero's wanderlust, a positive desire for a wider experience. It is true, though, that in the course of his travels, Ernest meets some of the influences that contribute to his development, notably the positive and negative examples of authorship in De Montaigne and Cesarini respectively and the love and, later, wisdom of Valerie de Ventadour.

Bulwer's attachment to the Byronic convention also confuses the issue of the relationship between personal merit and social rank.[45] Goethe's hero, a merchant's son, is presented and sees himself as limited by his bourgeois origins. He plans to and partly succeeds in using his training on the stage to acquire the harmonious self-culture that is the birthright of the nobility. As he writes to his child-hood friend Werner, in contrast to the bourgeois duty to specialize in some useful talent to the neglect of everything else, he finds in himself "an irresistible inclination to that harmonious cultivation which [his] birth denies [him]."[46] Goethe's ironic treatment of his hero's naïveté, as well as the action, indicates to the reader the limits of Wilhelm's prejudice, but at their best the nobly born characters support it, and Werner's philistine ambition is shown to result in a stunted personality.

Bulwer generally found the aristocracy deficient in education and culture, and inadequate to the task of improving society, and he presented the English middle class as the agent of progress.[47] In his attempt to return Ernest from his "Philosophy of Indifference" (also a stage in *Sartor*) to the "duties of active life," De Montaigne, the "large-souled" and practical French anglophile, points to "the Middle Class – the express creature of Civilization," as the new guarantor of progress.[48] His description of the burgher's discontent, despite his emancipation from serfdom, fits the general impulse, although not the goal, of Wilhelm Meister's rebellion against the limitations of his rank: "But the discontent does not prey upon the springs of life: it is the discontent of *hope*, not *despair*; it calls forth faculties, energies, and passions, in which there is more joy than sorrow."[49] There is, of course, also the difference between Goethe's novel being set before and Bulwer's after the French Revolution. Wilhelm remarks in the same letter on the limits set to bourgeois self-culture: "whether [the state of society] will ever change and how hardly concerns me."[50] In line with Bulwer's belief in merit, Ernest is preferred to a duke by Lady Florence on account of his literary genius. But Bulwer has it both ways: as a country gentleman from a family of "ancient name" and "ancestral estates," belonging to the class that Bulwer in *England and the English* calls the minor aristocracy, Ernest is constantly shown as commanding a legitimately superior position to the commoners in the novel and a place of equality in "the Great World."

However, in the most significant aspect of Ernest's apprenticeship, the moral one, and the only one announced in the preface of 1840, the message about Byronism is clearly Carlyle's: "Close thy *Byron*; open thy *Goethe*." Although the narrator explicitly distinguishes Ernest's pride from mere vanity, this central Byronic trait is chastised as a vice, rather than celebrated as a virtue, through the guilt that Ernest incurs in his love and loss of Alice and his near-incestuous love for her adopted daughter Evelyn. Deceived into believing Evelyn his daughter, he despairs: "He who had looked with haughty eyes on the infirmities of others, who had disdained to serve his race because of their human follies and partial frailties ... the Pharisee of Genius ... [his] Pride was shattered into fragments." This humiliation outlasts his undeception as to the practical facts, and with Alice at the grave of their child, "there vanished the last remnant of his stoic pride ... there did he pray to Heaven for pardon to himself, and blessings on the heart he had betrayed."[51] The motifs of guilty love in general and incestuous love in particular are major ones in *Wilhelm Meister*, as in all Romantic literature. For instance, although without Byronic pride, Wilhelm is humiliated in his self-righteous censure of Lothario's presumed betrayal of Aurelie when he discovers his own error of having condemned and abandoned Mariane and their child.[52]

Ernest's initial involvement with Alice, and to a lesser degree with Evelyn, borrows from Wilhelm's paternal/lover's care for Mignon, a figure of frequent English intertextual appropriation. Beauty, extreme youth, innocent simplicity, musicality, and devotion to the hero are the distinguishing features of all three. Alice's illicit love for the socially superior Ernest also alludes to Gretchen's love for the noble, gallant Faust: Gretchen pleads that, though resulting in sin, the impulse of her love was, "Oh God, so good! oh, was so dear!"[53] Since Alice is untutored in Christian morality and English propriety and consequently without remorse, it is Ernest and the narrator who have to make apologies for her pure love: "as she had not comprehended the danger, neither was she aware of the fall. In fact, she never thought of herself."[54]

Of particular interest in Bulwer's portrayal of Ernest's love of Alice is the implicit allusion to Schiller's essay "Über naive und sentimentalische Dichtung" (On naive and sentimental poetry [1795–96]). Especially for the idealism in Bulwer's aesthetics – Stang finds him the most articulate advocate of anti-mimetic art in his time[55] – Schiller provided less ambiguous critical and practical examples than Goethe. Objecting to the fashion of realistic art, Bulwer wrote in "On Art in Fiction": "the Ideal consists not in the imitation, but the exaltation of Nature; and we must accordingly inquire, not how far it resembles what we have seen so much as how far it embodies what we can imagine."[56] In the same vein he introduced his speculative novel *Zanoni* with the fictive author's discussion of the superiority of the Italian or Greek school to the Dutch: "the artist of the higher schools must make the broadest distinction between the real and the true, – in other words, between the imitation of actual life, and the exaltation of Nature into the Ideal."[57] In his essay "Über naive und sentimentalische Dichtung," Schiller similarly distinguished between real nature and true nature: the modern – that is, "sentimental" – poet, who lives in a state of culture, has to approach true nature, not through an imitation of the actual, but through a portrayal of the ideal.[58]

Bulwer's prefatory poem "The Ideal" in *The Pilgrims of the Rhine* (1832), revised as "The Ideal World" in 1849, seems to be the first of many allusions to Schiller's poem "Das Ideal und das Leben" (see chap. 1 above).[59] He translated the poem as "The Ideal and the Actual Life" for his collection *The Poems and Ballads of Schiller* (1844). In his introductory "Life of Schiller"[60] Bulwer distinguished the poet's journal, *Die Horen*, from British journals and their "broad and popular" topics because of its pursuit of "that Aesthetical cultivation – that development of Ideal Beauty, which, since his study of Kant, he regarded as the flower and apex of human accomplishment." The poet and the artist, he paraphrased Schiller's poem "Die Künstler" (The artists), "hold the highest intellectual rank Man can obtain" because in serving beauty they reveal truth.[61] Bulwer's work on Schiller as a poet and idealist completed the canonization of Schiller, whose English reputation had formerly been connected with Sturm und Drang plays and ghost and horror stories, such as *Die Räuber* (1781–82; trans. as *The Robbers* [1792]) and the novel fragment *Der Geisterseher* (1787–89; trans. as "The Ghostseer" [1795]).[62]

Schiller's theory, in his essay "On Naive and Sentimental Poetry," adds the idea of systematic progress to the association of Alice with Wordsworth's idea of benevolent nature and with Carlyle's natural supernaturalism.[63] To summarize the relevant argument in Schiller's essay, nature is "die Existenz nach eignen und unabänderlichen Gesetzen [existence according to its own and unalterable laws]"; consequently, our pleasure in natural phenomena is a moral, not aesthetic, pleasure: "Sie *sind*, was wir *waren*; sie sind, was wir wieder *werden sollen* ... [kindlich gesinnte Menschen] handeln und denken oft mitten unter den gekünstelten Verhältnissen der grossen Welt naiv [They *are* what we *were*; they are what we *ought to become* again ... persons of childlike mind act, and think naively even under the artificial conditions of the great world]." The path of both humanity and the poet lies from nature, which is at oneness (*mit sich eins*), through art, which is dividedness (*entzweit*), to the ideal, which seeks for unity in the infinite.[64]

Alice throughout is presented as "Nature's fairest child," "naively" obeying her own laws: "Amidst things foul and hateful had sprung up this beautiful flower, as if to proclaim ... the handiwork of God in scenes where human nature had been most debased by the abuses of social art."[65] Under her tutelage, Evelyn has retained a similar simple goodness, so that Ernest remarks to her, "I see already that from the world, vile as it is, you have nothing of contagion to fear ... Truth seems intuitive to you."[66] In contrast, Ernest, the "sentimental" modern genius, seeks nature in Alice and Evelyn as the sick man seeks health, in a conceit of Schiller's. The plot organizes Ernest's path from union with Alice and his own self, to separation from her and consequent divided aims, to a final reunion with her, blessed by nature. In its effective dedication to "the great objects that refine and elevate our race," his career now embodies, true to Schiller's third phase, the ideal of humanity (*Humanität*).[67]

Neither Ernest's political actions, which are now "infinitely more excellent," nor his theories, now "infinitely more wise," have been shown in the course of the work, except through their opposite, the actions and principles of Lumley Ferrers. The first we can deduce from Ernest's improvements on his estate, the second from the narrator's and Florence Lascelles's admiration for his idealistic essays and from his debates with De Montaigne, which point outside the work to Bulwer's own essay *England and the English*. The naturalistic specificity of the novels' historical-social context (which contrasts with Goethe's typical avoidance of naturalism as inartistic) relates them together with this essay to the literature of the Age of Improvement. As for Bulwer's use of statistics in De Montaigne's debate on progress,[68] Goethe had set a precedent in the *Wanderjahre* with the technical (although not statistical) report on the spinning and weaving industry. In a letter to his son on *A Strange Story*, Bulwer excused the inclusion of extra-literary genres in prose fiction with reference to Goethe's example: "It is clear that Goethe thought (as an artist) that prose narrative might include these dissertations [on Darwinism and metaphysics] which partially belong to essay. Thus in *Wilhelm Meister* he treats of an immense range of subjects."[69] Bulwer did not follow Goethe in the other notable interpolations: the novellas in the *Wanderjahre* (or the "Confessions of a Beautiful Soul" in the *Lehrjahre*).[70]

Bulwer subtitled *Alice* "The Mysteries," and to the 1851 edition of *Ernest Maltravers* he added the subtitle "The Eleusiana." The reference to gnostic initiation is not borne out by the general ethical and metaphysical context, which is more orthodox than that of *Wilhelm Meister*, apart from the occasional occult allusions, as, for instance, to Ernest's early astrological and alchemical studies in Germany and to Valerie de Ventadour's having "preceded [Ernest] through the 'MYSTERIES OF LIFE'" in learning "the real objects of being" and distinguishing "between the Actual and the Visionary – the Shadow and the Substance."[71] But in his next novel to deal with apprenticeship – and his own favourite – *Zanoni*, Bulwer portrays the conflict of the young hero, Clarence Glyndon, between the security of a conventional life as a British gentleman-painter and the promise of a perilous occult initiation into the mysteries of life, which in Glyndon's irreverent aspiration mean the power to "attain intercourse with the beings of other worlds ..., to influence the elements, and to insure life against the sword and against disease." Like the *Zauberlehrling* (sorcerer's apprentice) of Goethe's ballad, he fails his test; but he has nevertheless gained, according to his mentor, "an imperfect and new-born energy which will not suffer [him] to repose. As [he directs] it [he] must believe it to be the emanation of [his] evil genius or [his] good."[72]

This new theme in serious British fiction arose from Bulwer's interest in occult authors, many of German origin, and his apparent personal involvement in Rosicrucianism.[73] He found, of course, frequent examples of fictional heroes who are occupied in occult studies and practices in German Romantic literature, notably in Schiller's novel fragment *Der Geisterseher* ("The ghostseer" [1787–89]), E.T.A. Hoffmann's novellas, and Goethe's *Faust*, but the suitability of this milieu for an apprenticeship novel is exemplified in *Wilhelm Meister* itself: the initiation into a secret, high-minded society in Wilhelm's experience with the Society of the Tower in the *Lehrjahre* and the supernatural transcendence of time and space in the story in the *Wanderjahre* of Makarie's mystical union with the solar system and her concomitant benevolent wisdom towards her fellow humans, including Wilhelm.[74]

Makarie – her name means "blessed" in Greek – represents the highest level of insight into and union with nature and a commensurate ethical perfection. Periodically she in fact joins the starry sky, a transformation that Wilhelm once witnesses in a dream. Her attendant astronomer explains to Wilhelm that, in a way analogous to the sensible world being innate in the poet, the conditions of the solar system seem to be innate in Makarie. His initially skeptical calculations of her observations have demonstrated to him "dass sie sich ... geistig als ein integrierender Teil [im Sonnensystem] bewege [that she ... spiritually moves as an integral part in the solar system]."[75] When Zanoni, who also resembles Makarie in effective benevolence, bids farewell to his existence as an immortal initiate in order to sacrifice his life for his beloved, he summons a last vision of "the serener glories of creation": "Coursing through the fields of space, he beheld the gossamer shapes, whose choral joys his spirit had so often shared ... In his trance, all the universe stretched visible beyond."[76]

Again, it is characteristic of Goethe that Makarie's gifts come to her naturally, as does Natalie's goodness in the *Lehrjahre* (see chap. 2 above), in contrast with the hard-won and dearly-paid-for powers of Bulwer's "immortalists." This difference between Goethe and Bulwer – in Schiller's terms, between the "naive" and the "sentimental" author – is evident in their respective evaluations of Wilhelm's and Ernest's apprenticeships: Goethe's narrator leaves such questions as merit or luck and right mentors or benevolent nature open to the reader's judgment, whereas Bulwer's narrator asserts the moral certainties associated with Carlyle and *Sartor Resartus*. Bulwer admired in Goethe's style what Goethe himself prized: "Such effects with such ease," was his judgment of the *Wahlverwandtschaften* close to the time of writing *Ernest Maltravers* and *Alice*. "The interior meaning (without which no romance, no novel is worth much) so delicate, so noble; and yet the crowd of readers would call it the most ridiculous nonsense."[77] With his own work, however, he chose to make sure that the reader would miss neither the effects nor the interior meaning. As a result, his is not what he called Goethe's "perfectly pure *art*," but an art marred by rhetorical strain, what Trollope in his autobiography described as "the flavour of an effort to produce an effect ... He lived with his work, with the doctrines which at the time he wished to preach, thinking always of the effects which he wished to produce."[78]

Distaste for obvious rhetorical effort and for explicit authorial guidance has only grown since Trollope's criticism. Therefore today's literary historian and critic needs to allow for this "horizonal" prejudice in order to do justice to the cultural importance of Bulwer as a best-selling author who melded ideas from Goethe and Schiller with English ones, to fashion for English fiction a heterodox idealist aesthetics and an influential plot model.

4 The *Bildungsroman* as Foil: George Meredith's *The Ordeal of Richard Feverel* and *The Adventures of Harry Richmond*

Never popular like Bulwer's novels, George Meredith's were distinctly modern and highbrow. His reputation has fluctuated during and after his life as well as tending towards polarization. Having been honoured, including with the Order of Merit, as the leading English writer and a modern sage in his later life, he was generally dismissed after World War I in a generational reaction to the overvaluation of him as a champion of literary, intellectual, and moral modernity. E.M. Forster recorded, in *Aspects of the Novel* (1927), the change from "twenty or thirty years ago, when much of the universe and all Cambridge trembled." Current criticism generally confirms Virginia Woolf's reserved admission that his work, as that of an "innovator" and "great eccentric," "must inevitably be disputed and discussed."[1] Crucial in the development of English fiction are his "intellectualizing" of narrator and characters, his stress on interior perception, and his critique of gender roles.

In his departure from conventional English practice, Meredith found useful allies in German Romantic fiction in general and *Wilhelm Meister* in particular. After going to school in Germany, he became a competent and discerning friend of German letters. He included "the noble Goethe, the most enduring," in an account of his formative readings, and in a letter on the centenary of Schiller's death he described Schiller and Goethe as "the one poet and hero; the other poet and sage."[2] Both appraisals were addressed to German correspondents; depending on his correspondent, he would profess himself as sharing "the cult of Goethe" or declare himself more discriminating. For instance, Carlyle approved of and encouraged Meredith's admiration for Goethe from their first meeting, yet Meredith, in the *Pall Mall Gazette*, suggested the substitution of Goethe's poems for *Wilhelm Meister* for a selection of the best hundred books.[3] Despite the German content in his novels, German reception of his work was late and slow, starting with an essay in 1899 and the translation of his novels in 1904, *Richard Feverel* being the first. But German response was less divided than English, and it was appreciative of his philosophical ambitions for the novel.[4]

The ideal of *Bildung* and the genre of the *Bildungsroman* served Meredith in several novels as a strategy to critique the conventions of English life and of English fiction respectively. As instances of the diverse uses to which Meredith put the genre, *Diana of the Crossways* deals in part with the heroine's apprenticeship as a writer, *Beauchamp's Career* with the apprenticeship of a politician, and *The Amazing Marriage* with the heroine's critically selective adoption of an English lady's voice, both literally and figuratively. The reader's *Bildung* through the process of reading the fiction, a main characteristic of the genre, is typically the subject of the "subplot" between the narrator and the reader.[5]

The novels in which the German prototype is most evident are his first novel proper, *The Ordeal of Richard Feverel* (1859; substantially revised, 1878) and *The Adventures of Harry Richmond* (1870–71 in the *Cornhill Magazine*; 1871 separately). Although different in important respects, such as generic mode, narrative voice, and tone, they have in common a critical variant of a central feature of the *Bildungsroman* and the novel of development in general: in contrast to being fatherless (like Diogenes Teufelsdröckh, Ernest Maltravers, Pip, Jane Eyre, and Philip Carey, for instance, and like Wilhelm Meister early in the story) and consequently having to choose from surrogate mentors, Richard and Harry suffer from a surfeit of paternal guidance and need to create their identity in rejection of their fathers, a process that is made painful by the strong love that binds them.[6] The rejection is complicated by the fact that in each case the father has assumed the missing mother's love as well, like Arkady's father in Turgenev's *Fathers and Sons* and in contrast, for instance, to D.H. Lawrence's *Sons and Lovers*. Both fathers have devised a scheme that prescribes the son's path to adult identity, and in both cases the result is intended to vindicate an original suppositious wrong inflicted on the father.[7] That is, the father inhibits the son's organic individual *Bildung* and moreover, despite all professions of love, treats him as a means to his own end. In contrast to the *Bildungsroman* model, neither novel has a happy conclusion.

The idea of an ordeal in the title and in the content of *The Ordeal of Richard Feverel* suggests not so much a novel of development as the baroque genre of the *Prüfungsroman* (novel of testing), which portrays the testing of the Christian hero's courage in battle and constancy in love.[8] What is being tested in this secular novel, however, is at a first view the man-made "System" (more prominent in the first edition) by which the hero has been raised and its fitness to make him brave in battle and constant in love. At a second view the possibility of beneficent human guidance as such – also a subject for irony in Goethe's *Wilhelm Meister* – is being tested. Meredith does not always clearly distinguish between these two issues. The hero's failures are, then, those of his father's guidance, which finally result in the diminishment of Richard's humanity, the opposite of the aim of *Bildung*; at the end it is clear that he "will never be what he promised," the expression in his eyes being that of a blind man.[9]

Richard's father, Sir Austin, shares his name with the father in Bulwer's domestic novel *The Caxtons* (1849).[10] The contrast with the selfless benevolence that informs Austin Caxton's "schooling" of his son shows up the main flaw in Sir Austin's conception and application of his System. Unlike Sir Austin, Bulwer's Austin Caxton tempers his learned principles with subtle humour and plain wisdom, so that his son, according to the son's report as narrator, enjoys a rare filial intimacy with his father and, unlike other young men, consults him profitably on problems of career and love. The novel has a happy ending. Sir Austin also shares his name with another character in *Richard Feverel*, his cousin Austin Wentworth, whose influence on Richard is uniquely and wholly beneficent, both in the question of Richard's loyalty to a "friend-in-arms," Tom, and of his fidelity to Lucy and their child. The identity of the names of these two mentors emphasizes the contrast between their respective influence and consequently the error of Sir Austin's trust in his System. Unfortunately, while Sir Austin is ever-present, Austin Wentworth is mostly abroad, and his interventions are rare.

As we have seen, Goethe insisted on the component of chance in *Bildung*, but in Wilhelm Meister's life, chance tends eventually towards good. The factor of chance in Richard's case is compounded by the replacement of the ideal tutor by another cousin, the "wise youth" Adrian, whose frivolous skepticism and sensualism make him a Mephistophelean companion to Richard. Meredith satirizes Adrian's attitude as follows: "When one has attained that felicitous point of wisdom from which one sees all mankind to be fools, the diminutive objects may make what new moves they please, one does not marvel at them: their sedateness is as comical as their frolic, and their frenzies more comical still."[11] The attitude parallels that of Mephistopheles when, in the "Prologue in Heaven" in *Faust, Part One*, he compares a human being's rational aspirations to the cicadas forever trying to fly, yet falling back into the grass. He is of course contradicted by the Lord immediately and proven wrong finally.

Meredith had a personal interest in pedagogic theories and methods; he had attended a German school of the Moravian Brothers for nearly two years, and he chose a Pestalozzi school for his son. Juliet Mitchell supposes that in Sir Austin and his System Meredith possibly responded to Rousseau and his *Émile*.[12] In a letter he explained the moral of *Richard Feverel* as meaning "that no System of the sort succeeds with human nature, unless the originator has conceived it purely independent of personal passion."[13] Egoism as *the* hindrance to civilized humanity would become the subject of his best essay and his best novel, *The Essay on Comedy* (delivered as a lecture in 1877) and *The Egoist* (1879) respectively. Perhaps he considered the Moravian Brothers and Pestalozzi capable of such pure conception; his portrait of the Princess Ottilia's tutor, Professor von Karsteg, in *Harry Richmond* suggests that he believed it humanly possible. But to Sir Austin's guidance of Richard applies what Goethe shows in his novel and voices through the Abbé, "a child, a young person who gets lost on his own path is preferable ... to many who walk correctly on an alien path."[14]

It is true that Sir Austin uses for his System some organic metaphors for the anticipated phases of his son's development, such as the Wordsworthian "seed-time," but the generalizations as such run counter to the individualistic ideal of *Bildung*. Sir Austin calls himself a "Scientific Humanist," yet his scientific approach is compromised by his wounded pride, as a result of his betrayal by his wife and his friend before the action of the novel opens, and his humanism by the resultant "Manichaean tendency" in his view of human nature,[15] which is contrary to Meredith's own convictions and the view expressed in the ideal of *Bildung* and dramatized in the *Bildungsroman* in general and *Wilhelm Meister* in particular. Sir Austin's resolve to play Providence in a fallen world – "The boy had embarked ... and the devil on board piloting" – drives him to the punitive interventions in his son's education that he justifies, for instance, as "pollarding." Besides dogmatic prescriptions for Richard's development, he proscribes Richard's spontaneous imaginative inclinations, namely, the writing of poetry and the love of Lucy. The prohibition of the one has as its result that Richard's "spirit stood bare"; the interdiction of the other defeats what might indeed have been the triumphant conclusion of the System: "could Sir Austin have been content to draw the arrow to the head, and let it fly, when it would fly, he might have pointed to his son again, and said to the world, 'Match him!' " But Sir Austin lacks the wisdom of Prospero in his trust in Miranda.[16] Instead, his method suggests Carlyle's ascetic principles in *Sartor*.[17] (Carlyle does not seem to have read the novel as a refutation and expressed his approval of it to Meredith.)[18] By the end of the novel the narrator's earlier injunction, "Away with Systems,"[19] has been joined by Sir Austin's greatest admirer, Lady Blandish, who, in her final role as narrator, pronounces herself "sick ... of theories, and Systems, and the pretensions of men," and by Sir Austin's own admission of his presumption.[20]

Richard himself never exhibits the robust irritation with his mentors and their prescriptions that Wilhelm Meister repeatedly does. For instance, annoyed and suspicious, Wilhelm complains: "es wäre wunderbar, wenn jene geheimnisvollen Mächte des Turms, die immer so geschäftig sind, jetzt nicht auf uns wirken und, ich weiss nicht, was für einen seltsamen Zweck mit und an uns ausführen sollten [it would be marvellous if those secretive powers of the Tower, which are always so busy, were not to influence us right now and execute I know not what strange purpose with and on us]."[21] And he protests against the recitation of the maxims from his *Lehrbrief* (apprenticeship certificate): "Ich bitte Sie, ... lesen Sie mir von diesen wunderlichen Worten nichts mehr! Diese Phrasen haben mich schon verwirrt genug gemacht [I beg you, ... don't read me any more of these wondrous words! These phrases have already confused me enough]."[22] In contrast, when Richard's father has killed his love of poetry and of Lucy, Richard himself conceives, instead of *Bildung*, of spurious world-improving and self-punishing schemes, which are infected by false family pride. The ideal model for a positive enterprise is represented by his boyhood hero Austin Wentworth, who is establishing in South America a community of British poor and unemployed working men. While the conception is indebted to the Christian socialists' co-operative workshops in Britain and to Carlyle's doctrine of work, in its particularity the scheme alludes to the Migration Society in *Wilhelm Meisters Wanderjahre*.

On learning of the birth of his and Lucy's son, Richard experiences a short return to common sense and thus, in Meredith's terms, to true humanity. The conversion occurs, like crucial experiences in several of his other novels, in a German natural setting, here during a thunderstorm in the Black Forest. In a chapter entitled "Nature Speaks," Richard feels addressed by the lightning, the thunder, a leveret he is sheltering, and finally, in a forest chapel, by something he will not inquire into: "He was in other hands. Vivid as lightning the Spirit of Life illumined him. He felt in his heart the cry of his child, his darling's touch."[23] In his conception of nature as a benevolent guiding force, Meredith was rare among authors of his period, the majority view being represented by Tennyson and Hardy, for instance, but he shared his with Goethe. Whether it is a case of influence[24] or of inspiring confirmation is a matter of conjecture and, for my argument about the rhetorical use, immaterial. (In Eckermann's *Gespräche mit Goethe*, which Meredith found "always interesting and instructive,"[25] Goethe is recorded as saying, "Die Hauptsache ist, dass man eine Seele habe, die das Wahre liebt, und die es aufnimmt wo sie es findet [The main thing is that one have a soul which loves the true and which absorbs it wherever it finds it].")[26] Richard's return to nature does not, though, lead to the moral maturity achieved by Wilhelm Meister.[27] Wilhelm has transcended humanity's involuntary servitude to nature, most pathetically exemplified in the harper's story, through his self-culture, which has taught him to accept nature's laws. As the Abbé despairingly says of Aurelie, another character pathetically self-destroyed, "Ach! ... welche unendliche Operationen Natur und Kunst machen müssen, bis ein gebildeter Mensch dasteht [Alas! ... what infinite operations must nature and art perform until a cultivated person is produced]."[28]

The implicit allusion in Richard's news about his son to Wilhelm Meister's receiving new and lasting purpose from the knowledge that Felix, the boy in his care, is his own son is ironic. For Wilhelm, "[a]n diesem Tage, dem vergnügtesten seines Lebens, schien auch seine eigne Bildung erst anzufangen; er fühlte die Notwendigkeit, sich zu belehren, indem er zu lehren aufgefordert ward [On this day, the most cheerful of his life, his own self-culture seemed to truly begin; he felt the necessity of educating himself by being required to teach]."[29] For Richard, the awakening at the news of his paternity is ultimately futile, since on his return to England he is drawn back into the "humbug" of the Feverel pride and effectively sacrifices the love of his wife and child, as well as his full humanity, to a false idea of honour in a duel.

In *The Adventures of Harry Richmond* Meredith explicitly presents a positive alternative of *Bildung* to the deluded schemes of the father, Richmond Roy, for his son, in the education and self-culture of the German Princess Ottilia. Her *Bildung* for a life that will integrate her individual nature and her social duty contrasts with her fictional precursor, Disraeli's melodramatic archduchess in *Vivian Grey*. His Austrian princess is uneducated though talented and spirited, her noble German suitor revolting, and her renunciation of the hero in favour of a political marriage a bitter yielding to necessity.[30] Harry Richmond, Meredith's hero-narrator, recognizes, to his own grief, that "the laws of society as well as her exalted station were in harmony with her intelligence. She thought them good, but obeyed them as a subject, not slavishly: she claimed the right to exercise her trained reason."[31] Her name alludes to one of the four protagonists in Goethe's *Wahlverwandtschaften*, a novel that Meredith admired. His Ottilia is, however, a "schöne Seele" of a less quietist nature than Goethe's Ottilie, rather resembling Natalie in *Wilhelm Meister*. Contrary to Sir Austin's dictum in the "Pilgrim's Scrip" that "Woman will be the last thing civilized by Man," Princess Ottilia acts as the Goethean *Ewig-Weibliche* (the eternal feminine) who, as "[his] mentor and [his] glory,"[32] raises the hero by precept and example to a truer consciousness of his own self, his society, and his role in it.

That Meredith could express less idealistic views of the role of women in actual German society does not, of course, affect the persuasiveness of the allusion as a rhetorical gambit in this fiction. In the later *Essay on Comedy*, for instance, he wrote of the immaturity of the Germans' social intelligence: "They are kings in music, we may say princes in poetry, good speculators in philosophy, and our leaders in scholarship ... and when their men, as in France, and at intervals at Berlin tea tables, consent to talk on equal terms with their women, and to listen to them, their growth will be accelerated and shapelier."[33]

In her perfection as much as in her correction of her errors, Ottilia exemplifies the virtue implied in one of the precepts in Wilhelm Meister's *Lehrbrief*: "Handeln ist leicht, Denken schwer; nach dem Gedanken handeln unbequem [To act is easy, to think hard; to act according to thought burdensome]." Harry comes to accept his defeat in courtship because he understands "that she was a woman who could only love intelligently. She had the power of passion and it could be stirred; but he who kindled it wrecked his chance if he could not stand clear in her intellect's unsparing gaze." In his earlier optimistic attempts to win her, he has studied at a "famous German university, not far from Hanover" – that is, Göttingen – to remedy her view of him as "idle, worthless." The narrative rushes over his academic life in a short summary to return to his father's romance plotting on his behalf. Later on, wishing him "to work" in order to make her marriage to him and her consequent exclusion from German succession less painful to her father, Ottilia adds, "You will find that hard work in England."[34] The irony in the pun on "work" – Ottilia's command of English has improved since her early charming errors – reflects her tutor's unflattering comparisons of English and German society, to which I shall return.

Ottilia's intellectual and moral expectations of him make Harry feel like "a man on a monument," that is, impersonating, as his father did literally, a German prince instead of being his English "naked" self, which he can be with Ottilia's rival in his affections, Janet Ilchester, the favourite of his grandfather, Squire Belcham. Initially, each woman lacks a quality necessary for his heart's desire: "I thought of Janet – she made me gasp for air; of Ottilia – she made me long for earth." However, after Janet has come under Ottilia's idealizing influence, she is presented as having assimilated some of the princess's imaginative attraction, which makes her the hero's perfect mate. Against his will, Harry is impressed "by the air of high-bred friendliness" between the two. "Ottilia had caught the spirit of [Janet's] frank manner of speech; and [Janet], though in a less degree, the princess's fine ease and sweetness. They conversed, apparently, like equal minds."[35] In the reciprocal effect of the friendship between Ottilia and Janet, Meredith portrays naturalistically what Goethe in *Wilhelm Meisters Lehrjahre* presents symbolically through the juxtaposition of the practical Therese with Wilhelm's idealized image of Natalie as the Amazon and with the real Natalie, finally Wilhelm's spouse.

Specifically addressed to the hero's future role in English society are his discussions with Ottilia's tutor. Professor von Karsteg is preceded by Disraeli's Mr Sievers, the young prince of Little Lilliput's tutor, who had "nothing of the pedant, much of the philosopher."[36] Von Karsteg criticizes English society for being materialistic and stagnant, ruled as it is by an aristocracy and a merchant class who shirk their responsibilities. That is, by implication, he condemns as unworthy both Harry's father's scheme for him to claim his place as a royal descendant and his maternal grandfather's rival plan that he should claim his place as a magnate whose landed wealth has been increased by successful speculation. In a long debate in which Harry's responses are mostly annihilated, von Karsteg expresses his skepticism about the "scheme of life" that Harry might have as an Englishman: "Yes, you [English] work hard for money. You eat and drink, and boast of your exercises: they sharpen your appetites ... We strive and fail ... but we strive on, while you remain in a past age, and are proud of it. You reproach us with lack of common sense, as if the belly were its seat."[37]

Von Karsteg acts very much as Meredith's mouthpiece, expressing a view of British society that derives from Carlyle. At the time of writing the novel, Meredith frequently reflected on national differences in his letters on the occasion of the Franco-Prussian War and on the social-political evolution of British society in his letters to his friend Admiral Frederick Maxse. For instance, although sympathizing with the

French, he compared their "ignorance, or folly, or vanity" with the Germans' "persistently honourable career in civic virtue" in a letter to his son at school in Germany; and of England, "this pot-bellied country," he wrote to Maxse: "The aristocracy has long since sold itself to the middle class; that has done the best to corrupt the class under it. I see no hope but in a big convulsion to bring a worthy people forth."[38] Von Karsteg's discussions occupied considerably more space in the manuscript versions of the novel.[39] His criticism has weight because the German principality of Sarkeld and its ruling family, von Eppenwelzen – no comical names here – are treated seriously, especially the relation between privilege and responsibility. This approach resembles *Wilhelm Meister* but is unlike the humorous portrayals, for instance, of Weissnichtwo in *Sartor* and of the ducal town of Pumpernickel, with its reigning "Transparencies," in *Vanity Fair*, which both allude to Weimar, as does Sarkeld. It is part of Harry's education to learn to reject his father's deluded view of the principality as a romantic stage play or a German fairy tale. The extended metaphor of play-acting associated with Harry's father alludes to Wilhelm Meister's need to outgrow his infatuation with his "theatrical mission" and to perceive it, in the practical Jarno's words, as "playing with hollow nuts for hollow nuts."[40]

Not as desolate as the ending of *Richard Feverel*, the ending of *Harry Richmond* is nevertheless not as optimistic as that of *Wilhelm Meister*. The hero has been disabused of false goals, which recall Wilhelm's initial choice between the claims of the tragic muse and the muse of trade.[41] Harry's father's scheme for him to claim a position as a royal descendant, playing prince to Ottilia's princess, has come to nothing but shame, and his grandfather's plan that he should claim his place as a millionaire squire's heir, with Janet as hostess, has been shown up for its limitations. The fire that at the end destroys his grandfather's house and in it his father, and thus figuratively both men's dominance, alludes to Carlyle's symbolic "Baphometic Fire-Baptism" in *Sartor*,[42] an idea that Carlyle associated with Goethe. Unlike Goethe and Bulwer, Meredith ends his novel without indicating a vocation for the hero that would do justice to his self-culture and benefit a worthy community. The indeterminate conclusion compels readers to ask themselves the reason for this lack of fulfillment, and the German context directs them to try to find it in the particular conditions of British society, rather than in life itself.[43]

In *Beauchamp's Career* (1875 in the *Fortnightly Review*; 1876 separately) Meredith took an apprenticeship as far as the maturing of a political vocation, attempting, in his own words, "to show the forces round a young man of the present day, in England, who would move them, and finds them unutterably solid, though it is seen in the end that he does not altogether fail, has not lived quite in vain." (In contrast to Bulwer's favouring a Byronic cast for Ernest Maltravers's character, Meredith declares in his novel, "Beauchampism ... is the obverse of Byronism.") The novel's ending is more equivocal than Meredith's avowed intention here. When the hero's quest for love and vocation has resulted in a marriage and a political career both of which promise harmonious fulfillment, he dies in an attempt to rescue two boys from drowning. His friends bitterly compare his sacrifice with the saved life of one of the working-class boys. Their unspoken judgment is "visible in the blank stare at one another ... after they had examined the insignificant bit of mudbank life remaining in this world in the place of him": "This is what we have in exchange for Beauchamp!" The narrator does not establish any dissent from their bitterness. Arnold Kettle comments, "This is evolution, the survival of the fittest, the way the world progresses," without any evaluation of the author's attitude to this truth.[44] Yet in the phrase "the insignificant bit of mudbank life," Meredith rejects by allusion the social application of Darwin's valiantly optimistic conclusion to *The Origin of Species* that "to contemplate a tangled bank" is to be impressed by the "grandeur" of the evolutionary view of life as progress through the "Extinction of less-improved forms."[45]

The pointedly accidental end to Beauchamp's career resembles the spirit in which Meredith represents the death in a duel of the historical German socialist leader Ferdinand Lassalle in his fictionalized account, *The Tragic Comedians* (1880). Without being intentional on the protagonists' part, these premature deaths nevertheless imply the author's skepticism about the possibility of a beneficent political career,[46] in a way that is similar to Bazarov's accidental death in Turgenev's *Fathers and Sons*. A more explicit judgment on the futility of social-political action – in this case, Greek liberation – is expressed by the hero through his suicide by drowning in Hölderlin's *Hyperion*. In contrast, at the end of the *Wanderjahre*, Wilhelm Meister saves a young man from the fatal effect of drowning by applying his new mastery as a surgeon and then recognizes him as his son: "So standen sie fest umschlungen, wie Kastor und Pollux, Brüder, die sich auf dem Wechselwege vom Orkus zum Licht begegnen [So they stood in a close embrace, like Castor and Pollux, brothers, who have met on the path changing from Orcus to light]."[47] In saving his son from death, Wilhelm proves his adult responsibility, in contrast to his youthful irresponsibility, even ignorance, about his son, and in healing an apparent stranger, he proves his new rank as master of a vocation useful to the community.[48]

In both *Richard Feverel* and *Harry Richmond* the form and style contribute to each novel's critique of a prejudiced perception of life. Like Bulwer, Meredith cited Goethe (in addition to Shakespeare, Molière, and Cervantes) as authority for joining idealism to realism: "there is no natural conflict. This completes that."[49] Like Goethe, he abhorred naturalism; instead, he employed in these novels a variety of literary conventions in order to test them, in Gillian Beer's words, as "possible but limited ways of looking at his world."[50] Such preoccupation with *Weltanschauung* is typical of the *Bildungsroman*. The "medley"[51] of competing genres and modes in *Richard Feverel*, more varied than in any other of Meredith's novels, reflects on Sir Austin's futile attempt to trap the random manifoldness of life in his System.[52] The romance plot that shapes *Harry Richmond*, which exceeds the romance elements of any other of Meredith's novels and resembles *Wilhelm Meister*, represents a main theme of this *Bildungsroman* and the whole genre, namely, the self's wishful assumption of omnipotence vis-à-vis life, the world, and indeed, itself.[53]

In contrast to Bulwer, Meredith creates for his narrators a distance which resembles that of Goethe's narrator. In *Richard Feverel* he achieves this, first, by shifting the narrator's tone between identification, neutrality, and judgment and, secondly, by shifting the narrative point of view between the authorial narrator and several of the characters, compelling the readers to form their own conclusions. *Harry Richmond* is Meredith's only novel with a first-person narrative voice. Here the distancing occurs for readers through the need to adjust to the ongoing development of the protagonist-narrator's perception, from naive to mature, of the world and his place in it. The style itself changes with this development, accomplishing what the narrator says he intends: to "shape his style to harmonize with every development of his nature."[54] Beyond the hero's scrutiny of his motivation (this was more extensive and prominent in the version before proof),[55] his observations as narrator on "the busy little creature within [him], whom we call self,"[56] grow increasingly acute. His continued exposure of his youthful egoism is especially unsparing, in comparison, for instance, with the self-exonerating heroine-narrator of *Jane Eyre*. Note the different sense of entitlement in Harry: "The central *I* resembled the sun of this universe, with the difference that it shrieked for nourishment, instead of dispensing it. My monstrous conceit of elevation will not suffer condensation into sentences."[57]

As noted above, Meredith made substantial cuts in both novels: in *Richard Feverel* between the first and second edition, especially in the elaborations on Sir Austin's System; in *Harry Richmond* after proof, especially in Professor von Karsteg's discourses comparing German and English society. The subject matter in both cases is intellectual, which Meredith, like Carlyle and Bulwer, knew to be unpopular with British readers of fiction. Contemporary reviewers of *Richard Feverel* in its first edition generally disliked and dismissed the novel,[58] and nearly twenty years elapsed before the second, substantially revised edition. It was likely as a result of this experience that Meredith made the cuts to *Harry Richmond* even before publication. Throughout his novel-writing career he maintained his purpose to include "brain-stuff" in his fiction, to show, as he said of *Harry Richmond*, "the action of minds as well as of fortunes – of here and there men and women vitally animated by their brains at different periods of their lives – and of men and women with something of a look out upon the world and its destinies";[59] that is, retranslated into German, characters with a *Weltanschauung*. The revisions of the two novels are evidence of Meredith's struggle to represent each hero's *Bildung* through his reaction to a variety of *Weltanschauungen* and his forming his own, without alienating his readers with a surfeit of intellectual content. Failure in this task might have brought down such criticism as is voiced in Henry James's review, in form of a fictive dialogue, of George Eliot's *Daniel Deronda*, published five years after *Harry Richmond*: "I would as soon read a German novel."[60]

5 The "Philistines' Nets": George Eliot's *Middlemarch*

Rebelling against the pre-revolutionary social order, which denies self-culture to the burgher, Wilhelm Meister insists, in his letter to his philistine friend Werner, that like a nobleman he will pursue his "desire and purpose ... to cultivate [himself], completely as [he is], ... whether one day [the condition of society] will be changed at all, and what is going to be changed, are of little concern" to him in his urgency.[1] Mary Ann Evans experienced for herself the strain of developing her gifts and, as George Eliot, choosing the right vocation within the "dull medium," the "web," of her society's particular impediments. Her gender having exposed her to such strain at its worst – the pseudonymity of her fiction is symptomatic – she made both men's and women's needs for a vocation, a life filled with action "at once rational and ardent,"[2] and its frustration by their social milieu a central theme and plot of her last two novels. The possibility of social reform, as apart from political reform, is presented skeptically in *Middlemarch* (1871–72), as it is in *Felix Holt, the Radical* (1866); it is rejected together with England in favour of a utopian, proto-Zionist community abroad in *Daniel Deronda* (1876).

In *Middlemarch* and *Daniel Deronda* George Eliot uses standards alluded to as German to critique the English milieu, which in her presentation commonly breeds only "philistine" ambitions and frustrates ideal aspirations when they arise. In adopting this German perspective, she follows the example of Carlyle's early work; however, her models of German excellence are chosen less idiosyncratically and from a much more diverse field of intellectual and artistic activity. She wrote in an essay on Carlyle in 1855, "there is hardly a superior or active mind of this generation that has not been modified by Carlyle's writings."[3] Her study of German was apparently first inspired by him. She was also familiar with the novels of Bulwer, with whom the reviewers of her own novels frequently compared her.[4]

George Eliot's activity in the 1840s and 1850s as translator and reviewer in periodicals with a new cosmopolitan interest, particularly the *Westminster Review*[5] and the *Leader*, contributed significantly to establishing the currency of the German allusions in her two last novels. The most important examples of her work are, in the field of biblical criticism, her translations of David Friedrich Strauss's *Das Leben Jesu* (1835), *The Life of Jesus* (1846), and of Ludwig Feuerbach's *Das Wesen des Christentums* (1841); *The Essence of Christianity* (1853), in social history, a review of the first two volumes of Wilhelm Heinrich Riehl's revised *Naturgeschichte des Volkes* (1856); and in literature, her translations from Goethe for G.H. Lewes's *Life of Goethe* (1855) and her review "German Wit: Heinrich Heine" (1856). To quote her own summary of German achievements, based on her first-hand knowledge: "[Germany] has fought the hardest fight for freedom of thought, has produced the grandest inventions, has made significant contributions to science, has given us some of the divinest poetry, and quite the divinest music, in the world."[6]

A contemporary reviewer of *Middlemarch* and close friend of George Eliot's, Edith Simcox, praised the novel's originality: "The effect is as new as if we could suppose a *Wilhelm Meister* written by Balzac."[7] The novel excels in the realistic presentation of both the interior development of the individual and the exterior conditions (a favourite word of George Eliot's) of society, and moreover, of the reciprocity between the two. This last issue is a major focus of optimistic versus pessimistic interpretations within the novel, educing positive or negative connotations from the metaphor of the web. As we have seen in chapter 1, the humanistic persuasion, from Humboldt to J.S. Mill, was that the free intercourse of diverse individuals engaged in variously harmonious self-culture would bring about the desired social progress, namely, a more humane society.[8] What George Eliot shows is that such intercourse, even when relatively free from political control compared with Germany, pre- and post-revolutionary, is not exempt from social compulsions; nor is the pursuit of self-culture. In balance, the compromising effect of the Middlemarch ethos, including town and county, on even the most emancipated members of the community is indisputable, whereas their reforming purchase on this ethos is matter for ironic skepsis, if not pessimism. The conflicts between the individual's aspirations and the social medium constitute the main action of the novel, whereas the measure of defeat or victory is mostly taken in summary in the Finale. The backdating of the novel from the time of writing, which was that of the second Reform Bill (1867), to the time of the first Reform Bill (1832) – "those times when reforms were begun with a young hopefulness of immediate good which has been much checked in our days"[9] – implies the dismissal of political ameliora- tion, and thus agreement with the spirit of Wilhelm Meister's pre- revolutionary dismissal of the relevance of political change to his task of *Bildung*.

The alternative to the provincial life targeted in the novel's subtitle, "A Study of Provincial Life," is not London but cosmopolitanism as a perspective.[10] That is, Middlemarch stands for central English values, which can be interrogated from an eccentric position "abroad," a strategy which in *Daniel Deronda* becomes more prominent. That there are also indigenous standards present, such as the Wordswor- thian principle of the sympathetic imagination,[11] goes without say- ing. Germany provides George Eliot with most of the cosmopolitan allusions that serve as judgments of her English characters and of the English community. The backdating of the novel's action – 1832 was also the year of Goethe's death – avoids contamination with negative associations about Bismarck's "Prussianized" Germany, especially with the Franco-Prussian War of 1870–71.[12] The main issues in the novel that are evaluated in a German context are the search for a "key" of meaning and the desire for and dedication to a vocation in general and science, scholarship, and the arts in particular. An exami- nation of the German context will also result in a re-evaluation of the vexed status of Will Ladislaw.

The Prelude and the Finale affirm the primacy of the "Miss Brooke" story, one of the novel's two original impulses, and with it the primacy of the issue of women's vocation.[13] The fictional precursors in this de- bate, especially Jane Austen's *Emma* (1816) and Charlotte Brontë's *Jane Eyre* (1847), typically concluded that marriage – "Reader, I married him" – was the complete answer to the heroine's energy and desire for purposeful activity: "women feel just as men feel; they need exercise for their faculties, and a field for their efforts as much as their brothers do."[14] For the contemporary reader, the vocational theme of Dorothea Brooke's story responded to the questions that had been silenced in the marriage plot of these novels and others like them. *Middlemarch* continued more urgently the inquiry started by George Eliot in *The Mill on the Floss* (1860) by decreasing for Dorothea, a county heiress, the limits of understanding, education, and wealth of the miller's daughter Maggie Tulliver, which might otherwise be construed as the sufficient cause for women's compromised quest for a vocation. The author's promotion, then, of the rival interest of an "epic life ... of far-resonant action," rather than "the twanging of the old Troubadour strings,"[15] relates Dorothea's story to Wilhelm Meister's quest, with its idealism, disillusions, and realistic but satisfactory result.

In Dorothea's story George Eliot balances the typically masculine and optimistic *Bildungsroman* with the feminine and pessimistic *Entsagungsroman* (novel of renunciation; see chap. 2 above), of which Mme de Staël's *Corinne, ou L'Italie* (1807) is the famous precursor. George Eliot likely knew or knew of German examples, since some of their women authors were friends of hers. While writing *Middlemarch*, she probably read Wilhelmine von Hillern's *Ein Arzt der Seele* (Physician of the soul [1869]; trans., *Ernestine* [1879]).[16] George Eliot had met the young author in Freiburg in 1868. Von Hillern's heroine is "cured" of her ambition and incipient career as a published freethinker and scientist by the eponymous physician, who then marries her. More explicitly critical of sexual inequality in vocation and love is Ida von Hahn-Hahn's *Gräfin Faustine* (1841; trans., *Countess Faustina* [1844]), which in the young widowed heroine's life of free love and painting refashions Mme de Staël's *Corinne*, as George Eliot herself did in her dramatic poem "Armgart" (1871) and in the story of Daniel Deronda's mother, the Alcharisi. The "emancipated" von Hahn-Hahn's visit to London in 1846 created special interest in her novels. Both German authors enjoyed fair reputations in England during their lifetime.[17]

George Eliot reread *Wilhelm Meister* in 1870, during the writing of *Middlemarch*. In her review announcing the publication of Lewes's *Life of Goethe*, "The Morality of Wilhelm Meister" (1855), she concurred with his defence of the novel as moral: "[Goethe's] mode of treatment seems to us precisely that which is really moral in its influence ... [he] waits patiently for the moral processes of nature as we all do for her material processes."[18] What needs defending in this mode is the disinterested "intellectual contemplation" of "all human things" by the author, or narrator in today's usage: "Goethe ... writes like a passionless Mejnour."[19] Lewes wrote that, although "the Artist has been content to paint scenes of life, *without comment*," unlike a preacher, the work has "deep and healthy moral meaning."[20] Carlyle, without the taste for natural studies but with a preacher's disposition, had found Goethe's narrative tone more alien and reprehensible, describing the author as "[wearing] a face of the most still indifference," even a "slight sardonic grin."[21] Although George Eliot's narrative tone is not detached, she claims the scientist's truth of disinterested observation. Lewes's summary of Wilhelm's apprenticeship is fair, and it is close to the principles in George Eliot's last two novels: the novel portrays "the influence of life upon Wilhelm in moulding and modifying his character, raising it from mere impulse to the subordination of reason, from dreaming self-indulgence to practical duty, from self-culture to sympathy."[22]

Wilhelm Meister's reform missions and their frustrations, as well as his final achievement as a surgeon with the Migration Society, are conditioned by the social and economic changes in the pre-revolutionary German principalities. The narrator's attitude to these changes is neutral, and to his hero's final accommodations it is benevolent, even congratulatory: like Saul, who found a kingdom instead of the asses he went looking for, Wilhelm has achieved more than he feels he deserves. In contrast, George Eliot's tone is elegiac when she compares, in the Prelude and the Finale, the "blundering" life of her modern St Theresa, "foundress of nothing," with the medieval original's "epic life" in the reform of a religious order. As cause, she cites the lack of a "coherent social faith and order which could perform the function of knowledge for the ardently willing soul,"[23] a lack in modern English life which in her next and last novel, *Daniel Deronda*, is compensated for by the hero's assumption of his Jewish heritage.

George Eliot introduces ambivalence into this account of an objective historical change for the worse. By alluding to the classical literary genres – epic in the Prelude, tragedy in the Finale – she reminds the reader of her defence of the realistic novel in her reviews and in *Adam Bede* (1859). With a change of literary perspective, what is conventionally unhistoric, hidden, unvisited, without name,[24] is perceived as positive and thus equal to the standard of significance represented by medieval saints and Greek heroines. The blundering lives turn into beautiful works of art. This transformation is ultimately the reader's work, and the narrator's ambivalence has created a continuing critical debate about Dorothea's heroism and the narrator's attitude to it.

Her rank and wealth and her orphaned and single status free Dorothea from some constraints that affect the typical apprenticeships. However, her gender is the principal condition that makes her a victim of the social medium, her privileges merely serving to emphasize its powerful influence on any apprenticeship.[25] In her review essay on Margaret Fuller and Mary Wollstonecraft (1855), George Eliot argued that "we want freedom and culture for woman, because subjection and ignorance have debased her, and with her, Man."[26] Without culture, Dorothea's freedom leads to false choices, entrapment, and lack of purpose. Instead of culture in the sense imported from Germany, she has received the kind of education that her guardian, Mr Brooke, and society think fitting for the "lightness about the feminine mind – a touch and go – music, the fine arts, that kind of thing – they should study those up to a certain point," with the addition of that "toy-box history of the world adapted to young ladies."[27]

One of the consequences of this education is an undirected "yearning after some lofty conception of the world which might frankly include the parish of Tipton and her own rule of conduct there."[28] The narrator's attitude to the possibility of such a lofty conception is ambivalent: its unavailability is a judgment both on Dorothea's naïveté and on her society's philistinism.[29] The other consequence of her lack of culture is the absence of the necessary critical standards and habit of mind for evaluating what is offered her as keys to life, whether it is puritanic asceticism or Mr Casaubon's scholarship gathered for his "Key to All Mythologies." But through her experience of competing theories and the conflict of each with her own observations, she enters the process of conscious self-culture. George Eliot had already used the terms "key" and "clue of life" in *The Mill on the Floss*. In her family's misfortune, Maggie "wanted some key that would enable her to understand and, in understanding, endure, the heavy weight that had fallen on her young heart." Like Dorothea when she initially puts her faith in Casaubon's learning, Maggie imagines that "if she hád been taught 'real learning and wisdom, such as great men knew,' … she should have held the secrets of life."[30] George Eliot's educated contemporary readers would have recognized the German context for the notion of a "binding theory" or key to life, namely, the concept of *Weltanschauung*, the goal of the *Bildungsroman* hero as well as of the reader. They may also have recognized in her dramatization of an open-ended method in this quest the method of German literary, biblical, and historical hermeneutics, the "hermeneutic circle," which she herself had helped transmit to Britain through her translations and reviews.[31]

Dorothea finds strength in a most ascetic key, Carlyle's doctrine of work, after the key developed by her first husband, the scholarly Casaubon, instead of opening "wide vistas," has locked her into the labyrinthine tunnels of his jealous love and ambition, and after the key of romance seems to have opened only onto the scene of illicit lovemaking between the man she loves, Will Ladislaw, and her rival, Rosamond Vincy. Following a night of anguished protest against her injury, Dorothea "felt the largeness of the world and the manifold wakings of men to labour and endurance. She was part of that involuntary, palpitating life."[32] That is, in Carlyle's words, she closes her Byron and opens her Goethe. The motto of the next chapter continues in this spirit. It is from the beginning of *Faust, Part Two*, an apostrophe to Earth by Faust after Gretchen's death in prison and his restoration through nature, that is, through Ariel and his spirits' song: "Du regst und rührst ein kräftiges Beschliessen, / Zum höchsten Dasein immerfort zu streben [You stir and move a strong resolve to strive forever for the highest existence]."[33] Another allusion to this aspect of Faust is Dorothea's "delightful plans," when she feels barred by Casaubon's will from marrying Ladislaw and therefore from remarrying at all, to "take a great deal of land, and drain it, and make a little colony, where everybody should work, and all the work should be done well."[34]

But the author has prepared a more optimistic prospect, like Goethe's for Wilhelm Meister, for Dorothea. In *The Mill on the Floss*, George Eliot created for Maggie an escape from ascetic labour and endurance into a death that is an apotheosis through connection backward with the past, childhood, and familial love. Instead, Dorothea goes forward to a life that resembles, although cast in a lesser genre, the achievement of the saint's legend in the Prologue. The similarity of the metaphor alerts the reader to the difference from Maggie's death in the flood: "Her full nature, like that river of which Cyrus broke the strength, spent itself in channels which had no great name on the earth. But the effect of her being on those around her was incalculably diffusive: for the growing good of the world is partly dependent on unhistoric acts."[35]

The positive meaning of the ambivalent ending has generally been considered more problematic than the negative, mainly because the first requires the reader's approval of Will Ladislaw as a good choice for Dorothea. More even than the narrator's ironic treatment of Ladislaw's sensibility, the authorial self-indulgence in the undistanced description of his charms has provoked critics' exasperation with him as an "inadequate rescuer" and mate.[36] However, Ladislaw, whose name alludes to Ladislaw I of Poland, an eleventh-century saint and reformer,[37] brings essential gifts and attitudes to the transformation of Dorothea from a self-absorbed, "short-sighted," puritanic provincial into a beneficent, though modest and indirect, agent of reform. In the Finale the narrator avers that Dorothea has succeeded, although after the novel's dramatized action, at her self-imposed task, in her words to Ladislaw, of "widening the skirts of light and making the struggle with darkness narrower,"[38] and the reader has indeed witnessed examples of her interventions on behalf of Farebrother and Lydgate, which have saved both from the worst effects of entrapment in the Middlemarch web, namely, self-contempt and cynicism.[39]

Ladislaw is throughout associated with light: "The first impression on seeing Will was one of sunny brightness"; his smile is "a gush of inward light."[40] Unlike the "taper" of Casaubon's mind, Ladislaw's perspective illuminates positive connections to life for Dorothea. In its application to Ladislaw the metaphor strongly suggests an allusion to Matthew Arnold's concept of "sweetness and light" in *Culture and Anarchy*. The controversial and influential essays that made up his book appeared while George Eliot was planning her novel, and she certainly read the first essay, which forms the book's introduction, and "Sweetness and Light."[41] In summary, culture disinterestedly pursues "a harmonious expansion of *all* the powers which make the beauty and worth of human nature."[42] Arnold prescribes culture for England to compensate for faith in external machinery and to complement the exclusive pursuit of moral perfection. "Sweetness and light" – that is, beauty and intelligence – especially distinguish culture from philistinism. The main qualities of culture here – internal, becoming, harmonious, aesthetic, disinterested – all derive from the German idea of *Bildung*[43] and correct the changes that Carlyle made in favour of his own moral preoccupation. Arnold connected the pursuit of sweetness and light with the study of "the best that has been thought and said" in world literature, particularly in poetry. In an earlier essay, "On the Study of Celtic Literature" (1866), he had pronounced: "Our great, our only first-rate body of contemporary poetry is the German; the grand business of modern poetry, – a moral interpretation, from an independent point of view, of man and the world, – it is only German poetry, Goethe's poetry, that has, since the Greeks, made much way with."[44]

The German vantage point of Arnold's criticism of English philistinism is explicit in the precursor to *Culture and Anarchy*, the satirical 1866 "letters" to the *Pall Mall Gazette* which made up *Friendship's Garland*. Their fictive author is a young visiting Prussian, Arminius, Baron von Thunder-ten-Tronckh, named in allusion to *Candide* and "edited" by Arnold in allusion to *Sartor Resartus*. The letter writer represents Arnold's perspective from abroad after his visit to the Continent in 1865 to report on higher education, especially in Prussia.

In naming the middle-class type "Philistine" in *Culture and Anarchy*, in distinction from the aristocratic "Barbarians" and the working-class "Populace," labels that immediately stuck, Arnold made popular a German usage of the biblical term that Carlyle had introduced in 1827 as a German nickname for the "partisans" of the "partial abandonment of poetry, in favour of political and philosophical Illumination."[45] As an example of a more general meaning, Goethe's Werther complains about the philistine's (*Philister*) sensible, practical view of love;[46] but especially in their collaborative polemical distichs *Xenien*, Goethe and Schiller had made the philistine mentality a frequent target. To cite the distich entitled "Vorsatz" (Resolve), their "gay verse," which "only reveres the good," was to "annoy the philistine, tease the enthusiast, torment the hypocrite." For instance, the distich "To the Philistines" ironically warns them, "Don't take pleasure in the butterfly, the villain breeds you the caterpillar, / Which eats the marvellous cabbage, almost out of your bowl."[47] According to Arnold, in each class a few "aliens" emerge who differ from the class mentality and pursue their "best self" and disinterested truth. Their characteristic is their "humanity," rather than their class identity.[48]

Heinrich Heine, the German proto-intellectual par excellence,[49] was the other German authority whom Arnold and Eliot recruited for their English anti-philistine campaign.[50] After his elegy "Heine's Grave" (1862–63), Arnold published a lecture on Heine in the *Cornhill* in 1863. Attributing Carlyle's neglect of Heine to the eccentricity of "a genuine son of Great Britain," Arnold praises Heine as "the most important German successor and continuator of Goethe in Goethe's most important line of activity ... as 'a soldier in the war of liberation of humanity.'"[51] But unlike Goethe earlier, Heine was impatient with gradual reform after the post-Napoleonic political restoration: "His counsel was for open war. Taking that terrible modern weapon, the pen, in his hand, he passed the remainder of his life in ... a life and death battle with Philistinism." Arnold remarks, "*Philistinism!* – ... Perhaps we have not the word because we have so much of the thing."[52] In "Culture: a Dialogue," a rebuttal in the *Fortnightly Review* to "Culture and Its Enemies" (the first part of *Culture and Anarchy*), Frederic Harrison had a fictitious admirer say that "'there is a master of our English tongue, spiritual with true Teutonic *geist*, radiant as the sunniest France. Admit,' I cried, 'that Heines are of every soil, peculiar and confined to none.'"[53] George Eliot, in a letter of general approval, lodged her reservation with Harrison about his dismissal of culture: "I don't know how far my impressions have been warped by reading German, but I have regarded the word 'culture' as a verbal equivalent for the highest results of past and present influences."[54]

Arnold adopts the term "Philistine" because it describes "the [stiff-necked and perverse] enemy of the children of light or servants of the idea," and the middle class "not only do not pursue sweetness and light, but ... even prefer to them that sort of machinery of business, chapels, tea-meetings, ... which makes up the dismal and illiberal life" he has been attacking.[55] This use corresponds with George Eliot's portrayal of the Middlemarch community. She uses the term "Philistine" when Lydgate has sunk to the behaviour of the men who are betting at the Green Dragon.[56] And she has Casaubon research the origins of the Philistine god Dagon.[57] She had preceded Arnold in his observation on the lack of an English word for *Philister*. In her review of Riehl she notes it as "an epithet for which we have no equivalent, not at all, however, for want of the object it represents." She then substitutes for Riehl's definition "that the *Philister* is one who is indifferent to all social interests, all public life, as distinguished from private and selfish interests,"[58] a wider meaning gathered from her German reading, especially from Goethe: "We imagine the *Philister* is the personification and the spirit which judges everything from a lower point of view than the subject demands."[59] She cites Goethe's verse in which he claims his right to a national monument; as Blücher did from the French, he has freed Germany from the philistines' nets (*Philisternetzen*).[60] Goethe's metaphor is identical with her own frequent substitute for the web, as in Rosamond's netting.[61]

Will Ladislaw is presented positively with respect to his role as the missionary of *Bildung*. In the least sanguine reading of his actual effect on Middlemarch, he serves as a touchstone of its values, his cosmopolitanism showing up parochialism; his disinterestedness, self-interested partisanship; his bohemianism, propriety.[62] The Middlemarch judgments on him betray the judges' own prejudices: "Ladislaw is a sort of gypsy; he thinks nothing of leather and prunella" (Lydgate); "he wants to go abroad again … [for] what he calls culture" (Casaubon); "some emissary. He'll begin with flourishing about the Rights of Man and end with murdering a wench" (Hawley, the lawyer and town clerk, to Hackbutt, the rich tanner); "a quill-driving alien" (community gossip).[63]

Ladislaw's pursuit of self-culture is as manifold as his German namesake's. He has studied at Heidelberg, which, after Weimar and Jena, was the home of the third German Romantic "school," including Eichendorff, Brentano, and Arnim, and the place of origin for the Romantic collection of folk songs *Des Knaben Wunderhorn* (1805–8). That is, with respect to Arnold's advocacy of "German poetry, Goethe's poetry," for a "moral interpretation, from an independent point of view, of man and the world," the Heidelberg Romantics represent a less "classical" and less independent point of view, suited to a late-born's apprenticeship, and the sample of Ladislaw's poetry in chapter 47 is characteristically self-indulgent. Nevertheless, the author directs the reader to approve of Ladislaw's course by having Casaubon call it "anomalous": "And now he wants to go abroad again, without any special object, save the vague purpose of what he calls culture, preparation for he knows not what." In contrast, Dorothea, judging with imaginative sympathy, correctly sees its virtue: "After all, people may really have in them some vocation which is not quite plain to themselves … They may seem idle and weak because they are growing."[64] The narrator asks the reader's good faith in attending to Ladislaw's quest for a vocation, which is described as sincere and clear-sighted.[65] Read back from *Daniel Deronda*, Ladislaw's indecisions are cast in a positive light by Deronda's indeterminate quest for an ideal vocation and its final goal outside England in the service of Zionism, as Dorothea's hope to "lead a grand life here – now – in England"[66] is given ironic prominence.

Ladislaw next tries painting, an art about which Arnold was silent in *Culture and Anarchy*, as about all the arts except poetry, but which, as an object of contemplation, plays an important role in Wilhelm Meister's *Bildung*.[67] For this pursuit Ladislaw goes to Rome, where he studies with a representative of the German Nazarenes. In *Die Romantische Schule* (1833), which George Eliot included in her review essay, Heine recorded how the aesthetic-mystic theories of the Schlegels and the *Künstlerromane* by Tieck and Wackenroder[68] inspired some German painters at the beginning of the century to imitate pre-Raphaelite and early German religious painting.[69] They founded the St Luke Brotherhood, later dubbed "Nazarene," in Rome and, in George Eliot's words, "the youth of other nations who worked or idled near them were sometimes caught in the spreading movement."[70] The Nazarenes, whose most famous representatives were Johann Friedrich Overbeck and Peter von Cornelius, enjoyed much favourable publicity in England in the 1840s and 1850s, with Pugin as their main advocate and Prince Albert their most eminent patron.[71]

Ladislaw's German mentor, Naumann, functions like the members of the Society of the Tower in *Wilhelm Meister* and represents the type of the dedicated German artist, in contrast with the bungling English amateur, a precursor of the musician Herr Klesmer in *Daniel Deronda*.[72] Naumann calls Ladislaw's painting "pfuscherei," which is "his most opprobrious word." It means "bungling" and, in an idiom particular to Naumann's sense, "dabbling at another's trade." Justly, if with some conceit – and in a joke of the author against herself – he comments to Dorothea, "Oh, he does not mean it seriously with painting. His walk must be belles-lettres. That is wi——ide."[73] From a sad new understanding of her marriage to Casaubon, Dorothea takes up the word "bungling" in her next interview with Ladislaw: "I have often felt since I have been in Rome that most of our lives would look much uglier and more bungling than the pictures, if they could be put on the wall."[74] The judgment has been introduced from the start when, in the Prelude, the narrator describes modern women's lives as "blundering" in comparison with "epic life."[75]

Naumann's wit is more playful than Klesmer's and as atypical of a German as Heine's was, according to George Eliot's essay "German

Wit: Heinrich Heine." His facetious interpretation of Dorothea as "antique form animated by Christian sentiment – a sort of Christian Antigone"[76] alludes to a major German theme, the antithesis requiring synthesis, which Lewes, for instance, noted in much of Goethe's work, especially in *Iphigenie*, and which Arnold, borrowing the terms from Heine, represented as Hebraism and Hellenism in *Culture and Anarchy*. Desiring a balance but, like Heine in Germany,[77] finding too much of Hebraism in English society, Arnold emphasized the need for the Hellenic spirit: "The governing idea of Hellenism is *spontaneity of consciousness*; that of Hebraism, *strictness of conscience*."[78] George Eliot had treated the theme in her Renaissance novel, *Romola* (1863). In *Middlemarch* the conflict is dramatized as existing within Dorothea – for instance, in her ambivalent response to the jewels in the novel's first scene – and between her and Ladislaw in their debates about the good and the beautiful. The implication is that it is resolved through their marriage.

Naumann parodies Fichte's subjective idealism[79] when he claims the right to paint Dorothea, against Ladislaw's unprofessional prohibition: "the universe is straining towards that picture through that particular hook or claw which is put forth in the shape of me – not true?"[80] He also burlesques Ladislaw's jealousy of Casaubon, his mother's cousin, by alluding to Schiller's comedy *Der Neffe als Onkel* (The nephew as uncle): "in a tragic sense – *ungeheuer* [monstrous]!"[81] To free himself from familial obligation and the ludicrous implication that in Dorothea he loves his aunt, Ladislaw declines any further financial support from Casaubon. The triangle of course also alludes to the story of Tristan and Isolde and Tristan's uncle King Mark, newly topical through Wagner's opera (1865).

Having for the while "accepted his bit of work" as editor of Mr Brooke's reformist paper, the *Pioneer*, in order to stay near Dorothea, Ladislaw "studied the political situation with as ardent an interest as he had ever given to poetic metres or mediaevalism." The narrator comments: "never mind the smallness of the area; the writing was not worse than much that reaches the four corners of the earth."[82] That is, Ladislaw is writing "higher journalism" with the ardour that has been Dorothea's characteristic. Mr Brooke's assessment of him is typically hyperbolical: "a kind of Shelley ... he has the same sort of enthusiasm for liberty, freedom, emancipation – a fine thing under guidance."[83] On a smaller scale, a closer resemblance in both career and writing style is with Arnold and Heine. In Heine's own preferred description of himself, repeated by Arnold, Ladislaw is a soldier with a pen. There is, of course, also a resemblance with G.H. Lewes, whom Carlyle is reported to have called "the Prince of Journalists."[84]

George Eliot's four review essays on Heine had preceded Arnold's, appearing, unlike most other English evaluations except for two important articles by Lewes, even before Heine's death and constituting the most important introduction of Heine to England. In the major essay, "German Wit: Heinrich Heine" (*Westminster Review* [1856]), she described Heine's *Reisebilder* in terms that parallel her portrayal of Ladislaw's mentality: "letting his thoughts wander from poetry to politics, from criticism to dreamy reverie, and blending fun, imagination, reflection, and satire in a sort of exquisite, ever-varying shimmer, like the hues of the opal."[85] On the English, she quotes Heine, in place of "wholesome bitters": while acknowledging "the many brave and noble men who distinguished themselves by intellect and love of freedom," he found the mass hateful; they were "miserable automata – machines, whose motive power is egoism ... it seems to me as if I heard the whizzing-wheel-work by which they think, feel, reckon, digest, and pray."[86]

Ladislaw's status as a journalist receives further definition from George Eliot's review of Riehl's German social history, in terms of which Ladislaw is one of the "day-labourers with the quill, the literary proletariat." She found most interesting Riehl's chapters on this special segment of the fourth estate: "In Germany, the *educated* proletariat is the leaven that sets the mass in fermentation; the dangerous classes there go about, not in blouses, but in frock-coats."[87] However, while recommending his social definitions, she ignored his arch-conservative, *völkisch* evaluations and abstained from discussing his warning, after the 1848 revolutions, against this "inauthentic" (*unächt*) fourth estate, which in its vengeful resentment of the state's refusal to provide for it according to its role and reputation – "unnaturally" enhanced in Germany – negates the state and agitates to destroy the "historical society," its weapon not the sword but the wasp sting.[88] Heine would be a famous example; having agitated against despotism and for democracy during the period of restoration, he went into exile in Paris in 1831 and continued there until his death.

George Eliot's English version of the type is a reformer rather than a revolutionary.[89] As the unprovided-for grandson of Casaubon's disinherited aunt, Ladislaw also fits Riehl's type of the "aristocratic proletariat." In George Eliot's words, "[t]he custom [in Germany] that all the sons of a nobleman shall inherit their father's title, necessarily goes on multiplying that class of aristocrats who are not only without function but without adequate provision, and who ... [are] usually obliged to remain without any vocation."[90] In the England of Middlemarch, Casaubon tries to veto Ladislaw's career as a journalist in his own community by appealing to the genteel code, which, he writes in a letter, "should hinder a somewhat near relative of mine from becoming in anywise conspicuous in this vicinity in a status not only much beneath my own, but associated at best with the sciolism of literary or political adventurers." Lady Chettam is puzzled as to how to rank Ladislaw – "It is difficult to say what Mr Ladislaw is, eh, James?" – whereas Ladislaw himself is "rather enjoying the sense of belonging to no class," of never having "had any caste,"[91] except when he fears that this situation might disqualify him for Dorothea's regard.

Ladislaw's usefulness to Dorothea is represented in their debates about the good and the beautiful. Under the influence of puritanical notions, Dorothea has censored her natural sensitivity to the beautiful. The belief which she confesses comforts her most is "[t]hat by desiring what is perfectly good, even when we don't quite know what it is and cannot do what we would, we are part of the divine power against evil – widening the skirts of light and making the struggle with darkness narrower." Ladislaw counters that his religion is "[t]o love what is good and beautiful when I see it."[92] The allusion in Dorothea's name to the famous – and infamous – German Romantic Dorothea Veit, inspiration, lover, and later wife of Friedrich Schlegel, is therefore strictly partial, excluding the role of enthusiastic companion in free love, which Schlegel celebrated in his answer to Goethe's *Wilhelm Meister*, the novel fragment *Lucinde* (posthumous, 1799). In the terms of *Culture and Anarchy*, the partnership of Dorothea and Ladislaw implies her indirect support of reforms that are conceived in sweetness and light and his resolve, as parliamentarian, to make the good prevail. Dorothea's idealistic ardour has found direction in the practice of Ladislaw, the "ardent public man."[93] Thus their lives are redeemed from their early "bungled" appearance; instead of *Pfuscherei*, they resemble art.

Just as the success, however modest, of Dorothea's and Ladislaw's aspirations is presented in a German context, so too are the failures of the scholar Casaubon and the physician Lydgate. Casaubon is the man who is freest from external social pressures in the group that also includes Farebrother, Ladislaw, and Lydgate. Yet his dedicated work on the "Key to All Mythologies" is futile, and that for reasons – namely, British insularity and lack of conceptual scope – which are diagnosed with reference to German examples. Ladislaw points out to Dorothea, not without spite, that Casaubon's work is worthless, "as so much English scholarship is, for want of knowing what is being done by the rest of the world. If Mr Casaubon read German he would save himself a great deal of trouble."[94] The narrator comments, "Young Mr Ladislaw was not at all deep himself in German writers." But he is justified in that, unlike Casaubon, he is not jealously afraid of submitting his own attempts in poetry and painting to German experts. He is also right, which the author, who was deep in German writers, and her knowledgeable readers knew.

In opposition to Casaubon's Christian orthodoxy, she wrote, for instance, in her review of R.W. Mackay's *The Progress of the Intellect* (1850): "The introduction of a truly philosophic spirit into the study of mythology – an introduction for which we are chiefly indebted to the Germans – is a great step in advance of ... the orthodox prepossessions of writers such as Bryant, who saw in the Greek legends simply misrepresentations of the authentic history given in the book of Genesis."[95] Casaubon is only "crawling a little way after ... men like Bryant," in Ladislaw's words to Dorothea,[96] and duplicating in his search for a single key Georg Friedrich Creuzer's hypothesis, in *Symbolik* (1810–12), of a single source. George Eliot took issue with Creuzer's approach in connection with her reservations about Mackay's "allegorizing mania," which attempted to ground multiple polytheistic myths in a single monotheistic truth: "any attempt extensively to trace consistent allegory in the myths must fail."[97] Of the ubiquitous warnings in the novel against all a priori interpretation, the most famous is the narrator's parallel between the perception of concentric circles produced by a candle held to irregular scratches on a pier glass and a character's egoistic perception of events.[98]

It is true that Casaubon evokes the stereotype of the German *Gelehrter*, as George Eliot had herself caricatured him in her youthful invention of Professor Büchermann (bookman) for the amusement of her friends during her labours on Strauss's work in 1846.[99] But in her serious, mature estimate, Casaubon's failure to match his laboriousness with impartiality and a productive conception contrasts with what she had praised in Riehl and defined, in "A Word for the Germans" (1865), as typical of "the German mind": "largeness of theoretic conception, and thoroughness in the investigation of facts."[100]

Medical science is the other field in the novel where these German qualities count. In the *Wanderjahre* Wilhelm Meister apprentices himself for a while to a sculptor of anatomical models intended to advance medical science, and he owes his son's rescue from fatal drowning to a new technique.[101] In *Middlemarch* Lydgate's ambition, after postgraduate medical studies in Paris, is to go beyond Bichat's theory of primary tissues to discover their common basis, "the primitive tissue." That is, his is another search for a key – a key to all pathologies. His hypothesis of an *Urzelle* alludes to Goethe's morphological concept of the *Urpflanze*, which Lewes had made familiar in his *Life of Goethe*.

THINGS ONE WOULD RATHER HAVE LEFT UNSAID.

"Ach! gracious Laty, I hope zat my long Cherman Lecture on ze Boetical Aspects of ze Bliocene Beriod did not *bore* you fery much zis afternoon?"

"Oh, not at all, Professor Wohlgemuth. I don't *understand* German, you know."

Lewes judged the concept of the *Urpflanze* "misleading and infelicitous," but he credited Goethe with establishing morphology and concluded, "on some of the highest scientific testimonies in Europe," that "in the organic sciences Goethe holds an eminent place."[102] Through her collaborations with Lewes, George Eliot's knowledge about the state of Lydgate's research field was as good as her more immediate knowledge about Casaubon's field.

Lydgate fears that his courtship of Rosamond will conflict "with the diligent use of spare hours which might serve some 'plodding fellow of a German' to make the great imminent discovery."[103] German biologists did in fact disprove his hypothesis in 1833.[104] What makes Lydgate susceptible to being caught in the web of Middlemarch is his dislike of "barefooted doctrines, [his] being particular about his boots." He is radical only in relation to medical reform and scientific discovery, the narrator explains, "half from that personal pride and unreflecting egoism which I have already called commonness."[105] In "the rest of practical life" he is a philistine. The narrator warns, when first describing his youthful "moment of vocation," "that distinction of mind which belonged to his intellectual ardour, did not penetrate his feeling about furniture, or women, or the desirability of its being known ... that he was better born than other country surgeons."[106] In this quality he differs from the frugality that English visitors typically observed and often ridiculed about German men of note. Acknowledging this attitude in her article "Three Months in Weimar" (1855), George Eliot described Goethe's house in Weimar as disappointing "to English eyes": the "hardy simplicity" of the "dull study with its two small windows, and without a single subject chosen for the sake of luxury or beauty,"[107] suggested to her a contrast with Scott's study at Abbotsford.

Ironically, while one German context provides a standard for success, another one signals failure: the degradation of Lydgate's intellectual passion results, after the novel's action, in his practising during the season on wealthy patients in a Continental spa.[108] This end of his career fulfills an early warning, when he learned from Farebrother that a former roommate and fellow student of Lydgate's in Paris had given up his utopian plans to create a Pythagorean community and, instead, "is practising at a German bath, and has married a rich patient." Lydate's response then was scornful and sure of his own independence from "the harness" of social pressures that Farebrother was trying to caution him against.[109] Read back from *Daniel Deronda*, the final setting of Lydgate's career is suggestive of Leubronn, the scene of Gwendolen's gambling.

6 Regeneration in German Keys: George Eliot's *Daniel Deronda*

Four main subjects in *Daniel Deronda* (1876) are presented in a German context: gambling, music, the historical organic community, and Judaism. They are interrelated. Goethe and Heine are the historical German figures who are recruited most frequently and significantly to lend authority. The first scene of the novel is set, like Lydgate's final vocational defeat in *Middlemarch*, in a German spa; the fictive Leubronn (Lion's Well) fits into a series of German spas in English fiction, all scenes of spurious excitement and desperate risk, such as Bad Ems in Disraeli's *Vivian Grey* (1826–27), Baden-Baden, "the prettiest booth of all Vanity Fair," in Thackeray's *The Newcomes* (1853–55; chap. 30) and in Meredith's *The Amazing Marriage* (1895), and Bad Nauheim in Ford's *The Good Soldier* (1915). A novel by Turgenev, whose works George Eliot read in French translation and who became a favourite companion of the Leweses in 1878, parallels important aspects in *Daniel Deronda*. *Smoke, or Life at Baden* (1867; translated into French and English in 1868) plays largely in Baden-Baden and shares with *Daniel Deronda* the hero's involvement in the debate about the regeneration of his society, in this case Russia; the heroine's fatal gambling at marriage, to a cold brute, for the sake of her own social rank and power and her family's economic security; and the dynamic between the hero and heroine, which oscillates between his ambivalent erotic subjection to her and her intermittent moral submission to him. Henry James linked Turgenev and "the author of *Daniel Deronda*" as the "blessing of reviewers."[1]

Since the middle of the eighteenth century the Continental spas, with their gambling rooms, had become a principal playground for the English upper classes, who were also the wealthiest guests. For instance, Baden-Baden, the site of the marriage gamble in Meredith's *The Amazing Marriage*, had by the middle of the nineteenth century a large "English colony," who maintained villas, as did the most prominent occasional visitor, Queen Victoria, or who stayed at the best hotel, which from 1840 was named "Englischer Hof." However, after the unification of Germany, the Prussian "reign of Virtue" prevailed, and the gambling rooms at Baden-Baden and Bad Homburg were closed in 1873, bringing the salutary purpose and the natural beauty of these watering places into focus, as Henry James reported in his sketch on "Homburg Reformed" (1873).[2]

George Eliot had visited Bad Homburg with Lewes in 1872, before its closure, which had been announced for the following year, and again in 1873. Although she reported to her publisher Blackwood the scarcity of "dramatic 'Stoff'" to be picked up in the Kursaal, it made her cry to see Byron's young great-niece "in the grasp of this mean, money-raking demon."[3] While there, she read Leopold Kompert's stories *Aus dem Ghetto* (From the ghetto [1848]).[4] On both occasions she also visited Frankfurt and its Jewish quarter; that is, she pursued both strands of her "Jewish novel." A year earlier, in 1871, William Powell Frith's panorama painting *The Salon d'Or, Homburg* had been exhibited with popular success at the Royal Academy.[5] There is no evidence that Eliot saw that season's exhibition, but at least she very likely heard and read of the famous painting and possibly saw one of the many reproductions, and she could rely on the familiarity of many of her readers with it.[6] Frith's scene resembles the one that presents itself to Deronda: a serried crowd of various human types in different attitudes attends to a roulette table – two tables in the novel. In both works there is one exception: in the painting a pale, large-eyed young woman stands alone in the foreground with her back to the table and gazes at the viewer; in the novel a "melancholy little boy" gazes blankly towards the doorway, that is, facing the observing Deronda and representing Gwendolen in her aspect as moral supplicant.

The subject of gambling reflects on major issues in the novel. Of interest in the German context are the following three. First, based on luck, gambling contrasts with the idea of vocation and its requirement of personal gifts, dedication, and arduous progress, exemplified through music in the novel. In Herr Klesmer's words of warning to Gwendolen about a vocation in music, "it is out of reach of any but choice organizations – natures framed to love perfection and to labour for it; ready ... to endure, to wait."[7] Secondly, the vagaries of fortune's wheel, as Gwendolen experiences them, contrast with the idea of organic unity and continuity, in the moral economy of both the individual and the community. Finally, the shared interest in gambling creates a pseudo-community where, instead of mutual recognition and responsibility, "there was a certain uniform negativeness of expression which had the effect of a mask."[8] Here the cosmopolitan aspect of the crowd – "very distant varieties of European type" – indicates a mechanical, *unächt* (Riehl) principle of connection. The gambling community represents George Eliot's criticism of late-nineteenth-century English society, its implied obverse being the community that Deronda projects in his proto-Zionist enterprise.

The epigraph to the first chapter – "No retrospect will take us to the true beginning; and whether our prologue be in heaven or on earth, it is but a fraction of that all-presupposing fact with which our story sets out" – alludes to the beginning of Goethe's *Faust, Part One*. The play's third frame, "Prologue in Heaven," dramatizes the conflicting views of human aspirations as futile or redemptive. Mephistopheles scorns humanity: "Wie eine der langbeinigen Zikaden, / Die immer fliegt und fliegend springt / Und gleich im Gras ihr altes Liedchen singt [like one of the long-legged cicadas, which keeps flying and jumping in flight and soon sings again its old song in the grass]." Whereas the Lord counters: "Ein guter Mensch in seinem dunklen Drange / Ist sich des rechten Weges wohl bewusst [A good man, in his dark striving, is quite aware of the right path]."[9] And he is of course proven right in Goethe's Romantic version of the legend. George Eliot's alternative in the epigraph, of heaven or earth, emphatically suggests by omission the third realm in Goethe's play, hell: "Vom Himmel durch die Welt zur Hölle [from heaven through the world to hell]."[10] Hell corresponds to the questions at the start of George Eliot's narrative. Asked by the as-yet-unidentified Deronda, they read like authorial questions: "Was the good or the evil genius dominant in those beams? Probably the evil." These allusions relate the gambling scene to the sensualist diversions with which Mephisto tries to satisfy Faust and win his wager: the students' carouse in Auerbach's Cellar, the cavalier seduction of Gretchen, and the witches' Walpurgis Night. They raise the expectation that in Gwendolen too the evil genius may lose to the good genius, her good genius soon to be Deronda, of whom she senses in this scene "that he was measuring her, ... that he was of different quality from the dross around her, that he felt himself in a region outside and above her."[11]

Competing with the literary aspirations of her hostess, Mrs Arrowpoint, Gwendolen quotes Mephisto's observation in Auerbach's Cellar:

"die Kraft ist schwach, allein die Lust ist gross [the power is weak, yet the desire is great],"[12] with more truth about herself than she suspects at this stage. During Gwendolen's marriage the narrator compares Grandcourt's "stupidity" in his manipulation of her to the blunders that Mephisto would make if "thrown upon real life." The implicit parallel is between Grandcourt's imaginative blindness to Gwendolen's "remorseful half," with respect to her having made her own gain from Mrs Glasher's loss,[13] and Mephisto's quintessential negation of Faust's ideal and moral sense, the second of the two souls dwelling in Faust's breast.[14] At the end of her gamble on marriage, Gwendolen recognizes that she has been "following a lure through a long Satanic masquerade, which she ... had seen the end of in shrieking fear lest she herself had become one of the evil spirits who were dropping their human mummery and hissing around her with serpent tongues."[15] The allusion is to Mephisto's temptation of Faust in general and to their attendance at the witches' Walpurgis Night in particular. The critical alternative to Mephistophelean temptations proposed in the novel is the pursuit of a vocation either in music or in proto-Zionist leadership. Both vocations discipline the apprentice in selfless dedication and enable him or her to create a community aware of "a region outside and above" the Vanity Fair of English society. The fact that George Eliot denies her female characters either the gifts, the inclination, or the final joy in a vocation has been well discussed.[16]

In Victorian England, music as a serious art strongly suggested German music. (The earlier prestige of Italy is typified in Mme de Staël's novel *Corinne*, whose heroine finds it necessary to leave England for Italy in order to cultivate her artistic genius, especially as an *improvisatrice*.) Prince Albert's patronage helped to establish the reputation of German composers, musicians, music teachers, and instrument builders, and the London Philharmonic Society invited such celebrities as Mendelssohn, Wagner, Liszt, and Joseph Joachim. George Eliot wrote one of the earliest friendly appraisals of Wagner in England, in her essay for *Fraser's*, "Liszt, Wagner, and Weimar," in July 1855, after Wagner's first visit to London between March and June of that year as conductor of eight concerts, which included his own music.[17] Her report "Music of the Future" is based on an article of Liszt's, "The Romantic School of Music,"[18] which Eliot had translated a year earlier for Lewes's "Vivian" letters in the *Leader*. In her essay she acknowledged Wagner's important innovative role in the development of opera but expressed the reservation that "his musical inspiration is not sufficiently predominant over his thinking and poetical power, for him to have the highest creative genius in music."[19] In 1877 Richard and Cosima Wagner became regular acquaintances of

ADVANTAGES OF A FOREIGN EDUCATION.

Young Müller (from Hamburg) accompanies the Miss Goldmores in some of Rubinstein's lovely Duets – to the envy and disgust of Brown, Jones, and Robinson. (N.B. – Young Müller can also speak Six Languages, live on a Pound a Week, work Eighteen Hours out of the Twenty-Four, and do without a Holiday.)

the Leweses, but his music never came to appeal to their conservative taste. In Weimar in 1854, despite their interest in Liszt's conducting, they "had not patience to sit out more than two acts of Lohengrin,"[20] and after a visit to the Berlin Opera in 1870, Lewes wrote to his son: "The Mutter and I have come to the conclusion that the music of the future is not for us – Schubert, Beethoven, Mozart, Gluck or even Verdi – but not Wagner – is what we are made to respond to."[21]

However, in an interview George Eliot had found Liszt better than the rumours about his person: "a man of various thought, of serious purpose, and of a moral nature."[22] And it is the moral effect of music on the practitioner and the listener that signifies in *Daniel Deronda*, possibly in allusion to Schopenhauer's theory, in *Die Welt als Wille und Vorstellung* (The world as Will and Idea [1819]), that music as an immediate expression of the Will suspends self-will. George Eliot read the work in 1873 and had known about it from John Oxenford's review in the *Westminster Review* in 1852 under her editorship.[23] Klesmer's words of censure to Gwendolen about an aria of Bellini's are typical: "that music … expresses a puerile state of culture … no cries of deep, mysterious passion – no conflict – no sense of the universal. It makes men small as they listen to it."[24] He then plays as a positive example a fantasia called "*Freudvoll, Leidvoll, Gedankenvoll*" (Joyful, sorrowful, thoughtful), which is his own composition – "to be quite safe," the narrator adds with the irony which is missing in Klesmer's view of himself and from which, even among the admirable characters, only Mirah and Mordecai are spared. That Gwendolen, in spite of her wounded egoism, "had fulness of nature enough to feel the power of this playing" also indicates her moral potential. Klesmer's music and his person – "a felicitous combination of the German, the Sclave, and the Semite"[25] – suggest a composite of the famous virtuosi of the time: Liszt, Anton Rubinstein, and Joachim.[26]

In the novel Klesmer is compared with Liszt and Mendelssohn. His defence of the social role of the musician against the low opinion of the politician Mr Bult is typical of German Romantic ideas and also alludes to Shelley's *Defence of Poetry*: "We are not ingenious puppets, sir, who live in a box and look out only when it is gaping for amusement. We help to rule the nations and make the age as much as any other public men. We count ourselves on level benches with legislators."[27] The comparison has added authority coming from a political exile, who is obliged "to make a profession of his music," an allusion to Wagner's revolutionary activity and exile, as well as, possibly, to the fictive story of Ladislaw's Polish father in *Middlemarch*.[28] The narrator endorses Klesmer's self-appointed role as missionary to a nation of amateurs by adopting his diagnosis to explain Gwendolen's discomfort at the view of Klesmer's "width of horizon":[29] "she had moved in a society where everything, from low arithmetic to high art, is of the amateur kind politely supposed to fall short of perfection only because gentlemen and ladies are not obliged to do more than they like."[30] "Dilettante" is also the ultimate censure expressed by the German music teacher Lemm in Turgenev's novel *Home of the Gentry* (1859). Similar in temperament and convictions, he is less fortunate in career and love than Klesmer.

An earlier English novel, Elizabeth Sheppard's *Charles Auchester* (1853), had also fused music, Germany, and Jewry into a composite value of excellence, represented by Seraphael, an idealized portrait of Felix Mendelssohn. The young English hero, who is proud of his German and Jewish ancestry, realizes early in his musical education that "[c]ertainly it is out of English life in England one must go for the mysteries and realities of existence."[31] On dismissing Auchester from his preparation for the conservatory, his violin master in Germany agrees with his pupil's comparison of music with religion, with the reservation that "there is no right to say so anywhere now, except in Germany, for here alone has music its priesthood."[32] The reputation of Leipzig, the town implied by Sheppard, is demonstrated in the

MUSIC AT HOME.

Mrs. Gushington (who is always to the fore). "Oh! thank you so much, Fraülein, for your quite *too* delightful Singing! – such exquisite *Enunciation*, you know!! – so rare!!! I *should* so like to hear you sing a Song in *English!*" *Fraülein Nachtigall*. "Ach, Lieber Gott! Vy, my last Sree Zongs zat I haf choost peen Zinging, zey *vere* in Enklish!"

career of Dame Ethel Smyth, the path-breaking woman composer, who studied there, at the Conservatory and privately, from 1877 and had her first works performed there.

A more serious and powerful version of the painter Naumann in *Middlemarch*, Klesmer legislates artistic perfection as a moral value affecting both the individual and the community. It is, significantly, three female characters whom he influences directly – his name rhymes with Mesmer[33] – in parallel with Deronda's central relation with Gwendolen and in allusion to Goethe's play *Torquato Tasso* (1790), which Mrs Arrowpoint claims to have upstaged in her own treatment.[34] In Goethe's play it is the ladies of the court who give the poet the greatest measure of support in the conflict of art with politics. For Gwendolen Klesmer sets a new high standard by demonstrating to her that she would only be fit to make music inferior to her best moral sense. He confirms Mirah's own values, which the narrator approves, when "like a great musician and a kind man," he judges her singing perfect for the drawing room but not suitable for the stage, which she has hated. She correctly imagines that to conclude his examination "he would now like to hear her sing some German," and she sings a composition of Gretchen's songs from

Goethe's *Faust*.[35] As a final sign of their consonance, she caps Klesmer's quotation of Goethe's words, which also serve as the chapter's epigraph, on the certainty to be derived from the expert's advice.[36]

Klesmer's enthusiastic teaching and successful courtship of the heiress Catherine Arrowpoint, defeating his rival, the politician and expectant peer Mr Bult, suggest the possibility of English regeneration in the artistic and private spheres but not in the social and political ones. This implication, as well as the Jewish origin of Klesmer's name, which means "itinerant musician" in Yiddish, and his description of himself as the Wandering Jew[37] set the stage for Deronda's choice of proto-Zionism as the alternative to unregenerate English life. Unlike the visual arts, which are subject to the mosaic *Bilderverbot*, or "hostility," as the motto from Heine to chapter 63 reminds, music is the art that most readily typifies the *Künstlergeist* (artist's spirit) in Jewry. However, the most important evidence of Jewish art, according to the motto from Heine, is Moses' creation of the people of Israel: "er baute Menschenpyramiden, meisselte Menschen-Obelisken, er nahm einen armen Hirtenstamm und Schuf daraus ein Volk, das ebenfalls den Jahrhunderten trotzen sollte ... er Schuf Israel [he built human pyramids, he carved human obelisks, he took a poor tribe of shepherds and created a people which (like the Egyptian pyramids) was to defy the centuries ... he created Israel]."[38]

George Eliot observed that the "fundamental idea of Riehl's books" was the "conception of European society as incarnate history,"[39] a conception which she would have known to derive from "the great Herder."[40] Just as Riehl's rural novellas do for Germany, her earlier novels, dealing with backdated rural life, portray English communities as incarnate history. Even in the transitional *Middlemarch* all self-willed attempts to ignore the past and its moral meaning for the present, such as Casaubon's fudging of Ladislaw's rightful inheritance, Lydgate's delusion that his earlier sentimental error about Laurie was uncharacteristic, and Bulstrode's dishonesty about his former criminal association, are ultimately frustrated. *Daniel Deronda* deals with contemporary England, and with higher and politically more powerful strata of society, and it portrays a society that has lost all meaningful connection to its past; in Riehl's terms, it is no longer an organic society. Familial discontinuity (more emphasized here than in *Middlemarch*) is emblematic of this condition: Deronda, Gwendolen, and Mirah are all orphaned and dispossessed of their personal histories, Sir Hugo has no son for an heir, and Grandcourt makes an heir of his illegitimate son.

In her essay "The Modern Hep! Hep! Hep!" (1879), George Eliot argued that "[t]he eminence, the nobleness of a people, depends on its capability of being stirred by memories, and of striving for what we call spiritual ends," and that the nobleness of the individual citizen depends on a noble national consciousness.[41] A symbol in *Daniel Deronda* for the degeneracy of English society is the use of the "fine old choir" of the abbey on Sir Hugo's estate as stables.[42] Disraeli had employed the same symbol in *Sybil, or The Two Nations* (1845) to advocate a return to England's Catholic past as a cure for the domestic war in industrial England between the "two nations," the rich and the poor. His hero finds cattle sheltering in the former nave of the ruined abbey church on his uncle's estate.[43]

In the same essay on Jewry, George Eliot argued against cosmopolitanism for the time being – "A common humanity is not yet enough to feed the rich blood of various activity which makes a complete man" while she acknowledged that "[t]he tendency of things is towards the quicker and slower fusion of races," the current prime minister, Disraeli, being a case in point.[44] In the novel, Klesmer is reported to have "cosmopolitan ideas" and to "[look] forward to a fusion of races";[45] but more emphatically, cosmopolitanism appears, as we have seen, in a negative aspect in the pseudocommunity in the casino at Leubronn. For Deronda to become a "complete man," he has to discover and elect his membership in a people that, unlike the English, cherishes the continuity guaranteed by memories of and aspirations for spiritual goals. The Jewish people are exemplary in this respect, Eliot argued in her essay, as she speculated on the alternative to fusion with the host nations, namely, the restoration of a Jewish state. The physical and intellectual places for Deronda to discover and understand his Jewish heritage are largely German. In her essay on Riehl, Eliot had concluded that the "vital connexion with the past is much more vividly felt on the Continent than in England."[46] And this link she shows to be true for Jews too, in disregard of Riehl's anti-Semitism.[47]

Daniel Deronda is a *Bildungsroman* hero. His talents are typically many-sided: "one thing was as easy as another if he had only a mind to it." He consciously seeks self-development – at Cambridge "he longed to pursue a more independent line of study abroad … to have the sort of apprenticeship to life which would not shape him too definitely, and rob him of that choice that might come from a free growth" – and he comes to understand that his vocation will need to "[gather up knowledge and practice] into one current with his emotions."[48] The movement of his love between Gwendolen and Mirah expresses fluctuations and a final choice between aspects of his nature, and thus of his vocation. The characterization of Mirah in allusion to Wilhelm Meister's charge, the pathetic, exotic child-woman Mignon, who symbolizes the imagination,[49] makes Mirah a satisfactory choice in thematic terms, if not in realistic ones.

Unlike the main characters in *Middlemarch*, whose elders are derelict guardians, Deronda receives powerful guidance from Jewish elders, resembling that of the Society of the Tower in *Wilhelm Meister*. His collection of the chest of papers that his grandfather has left for him in the care of his friend Kalonymos suggests Wilhelm's reunion in the Tower with his grandfather's paintings at the conclusion of his apprenticeship.[50] Deronda's departure, at the end of the novel, in the service of Zionism echoes Wilhelm's final joining, as surgeon of the Migration society, the group that will colonize within Germany. In the *Wanderjahre* the choice between Germany and America is framed as one between culture and freedom, in the Uncle's return to Germany from America and Lenardo's emigration there.[51] In the England of *Daniel Deronda*, freedom without culture, both as self-culture and as national culture, is generally corrupted to licence, most strongly desired by Gwendolen and most completely enjoyed by Grandcourt. Deronda's status as an English gentleman implies Sir Hugo's licence as his supposed illegitimate father – the baronet "was pleased with that suspicion"[52] – and denies Deronda both rights and duties. His uncertain birth inhibits him from becoming "an organic part of social life, instead of roaming in it like a yearning disembodied spirit, stirred with a vague social passion, but without fixed local habitation to render fellowship real."[53] More nearly than Ladislaw, he fits Riehl's type of the aristocratic proletariat, who, in George Eliot's paraphrase, "is usually obliged to remain without any vocation, ... to the ends of his days ... a dilettante." She quotes Riehl: "But the ardent pursuit of a fixed practical calling can alone satisfy the active man."[54] However, instead of seeking revolutionary activity born of resentment, as Riehl analyzed it in the German type, Deronda finds a utopian cause outside England, in an intensification of Ladislaw and his reformist English politics.[55] As we have seen, in *Middlemarch* George Eliot was skeptical about the possibility of socially efficacious political reform in England, just as she was in *Felix Holt the Radical* and as Meredith was in *The Adventures of Harry Richmond* and *Beauchamp's Career*.

Deronda's self-culture leads to the culture of Judaism and the discovery of his duty. He explains to his mother, the Princess of Halm-Eberstein, who rejects his more immediate filial duty: "I consider it my duty – it is the impulse of my feeling – to identify myself, as far as possible, with my hereditary people, and if I can see any work to be done for them that I can give my soul and hand to, I shall choose to do it." As is typical of the *Bildungsroman*, the novel ends with the hero entering on his ultimate vocation, so its practical execution remains undemonstrated. But the political dimension has been indicated in the speech of his mentor, Mordecai, to the Philosophers club: "Looking towards a land and a polity, our dispersed people in all the ends of the earth may share the dignity of a national life which has a voice among the peoples of the East and the West." Mordecai offers Deronda, even before he suspects his Jewish lineage, "the complete ideal shape of that personal duty and citizenship which lay in his own thought like sculptured fragments certifying some beauty yearned after but not traceable by divination."[56]

The mentalities that in an ascending order rationalize, as it were, the exotic vocation of this Victorian fictional hero are religious humanism, kabbalistic Judaism, and Zionism. All three were familiar to George Eliot from largely German sources. She contributed to her contemporary readers' familiarity with them through her translations and review essays, and they are largely associated in the novel with German contexts.[57] The main German source of nineteenth-century English religious humanism was German historicism and its special branch, biblical criticism, or the "higher criticism."[58] One of George Eliot's contributions was her anonymous translation of David Friedrich Strauss's *Das Leben Jesu, kritisch bearbeitet* (1835; 2nd ed. 1840), *The Life of Jesus Critically Examined* (1846), which replaced a cheap serialized translation of 1841. Her translation is still in print, even in a paperback edition. In his thorough criticism of the Gospel narratives, Strauss established the basis for a material critique of the Gospel history. Superseding the supernaturalist and the rationalist approach, his method was the new "mythical point of view."[59] An article, "Tübingen in 1846," in *Macmillan's* described the Tübingen school of theology, of which Strauss, with his teacher F.C. Baur, was the main representative, as being "terrible" to the English "for its powerful scientific development of Rationalism."[60] Typically, a contributor to the *Fortnightly* scolded G.H. Lewes for opposing religion and science to theology and for prophesying "that the Religion of the future will discard the Theology now dominant, and will be fed through Science."[61]

George Eliot next translated, again anonymously, Ludwig Feuerbach's *Das Wesen des Christentums* (1841) under the title *The Essence of Christianity* (1853). The translation has been reprinted, with an introduction by Karl Barth and a foreword by Reinhold Niebuhr. Taking the rationalist critique of Christian dogmas as his departure, Feuerbach argued that religion had psychic, rather than metaphysical, origins, being essentially emotion, and that God was a projection of humanity's needs and desires, that genuine religiosity was expressed in the I-thou relation, especially of a sexual nature, and that in consequence, theology needed to be replaced with secular disciplines. Feuerbach wrote in the "Concluding Application": "*Homo homini Deus est;* – this is the great practical principle: – this is the axis on which revolves the history of the world."[62] In Germany his ideas were taken up by the 1848 revolutionaries, contributing to the Marxist concept of alienation. George Eliot compared the book's effect in Germany and England: "it is considered *the* book of the age there, but Germany and England are *two* countries. People here are as slow to be set on fire as a *stomach*."[63] The *Spectator* commended her on her achievement while censoring the message: "In plain English, this system is rank Atheism."[64] Feuerbach's humanism aided George Eliot in her condemnation of dogmatic and punitive religiosity, as, for instance, in her essay "Evangelical Teaching: Dr Cumming" (1855), where she wrote: "The idea of a God who not only sympathizes with all we feel and endure for our fellow-men, but who will pour new life into our too languid love … is an extension and multiplication of the effects produced by human sympathy."[65] Her first work of fiction, *Scenes from Clerical Life* (1857), had as a major theme the moral superiority of a religion of the heart, including an erotic dimension, to a religion based on dogma; in Bulstrode and Farebrother in *Middlemarch* she dramatized the contrast. In part, her fiction can be read as an answer to Feuerbach's call for the replacement of theology with anthropology.

In conformity with Feuerbach's ideas, religiosity in *Daniel Deronda* is a matter of temperament, of psychic disposition, rather than of dogma or ritual. This characteristic appears, in ascending order, in Gwendolen's susceptibility to terror, first shown in the episode of the hidden movable panel picturing a dead face and fleeing figure; in Deronda's ability to be piously awed, as in the abbey choir converted to stables; and lastly, in Mordecai's visionary enthusiasm, which Deronda distinguishes from "narrow and hoodwinked" fanaticism, Mordecai belonging to "the highest order of minds – those who care supremely for grand and general benefits to mankind. He is not strictly an orthodox Jew." In addition, and most important for the plot, Deronda's "ready sympathy," his receptiveness to another soul, is "a rare and massive power," in the narrator's words, and it bestows on him quasi-religious roles, which affect him as profoundly as they do his opposites.[66] He acts as Gwendolen's conscience and confessor in her guilt for her murderous hatred of her husband and in her desire to live a less selfish life, his only command being that she endeavour not to gain from another's loss.[67] This role culminates in an allusion to Jesus' words to his disciples when Deronda tries to comfort Gwendolen over his departure from England for an indefinite period: "I shall be more with you than I used to be."[68] He also becomes Mirah's rescuer and benefactor, a role that imposes an irksome reticence on his lovemaking and on his rivalry with Hans Meyrick. And finally, he fulfills Mordecai's expectation of him as his disciple and "second soul."

Wilhelm Meister also includes a mystic in each part: the "Beautiful Soul" and her autobiographical account in the *Lehrjahre* and Makarie in the *Wanderjahre*.[69] The first exemplifies pietist enthusiasm and ascetic other-worldliness; the second, theist oneness with the cosmos and its laws (see chaps. 2 and 3 above); that is, not historical world religions, as in George Eliot's novel. Neither character seeks to transmit her mystical knowledge for "grand and general benefits to mankind" or to be effective in the world through a disciple, as Mordecai does – their gender no doubt plays a part in this difference – but their experiences are indirectly communicated to Wilhelm and contribute new dimensions to his *Bildung*.

Both the psychological conception of Christianity as the religion of the heart and the historicizing conception of it as a product of myth-making permit the stress in the novel on its essential continuity with Judaism; that is, the psychological conception is in affinity with the kabbalistic tradition, and the historicizing conception is in affinity with Old Testament typology. In Hans Meyrick's persiflage of Mordecai's idea, "a whole Christian is three-fourths a Jew."[70] With the novel's stress on these aspects, Judaism here does not represent the moral ethos that Heine, Arnold, and George Eliot opposed as Hebraism to Hellenism (see chap. 5 above). Instead, it is associated with light, which symbolizes prophetic inspiration, as in the scene when Deronda in a boat on the Thames and Mordecai on Blackfriars Bridge are revealed to each other in the "western light" as long-awaited disciple and much-needed mentor. When Deronda accepts his Jewish heritage, he does not accept orthodoxy. He responds to the authoritarian pressure of his grandfather's friend Kalonymos: "But I will not say that I shall profess to believe exactly as my fathers have believed ... But I think I can maintain my grandfather's notion of separateness with communication."[71]

Although Mordecai is conceived, as it were, in opposition to Disraeli's character Sidonia in *Coningsby* (1844), who is a great success as an international banker, political adviser, and favoured guest in high society, they both function as mentors. In George Eliot's proto-Zionist context, the less-powerful Mordecai can expect his dreams to be converted to action, while Sidonia confesses to the adulatory Coningsby that as a Jew he can never be a hero: "I am and must ever be ... but a dreamer of dreams."[72]

George Eliot's most immediate source of information on the kabbalah and on Zionism was her friend Emmanuel Deutsch, a German refugee after 1848 and a biblical Orientalist and cataloguer in the British Museum, who as the sole member of the "Deutsch-party," in his own words, was an enthusiastic advocate of a Jewish national home.[73] He taught her Hebrew, and she read, for instance, an article of his on the Talmud. His death in 1873 on his way to Palestine, while she was planning her "Jewish novel," inspired her portrayal of the dying Mordecai. In her own discursive treatment of Jewry, "The Modern Hep! Hep! Hep!" she speculated on Zionism as the alternative to assimilation, or "fusion": "there may arise some men of instruction and ardent public spirit, some new Ezras" – Mordecai's familial name is Ezra – who would bring about the restoration of a Jewish state from the "organized memory of a national consciousness."[74] In the novel Deronda and Mordecai divide the offices of instruction and public spirit between them, Deronda becoming Mordecai's hand and soul – his hand by virtue of his qualities as an English gentleman and his soul in the kabbalistic conception of the second soul.[75]

Like George Eliot herself, Deronda finds his information about Jewry in German books and places. Unsuspecting of his own Jewish origins but curious about modern Judaism and Jewish history on account of Mirah and his ambivalence about her wish to find her brother, he explores the Judengasse (Jews' Lane, or Jewish quarter) in Frankfurt, buys books on Jewish subjects, and attends service at the synagogue, where he is for the first time identified as a Jew by his grandfather's friend.[76] George Eliot had herself attended service at the synagogues in Frankfurt and Bad Homburg. The Jewish quarter in Frankfurt, Goethe's native city, was familiar to his readers from his description, in his autobiographical *Dichtung und Wahrheit*, of his fascinated visits to the Jewish ghetto as a boy and youth whose sensations developed, like Deronda's, from a mixture of revulsion, fear, and reverence to sympathetic interest.[77] A summary of Goethe's account could also be read in the second edition of Lewes's *Life of Goethe*.[78] Frankfurt Jewish life is also the topic of Heine's novella fragment *Der Rabbi von Bacharach* (1840).

After accepting his Jewish heritage, Deronda returns to Mainz to collect the chest with his grandfather's papers. His grandfather's friend Kalonymos, a banker, observes to him that Jewish fortunes in Mainz have changed for the better since Charlemagne's introduction of Jewish scholars – Kalonymos is the name of a famous medieval poet in Mainz:[79] "we increase our wealth in safety, and the learning of all Germany is fed and fattened by Jewish brains – though they keep not always their Jewish hearts."[80] Deronda's first meeting with Mordecai in London results from his purchase of *Salomon Maimon's Lebensgeschichte* (Life story [1792]). On his way to accompany Mordecai to the Philosophers club, where the future of Jewry will be debated, he recalls a passage from Leopold Zunz's book on medieval Jewish literature, *Die synagogale Poesie des Mittelalters* (1855), which also serves as the epigraph, in German, to the chapter. In it Zunz claims the superiority of the Israeli "tragedy" even to Greek literary tragedy, since it "has lasted one and a half thousand years, created and played by the heroes themselves."[81]

This equation of Jewish history with art recurs in the German epigraph to chapter 63, in which Deronda returns to Mordecai from Germany to receive his Jewish bride and vocation. The epigraph, from Heine's *Geständnisse* (already referred to above), speaks of Moses as a great artist, comparable to Egyptian creators of pyramids and obelisks, but who created a nation, Israel. The resemblance to Zunz's argument is no coincidence. While a student in Berlin, Heine joined Zunz as teacher and secretary of the Society for Culture and Science of the Jews, co-founded by Zunz in Berlin in 1819. The statutes of the Culturverein determined that it "bring the Jews into harmony with the age and the countries in which they live by means of a program of internal education developing outwards."[82] Zunz called such a program "science" (*Wisssenschaft*), by which he meant a scientific – that is, unbiased – knowledge of Judaism. Heine probably sought in the Culturverein "an alternative middle ground between benighted Orthodoxy and the Jewish Reform."[83] The period of his collaboration was 1821–23, when he also attended the salon of Berlin's most celebrated emancipated Jewess, Rahel Levin, and before his conversion to Protestant Christianity in 1825.

A major implied authority in *Middlemarch*, Heinrich Heine is the principal German muse in *Daniel Deronda*, combining in his person, like the fictional Klesmer, the themes of anti-philistinism, music, and Jewry. George Eliot and Lewes read Heine's *Geständnisse* during their first winter in Berlin, when they often discussed Heine with Varnhagen, Rahel Levin's husband and Lewes's most important personal source for his *Life of Goethe*.[84] Consequently, George Eliot's idea of Heine was probably not that of a Jew like Pash, Mordecai's opponent at the Philosophers club, who, in the words of a contemporary Jewish reviewer, "is the representative of what might be called the Heine side of Jewry – the wit and cynicism that reached their greatest intensity in the poet of Young Germany."[85]

Her use of Heine in the novel rather suggests the generous view of his modern biographers Max Brod and Ludwig Marcuse. In Brod's words, "Heine succeeded in doing what no one else did in his day: in striding out in opposite directions ... [h]e walked out of the Jewish Middle Ages into the modern era laughingly, even, to a certain extent frivolously, and yet succeeded in preserving his continuity with living Judaism."[86]

The novel's other epigraph by Heine on a Jewish subject supports the claim. The excerpt from his poem "Prinzessin Sabbath,"[87] which describes the transformation of the bewitched weekday cur to the Sabbath human, introduces chapter 34, in which Deronda shares the Cohens' Sabbath celebration and revises his prejudice on finding "that this pawnbroker proud of his vocation was not utterly prosaic."[88] Matthew Arnold, in his essay on Heine, had paraphrased the poem and also translated Heine's humorous prose account of the Sabbath transformation of Moses Lump, the huckster from Hamburg.[89] He inserted these Jewish tales because Heine treated his race "with the same freedom with which he treated everything else, but he derived a great force from it ... He himself had in him both the spirit of Greece and the spirit of Judaea."[90] Contrasting with the spirit of the Sabbath, the return of Mirah and Mordecai's derelict, "unreverend" father in chapter 62 is also introduced with an epigraph from Heine, a lyric on the fickle maid Fortune and the constant matron Misfortune.[91] The German places where Mordecai studied after his first Jewish studies in Holland, "that [he] might take a larger outlook on [his] people, and on the Gentile world,"[92] are associated with Heine's life, though not with his attitude to them: Hamburg, his second home, with his uncle Salomon Heine, a banker, and the scene of his short business career under his uncle's wing, and Göttingen, where he studied law, hating both the subject and the town. An allusion to Heine also appears in the Gentile world of the novel, when Gwendolen compares her accursed cruising with Grandcourt to the voyages of the Flying Dutchman.[93] George Eliot knew that Wagner's "beautiful" opera was based on Heine's version of the legend.[94] However, the strongest association of Heine with music is through his lyrics, which are remembered as lieder by Schubert, Schumann, Mendelssohn, and Hugo Wolf. It is with his composition of Heine's poem "Ich hab' dich geliebet / und liebe dich noch! [I have loved you and love you still!]" that Klesmer declares his love to Catherine Arrowpoint.[95]

In accepting Klesmer, Catherine defies her parents' philistine prejudice against the cosmopolitan artist. As the narrator observes, the prejudice is particularly ironic in Mrs Arrowpoint, who has written a defence of Tasso, about whom the many previous authors "are all wrong."[96] The most immediate contender would be Goethe's drama *Torquato Tasso*, which balances the claims of imagination, art, and love, personified in Tasso, with the claims of pragmatism, politics, and decorum, personified in the courtier Antonio, although the poet's claims are made more affecting. In practice, Mrs Arrowpoint responds in the spirit of the court to her daughter's "[enacting] what she had safely demanded of the dead Leonora": both her patronage of music and her defence of love give way to social ambition; Klesmer, formerly the genius, is now "nobody knows what – a gypsy, a Jew, a mere bubble on the earth ... a mountebank or a charlatan," and a woman in Catherine's position as an heiress "must follow duty" when it and inclination clash. Her duty is to marry "a man connected with the institutions of this country,"[97] that is, Mr Bult, who stands in relation to Klesmer as the courtier and diplomat Antonio does to Tasso in Goethe's play. At the end of the play, Tasso leaves the court and its values, self-banished, but treasuring nature's gift to him of "melody and speech / to tell the full depth of [his] distress."[98] George Eliot permits some English regeneration in having Klesmer and Catherine marry and live in London, "rather magnificently now," Klesmer "a patron and prince among musical professors."[99] But the novel's hero has to leave the philistine milieu behind in the manner of Tasso in order to pursue his vocation, his quasi-priestly care having had a morally beneficent effect on Gwendolen, who represents the slim potential for regeneration in English life.[100]

In *Middlemarch* George Eliot's innovative gesture is towards an epic of intellectual passion and vocation, in departure from the romance of love. But vocation is still conceived within the conventional professions and occupations of the England of the novel's era. Similarly, the narrator's uncommonly wide range of discourses does not go outside the conventional fields of inquiry as they were covered in the perodicals and were shaping into disciplines at the time of writing. In *Daniel Deronda* Eliot pushes the experiment further: her portrayal of the vocation of music, pursued in a manner that is signalled as un-English, or German, leads to the portrayal of a vocation of spiritual politics which, she implies, can only be imagined as outside England and in the future. Where the backdating of the action in *Middlemarch* leaves a margin of optimism about the future reform of the Middlemarch mentality, *Daniel Deronda* portrays contemporary England as without any significant scope for regeneration. By extension to the author, *Middlemarch* reflects George Eliot's own professional concerns,[101] while her last novel may mirror her doubts about the efficacy of her fiction as a means of reform, through the reader's imagination, of English life. Thus *Daniel Deronda* is an elegy both to Carlyle's and to Wordsworth's program for England.

The narrator's range of discourses includes the sphere of Deronda's spiritual vocation, starting with the first epigraph, which opens the space of an English novel concerned with social convention and morality, typified by Jane Austen's novels, to Goethe's *Welt-Theater*, comprising heaven, earth, and hell and treating man's and woman's relations to these dimensions. Thus from the start, the author indicates a horizon of expectations which, unlike, for instance, the horizon of Thackeray's *Vanity Fair* (1847–48), contains the pilgrim's progress as well as that of the rake.

Negative critical response to George Eliot's experiment has generally played off the "English" part of the novel against the "Jewish" one,[102] as though they were separable instead of dialectically united, the realistic presentment of the Gentile English milieu producing the desire for a redemptive alternative whose visionary nature entails a non-realistic style. Positive critical response has valued George Eliot's self-conscious departure in her last novel from the mainstream of English realist fiction and her inclusion of other generic conventions, especially since current critical theories promote interest in past works that evidence the author's subversion of dominant conventions or the juxtaposition of competing ones.[103] At the start of book 6, titled "Revelations," George Eliot directly engages the issue of realism when she presents Deronda's reflections about the meaning of Mordecai's visionary election of him. He contrasts the perspective that recognizes "momentous and sacred [crises] in the historic life of men" with what he knows would be Sir Hugo's perspective of "a man of the world." Deronda shrinks more from the "moral stupidity" of erring on the side of Sir Hugo's skepticism than from erring on the side of credulity.[104] His inner debate and judgment serve as commentary on the novel's generic disjunction and constitute an appeal to the implied reader on behalf of the speculative tone of the novel, or, in Henry James's words, its German tone.[105]

In accordance with George Eliot's discussion of philistinism in her essay on Riehl and with her dramatization of it in *Middlemarch*, the reader is asked to dissociate himself or herself from the philistine spirit, "which judges everything from a lower point of view than the subject demands."[106] The narrator of *Middlemarch* is ambivalent about Dorothea's visionary idealism and frequently adopts irony, as it were in indirect style, as a concession to the Middlemarch mentality. In her last novel George Eliot is less equivocal in her presentation, leaving her reader less room for evasion and comfort. *Daniel Deronda* can usefully be read as a modern epic poem, the author's "Divine Comedy"

for the nineteenth century, in the orbit of Victorian philosophical poetry and fiction.[107] However, by virtue of the novel's German referen-
tiality, the most instructive intertext – or hypotext, to use Gérard
Genette's term – is *Wilhelm Meister*, which George Eliot had reread in
1870 and which in its inclusiveness of genres, discourses, and presented worlds modelled the novel as *the* Romantic genre in German
Romantic aesthetics.[108]

7 Infidel Novels

Where the most popular nineteenth-century loss-of-faith novel,[1] Mrs Humphry Ward's *Robert Elsmere* (1888), succeeds as fiction, it is modelled on George Eliot's novels. George Eliot, however, did not make the loss of Christian faith a subject of her fiction. She had herself gone through one kind of religious crisis typical of the period, in rebelling against her evangelical upbringing and, with it, against her father and her feminine role; and she had contributed two major instruments of crisis in others with her translations of Strauss's *Life of Jesus* and Feuerbach's *The Essence of Christianity* (see chap. 6 above). In her essay "Silly Novels by Lady Novelists" (1856), she singled out as the "most pitiable" kind "the *oracular* species – novels intended to expound the writer's religious, philosophical, or moral theories."[2] Both her aesthetic rejection of anything as "diagrammatic" as the *Tendenzroman*, or *roman à thèse*, and her general reticence in her fiction about the controversial features of her own life – in addition to her atheism, her profession and her marital status – explain the obliqueness with which her own spiritual autobiography enters into her fiction.

George Eliot's good clergymen, such as Mr Tryan in "Janet's Repentance," Mr Irwine in *Adam Bede*, and Mr Farebrother in *Middlemarch*, all derive their conduct, not from dogma, but from their imaginative sympathy and sense of duty; that is, they resemble the pattern of the good agnostic. Conversely, dogmatism precludes pastoral care. Adam Bede speaks for his author when he compares Mr Irwine with his zealous successor: "I've seen pretty clear, ever since I was a young un, as religion's s'thing else besides notions. It isn't notions sets people doing the right thing – it's feelings."[3] Also, George Eliot presents a youthful character's need for a "key of life" other than traditional Christian religion as a matter of course in the case of Maggie Tulliver, Dorothea Brooke, and Daniel Deronda. For instance, Dorothea's Christian training and environment have provided her with nothing to dispel the "[oppressive] indefiniteness which hung in her mind, like a thick summer haze, over all her desire to make her life greatly effective."[4]

In Victorian narratives of a crisis of faith, both factual and fictive, German biblical criticism, or higher criticism, most importantly Strauss's *Life of Jesus*, is usually cited as one of the two main causes, the other being scientific knowledge. A third cause, which is also often connected with Germany, is a competing dedication to aesthetic ideals. Further causes cited are ethical qualms about Old Testament morality and about Christian doctrines, such as atonement, and disillusionment with worldly or hypocritical clergy, such as we meet in Trollope's Barchester. As an example of the commonplace connection of biblical criticism and natural science with Germany, Matthew Arnold's acknowledgment of it in his preface to *Literature and Dogma* (1873) may serve: "To get the facts, the data, in most matters of science, but notably in geology and Biblical learning, one goes to Germany."[5] However, for right conclusions about the Bible's truth, he proposed a better, English approach, namely, literary criticism. The foregoing discussions of *Middlemarch* and *Daniel Deronda* have already touched on the German context of aestheticism; I shall deal with this last aspect in my discussion of *Robert Elsmere*.

It is a matter of interpretation, with respect to both the factual and the fictive crisis-of-faith stories, whether these causes are sufficient causes, and, indeed, whether the crises represent actual crises in faith or mediate normal crises in personal development or, in some instances, the period's crisis over new intellectual legitimation and professionalization.[6] The interpretation will depend on the role of spiritual faith in the reader's own experience and on the common evaluation of faith in an era's critical discourse, that is, on critical fashion. For instance, acting as his own literary critic, Edmund Gosse offered his reader two interpretive models for his autobiographical *Father and Son* (1907): it is "the narrative of a spriritual struggle" and also "the record of a struggle between two temperaments."[7] In addition, for the reader of Gosse's poetry and criticism, the work told the early history of his literary career as the rejection of the two vocations exemplified, in notorious incompatibility, by his father, namely, those of the preacher and the scientist. For the purposes of this study, the novelists' narratives themselves and the causes they represent matter, however overdetermined, not their relation to some hypotheticized reality.

To start with the physical sciences and stay with Gosse's father, advances in geology and evolutionary biology were most antagonistic to bibliolatry. While a member of a prospective "body-guard of sound and experienced naturalists,"[8] organized by Sir Charles Lyell in 1857 in anticipation of the publication of Darwin's *Origin of Species* (1859), Philip Gosse published a sincere and ingenious attempt at reconciling the scientific and the revealed truths about physical life. However, *Omphalos: An Attempt to Untie the Geological Knot* (1857) proved religiously useless and professionally disastrous.

The major names and titles in science commonly cited as causes for religious doubt are British: Lyell's *Principles of Geology* (1830) and *Elements of Geology* (1838), Robert Chambers's *Vestiges of the Natural History of Creation* (1844), and most critically, Charles Darwin's *On the Origin of Species by Means of Natural Selection* (1859), with its scandalous promise of a work on the descent of man. Nevertheless, the connection of the scientific enterprise with notions of German rigour, industry, and professionalism, as we saw in Lydgate's fear of German competition (chap. 5 above), was becoming ever more established through frequent visits by English scholars to German universities and the reform of English universities along German lines.[9] And of course the Doctors Faust and Frankenstein guaranteed the popular implication of atheism with a German odour.

The main German names to conjure with were two popularizers of Darwin on the Continent and self-appointed champions in the battle between religion and science, the geologist Karl Vogt and the medical doctor Ludwig Büchner.[10] Vogt, who also translated Chambers's *Vestiges*, agitated the European controversy with quotes from his lecture tours such as the following: "Thoughts come out of the brain as gall from the liver, or urine from the kidneys."[11] Büchner's book *Kraft und Stoff* (1855), translated as *Force and Matter* (1864), lost him his university post, and it is, for instance, the materialist's bible for the nihilist physician Bazarov in Turgenev's *Fathers and Sons*.[12]

These German scientific materialists derived their axioms from the writings of Strauss and especially Feuerbach.[13] The connection between the two enterprises is nicely stereotyped in the name of Guelph Frankenstein for the malevolent German rationalist of Tübingen provenance in the anonymous English novel *Enthusiasm not Religion* (1848).[14] The scientific (*wissenschaftlich*) inquiry into the historical and philological facts of the Scriptures had in Germany developed from the Deutsche Bewegung (German movement), or *Historismus*,[15] that is, a genetic-organicist perspective which came to inform first German classical philology and then theology and political and legal history.

Of the historians, Barthold Georg Niebuhr, author of the *Römische Geschichte* (Roman history [1811]), and his Bonn circle exercised special influence, first on the Cambridge Apostles in the 1830s, which can be traced in the historical and speculative attitude in Tennyson's *In Memoriam* (1850), and secondly on Thomas Arnold and his pupils at Rugby.[16] Arnold, who produced a popularized version of Niebuhr's *History of Rome* (1838–43), listed as the "intellectual means of acquiring a knowledge of the Scriptures in themselves," apart from the far more complex "knowledge of their right application": "Philology, Antiquities, and Ancient History."[17] This German rationalism, or higher criticism, dreaded in nineteenth-century England, in turn derived from English eighteenth-century rationalist, deist writers, the two countries being out of phase as a result of differences in their respective relations of church and state and in their experiences with the French Revolution and Napoleon.[18]

Meredith used the stereotypical combination of political and religious radicalism when, in *The Adventures of Harry Richmond*, he had the Princess Ottilia's tutor, Professor von Karsteg, retire from her service to write, in her aunt's words, "a book – a horror! all against Scripture and Divine right." The princess, however, admits to having read his book and defends the "cut-throat" as a hero.[19] In Trollope's *Barchester Towers* (1857) the cosmopolitan young Bertie Stanhope wickedly shocks the chancellor's nervous system when he announces to an assembly of conservative clergymen that Englishmen could learn from German professors.[20] The chancellor's sentiments match those of Dr E.B. Pusey, the guardian of the Oxford Movement, who himself had studied in Germany: "all the troubles of the Church since the Reformation can be ascribed to German Professors."[21]

The likely German professors implied here are Kant, Hegel, Schleiermacher, and the neo-Hegelians David Friedrich Strauss, Ferdinand Christian Baur, and Ludwig Feuerbach. Kant seemed to reduce religion to the mere outer form of morality; and Hegel, to a medium for the Absolute, that is, for an intellectual idea; while Schleiermacher, in contrast to both, stressed the subjective, intuitive feeling of piety. Dubbed the "father of modern Protestant theology" and "the Second Reformer," Schleiermacher was the first to lecture on the life of Jesus, repeatedly from 1819 at Berlin, and his *Critical Essay on the Gospel of Luke* (1817), in Thirlwall's anonymous translation of 1825, made his name a "bogey word" in England.[22] Following his lead, the Tübingen professors Strauss and Baur both examined the Gospels critically in order to establish, for the sake of true religion, the historical, non-supernatural Jesus. In a partisan and widely influential study published in 1863, *The Tübingen School and Its Antecedents: A Review of the History and Present Condition of Modern Theology*, R.W. Mackay described the school's work as "an exceptionally creditable reaction against the halting, irresolute liberalism forming the ordinary staple of theological compromise during the past and present centuries"; "Christianity becomes intelligible as a natural development."[23] Baur's historical method improved on Strauss's internal textual comparison, but Strauss had the more general impact. His *Leben Jesu*, which rationalized the supernatural aspects of Jesus as the product of legend and mythmaking, was considered the most radical work of the Tübingen school.[24] In response to the unforeseen scandal of the book, Strauss revised it several times over the years. All the philosophical and theological impulses I have summarized here climaxed in Feuerbach's substitution of anthropology for theology and his advocacy of the religion of man (see chap. 6 above).[25]

Strauss's name signals, for instance, a stage in the intellectual history of Charles Kingsley's hero in *Alton Locke, Tailor and Poet* (1850). In the hero's progress from his evangelical childhood via skepsis and Chartism to the "new Church" of Christian social work, Strauss's rationalist examination of the Gospel miracles constitutes the hero's "greatest stumbling-block," "and, till clergymen make up their minds to [read Strauss], and to answer Strauss also, they will … leave the heretic artisan just where they found him."[26] The time is the 1840s. In *The Way of All Flesh* (posthumous, 1903), which attacks all Christian teaching as "humbug," Samuel Butler described the period of the 1840s and 1850s as the calm before the "commencement of the storm" created by the publication of *Essays and Reviews*, Bishop Colenso's *Lectures on the Pentateuch*, and Darwin's *Origin of Species* – a superficial calm since "the wave of scepticism … had already broken over Germany."[27]

The publication in 1860 of *Essays and Reviews* (edited by the Reverend Henry Bristow Wilson) and the subsequent debate demonstrated to the general educated public that important clergymen connected with Oxford had both read and answered Strauss. Nicknamed the "Septem contra Christum," its authors agreed with the German scholars' precept "Interpret the Scripture like any other book,"[28] that is, critically, or scientifically. They admired with reserve – "My lips but ill could frame thy Lutheran speech, / Nor suits thy Teuton vaunt our British pride"[29] – and they found an English way of reconciling higher criticism with Christian faith by stressing the psychological and moral facts of the Bible: "A confusion of the heart and the head may lead sensitive minds into a desertion of the principles of the Christian life, which are their own witness, because they are in doubt about facts which are really external to them."[30]

Matthew Arnold reiterated this dichotomy of German head and English heart in *Literature and Dogma*, a work that was first serialized in the *Fortnightly Review* and then became a very popular book: "English religion does not know the facts of its study, and has to go to Germany for them ... But perhaps the quality specially needed for drawing the right conclusion from the facts ... is best called *perception*, justness of perception," which, being a result of culture, is missing in theologians in general, but particularly the typically German specialist, such as Strauss.[31]

Next to *Essays and Reviews*, a principal book that popularized the higher criticism in England was Ernest Renan's *Vie de Jésus* (1863; translated into English and other European languages in the same year). Based on the scholarship of the Tübingen school, but not following it in "taking up the theological ground too much, and the historical ground too little,"[32] it was the first biography of the man Jesus in history and was written for the general public. Like *Essays and Reviews*, Renan's book caused a furious controversy, despite his purpose of going beyond German skepsis, with regard to the supernatural dimension of the Gospels, to devotion to Jesus, the inspired teacher and emancipator. Renan summed up "the religion of Jesus" as follows: as an "inexhaustible principle of moral generation for humanity," Jesus may be called divine "in the sense that [he] is the one who has caused his fellow-men to make the greatest step toward the divine."[33] In his *Notes on England, 1860–1870* (1872, original publication and translation), Hippolyte Taine reported: "What is now the rule with us, is the exception here ... Three-quarters of the newspapers and books published censure 'French scepticism and German free-thinking' with every appearance of conviction."[34]

The authors of nineteenth-century English crisis-of-faith novels could count on the familiarity of many of their readers with and even their gratitude for two important precursors: Carlyle's *Sartor Resartus* (1833–34) and Tennyson's *In Memoriam* (1850). Both works participate in the genres of the fictionalized spiritual autobiography and the *roman à thèse*, and both conduct an intellectual debate on the conflict between materialist fact and idealist truth, concluding with an affirmation of spiritual faith. Professor Teufelsdröckh's *Bildungsroman* and his writings suggest that the path of German speculative philosophy is risky but that it leads to the "Everlasting Yea" of moral and spiritual health, which defeats the "Everlasting Nay" resulting from

British materialism. Carlyle thanks German idealist philosophers and Romantic writers for the gift of new clothes for the old faith, as we have seen. Tennyson is less explicit, but he alludes, for instance, in the first section of *In Memoriam* to Goethe:

I held it truth, with him who sings
To one clear harp in divers tones,
That men may rise on stepping-stones
Of their dead selves to higher things.

Yet his past belief is now cast in doubt:

But who shall so forecast the years
And find in loss a gain to match

The phrase echoes the title of John Henry Newman's autobiographical novel about his own religious crisis, *Loss and Gain: The Story of a Convert* (1848). Tennyson's treatment in poetry of current scientific knowledge about astronomy, geology, and biology resembles Goethe's in its authority, and it differs significantly from the unscientific, sentimental portrayal of nature's moral ministrations in Wordsworth's *Prelude* (1850), another major poetic model of an unorthodox spiritual journey.[35] However, Tennyson's defence of "honest doubt" (elegy 96) comprises an agony of religious conflict that is absent from Goethe's work.

To illustrate the range of typical representations of German contexts in English crisis-of-faith novels, I shall consider James Anthony Froude's *The Nemesis of Faith* (1849), Mark Rutherford's *Autobiography* (1881) and *Deliverance* (1885), George Gissing's *Workers in the Dawn* (1880), and Mrs Humphry Ward's *Robert Elsmere* (1888).[36] In all these novels and others like them, religion stands for *Weltanschauung*, bringing them more or less close to the genre of the *Bildungsroman*. However, in their use of explicit moral didaxis, these authors differ from Goethe and follow Carlyle. So it was as *Tendenzromane* (novels with a purpose) that the novels provoked debate and censure. For his story of loss of faith and consequent guilty love, Froude borrows the narrative form and plot elements from novels by Goethe and thereby indirectly recruits Goethe for the legitimization of unorthodoxy. The Mark Rutherford novels employ the same narrative form, but they also deal explicitly with the destructive effects of "German" knowledge on a mind less well equipped than Carlyle's and George Eliot's. Gissing's crisis-of-faith story, which constitutes only part of his novel, is rare in that the protagonist is a woman who goes to study at Tübingen and also in that the effects of the higher criticism are pure gain. Finally, Mrs Humphry Ward's hero has all the sensibility, intellectual ability, and professional training to experience both the loss and the gain that German scholarship could entail.

Markham Sutherland, the hero of *The Nemesis of Faith*, has graduated from Oxford and is anxiously questioning his future vocation as an Anglican clergyman in 1843; that is, his crisis coincides with what his fictional successor, Robert Elsmere, in the early 1880s describes as "the destructive wave ... the beginning of the Liberal reaction, which followed Tractarianism, and in twenty years transformed the University."[37] Froude's novel created a controversy: it was preached against and publicly burnt in his college and caused its author's resignation of his fellowship; on the other hand, George Eliot, whose translation of Strauss's *Life of Jesus* Froude had read and to whom he had their common publisher send a copy of his novel, wrote an enthusiastic review in the *Coventry Herald*.[38]

The story is typical of the period's factual and fictional narratives, and it is "perhaps the most interesting imaginative (as opposed to controversial) statement of the case against Christianity in [the] period" from 1840 to 1890.[39] After his family's fashionable change from rigid Protestantism to ritualism, Markham Sutherland encounters Tractarianism at Oxford. He reads first English and then also Continental critics and comes to reject several of the Thirty-Nine Articles and, indeed, "the Christian religion," as opposed to "the religion of Christ." "Puseyism is the error on one side, German rationalism on the other," his friend warns him.[40] Sick from the conflict within himself and with his family over his prospective clerical vocation, he goes to recover on the shore of Lake Como. There, in implicit imitation of Rousseau, he finds peace in nature, in giving medical help to the cottagers, and in writing, until he becomes the soulmate of a married woman. When her child dies as a consequence of their absorption in each other, he attributes his moral fault to his loss of religion and tries to repent in a monastery under the influence of a figure reminiscent of Newman, but he soon dies in despair.

The novel records no direct German influence on the hero's crisis. At Oxford he is under the sway of Newman, of whom Mrs Ward records Dean Arthur Stanley as saying "that the whole course of English religious history might have been different if Newman had known German."[41] As a student, Froude's hero is not what Newman, in his own novel *Loss and Gain*, criticized as "'viewy,' in a bad sense of the word."[42] Markham reports of himself that his subsequent independent doubts were caused by his English reading: "I was not yet acquainted with any of the modern continental writers." He lacks the vigour for Carlyle's message – "Carlyle! Carlyle only raises questions he cannot answer" – but he acknowledges him as one of the two "greatly gifted [men] then living in this England," Newman being the other, and Goethe's poetry as completing the sources of his inspiration. When he turns to philosophy as an alternative to theology, reading, for instance, Spinoza and Leibniz – both influenced Goethe at the same age – he extracts no comfort from their "cold system[s]."[43] However, the narrative form of the novel, the characterization of the hero, and the climax of the plot are derived from Goethe and thus evoke the unorthodoxy of Goethe's works as well as the positive evaluation of his "teaching" in general by Carlyle, Froude's mentor and later the subject of a biography by him. By implication, Froude's contemporary reader is invited to extend the respect granted to Goethe's portrayals of unorthodox protagonists to Froude's own "Tragedy" of honest doubt.

Goethe's last recorded conversation with Eckermannn, only days before the former's death, dealt with biblical criticism. Goethe predicted the emergence of "die reine Lehre und Liebe Christi [Christ's pure teaching and love]" and consequently a gradual change from a "Christenthum des Wortes und Glaubens immer mehr zu einem Christenthum der Gesinnung und That [Christianity of word and faith more and more to a Christianity of attitude and deed]."[44] One of the topical debates that eclipsed the publication of Eckermann's book in 1836 was in fact about Strauss's *Leben Jesu*, published a year earlier.

Froude's choice of the epistolary form and a fictive editor was designed to distance him from his hero in the reader's mind; he protested in the preface to the second edition: "I wrote a Tragedy; I have been supposed to have written a Confession of Faith."[45] The model for a novel of unilateral letters written by a sensitive soul to a sympathetic but more prudent friend, who acts as editor and commentator, was Goethe's first and most famous novel, *Die Leiden des jungen Werther* (1774; revised 1786).[46] As in Froude's case, the novel is strongly autobiographical, and the writing of it was cathartic. Werther, the "worthy" one, finds a temporary cure for his *Weltschmerz* – that is, for the pain caused by life's limitations – in nature and in his love for Lotte. On the return of Lotte's betrothed, the sensible Albert, nature reveals to Werther a new visage, like nature in *In Memoriam*, "red in tooth and claw": "[der] Abgrund des ewig offenen Grabes ... ein ewig verschlingendes, ewig wiederkäuendes Ungeheuer [the ever-open grave ... an ever-swallowing, ever-ruminating monster]."[47] Werther leaves his rural Wahlheim (home of choice) for the court in an attempt to settle his vocation. Alienated by the philistinism and snobbery of the nobility, he returns to Lotte and Albert, resigned to suffer. He kills himself in the hope of returning to his divine Father – Goethe's Neoplatonic, pantheistic conception – no clergyman attending his funeral.

Stylistically, Froude's novel is discursive where Goethe's is lyrical, but some of Markham Sutherland's letters start, as Werther's typically do, with emphatic emotional statements before filling in the narrative situation, as, for instance, in letter 6: "Well, Arthur, we are come to a crisis now … But I am running on as usual with my own feelings, and I have not told you what it is which has happened." The Editor's description of Markham as one of the natures who would better not have been born reads like a prosaic analysis of Werther: "natures which fail … from delicacy of sensitive organization, to which their moral energy of character bears too small proportion." Just as Werther rejects a vocation, so Froude's hero spurns the three traditional vocations as inauthentic: "a lawyer …, a doctor, or a professional clergyman … are not simply men, but … something not more but less than men – men who have sacrificed their own selves to become the paid instruments of a system."[48] Like Werther, Markham loves nature and children, and he entangles himself half-consciously in a guilty love with a woman who sympathizes with his *zerrissen* (torn) self and whose husband is a foil to the hero. He dies early and outside conventional religion.

During his convalescence in Italy, Markham has written a "retrospective sketch," which the Editor includes as a valuable "analysis of a process through which in these last years so many minds besides his own have been slowly and silently devolving."[49] Its title, "Confessions of a Sceptic," alludes ironically to the "Confessions of a Beautiful Soul," which form one book of *Wilhelm Meister* (see chap. 1 above). Despite the differences entailed in a pietist woman's account of her ascetic devotion to Christ, the juxtaposition stresses the similarity of the two characters' honest unorthodoxy and lonely martyrdom.

The plot comes to a climax when Markham and Mrs Leonard are sailing on Lake Como and their lovers' talk makes them oblivious to her little girl, who gets herself drenched by leaning overboard unobserved. As a result of the chill, the child dies, a catastrophe that to the mother seems to be God's punishment for her untrue marriage, not for her adulterous but true love. To Markham, his remorse reveals that he has never truly loved Mrs Leonard and that his immoral conduct has been a direct outcome of his irreligiosity. In the words of the Editor, "he experienced at last what so long he had denied, that to attempt to separate morality from religion is madness."[50]

The incident is a direct borrowing from two contrasting episodes in Goethe's novel *Die Wahlverwandtschaften* (Elective affinities [1809]).

Froude doubtlessly knew the novel, which he was to translate pseud-onymously in 1851.[51] The translation was published as part of a collection, *Novels and Tales by Goethe*, three years later. The comparison of his novel with Goethe's *Wahlverwandtschaften* throws into relief, both for this critic and for the reader of Goethe in Froude's time, the different moral tone. Goethe's novel portrays the "elective affinities" – that is, the naturally lawful attraction – between Charlotte and her husband Eduard's old friend the Major, on the one hand, and between Eduard and Charlotte's ward, Ottilie, on the other. The two episodes deal with declarations of love beside the same lake. In the first scene the "sensible" pair, Charlotte and the Major, express their devotion to each other at the end of a boat ride but agree that they must part in order to make their embrace worthy of themselves.[52]

The second scene occurs when Eduard has returned to his estate, from which his wife had banished him while keeping Ottilie with her.[53] Instead of finding his wife, with whom he wishes to arrange a divorce to be followed by his marriage to Ottilie, he happens on Ottilie by the lake, where she is tending the child born to Charlotte after Eduard's departure. He explains the boy's marvellous resemblance to his wife's friend and to Ottilie, rather than to his biological parents, with the "double adultery" that he and his wife committed when they made love to each other while their hearts were occupied by their respective friends. Taking this marvel as a sign of their rightful love, Eduard and Ottilie kiss for the first time and take a passionate leave from each other. To hasten her late return with the child to Charlotte, Ottilie decides to row across the lake rather than walk around it. Pushing the boat off, she loses her balance and drops the child, who drowns. Ottilie sees the accident as a divine sign of her sin against marriage, and she imposes on herself a vow of silence and starvation, without, however, revoking her love; Eduard, still hopeful until her death, imitates her martyrdom. They are entombed side by side in a chapel, which the all-forgiving Charlotte dedicates to them alone.

In later years, Froude declared Goethe's novel a "monstrous book."[54] His borrowing from Goethe puts into relief his ambivalence about honest doubt. Goethe in both novels presents illicit love as pure, though destructive in its tragic conflict with other, equal claims – that is, as "daemonic" in his use of the word – and he conceives of a religiosity that holds sacred, even apotheosizes, such love, the narrator of *Wahlverwandtschaften* calling the lovers "saints" and "blessed."[55] In contrast, Froude's punitive plot and moralizing Editor insist on the causal connection between religious doubt and immoral love and on the necessary outcome: pathetic waste. The Editor admonishes the reader: "If there be one prayer which, morning, noon, and night, one and all of us should send up to God, it is, 'Save us from our own hearts.' "[56]

It is only in Mrs Leonard that Froude follows Goethe by making her cling to the truth of her heart against all dogma. As well as the allusion to *Wahlverwandtschaften*, she is reminiscent of Gretchen in Goethe's *Faust*, who says of her illicit love for Faust that it was a sin, yet its motivation, "Gott! war so gut! ach war so lieb! [God! was so good! oh, was so dear!]"[57] and who is granted salvation and even beatification. But as a minor character, a woman, and one who is naive and possibly mad, Helen Leonard is no counterweight to the male protagonist in the novel's argument. Nevertheless, at the time of publication the moralistic tone and plot did not sufficiently soften the scandal of Froude's sympathetic portrayal of the sufferings of a skeptic.

William Hale White also used the fiction of a manuscript edited by its author's friend in his pseudonymous novel *The Autobiography of Mark Rutherford, Dissenting Minister*, and its sequel, *Mark Rutherford's Deliverance: Being the Second Part of his Autobiography*. As was the case with Froude and his hero, Hale White made his hero's crisis of faith more damaging to life and career than his own, taking him through a descending sequence of employments and loves to an early death. Where Froude's protagonist lacks the Carlylean vigour that was generally thought a necessary requisite for the freethinker, Mark Rutherford lacks the intellectual power and training. In the preface to the second edition the author describes the hero as an "example of the danger and the folly of cultivating thoughts and reading books to which he was not equal, and which tend to make a man lonely."[58] A minor character, Clark, in *Deliverance* mirrors the protagonist's early self: "just in proportion to his lack of penetrative power was his tendency to occupy himself with difficult questions … and an unlucky day it was for him when he picked up … some very early translation of some German book on philosophy."[59]

The novel's milieu is provincial Nonconformity, an earlier period of which George Eliot had portrayed. She is present in the novel as a model for the realistic scenes of provincial social life, for the hero's ultimate ethos, and indeed, for a minor character. The story tells of the hero's "sham" training at a dissenting college, where the president's ignorance of German literature permits him to preach against the "shallow infidel," using the word "German" as a vague term of reproach, without preparing his charges to "meet the doubts of the nineteenth century." "It was a time in which the world outside was seething with the ferment which had been cast into it by Germany and by those in England whom Germany had influenced." Once outside and exposed to "German" questions about the Scriptures, the hero loses his faith in immortality and the Christian God, replacing him with Wordsworth's "God of the hills, the abstraction Nature."[60] When a leading member of his congregation denounces the "German gospel" of his sermons in the local newspaper,[61] he himself realizes that he has no gospel to preach and he resigns his ministry. For a while he finds clerical work with a London publisher of "books of a sceptical turn," and he falls in love, unrequited, with his niece. The models for Wollaston, the publisher, and his niece, Theresa, are John Chapman and Mary Ann Evans (George Eliot), who lived in Chapman's house while she was editing the *Westminster Review* for him; while there, she befriended Hale White, who himself also worked for Chapman for a period. Mark Rutherford describes Theresa as a woman whose "brain seemed to rule everything."[62]

The sequel picks up the narrative some years later when Rutherford joins a freethinking fellow journalist in missionary work in London's East End.[63] With very rare successes, they attempt to "create in [their] hearers contentment with their lot, and even some joy in it," preaching "the religion of the Reconciliator, the reconciliation of man with God." Besides the Wordsworthian worship of nature, which nurtures him and his family on their rare outings from London and their cramped life, a religion of human love is finally revealed to Rutherford through his stepdaughter's unexpected loving care of her dying mother and through his own resultant love of the child: "My love to Marie was love of God Himself as He is – an unrestrained adoration of an efflux from Him."[64] The experience is the climax of earlier ideas of altruism as the true religion and of marital love as a revelation of divine love.[65] Detached as they are from church and Scripture, these beliefs allude to Feuerbach's *Essence of Christianity* and the religion of humanity (see chap. 6 above), although Hale White implies the existence of God where Feuerbach reduces God to the idealized conception of humanity.

While Carlyle, Newman, and Wordsworth are mentioned by name, the influence of writers such as Strauss and Feuerbach appears only under the generic term "German." By the 1880s the "German gospel" needed no gloss either for Mark Rutherford's readers to understand its serious challenge to an uncritical Christianity or for the provincial readers of Mr Snale's zealous denunciation of Mark Rutherford's sermons to understand its heresy.

George Gissing, in his first published novel, *Workers in the Dawn* (1880), made a double departure by creating an English student of the Tübingen school who is a woman and who profits from its rationalist gospel. The commonplace view of the unlikeliness of female skepticism appears, for example, in John Morley's "fierce and famous mani-festo" (in Mrs Ward's words)[66] *On Compromise* (1874): "It constantly happens that the husband has wholly ceased to believe the religion to which his wife clings with unshaken faith." For Morley, a principal fig-ure of philosophical Radicalism, the reason is that women "are at present far less likely than men to possess a sound intelligence and a habit of correct judgment," and they will remain so as long as they have "less ready access than men to the best kinds of literary and scien-tific training" and, more importantly, are excluded from responsible public activity.[67]

It was frequent practice and strategy for radical thinkers on theo-logical matters to express conservative views on the feminine role.[68] In fiction, Mrs Humphry Ward, who herself recognized fem-inine educational disadvantages and helped to remove them, con-trasts Robert Elsmere's heroic intellectual doubt with his wife's simple piety, in obedience to her dead father, a contrast whose pro-totype is that between St Augustine and his mother, Monica, in the *Confessions*. When Ward created a female skeptic in the best-selling novel *Helbeck of Bannisdale* (1898), her doubt is not earned but in-herited from her father, and her lack of intellectual foundations for it makes her vulnerable in the conflict with a better-educated male, in this case a Roman Catholic. Even in Samuel Butler's iconoclastic novel *The Way of All Flesh*, Ernest's freethinking, independent Aunt Alethea, while presented most favourably, is condemned to an early death reminiscent of the punitive plots we have seen. Thomas Hardy's Sue Bridehead in *Jude the Obscure* (1896) accepts the fateful disasters in her life as divine punishment and surrenders her emancipated paganism to religiosity, changing places with Jude.

The standard fictional treatment of religious unorthodoxy in women is well exemplified, though without any German context, by a novel of the best-selling author Charlotte Yonge, who was also pop-ular in Germany and who was both socially and religiously conserva-tive. In *The Clever Woman of the Family* (1865) she portrays a young woman who finally comes to recognize and accept the feminine handicaps listed by Morley and to submit her moral and religious judgments to male counsel. Encouraged by her widowed mother, her sister, and their social circle to mistake her unusual "honest truth-seeking"[69] for intellectual power, Rachel Curtis has acted on her inde-pendent judgment, with disastrous results for others, including a child's death, and shame and remorse for herself.

The author, a High Anglican disciple of Keble, attributes the hero-ine's misguided actions to her skepticism and materialism. To Rachel's regretful admission of religious confusion that she "cannot rest or trust for thinking of the questions that have been raised!" her suitor and the mentor of her correction replies, "It is a cruel thing to represent doubt as the sign of intellect."[70] Under the influence of her suitor's ironic subversion of her self-conceit and of a truly learned and pious clergyman's inspiring example, she finds her way back to her Christian faith. The narrator comments that, "happily for herself, a woman's efforts at scepticism are but blind faith in her chosen leader, or, at the utmost, in the spirit of the age."[71] Whereas male skepticism usually suggests Lucifer and the German doctors Faust and Frankenstein, the cultural prototype for female skepticism is Milton's Eve, who is merely reacting to the temptation and correction, respectively, of the two antagonistic male figures of the epic. Yonge does not specify Rachel's reading as German, giving only general indications, such as Rachel's remark that she has taught herself enough Hebrew "to appreciate the disputed passages" in the Scriptures.[72] The author seems to assume a sufficient common knowledge of the debate that, even without further explanation – to adopt Mrs Ward's words about her own novel – "the popular consciousness may feel its force" in the protagonist's life.[73]

A German novel that portrays a similar return to faith by an emancipated woman, Wilhelmine von Hillern's *Ein Arzt der Seele* (A physician of the soul [1869]), is of some interest here since the author enjoyed a fair reputation in England. As we have seen, George Eliot probably read *Ein Arzt der Seele* in 1869 while writing *Middlemarch*, and Meredith used her *Geier-Wally* (The vulture maiden [1875]) to fashion his heroine, her setting, and some incidents in *The Amazing Marriage* (1895). The intellectual and religious emancipation of von Hillern's heroine goes well beyond anything portrayed in an English novel of the time, to my knowledge. Ernestine's scientist-uncle and guardian has privately trained her, for his own selfish reasons, as an experimental scientist and has indoctrinated her in absolute materialism. An anonymous original essay of hers in physiology wins an academic prize, but as a woman, she is denied attendance at the university for doctoral studies. Feeling rejected both by academe and, mistakenly, by the man she loves, she exclaims: "Die Männer wollen nun einmal kein Weib zum Professor – und der Mann – will keinen Professor zum Weib! [After all, men don't want a woman as professor – and man – doesn't want a professor for a wife!]."[74] Shaken by traumatic experiences – the novel is as melodramatic as it is intellectual – she becomes receptive to the "bitter medicine" which the *Seelenarzt*, himself a physician and scientist, prescribes, out of love for her, against her guardian's "unnatural" education in science and atheism to the exclusion of love – that is, unnatural for a woman. But in recog-

nition of her independent will, he subsequently obtains for her the offer of a professorship in natural science at Petersburg so that she may
freely choose between scholarship and fame, on the one hand, and
love and family, on the other. She chooses the latter and becomes happily reconciled to woman's lot as wife and mother, the author granting
her the honour of being her husband's scientific assistant as a concession to her talents. Despite the author's explicit conservative advocacy, which also seems to account for the fact that the title does not
refer to the principal character but to her male mentor, she gives the
emancipatory side equally persuasive arguments, creating an ambivalence that we also find in George Eliot – as for instance, in her treatment of the Princess Halm-Eberstein in *Daniel Deronda*.[75]

Of Gissing's *Workers in the Dawn* only a few dozen copies were
sold at the time. But as a consciously experimental novel, it indicates typical preoccupations of a novelist who wished to present
radical subjects and, in their treatment, to graft Continental social
and psychological realism onto the English tradition of interior
character development, as represented by Charlotte Brontë and
George Eliot.[76] Gissing explained in a letter to his brother Algernon:
"The book ... is not a novel in the generally accepted sense of the
word, but a very strong ... attack upon certain features of our
present religious & social life." Intending to be "the mouthpiece of
the advanced Radical party," he sought in religious matters "to
show the nobility of a faith dispensing with all we are accustomed
to call religion, & having for its only creed a belief in the possibility
of intellectual & moral progress."[77] In his later novel *Born in Exile*
(1892), the semi-autobiographical hero discovers that a wider range
of unorthodoxy, from broad church to atheism, is common in both
men and women with an education in the 1880s than his narrow
social experience has led him to expect.

Growing up in the 1860s, Gissing's heroine, Helen Norman, has experienced in her father, an Anglican clergyman, a learned and virtuous agnosticism while observing hypocritical, vulgar piety in his
curate. Mr Norman has devoted himself to his motherless child's education, and he acts in accordance with John Morley's advice on the
relationship between child and parents: "Those parents are wisest
who train their sons and daughters in the utmost liberty both of
thought and speech."[78] Mr Norman responds honestly to his young
daughter's question about God by saying that God is that "something in your mind which gives you the power of distinguishing between a good and a bad action, a beautiful and an ugly thing, and
also bids you choose the good and the beautiful."[79] (We have seen
this belief in the discussions between Dorothea and Ladislaw.) An

inheritance helps him to resign his living and end the hypocrisy of preaching a gospel he does not believe. For the sake of his health and to give Helen a Continental education, they move to Mentone.

In her grief over her father's early death from consumption, Helen turns devout under the influence of a French Catholic family with whom she has lived, but she discovers a new, invigorating gospel when she returns to England to live with her guardian and his daughter, both of them cynics, and comes across Strauss's *Leben Jesu*.[80] The narrator eulogizes Strauss as the thinker "whose eyes saw with surpassing clearness through the mists of time and prejudice, whose spirit comes forth ... to greet those toiling painfully upwards to the temple of truth." As a result of this reading and in the hope of forming "some definite convictions," Helen decides to study at Tübingen, where "her master's influence would ... be most pronounced."[81] Gissing sets her stay there from 1868 to 1869, by which time Strauss himself had long left Tübingen, his *Leben Jesu* having brought his academic career to an end in 1835.

Helen's German experience is portrayed in her diary, which forms a chapter entitled "Mind-Growth," a synonym for *Bildung*. With this chapter Gissing had the help of his German friend Eduard Bertz, a socialist in exile in London.[82] In Tübingen Helen studies the New Testament in the original, finding her rationalism strengthened despite her clerical tutor; she concludes that the speculations of Fichte, Schelling, and Hegel can have no influence on her practical life; and she reads Darwin's *Origin of Species* in German, with an enthusiasm only equalled by her discovery of Strauss. After a respite of German poetry and romance, she is introduced to Comte and Schopenhauer by a new mentor. Taking from Schopenhauer's pessimism his sympathy for suffering humanity and from Comte an optimistic plan for its alleviation, she constructs for herself an answer to the question "What can a woman do in the world?"[83] She returns to England to serve the "religion of humanity," and under the guidance of a dissenting clergyman, she dedicates herself to helping the poor in London's East End, with gifts of money but principally by starting an evening school for young working women.

Embodying the type of the "devout skeptic" derived from Strauss,[84] Helen is never shaken in her convictions, neither by her guardian's and his daughter's scandalized incomprehension nor by the hardships and disappointments of her work. When she falls ill and soon dies of consumption, Gissing stresses the "hereditary" nature of the disease, rather than the unhealthy conditions of her work or any spiritual cause. Nearing death, Helen answers her clergyman-friend's solicitous question, whether she has "no hopes of a future life; no hopes of anything beyond this world of misery?": "None. I do not deny that there may be such; but my reason is unable to conceive of it."[85] Unlike the authors considered so far, Gissing makes no moralizing comment. He presents Helen's agnosticism and the choices it results in as true and good by contrasting her altruistic idealism – her "schwärmerei" (sic), as her guardian's daughter, Maud, calls it – with Maud's cynical egotism and with the self-destructive dividedness of purpose in the hero, Arthur Golding, whose life intersects with Helen's at several stages. Arthur vacillates between the "double life" of art and philanthropy, between socialist militancy and Carlylean self-education, and between his ideal devotion to his muse, Helen, and his sensual passion for the vulgar and vicious Carrie. His sense of purposelessness and his consequent suicide when he learns of Helen's death seem to express Gissing's equivocal attitude, at this early stage in his career, to the choice between the beautiful and the good, that is, to the possibility of a socially useful fiction that is also art.

The most successful crisis-of-faith novel, with regard both to popularity and to artistry, was Mrs Humphry Ward's *Robert Elsmere*. It also treats most thoroughly the German influence on religious skepsis. The great sway and rapid obsolescence of Ward's reputation testify to her role as a mouthpiece for her era. As a "picture of actual life and conduct," the novel was intended to "defend the 'Liberal host'"[86] against the implication of skepticism with sin; that is, it operates in three generic modes: the *roman à clef*, the *Tendenzroman*, and the *Bildungsroman*. With respect to the first, the novel portrays a crisis of faith typical of the Oxford environment of the 1870s and 1880s,[87] and it uses as models for the hero's diverse mentors major figures at Oxford, with whom Ward, as an Arnold and the wife of a liberal Oxford fellow, was friends. Secondly, for her thesis, which she had already argued in 1881 in a pamphlet entitled "Unbelief and Sin," she tried, according to her memoirs, "so to suggest the argument, that both the expert and the popular consciousness may feel its force. And to do this without overstepping the bounds of fiction."[88] The novel's popularity testifies to her having achieved this balance. Despite Oscar Wilde's quip that *Robert Elsmere* was "simply Arnold's *Literature and Dogma* with literature left out,"[89] the third generic mode of the novel as *Bildungsroman*, as adapted by George Eliot, is effective in showing the interplay between intellectual ideas and sensibility, between differently oriented characters, and between the individual and the social-cultural milieu. In the manner of the classical *Bildungsroman*, these dynamic relations are presented as tending towards personal growth and, in a distant future, towards a general increase in humanity.

The novel immediately made Ward a "cult author ... despite the coolness and delay of the reviews."[90] In response to the popular success, the important periodicals finally weighed in with negative reviews, Gladstone's in the *Nineteenth Century*[91] (a journal to which the hero contributes articles on biblical criticism) being the most eminent. Robert's crisis takes place in the 1880s; the story tells of a young Oxford-trained clergyman's courtship and beneficent married life as a country parson, the doubt created by his historical research and goaded by the German-trained atheistic Squire Wendover, and his decision to resign his living and instead do social work in London, which soon results in a fatal illness. In contrast to Froude's conception, Robert's early death is not so much a punishment for his unorthodoxy as a sanctification of his martyrdom. His honest doubt, after causing severe marital suffering,[92] has produced in his wife, Catherine, a truer, more loving, rather than judging, Christianity, and in himself it has led to a new faith in Jesus as *the* moral type for Europeans. The narrator reports that Robert's "new church," the New Brotherhood of Christ, continues to grow after his death. His life and death illustrate Tennyson's assertion in *In Memoriam* that "There lives more faith in honest doubt / Believe me, than in half the creeds" (elegy 96).

Most of the German allusions are found in the middle part of the novel, which portrays Robert's struggle against Squire Wendover's challenge to his uncritical faith. The symbolic site of the conflict is Wendover's library, one section of which is stocked with German texts, which constitute, in the narrator's words, a "history of modern thinking Germany, of that 'unextinguished hearth' of whence the mind of Europe has been kindled for three generations."[93] Many are autographed, testifying to Wendover's ten years in Germany in the 1840s and 1850s. True to her purpose of satisfying the expert as well as the popular reader, the author specifies more German scholars and universities than we have seen in the other novels. Strauss's *Leben Jesu* and Tübingen are, of course, included.[94]

Ward modelled Wendover partly on Mark Pattison, giving him the Oxford scholar's two main traits, "great learning and a general impatience of fools." During her youthful friendship with Pattison, she had often listened to him "[pour] scorn on Oxford scholarship ... as compared with the researching ideals of the German universities, which seemed to the Rector [of Lincoln College] the only ideals worth calling academic."[95] In his role as irresponsible landlord, the scholarly squire is a pointed elaboration of Mr Brooke, intellectual dabbler and neglectful landlord in *Middlemarch*. The author attributes Wendover's "contempt for all forms of altruistic sentiment" to his German mentors, Bismarck and Mommsen,[96] the practitioner of *realpolitik* and the historian who dismissed the idea of a universal morality.[97]

Wendover's cynical motivation for destroying Robert's faith suggests a link between his library and Faust's study, scene of the wager with Mephisto in Goethe's *Faust*, and between Wendover and Mephisto, "der Geist, der stets verneint [the spirit who always negates]," but who "stets das Böse will, und stets das Gute schafft [always intends evil, and always creates good]."[98] In the same context, Catherine's direct questions about Robert's faith – "*can* you doubt – *do* you doubt – that He rose – that He is God – that He is in heaven – that we shall see Him?" – allude to the "Gretchen question" in *Faust*: "Nun sag, wie hast dus mit der Religion? ... Glaubst du an Gott? [Tell me what manner is your religion? ... Do you believe in God?]."[99] Wendover's end also strongly suggests Frankenstein's final recognition that he has sacrificed all affectionate bonds to his intellectual pride, when Wendover despairs, "among his German books," over his misused intellectual powers in the perverse alienation of his only intellectual companion, potentially a son to him.[100] In an echo of Matthew Arnold's strictures in *Literature and Dogma*, he comes to denounce "the Germans, [who] are beginning to founder in the sea of their own learning."[101]

The development of Robert's doubt recapitulates the course of German biblical criticism as originating from historiography. Modelled on Ward's own researches for a history of early Christian Spain, for which she had found German critics to be "the only [ones] worth following,"[102] Robert's historical project on Gaul brings him up against the problem of testimony. Wendover, himself involved in his life's main work, "A History of Testimony," compels Robert to realize the implications for biblical testimony. Robert emerges from the ensuing crisis with the self-confession "Every human soul in which the voice of God makes itself felt, enjoys, equally with Jesus of Nazareth, the divine sonship, and '*miracles do not happen!*'"[103] The first part of this creed is close to Feuerbach's religion of humankind; the second is a direct quotation from Arnold's *Literature and Dogma*. At least partly as a result of the intervention of George Eliot's fiction,[104] Ward makes a strong point about the independence of morality from dogma and church by implicitly contrasting the story of her precursor, Froude, about guilty love with her own hero's immunity to adulterous seduction.[105] In this claim, her thesis leads her beyond Arnold's position in *Literature and Dogma*, where he stresses the moral benefit of Christianity: the object of religion is conduct, which is "three-fourths of life."[106]

In his conclusion to *Literature and Dogma*, Arnold acknowledges that in *Culture and Anarchy* he stressed the remaining fourth of life – the "sweetness and light" of culture, that is, Hellenism – over morality, that is, Hebraism, as particularly neglected in the contemporary English mentality.[107] In this conflictual sense of Hellenism and Hebraism, some crisis-of-faith stories portray aestheticism as the enemy of conventional religion. Examples without a German context include Jane Eyre's love of beauty in rebellion against the puritanism of Mr Brocklehurst and his school and, in Gosse's *Father and Son*, the author's love of the imaginative life in conflict with his father's puritanical religion. In *Robert Elsmere*, aestheticism is associated with Germany, as it is in *Middlemarch*. Catherine's youngest sister, Rose, suggestively called by the German diminutive "Röschen" by her sisters, fiercely rebels against the ascetic evangelicalism of Catherine, who acts as parent because of their mother's ineffectiveness and the death of their father. Rose's Pre-Raphaelite hair and dress declare her dedication to beauty, as does, more substantially, her passionate musicality, in defiance of Catherine's censure that "art is not religion."[108]

As in *Daniel Deronda*, serious musicianship connotes German music. From studying the violin with a German teacher in Manchester, Rose returns "thirsty for the joys and emotions of art, … with Wagner and Brahms in her young blood." With her next ambition, to study music in Berlin, she receives Robert's help. Of a wider culture and an easier temperament than Catherine, he "tried to lift her to a more intelligent view of a multifarious world, dwelling on the function of pure beauty in life, and on the influence of beauty on character, pointing out the value to the race of all individual development."[109] The narrator attributes this line of argument to Kingsley; indirectly it derives from the concept of *Bildung*, as promoted by Humboldt, Schiller, and Goethe. Towards the end of Rose's successful German stay, which, however, is only reported offstage, the famous Joachim himself takes her on as a student. The Austro-Hungarian violinist, conductor, and composer made his career in Germany at the courts of Weimar and Hanover and, from 1860, at the Berlin Royal Academy of the Arts. From his annual concerts in London from 1862 until his death in 1907, his name would have been well known to Ward's readers.

Rose's talent and beauty are most appreciated by Robert's former tutor, Edward Langham, whose musical experience includes annual visits "to Berlin and Bayreuth to drink his fill of music." Based on a composite of models, including the English priest of aestheticism, Walter Pater, Langham represents the futility of intellectual power and aesthetic sensibility when divorced from "moral muscle."[110] Rose's ambivalence to his courtship indicates that there is a risk in her substitution of art for religion. She finally marries her other suitor, who combines culture with energy and philanthropy – a strikingly un-"Barbarian" aristocrat – and whose recent mathematical prize at Berlin nicely matches Rose's musical success there. As with Robert's resistance to temptation, the author shows that the risk of unorthodoxy can be overcome and that a life conducted on other principles than those of traditional religion can be good.

The four main crisis-of-faith novels under discussion here continue the debate about the good, the true, and the beautiful. We have already seen it in Carlyle's substitution of the true for the beautiful in Goethe's triad: the whole, the good, and the beautiful; in the restoration of the beautiful in Bulwer's *Ernest Maltravers* and George Eliot's *Middlemarch*; and in Matthew Arnold's shifting balance of the good and the beautiful in his culture criticism. The novels participate only marginally in the genre of the *Bildungsroman*, since they focus more or less narrowly on their young protagonists' quest for a religious orientation and on its effects on their development. The authorial attitude in all four makes them *Tendenzromane* (or *romans à thèse*), an eccentric genre in the English tradition of realist fiction but the preferred genre, for instance, of the German authors associated with Jung Deutschland (Young Germany) and the *Vormärz* (pre-1848) of the 1830s and 1840s, such as Karl Gutzkow and Fanny Lewald. Since the referential frame of the English novels is German, the French example of the *roman à thèse* does not as obviously come into play. Ward defended "the novel with a purpose" and its "thought-stuff" and propaganda against her negative reviewers by setting it in the larger historical and European tradition of Cervantes, Rousseau, and Goethe, citing their novels' inclusivity of discourses: "Theology, politics, social problems and reforms, they have laid hands on them all, and have but stirred the more vibrations thereby in the life of their time."[111]

8 Pessimism and Its "Overcoming": Schopenhauer and Nietzsche

A consideration of allusions to the ideas of Arthur Schopenhauer and of his renegade disciple, Friedrich Nietzsche, brings into sharp focus the difficult but necessary distinction between influence, affinity, and independent similarity. For instance, what was long the strongest case of Schopenhauerian influence, Thomas Hardy, has been dismissed: Hardy appears to have arrived at his metaphysical pessimism independently and prior to any familiarity with Schopenhauer's writings. However, the ready association of his novels and *The Dynasts* (1904–8) with Schopenhauer's pessimism, originating with a review of *The Return of the Native* (1878), testifies to the prominence of Schopenhauer on the readerly horizon.[1] Again, Nietzsche's chief popularizer in England, G.B. Shaw, protested vigorously in the preface to *Major Barbara* (1907), for instance, against allegations of indebtedness to Schopenhauer and Nietzsche – in a caricature by Max Beerbohm he protests to the critic Georg Brandes the originality of the patches on his clothes borrowed from Schopenhauer, Nietzsche, and Ibsen[2] – and indeed, he recruited their ideas for his own campaigns entirely as they suited his purposes.

The reception of Schopenhauer's philosophical system and of what is best described as Nietzsche's philosophy of culture or culture-criticism was delayed in England, as it was in Germany.[3] Both thinkers argued against and outside the Hegelian orthodoxies of German philosophy, which then was typically professorial, and wrote in a non-academic, literary style, disqualifying themselves from fair academic recognition. With a touch of sour grapes but not altogether un-

GEORG BRANDES ('Chand d'Idées): "What'll you take for the lot?"
GEORGE BERNARD SHAW: "Immortality."
GEORG BRANDES: "Come, I've handled these goods before! Coat, Mr. Schopenhauer's;
waistcoat, Mr. Ibsen's; Mr. Nietzsche's trousers –"
GEORGE BERNARD SHAW: "Ah, but look at the patches!"

justly, Schopenhauer railed against German *Kathederphilosophie*
(lectern, or academic, philosophy) as analogous to prostitution of the
truth to the expediencies of the state.[4] The influence of both intellectual rebels became as powerful in literature, the arts, and lay thought
as it remained limited in academic philosophy, except for the recruitment of Nietzsche as a precursor of existentialism and the recent
reception of his epistemology.

Fittingly for the anglophile Schopenhauer, it was an English review that led not only to English familiarity with his main work, *Die Welt als Wille und Vorstellung* (The world as Will and Idea [1818]), and the subsidiary essays, *Parerga und Paralipomena* (1851), but also to a wider interest and even cult in Germany. John Oxenford's "Iconoclasm in German Philosophy" appeared in the *Westminster Review* in 1853, that is, while George Eliot acted as editor.[5] After the publication of Darwin's *Origin of Species* in 1859, Schopenhauer's pessimistic world view, the first such metaphysical system in Western thought, seemed to complement the findings of science that humankind was ruled by deterministic but non-purposive principles. Darwin in fact acknowledged "the German philosopher" Schopenhauer as a forerunner in the second edition of *The Descent of Man*.[6] By the time of the English translation of Schopenhauer's complete works in 1883, his chief ideas were well disseminated, helped by the philosophy of the unconscious developed by his disciple, Eduard von Hartmann, and by critical writings on Wagner's essays; soon after, his ideas came to coincide with the *fin-de-siècle* mentality. Nevertheless, in a comparison with Schopenhauer's Continental influence, Edmund Gosse polemicized in 1890, "The Anglo-Saxon race is now the only one that has not been touched by that pessimism of which the writings of Schopenhauer are the most prominent and popular exponent." (Gosse himself introduced *Father and Son* with an epigraph from Schopenhauer.)[7] A more self-satisfied observation than Gosse's is S. Laing's in his best-selling popularizing work *Modern Science and Modern Thought* (1885): the doctrine of Schopenhauer and Continental Pessimists could only find acceptance with men of "cultivated intellects, sensitive nerves, and bad digestion." In England he finds little effect of it.[8]

Nietzsche would have accounted for Gosse's observation with the reason, given around this time, that because of the actual hegemony of Christian valuation, despite its "forgotten" origin, "[f]ür den Engländer ist die Moral noch kein Problem [for the Englishman morality is not yet a problem]." He judged the English an unphilosophical race. His own *Umwerthung aller Werthe* (trans-valuation of all values) had to wait for its promotion and fame until the last year of his active, sane life, when in 1888 the Danish critic, friend, and advocate of Ibsen Georg Brandes lectured and subsequently published on Nietzsche's "aristocratic radicalism."[9] Until the complete but still unreliable translation of his works in 1909–13, English familiarity with Nietzsche was confined, for non-German readers, to French translations – the French were his best and favourite public – to an earlier incomplete and faulty English translation, and, disastrously, to the pillorying of his "egomanic" "philosophy of 'bullying'" in Max Nordau's notorious denunciation of the *fin-de-siècle* mentality in *Degeneration* (1895).[10] Together with the hostility gen-

WHY HAVE WE NO SUPERMEN LIKE THE GERMANS?

How they might brighten Regent Street.

How they might wake up our restaurants.

And honour us with their gallantry.

And, best of all, how amusing to see them meet a super-superman.

erated in British Wagner circles by Nietzsche's apostasy from Wagner, these mediations resulted in a pronounced split into fierce pro- and contra-Nietzscheans, with Shaw as the main popularizer of Nietzsche "the Diabolonian" and G.K. Chesterton as the voice of protest against the "heretic."[11]

The short "Nietzschean decade" of serious study was interrupted by the casting of World War I as the "Euro-Nietzschean War," which made Nietzsche taboo.[12] Programmatically unsystematic, ironic, and self-contradictory, Nietzsche lent himself to being recruited as an ally in diverse, even opposite, campaigns, such as Darwinian and anti-Darwinian, reactionary and socialist, cosmopolitan and nationalist. His concepts were adopted selectively, such as the superman by Shaw and the eternal recurrence by W.B. Yeats. The most positive British readings of Nietzsche naturalized him as the successor of Blake. Following J.A. Symonds and Yeats and in contrast to the assimilation of Nietzsche to Nazism,[13] W.H. Auden, in his *New Year Letter* of 1941, apostrophized Nietzsche: "O masterly debunker of our liberal fallacies, ... you stormed, like your English forerunner Blake."[14]

Of Nietzsche's writings, *Also Sprach Zarathustra* (Thus spoke Zarathustra [1883–85]), which presents the gospel of the *Übermensch* (overman, or superman), became the bible, complemented by the *Umwerthung* (transvaluation) of the Christian *Sklavenmoral* (slave morality) proposed in *Zur Genealogie der Moral* (Genealogy of morals [1887]). The dynamic polarity of the Apollonian and Dionysian principles in *Die Geburt der Tragödie* (The birth of tragedy [1872]) appealed particularly to artists. The notion of a Nietzschean is strictly a solecism; Zarathustra counsels his disciples: "Nun heisse ich euch, mich verlieren und euch finden; und erst, wenn ihr mich Alle verleugnet habt, will ich euch wiederkehren [Now I bid you lose me and find yourselves; and only when you have all denied me will I return to you]."[15]

Because of the delayed and indirect reception of Schopenhauer and Nietzsche in England, we need not here consider the development of their ideas closely. (However, for a just account of Nietzsche and for a partial explanation of his contradictory reception, attention to the major changes, in the later 1870s, in his revised views of nationalism and war and his new values of cosmopolitanism and self-conquest is crucial.)[16] In total rejection of Hegel's "charlatan" optimistic metaphysics and in a radical reading of Kant, Schopenhauer "intuited" as the ultimate truth of existence an unconscious and irrational *Wille zum Leben* (Will to Life), of which the Ideas (in Plato's sense) are second-order representations.[17] Competition and sexuality make men and women, like all creatures, mere tools of the Will, trapping them in the misery of either pain or boredom. For escape from the futile struggle, Schopenhauer proposes three rational routes: the ethical, namely, pity towards all other living beings as fellow victims; the artistic, namely, disinterested contemplation of the phenomena in the world; and the highest, namely, the philosophical, the recognition of this truth and the consequent refusal to participate in the struggle of life (for this quietist attitude, he was indebted to Hinduism). Only an elite of minds is eligible for these reflective routes, most men being mere

Fabrikwaare der Natur (mass products of nature).[18] Women are further disqualified by their stronger biological subjection to the Will to Life, an argument that led to the notoriety of Schopenhauer as a misogynist. Compared to men, women represent the Will in contrast to the Idea.[19]

Nietzsche initially read Schopenhauer, his *Lehrer und Zuchtmeister* (teacher and disciplinarian), "als ob er für [ihn] geschrieben hätte [as though he had written for (him)]," but later he rejected him, together with his fellow disciple Richard Wagner. In *Zarathustra* Schopenhauer appears as "der Wahrsager" (the soothsayer), who preaches the doctrine that "Alles ist leer, Alles ist gleich, Alles war! [All is empty, all is the same, all has been!]." He later comes to seduce Zarathustra to his "final sin," pity for the *höheren Menschen* (higher humans), that is, for the followers of Zarathustra, who are no more than a bridge to the *Übermensch*.[20] For Nietzsche, strife nurtures development (*Bildung*), and consequently the Will, in the form of the *Wille zur Macht* (Will to Power), is asserted nobly, especially as *Selbst-Überwindung* (self-overcoming).[21] The domesticated, civilized, good man, epitomized in the decadent nineteenth-century European, needs "overcoming" to reach the goal of the "overman," who, in Nietzsche's idiosyncratic variation on Goethean *Bildung*, will be a higher, purified metamorphosis of the primitive *blonde Bestie* (blond beast) of the *Genealogie der Moral*.[22] What to Schopenhauer is a pitiable universal and permanent condition of humankind is to Nietzsche foremost a modern cultural crisis, which can be overcome. Now that materialism has killed the divine – "Gott starb: nun wollen *wir*, – dass der Übermensch lebe [God died: now *we* want the overman to live]" – and now that democracy has created the *Heerden-Mensch* (mass human), contempt and despair over the littleness of life must be transcended through dance and laughter.[23]

With their uncommon stress on individual psychological experience – in Nietzsche's words, "Menschliches, Allzumenschliches [the human, all-too-human]" – these two "existentialist" philosophers were working in the domain of the novelists. Consequently, their *Lebensanschauungen* lent themselves readily to adoption, comparable to Freud more recently, for a fictional character or for the narrator, if not indeed by the author. As was the case with the two philosophers themselves, we find their ideas are sometimes presented in close relation to or development from each other. For an all-inclusive example of Schopenhauer's philosophy in a novel's protagonist, narrator, and author, I shall consider Gissing's *The Whirlpool* (1897). The other principal novelists I shall examine are E.M. Forster, Joseph Conrad, and D.H. Lawrence. I treat the association of Nietzsche with imperialism in the next chapter.

John Oxenford had lamented in Schopenhauer the waste of "the most general, the most ingenious, the most amusing" treatment of pessimism, "the most disheartening, the most repulsive, the most opposed to the aspirations of the present world." As editor of Oxenford's article on Schopenhauer, George Eliot had highly recommended it to a friend.[24] The main allusion she makes in her fiction to Schopenhauer is in her treatment of the superior truth and power of music and of its prophet, Herr Klesmer, in *Daniel Deronda* (see chap. 6 above).[25]

Mrs Humphry Ward, who was for many of her readers the successor to George Eliot, is a good indicator of the general public's receptivity to allusions to Schopenhauer and Nietzsche. A serious and best-selling novelist, she disseminated her period's radical religious and social-political ideas to a large public. She frequently constructed gender relations in a modified version of Schopenhauer's terms. In a recurrent pattern in her best political novels, *Marcella* (1894), *Sir George Tressady* (1896), and *Eleanor* (1900), for instance, the hero dreads his chronic sense of futility, "that pessimist temper of his towards his own work and function," and welcomes rescue by the enthusiastic heroine into the healthy struggle of public life.[26] The heroine's "natural" social pity adds motivation to men's rational convictions and even converts otherwise indifferent men to political engagement. That is, the difference from Schopenhauer lies in the fact that the natural vitality of Ward's heroines does not serve the irrational will to procreate but is expended on social pity, which in turn is not a product of rational contemplation, as in Schopenhauer, but of the heart, and results in true progress. In *The Marriage of William Ashe* (1905) she created a secondary character, Geoffrey Cliffe, the poet, Don Juan, traveller, and political correspondent and adviser, in the popular modern version of the Byronic hero, namely, the Nietzschean "immoralist." Trying to persuade the heroine to join him in adultery and a war of liberation in Bosnia, he argues that "the modern judges for himself – makes his own laws, as a god, knowing good and evil."[27]

Ward considered Henry James and George Meredith the two novelists who "at that time stood at the head of [her] own art." In the "tonic" and "bracing" Schopenhauer, Meredith discriminated between the superior "analysis of the elements by which we live" and the faulty "personal judgment on his exposition"; he thought Nietzsche "a wrong-headed madman of morbid tendencies"; and he did not allude to either in his fiction. According to G.K. Chesterton, Meredith was the champion of "open optimism" versus Hardy's championship of "open pessimism," the clash bringing to an end the Victorian peace.[28]

In contrast to Meredith, Henry James, who had first encountered Schopenhauer's work as a youth in 1858, made pessimism the basic note of the authorial voice in his two novels on social-political reform, *The Bostonians* (1885) and *The Princess Casamassima* (1886).[29] In the latter the protagonist, little Hyacinth the bookbinder, values Schopenhauer's opinions as "important to have," although he gallantly disagrees with his misogyny, which the novel, however, generally supports. Particularly close to Schopenhauer is Hyacinth's abandonment of revolutionary politics and his new commitment to fight for the beautiful, the "monuments and treasures of art," even to the point of self-sacrifice. As James's mouthpiece, Hyacinth's mentor and a former socialist, the fiddler Mr Vetch, believes that "there was no way to clear it up that didn't seem to make a bigger mess than the actual muddle of human affairs ... The figures on the chess-board were still the passions and jealousies and superstitions and stupidities of man." In both novels James shows the truth of Basil Ransom's criticism of the feminist reformers: "what strikes me most is that the human race has to bear its troubles."[30]

More radically reflecting on progress is H.G. Wells's portrayal, in one of the early pessimistic scientific romances, *The Island of Doctor Moreau* (1896), of the eponymous hero's evolutionary experiments in the "plasticity of living forms" – a travesty of Goethean *Bildbarkeit*.[31] Although Wells had developed his Darwinian ideas independently of Nietzsche, he found him a useful ally against democratic humanity.[32] Doctor Moreau takes literally and materially, as the eugenics movement did, Zarathustra's words "Der Mensch aber ist Etwas, das überwunden werden muss [Humankind, however, is something that must be overcome]," and he "overcomes" physiologically his animal specimens' limitations, explaining to the narrator: "To this day I have never troubled about the ethics of the matter. The study of Nature makes a man at last as remorseless as Nature." Doctor Moreau thus acts "jenseits von Gut und Böse [beyond good and evil]." The narrator's horror first at the scientist's dispassionate cruelty and later at the Beast People's malice is transformed into a yet more devastating insight when, on his return to London, he "could not persuade [him]self that the men and women [he] met were not also another, still passably human, Beast People, animals half-wrought into the outward image of human souls, and that they would presently begin to revert."[33]

The narrator has earlier observed that the Beast People, in their hybrid state "in the shackles of humanity," are inferior to their previous state, "their instincts fitly adapted to their surroundings."[34] Similarly, Zarathustra repeatedly takes refuge with his animals, the eagle and the serpent, from humankind, including his followers, the "higher men," who are mere pitiable "bridges" to the prospective *Übermensch*. However, like his author, he always returns to his optimistic mission of "overcoming" humankind. Wells would go on to write his optimistic utopias, but while *The Island of Doctor Moreau* indirectly agrees through Doctor Moreau with Nietzsche's diagnosis of humankind's need of improvement, it rejects through the narrator and the plot his prognosis of progress. The "plasticity of living forms" is not matched with plasticity of spirit.

It is small wonder that Thomas Hardy's novels have long been associated with what he, in *Tess of the d'Urbervilles* (1891), called Schopenhauer's "renunciative philosophy," even though Schopenhauer's role seems to have been limited to a late confirmation of Hardy's own independent views. Where James's pessimism is controlled, implicit, and "dramatized," Hardy's obtrudes in authorial commentary and plot bias, what Chesterton called his new "game" of "the extravagance of depression."[35] Uncommonly in the English tradition, Hardy explicitly relates the characters' fate to a metaphysical world view, which has, moreover, the ultimate ruling principle as unconscious, irrational, and indifferent to human life, if not malignant. For instance, the rape of Tess by Alec occurs in a darkness and silence that goes beyond the Chase, in the absence of guardian angel or providence.

In *Jude the Obscure* (1895), his last and most pessimistic novel, Hardy constructs Jude's conflict between idealistic learning and naturalistic sex as a conflict between him and Arabella or, in Schopenhauer's terms, between male and female as representing the Idea and the Will.[36] That Jude laments the increased suffering caused by consciousness, and that Little Father Time kills the children and himself because it would be better not to have been born, goes against Schopenhauer's teaching, but only as it counsels elite minds, not as it describes ordinary experience.

According to Gosse's report, Hardy "did not admit any influence of Schopenhauer on his work."[37] His German was minimal, and his occasional quotations from German authors are second-hand – from Carlyle's German essays, for instance. He followed the discussion of Schopenhauer's ideas in the periodicals and read, and copied from, some of his works in translation.[38] As well, he read Eduard von Hartmann's *Philosophy of the Unconscious* (trans. 1884). As Hardy's notebooks show, he also closely attended to discussions of Nietzsche's ideas. He was repelled by the "superman," but intrigued by the Apollonian and Dionysian as epistemological concepts.[39] In *The Dynasts* (1904–8) Hardy espoused evolutionary meliorism. He ends the "epic-drama" with the hopeful answer by the chorus to "the question ... / Of the Will's long travailings": "Consciousness the Will informing, till It fashion all things fair!" This conception resembles the philosophy of Schopenhauer's disciple, critic, and popularizer von Hartmann, who combined Schopenhauer's "eudaemonological pessimism" about individual life with Hegelian "evolutionary optimism" about the cosmos.[40]

Of the novelists treated here, George Gissing found Schopenhauer's pessimism the most congenial and useful, and *The Whirlpool* is the novel that is most thoroughly informed by it.[41] Gissing was introduced to Schopenhauer in German by his German friend, Eduard Bertz, while the latter sketched the Tübingen chapter for *Workers in the Dawn* (see chap. 7 above) – the heroine reads the *Parerga und Paralipomena* in Tübingen. Bertz also introduced Gissing to Nietzsche, but Gissing found little use for the "Man-worshipper."[42]

In 1882, two years after his first introduction to Schopenhauer, Gissing wrote an essay, "The Hope of Pessimism." In it he extracted from Schopenhauer a system of metaphysical, ethical, and aesthetic ideas which served him for his remaining writing career and which is evident in all his novels. Taking as "the eternal truth that the world is synonymous with evil," Gissing held that a "conscious and consistent pessimism" can be the only rational attitude to life, and pity the only rational attitude to oneself and one's fellow beings. The only activity that does not share the evil egotism of the "battle of life" is art: "In the mood of artistic contemplation the will is destroyed, self is eliminated, the world of phenomena resolves itself into pictures of absolute significance, and the heart rejoices itself before images of pure beauty."[43]

Schopenhauer's theory of art accorded well with English aestheticism as Gissing knew and admired it in Ruskin, Swinburne, Rossetti, Morris, and its English forerunners, Shelley and Arnold. However, in contrast to Ruskin and Morris, Gissing gave up for good any hope of influencing social progress, Schopenhauer's pessimism providing him with a theory that matched his own experience. He expostulated when, in 1885, Morris's socialist activities had brought him into a police court: "Why cannot he write poetry in the shade? He will inevitably coarsen himself in the company of ruffians. Keep apart, keep apart, and preserve one's soul alive – that is the teaching for the day."[44]

Gissing apparently did not publish his "pessimistic article" for fear of alienating Frederic Harrison with his apostasy from Agnostic Positivism, Harrison having helped him publish a series of articles on Continental socialism in the *Pall Mall Gazette*.[45] From now on, he gave clear preference in his novels to the life dedicated to art and the imagination over that dedicated to social-political reform, a choice which in his first published novel, *Workers in the Dawn*, had been debatable as "the double life," represented respectively by the two protagonists (see chap. 7 above). Waymark, in *The Unclassed* (1884), speaks for Gissing when he explains to his friend the aesthetic, rather than social, object of his first novel, despite its naturalist subject matter: "I have no longer a spark of social enthusiasm. Art is now all I care for, and as art I wish my work to be judged."[46]

The Whirlpool is a late, well-fashioned work that shows consistent parallels between Schopenhauer's ideas and the judgments which Gissing makes in his presentation and discussion of the novel's main issues: marriage, family, and modern life in general. Gissing was re-reading Schopenhauer at the time he started to think about the novel. He discarded two earlier titles in favour of "The Whirlpool," an image that he had chosen in "The Hope of Pessimism" to replace "that phrase, 'the battle of life' ": "We are shipmates, tossed on the ocean of eternity, and one fate awaits us all. Let this excite our tenderness. Let us move on to the real gulfs hand clasped in hand, not each one's raised in enmity against his fellow." Here Gissing extracts hope from Schopenhauer's simile which compares the egotistic confidence of unreflective humanity in the midst of an infinite world of suffering with a sailor's foolish trust in his weak vessel in the middle of a raging sea.[47]

A perception of the reality of the whirlpool distinguishes a few of Gissing's characters from the majority, the "*Fabrikwaare der Natur*," in Schopenhauer's term. The image of the whirlpool recurs throughout the novel, always connoting modern social life, especially in London, in contrast with old-fashioned virtues, such as simplicity, stability, and rationality. For instance, Harvey Rolfe, the protagonist, on leaving the city with its anxieties, scandals, and crime for a week's break in a provincial town, writes to his friend, "I feel as if we were all being swept into a ghastly whirlpool which roars over the bottomless pit."[48]

Schopenhauer's view of the world as Will and Idea corresponds with the novel's main conflict between the two modern trends expressed in, first, imperialism, commercialism, barbarism, and the whirlpool of city life, and secondly, pacifism, art, self-culture, and simple country life. The friends Hugh Carnaby and Harvey Rolfe embody the two trends: "The one's physical vigour and adroitness, the other's active mind, liberal thoughts, studious habits, proved reciprocally attractive"; other characters are grouped accordingly.[49] Gissing favours the second trend; his authorial comments are in sympathy with it, he makes Harvey's point of view the prevalent one, and he stresses, as in the essay, that it is the result of mature reflected experience.[50] Yet to the end of the novel Gissing and his protagonist concede the validity of the first trend, the assertion of the will. The characters who represent it may be criticized for their lack of reflection, but their success in life makes this lack no cause for regret; nor are they presented as contemptible.

The authorities cited in the novel in support of the first trend are Darwin and Rudyard Kipling. Darwin appears by allusion to Herbert Spencer's term for his theory, "the survival of the fittest,"[51] and Kipling in an explicit reference in the last chapter, when Harvey reads aloud to his friend Morton from *Barrack-Room Ballads* and comments, as Gissing himself did similarly in letters to Bertz, in a mixture of admiration and condemnation: "Here's the strong man made articulate … It's the voice of the reaction … The brute savagery of it! The very lingo – how appropriate it is! The tongue of Whitechapel blaring lust of life in the track of English guns!"[52]

Schopenhauer's name appears only once in the novel, in reference to the friends' anticipated life of resigned cheerfulness.[53] According to Schopenhauer, a philosophical perception of life and a consequent altruism would generate "eine gewisse Gleichmässigkeit und selbst Heiterkeit der Stimmung [a certain equanimity, even cheerfulness]." Neither in the novel nor in his essay on pessimism does Gissing advocate the option of hastening death, a choice that Schopenhauer judges a merely apparent, physical deliverance, signifying not a denial of the Will but its ultimate assertion.[54]

Gissing's portrayal of his female characters, in their relations to men, children, other women, society, and intellectual and artistic endeavour, closely follows Schopenhauer's theories on women. The difference lies in Schopenhauer's maintaining that women are naturally inferior to men and therefore ill-equipped to use the equality granted them in European society to any but harmful ends, a conviction that he privately changed in later life under the influence of several women disciples. Gissing's belief in women's potential equality lends force to his criticism of their actual, socially conditioned inferiority.

According to Schopenhauer's essay "Über die Weiber" (On women), woman considers love "ihren allein ernstlichen Beruf [her only serious vocation]"; she must capture a member of the stronger sex so that he can take care of her. As a partner, she compensates for her physical and mental inferiority with instinctual deception: "daher ihre instinktartige Verschlagenheit und ihr unvertilgbarer Hang zum Lügen [therefore her instinctive slyness and her ineradicable tendency to lie]." Her *geistiger Myops* (mental short-sightedness) knows only expediency, not honesty and justice. It also confines her vision to her material environment, which frequently results in "bisweilen an Verrücktheit grenzende[n] Hang zur Verschwendung [an inclination for luxury occasionally bordering on madness]." Dependent on her husband for her social standing, she is more conscious of rank than he: "die Weiber sind … die gründlichsten und unheilbarsten Philister [the most thorough and incurable philistines]." This dependence makes her view other women as rivals. She only cares for her children instinctively, while they are helpless infants, since she is incapable of developing, as a father does, a continued love "auf Gewohnheit und Vernunft gegründet [based on habit and reason]." Finally, any interest that a woman may show in the arts or in books is never objective, but an indirect way of conquering men; this is Schopenhauer's reason for calling her "das unästhetische Geschlecht [the unaesthetic sex]."[55] In all, woman's weaker power of reasoning makes her more subject to nature and thus party to the Will, which puts her in conflict with the man, who seeks to deny the Will and live by the Idea.

In his *Commonplace Book*, Gissing remarked on "the profound cynicism (or naturalism) of the common woman." In *The Whirlpool* he makes it clear that his two main female characters capture their husbands by feminine skills that the men hardly understand. The irresistible attraction that the whirlpool of high society has for the women corresponds with what Schopenhauer says of woman's extravagance and concern with rank. Alma's growing jealousy of Sibyl because of the capitalist Redgrave's favours does not arise from love but from her wish for social success, to which his influence can help her. In accord with Schopenhauer's observations on this *"odium figulinum"* (trade jealousy), Gissing remarks, "jealousy without love, a passion scarcely intelligible to the ordinary man, is in woman common enough, and more often productive of disaster than the jealousy which originates in nobler feeling."[56] In all the other London marriages it is similarly the wife's attraction to the whirlpool of social life which for the husband means scandal, overwork, and debts and for the children, neglect.

Although Gissing shows women to be the immediate cause of domestic misery, he blames modern urban life for providing the conditions. He stresses that the exceptional Mrs Morton, as wife of a small-town merchant, "was so fortunate as to find no obstacle in circumstance" to being the perfect hausfrau. For Alma and Sibyl, as well as for the other London New Women, there is no contentment in a return to a simpler life, in Wales for Alma and Harvey, in Australia for Sibyl and Hugh. Freedom from the anxieties of the whirlpool only brings them boredom, which Schopenhauer argues is the inevitable alternative to suffering: "denn zwischen Schmerz und Langeweile wird jedes Menschenleben hin und her geworfen [for all human life is pitched hither and thither between pain and boredom]."[57]

The care of children is a major problem in the novel, and Gissing's treatment of it is his most unequivocal rejection of the idea of progress. Harvey discusses the problem with Mrs Abbott, who in her nursery school takes care of his and of other middle-class children whose mothers will not: "Naturally, children are a nuisance; especially so if you live in a whirlpool ... men and women practically return to the state of savages in all that concerns their offspring."[58]

Finally, Gissing exposes his female characters' intellectual and artistic interests, in sharp contrast to the male characters', as the mere means to social ends, which Schopenhauer says they always are for women. Despite appearances, Sibyl "did not read much, and not at all in the solid books which were to be seen lying about her rooms; but Lady Isobel Barker, and a few other people, admired her devotion to study." Alma plans to come out as a professional violinist because, "[i]n one way, and one way only, could she hope to become triumphantly conspicuous ... And she must make use of all subsidiary means to her great conquest – save only the last dishonour."[59]

Among the objects of disinterested contemplation that can aid human beings in negating their will, Schopenhauer ranks nature lowest and music of all the arts the highest. Music is an immediate representation of the Will, not like the other arts a representation of the Ideas, which in turn objectify the Will: "der Komponist offenbart das innerste Wesen der Welt und spricht die tiefste Weisheit aus [the composer reveals the inmost essence of the world and expresses the deepest wisdom]." Without following Schopenhauer's hierarchy in detail, Gissing in "The Hope of Pessimism" also singles out music as "the most perfect utterance of the deepest truth."[60] Alma's perversion of music to a social ruse is a strong condemnation of the whirlpool.

The optimism about art which Gissing shares with his protagonist is also evident in his care for the form of his pessimistic novel. According to his essay on pessimism, the artist improves the human lot by increasing the beautiful and by exercising his audience's denial of egotism in the disinterested, objective contemplation of it. The foregoing discussion of The Whirlpool provides examples of this aesthetic: in terms of objectivity, the choice of subject matter and its honest and dramatic presentment; in terms of beauty, the thematic grouping of characters; and in terms of both, the careful style, with its characteristically distanced, highly latinate diction.

Nietzsche is a rare and minor presence in Gissing's fiction.[61] In The Whirlpool one of the two modern trends, that which values strength and struggle and is explicitly associated with Darwin and Kipling, is also implicitly associated with Nietzsche. An explicit reference in *Our Friend the Charlatan* (1901) voices Gissing's own criticism. During the short period when the two protagonists, Dyce Lashmar and Constance Bride, see profit in sharing their self-interests, they both read "a book of Nietzsche," making him their "intimate" philosopher, each secretly liking "this insistence on the right of the strong." But in words echoing Harvey's on Kipling in *The Whirlpool*, they warn against Nietzsche's influence on others: "He'll do a great deal of harm in the world ... The jingo impulse, and all sorts of forces making for animalism, will get strength from him, directly or indirectly ... And he delivers his message so brutally."[62]

Averse to any kind of dogma, to what in "What I Believe" (1939) he called "mental starch," E.M. Forster nevertheless used allusions to Schopenhauer and Nietzsche for the realistic portrayal of the modern intellectual milieu of both his characters and his moralizing narrators and their implicit readers.[63] Such allusions contribute the force of familiar philosophical arguments, approximating commonplaces, to the questioning of the novels' apparently dominant liberal humanist optimism, to what Lionel Trilling called Forster's "war with the liberal imagination." Forster had gone as a tutor to Germany in order to learn German. One of his early adult-education lectures had for its title "Pessimism in Literature." When in 1939 he thought it necessary in self-defence against the prevalent militant creeds to "formulate a creed of [his] own" in "What I Believe," he acknowledged with Schopenhauer and Nietzsche that force and violence are "alas! the ultimate reality on this earth." But he disagreed with "the Nietzschean [who] would hurry the monster up" and, instead, advocated creativity in art and human relations during the "intervals when force has not managed to come to the front," intervals that are fashionably decried as decadent but are really "civilization."[64] Forster here rejects popular Nietzschean clichés rather than Nietzsche's own later ideas. The "Nietzschean" warmonger is here the very type of jingoist whom Nietzsche, the self-proclaimed "good European," repeatedly attacked, and Forster's conception of civilization in contrast to war resembles Nietzsche's several statements on the "antagonism" between culture, which at its best is "unpolitisch, selbst *antipolitisch* [unpolitical, even anti-political]," and the state and its "grosse Politik [big politics]."[65]

In *Maurice* (posthumous, 1971; written 1913–14) Forster typically contrives to both alert his readers to a Nietzschean context and permit them to ignore it, when the protagonist denies that he is a disciple of Nietzsche and owes him his social observation that "the poor don't want pity, won't get love." The citing of Nietzsche points beyond the immediate topic to the larger theme in the novel, a revaluation of Christian heterosexual morality: "Those who base their conduct on what they are rather than what they ought to be always must throw it over in the end." The new morality is guaranteed by a post-materialist humanism whose heroism Forster stresses. After parting from his first lover, Maurice "was doing a fine thing – proving on how little the soul can exist. Fed neither by Heaven nor by Earth he was going forward, a lamp that would have blown out were materialism true ... struggles like his are the supreme achievements of humanity."[66]

In an earlier attempt on the themes of *Maurice*, the pessimistic *Bildungsroman The Longest Journey* (1907), Schopenhauer's and Nietzsche's ideas contribute to the dichotomies in Forster's critique of modern English life and to his prescription for the continuity of traditional English values. The contending "inheritors" of England are contrasted schematically, although not without internal contradictions, in camps denoted as aestheticism versus athleticism, sickness versus health, country versus suburb, real versus conventional, modern English versus classical Greek. The protagonist, Rickie Elliott, is the champion of the imaginative, sensitive, and conscious life, but he is physically crippled, whereas his rival, Gerald, and his half-brother, Stephen, are athletic and physically beautiful but brutal and self-destructive. Lacking self-consciousness, Gerald and Stephen require Rickie's value-giving consciousness (which is born of his longing for their qualities) to make them "real."[67] Forster dramatizes the "salvation" of unconscious life through Rickie's urging of Gerald's fiancée, Agnes, to "mind" Gerald's death as her "greatest thing," and through Rickie's rescue, fatal to himself, of the drunk Stephen from the railway line. That is, in an implicit dialogue with Nietzsche, and in rejection of mere Nietzschean clichés, Forster contradicts Agnes's earlier angry reflection that it is weak, crippled people like Rickie who survive the strong and beautiful people like Gerald.[68] The final judgment by Rickie's cynical aunt, that "he has failed in all he undertook," is contradicted by Stephen's epitaph: "[Rickie's] spirit had fled, in agony and loneliness, never to know that it bequeathed him salvation."[69]

However, this sublimation of the conflicting mentalities is more asserted than realized and less persuasive than the novel's pessimistic sense of the futility of human effort to create meaning.[70] Rickie's intellectual Cambridge friend Stewart Ansell discovers "the Spirit of Life" in Stephen; that is, like Shaw, he transforms Schopenhauer's malevolent Will to Life into a positive force. But this belief does not cancel the effect on the reader of Ansell's earlier frustrated quest for the "real," when he draws a circle within a square and within it a circle and so on, explaining to Rickie that only the very centre is real, but that there is never enough room to draw it.[71] Schopenhauer's pessimism, which Ansell (whose role was larger in an earlier draft of the novel) has taught Rickie, accounts better than Stephen's optimistic epitaph on Rickie's self-sacrifice, and better than the author's scheme of hopeful reconciliation, for the spirit in which Rickie rescues Stephen, wearily and solely from a sense of duty. Having despaired at Stephen's broken promise and renewed self-destructive drinking, Rickie's final judgment of himself is "Gone bankrupt ... for the second time. Pretended again that people were real."[72]

Howards End (1910) is organized in dichotomies similar to those in *The Longest Journey*: culture versus business or inner versus outer life, as represented by Howards End versus London and the Schlegels versus the Wilcoxes.[73] Schopenhauer's principle of the Will to Life appears in what Margaret Schlegel sees as the "logical, yet senseless train" of events, including her marriage, which she is trying to transform from battle into comradeship: "Are the sexes really races, each with its own code of morality, and their mutual love a mere device of Nature to keep things going?"[74] In an explicit allusion and typical of the mistaken popular understanding, the Nietzschean "superman" is associated by Helen Schlegel and the autodidact Leonard Bast with the men of the "outer life," who "can't say 'I,'" such as Pierpont Morgan, Napoleon, and Bluebeard.[75] In a significant variation on Nietzsche's "beyond good and evil," the characters who most closely speak for Forster refuse to lay blame because of their knowledge of the inextricable connection, or "muddle," of "good-and-evil."[76]

The novel seems more optimistic than *The Longest Journey* about the possibility of reconciliation, of the ability to "only connect," against a background of an unknowable but certain "ultimate harmony," glimpsed "from the turmoil and horror," like stars by a prisoner.[77] The happy ending in the old farmhouse reconciles the novel's dichotomies in the infant inheritor, in Margaret's marriage, and in Helen's friendship with Margaret's husband, the man of business; but it reads more bleakly when the exclusions are registered. Symptomatically, Howards End has no future, the big crop of hay being a fulfillment rather than a promise.[78]

Forster acknowledged the wishful contrivance, and hence lack of truth, in the happy ending of *Maurice*.[79] In the post-war novel *A Passage to India* (1924), where the surface conflict is national and racial, he relates his vision of human futility and cosmic malevolence, here as elsewhere in contest with the narrator's liberal humanist affirmations, to Hinduism, the religion that had proved influential for Schopenhauer's view both of the true nature of life and of the right response to it. The spiteful goblins which in *Howards End* Helen hears in the second movement of Beethoven's Fifth Symphony – "They merely observed in passing that there was no such thing as splendour or heroism in the world ... Panic and emptiness!" – develop in *A Passage to India* into the evil echo in the Marabar Caves, which murmurs to Mrs Moore: "Pathos, piety, courage – they exist, but are identical, and so is filth. Everything exists, nothing has value."[80] And Margaret's final quietism, in emulation of Mrs Wilcox, in *Howards End* is further developed in Mrs Moore's renunciation of life under the tutelage of Professor Godbole's mysticism.

Like Schopenhauer, Forster exempted art from the futility of human effort. Rickie asserts to his prosaic wife that poetry, as he is trying to capture it in his fantastic stories, not the prose of actual life, "lies at the core" of life. In Forster's lecture "Art for Art's Sake" (1949), finding no present possibility of order "in daily life and in history, ... in the social and political category," he could see only two prospects in the entire universe: the first, in contrast to Schopenhauer, "the divine order, the mystic harmony," and the second, in accord with Schopenhauer, "in the aesthetic category ...: the order which an artist can create in his own work."[81] This aesthetic order Forster created more persuasively in analogy to music through leitmotiv and the rhythm of symbols than through the intellectual categories that I have examined here. Like Schopenhauer, he ranked music as "more 'real' than anything," "the deepest of the arts and deep beneath the arts."[82]

Forster dismissed Joseph Conrad's claim to a philosophy: "Only opinions, and the right to throw them overboard when facts make them look absurd. Opinions held under the semblance of eternity, girt with the sea, crowned with the stars, and therefore easily mistaken for a creed."[83] While the observation ironically reflects on Forster's own professed dislike of dogma and on his difficulties, noted above, with the realization in his fiction of a coherent vision, it is also a common, as well as a just, response to Conrad's insistent gestures at metaphysics. In a close parallel with Schopenhauer's definitions of the artist's gift, to see the essentials, and his or her technique, to let us see with the artist's eyes, Conrad emphasized, in the preface to *The Nigger of the "Narcissus"*, that his own task was "to make [the reader] *see* ... perhaps, also that glimpse of truth for which [he or she has] forgotten to ask."[84] Conrad's advice to an aspiring writer was "Everyone must walk in the light of his own heart's gospel. No man's light is good to any of his fellows. That's my creed."[85] The gospel of the novels under consideration wavers uncertainly between the metaphysical and the practical, the first indebted to Schopenhauer and Nietzsche, the second to Conrad's conception of an ethic both English and marine.

Joseph Conrad created both German scoundrels and German sages, connecting the first explicitly with the new German Reich and the second with Schopenhauer's pessimism and Nietzsche's "immoralism."[86] In *Heart of Darkness* (1902) he combined the two types in Kurtz. In *Lord Jim* (1900) the captain of the *Patna* is an example of the first, and the trader and entomologist Stein, of the second. Stein sympathetically "realizes" Jim as a man who has pursued "the dream" of his ideal, heroic self and is now facing "the real trouble – the heart pain – the world pain." ("World pain" is a literal translation of *Weltschmerz*, the famous first sufferer of which was Goethe's Werther.) The narrator himself explains Jim's paralysis of will on the *Patna* by appealing to his audience: "Which of us here has not observed ... or maybe experienced ... this extreme weariness of emotions, the vanity of effort, the yearning for rest? Those striving with unreasonable forces know it well."[87]

The protagonist in *Victory* (1915), Heyst, is an elaboration of Stein, just as the "Teutonic" hotelier Schomberg is of the captain. Since the novel was published during World War 1, Conrad softened the German connection, making Heyst a Swedish baron; but his name, like Kurtz's, signifies in German: Heyst (*heisst*) alludes to the various names, such as "Enchanted Heyst" and "Heyst the Enemy," through which people have tried to comprehend a man whose conduct is mysterious because it is motivated by pessimism.[88] Heyst exhibits the rational of the three responses to life according to Schopenhauer, Mr Jones representing boredom and his man Ricardo, struggle. Taught to see life as "the Great Joke" by his scholarly father, whose comprehensively pessimistic writings suggest Schopenhauer's, Heyst has tried to "elude" the evil world as an "independent spectator" from the bank of "life's stream, where men and women go by ... revolving and jostling one another,"an image reminiscent of Schopenhauer's sailors on a raging sea.[89] However, subject to life and despite his resolve to be stone- (*Stein*) like, he is fatally drawn into action through pity and love. Conrad here contradicts Schopenhauer: he both denies that pity can be an escape from the Will to Life and asserts the transcendent power of sexual love in Lena's final apotheosis. Nevertheless, the last word of the novel, the narrator's repeated "Nothing," reasserts the spirit of "negation" of Heyst's father and of Schopenhauer.

Even before the English translation, Conrad seems to have been familiar with Nietzsche's ideas through French translations and through his English friends, especially Edward Garnett. (Nietzsche's claim to Polish ancestry may have added to his interest.) Conrad included Nietzsche among *les grands-esprits* who look at life from afar, to oversimplify it, and judged that his "mad individualism" would pass away.[90] Instead of metaphysical speculation, in his essay "Well Done" (1918) he argued: "For the great mass of mankind ... what is needed is a sense of immediate duty, and a feeling of impalpable constraint."[91]

Heart of Darkness and *The Secret Agent* (1907), two particularly powerful and successful works, show Conrad's engagement with both Schopenhauer and Nietzsche. In both works he portrays evil ambiguously, as a temporary and local condition as well as a universal human one. In the earlier work the dark truths of humankind's instinctual depravity and of life's futility are repressed by the optimism of modern European imperialism and its missionary ideal of progress, "the whited sepulchre." Its most gifted emissary to the Congo is the trader and idealist Mr Kurtz, who seems to vindicate it: he extracts the most ivory from the Dark Continent. However, in this pursuit incalculable "powers of darkness claimed him for their own," so that his abrupt final verdict, the postscript to his report on his civilizing efforts – "Exterminate all the brutes!" – implicitly includes himself and with him "civilized" Europe. ("All Europe contributed to the making of Kurtz.")[92] That is, Conrad both invokes and critiques Nietzsche's positive concepts of the Apollonian, in Kurtz's eloquence; of the Dionysian, in the African savagery; and of the Will to Power, in Kurtz's quest.

Marlow, the narrator and Kurtz's last companion, judges Kurtz's self-degradation worth the acquired self-knowledge since it has resulted in "moral victory" when Kurtz cries, "The horror! The horror!" (In his spiritual journey Kurtz's crucial ancestor is Faust in Goethe's ambivalent version, an allusion that Conrad strengthens through the young Russian adventurer's translation of the German name "Kurtz" [short] and through Marlow's description of the nominal brickmaker and spy as "this papier-mâché Mephistopheles.")[93] More problematically, Marlow prefers the partnership with the "immoralist" overman Kurtz to that with the other traders, the "pilgrims," who serve the "flabby, pretending, weak-eyed devil of a rapacious and pitiless folly," and he extends his contempt to his listeners' hypocritical civilized life "between the butcher and the policeman," his listeners being a director of companies, a lawyer, and an accountant.[94]

But both Marlow and his author, according to Conrad's critical statements, cited above, are ultimately advocating no more than a vicarious, imaginative engagement with the "heart of darkness," human life being best dedicated to "the work of the world": Marlow finds himself too busy repairing his boat to "go ashore for a howl and a dance. After all, for a seaman, to scrape the bottom of the thing that's supposed to float all the time under his care is the unpardonable sin." He does not hold himself responsible for the purpose of his boat's voyage. Marlow likes "what is in the work – the chance to find yourself. Your own reality."[95] Conrad's conception of work as a source of identity is closer to Carlyle (see chap. 2 above) than to Nietzsche, for whom activity is an expression of the self, as immediate self-affirmation in the strong, which in the weak is mediated through negation of the other.[96] Conrad's conception also differs from Nietzsche's more dynamic idea of *Bildung*, the overcoming of one's self.

In *The Secret Agent*, a novel based on the Greenwich Bomb Outrage of 1894 and in some measure indebted to James's *Princess Casamassima*, Conrad focuses on life "between the butcher and the policeman," or here between the terrorist and the policeman, who, according to "the Professor," "both come from the same basket. Revolution, legality – counter moves in the same game."[97] London in this novel functions as another heart of darkness, Conrad describing it uniformly in the following terms: "[the assistant commissioner of Scotland Yard] advanced … into an immensity of greasy slime and damp plaster interspersed with lamps, and enveloped, oppressed, penetrated, choked, and suffocated by the blackness of a wet London night, which is composed of soot and drops of water."[98]

The Professor, who makes bombs and is dedicated to developing the perfect detonator, is a double of Kurtz and the mouthpiece for Conrad's most radically anti-democratic views. He alone is willing to die for his revolutionist beliefs – that is, to live life not as a game – and he communicates them in the Silenus bar. The allusion is to Silenus's "terrible wisdom," taught to Midas and cited by Nietzsche in *Die Geburt der Tragödie*, that it were best for men not to be born.[99] The Professor considers the weak "the source of all evil! They are our sinister masters – the weak, the flabby, the silly, the cowardly, the faint of heart, and the slavish of mind … They are the multitude … Exterminate, exterminate!" Although disillusioned by the mass of humanity, whom nothing can move, he rejects pessimism and plans for "a clean sweep and a clear start for a new conception of life." His opposite, the compassionate "Apostle" Michaelis, is projecting in his autobiography a reformed world that Conrad, through the Nietzschean Professor, ridicules as an "immense and nice hospital … in which the strong are to devote themselves to the nursing of the weak."[100] Conrad shows the futility of such nursing through the fatal results, to both the strong and the weak, of the devoted plottings for the half-wit Stevie's welfare by his shrewd mother and sister.[101]

The characters who are less clear-sighted than the Professor, notably Verloc, his wife, Winnie, and Comrade Ossipon, are forced to discover to their horror the reality of life hidden by "the game," despite all their efforts to avoid, like Marlow, "scraping the bottom"; Winnie Verloc, after resolutely refusing to look "under the surface of things," is finally forced to see life as "blood and dirt."[102] Conrad represents the ultimate truth about life through Stevie's obsessive drawings: "a coruscating whirl of circles that by their tangled multitude of repeated curves, uniformity of form, and confusion of intersecting lines suggested a rendering of chaos, the symbolism of a mad art attempting the inconceivable."[103] The symbolism is reminiscent of Schopenhauer's whirlpool of human agony. (We have seen an analogous graphic metaphor in Ansell's drawing in Forster's *Longest Journey*, published in the same year.) The unremitting irony of fate of Conrad's plot, which turns all the major characters' well-laid plots against themselves, seems to teach the reader the Schopenhauerian lesson of fatalism, as it does Verloc.

Like Nietzsche, and in contrast to Schopenhauer and to his own later *Victory*, Conrad exposes pity as born from resentment and as a weak response to others' suffering: Stevie's pity and accompanying rage result from his own early victimization, and they are indiscriminate and ultimately self-destructive when he is tricked into carrying the bomb and blowing himself up, without achieving either his own aim or even the secret aim of the double agent, Verloc. The implicit comparison of Stevie with Dostoyevsky's holy fool, the truly wise and noble Prince Myshkin in *The Idiot*, brings out Conrad's ambivalent treatment of Stevie as both touchstone of society's corruption and symptom of the gullibility of the "mass of mankind," or Schopenhauer's *Fabrikwaare der Natur* and Nietzsche's *Heerdenmensch*. It is the latter function of Stevie that is reflected in the narrator's indifferent or contemptuous attitude towards him throughout the novel. This treatment sharply departs from Conrad's prescription for truth in fiction, as presented in his preface to *The Nigger of the Narcissus* (1897): "the bewildered, the simple and the voiceless" deserve a "glance of wonder and pity."[104]

As in *Heart of Darkness*, Conrad juxtaposes the uncompromising attitudes that allude to Schopenhauer and Nietzsche with an unreflected implicit respect for "the work of the world," in particular the English way of running things, despite the fact that the work is understood to be a mere game in a corrupt world.[105] Although he expresses Conrad's own extreme thoughts, the Professor is much more a caricature than are Chief Inspector Heat and the assistant commissioner, who both work hard at maintaining the English status quo.

According to Heat, to act on insight into the true state of things, as Verloc finally resolves to do, is "sorry, sorry meddling."[106] Despite Conrad's use of multiple perspectives, his ambiguity is ultimately not without personal bias, his skepsis not absolute.[107] Nevertheless, his persuasiveness in favour of the Professor's Nietzschean philosophy has recently been fatally testified to by his fan Ted Kaczynski, the "Unabomber."

D.H. Lawrence could not "forgive Conrad for being so sad and giving in."[108] He saw in the unconscious, even its horror, the only remedy for the horror of Western decadence and "dissolution." Both Schopenhauer and Nietzsche, the latter "one of Lawrence's greatest passions," had figured importantly in Lawrence's omnivorous youthful reading, and his marriage to Frieda Richthofen Weekley strengthened the German interest.[109] Of Schopenhauer's ideas he continued to engage in his novels the primacy of the will to life, its stronger hold over woman than over man, with the resultant male-female conflict, and the possibility of a denial of the will for a natural aristocracy of men. His first novel, *The White Peacock* (1911), shows this influence: the protagonists feel fatally entrapped, like "chess-men," by nature and society, whereas the narrator escapes by means of detached contemplation, but without joy. One of the chapter titles is "The Dominant Motif of Suffering."[110]

Subsequently, Schopenhauer's ideas appear in Lawrence's fiction as they are refracted by Nietzsche's philosophy, both being modified by Lawrence's other wide readings and continuously developed under the pressure of his own experience. In Gérard Genette's terms, his novels are metatexts on Schopenhauer's and Nietzsche's philosophies. He was a true disciple of Nietzsche's advice "Vademecum – Vadetecum."[111] Of the manifold sources, including evolutionary biology, sociology, anthropology, and comparative religion, which contributed to Lawrence's conceptions, Nietzsche was for his readers one of the most generally recognizable and notorious. Central Nietzschean ideas in the fiction concern the crisis of European civilization, of which rule by the masses and by the machine are the symptoms, and its radical remedy, a rebirth of humanity through a transvaluation that restores the instinctual, the unconscious, as a ruling principle and recreates community under the leadership of a natural aristocracy. If timely and in service of rebirth, war can be, in alternation with love, a "necessary disintegrating autumnal process."[112] For T.S. Eliot, this program marked Lawrence as "an almost perfect heretic," whose fictional characters lacked any moral or social sense.[113]

Even more distinctive than Nietzschean ideas is Lawrence's Nietzschean persona as a critic of culture-cum-prophet and one who, unlike Carlyle or George Eliot, shares Nietzsche's self-mockery. Like the other authors in this study, Lawrence advocated and practised the integration of fiction and philosophy. Disillusioned with humanity during the war, he even reported his own growing preference for philosophy over fiction.[114] More typically, he argued, in "Why the Novel Matters" (1925), that at its best the novel "supremely" helps the reader to "be alive … to be whole man alive," since, as he wrote in *Kangaroo*, it is not only a record of emotions but "also a thought-adventure."[115] Lawrence's characteristic Nietzschean manner includes explicit philosophical speculations by the narrator or a character – not always separate – which are contested throughout a novel, an incantatory and rhapsodic style, new compound words to represent new ideas, a plot that exhibits a world view but ends inconclusively, and the investment of the physical environment and physical objects, both animate and inanimate, with noumenal qualities.

Both Nietzsche the philosopher and Lawrence the novelist crossed genre boundaries to communicate their heretical ideas, and both self-consciously drew attention in their representation to the paradoxical attempt of teaching through a literary medium a new consciousness that was radically personal, experiential, and anti-rationalist.[116] Nietzsche wrote, "Wir selber wollen unsere Experimente und Versuchs-Thiere sein [We ourselves want to be our experiments and guinea pigs]."[117] And Lawrence, in the poem "Thought," exclaimed:

Thought, I love thought.
But not the jiggling and twisting of already existent ideas
I despise that self-important game.
Thought is the welling up of unknown life into consciousness.[118]

As examples, I shall consider *Women in Love* (1921), *Aaron's Rod* (1922), and *The Plumed Serpent* (1926). Together with its companion work, *The Rainbow* (1915), *Women in Love* is now generally considered Lawrence's best novel, and he himself judged it so. For a time, *The Plumed Serpent* seemed to him his most important novel.[119] Confirmed by World War I in his bleakest views of European civilization, Lawrence in these three novels respectively condemns English life, tests the old and the new Italy for regenerative potential, and turns, after a vain detour to Australia in *Kangaroo* (1923), to the pre-Aztec culture of Mexico for a model of human regeneration through the revival of primitive animistic cults everywhere.

The original, suppressed prologue to *Women in Love* has the novel's Lawrence figure, Rupert Birkin, "holding forth against Nietzsche."[120]

Conceived as an apocalyptic account of European civilization – "Dies Irae" and "The Latter Days" were tentative titles – the novel represents and debates both decadence and rebirth in terms of the will in its destructive and creative properties, as conceptualized by Schopenhauer and Nietzsche. As Birkin and his lover, Ursula, watch his tomcat assert its will over a female, they differ in their evaluations: Ursula as a woman sees the action as "a lust for bullying – a real Wille zur Macht – so base, so petty," whereas Birkin approves of it as "a volonté de pouvoir."[121] Lawrence here linguistically associates only the negative aspect with Nietzsche, but unjustly so and probably as a reflex of his "anxiety of influence," as well as the result of a disproportionate reliance on or topical allusion to the misleading posthumous work *Wille zur Macht*, edited by Nietzsche's sister.[122] Birkin's French interpretation is in fact typical of Nietzsche's conception in his authorized writings. For instance, in the *Genealogie der Moral* he defines the noble morality of the warrior caste in terms of the identity of self-affirmation, strength, and self-directed will, in contrast to the other-directed revenge of the slave morality,[123] and in *Zarathustra* he stresses the overman's power of "self-overcoming."

In the novel's decadent post–World War I world, the destructive will to power and its converse, slavish submission to it, are prevalent. The mine owner Gerald Crich, as the "God of the machine," and the miners, as "mere mechanical instruments," represent "the great social productive machine." Emotionally and physically violent power struggles dominate the novel – Lawrence distinguished it from *The Rainbow* as solely destructive – struggles between miners and owners, women and men, humans and animals, and, in the novel's background, nations and nations. This destructiveness is presented by the narrator and experienced by the characters as a negative and repellent symptom of decadence, on the one hand, and as a positive and attractive preparation for "creative change," on the other. In an allusion to Nietzsche's cyclical alternation of the Dionysian and the Apollonian principles, Gerald understands his modernized impersonal mining system as "the first great step in undoing, the first great phase of chaos, the substitution of the mechanical principle for the organic."[124] Himself merely a wheel in the machinery, Gerald, a "hollow" man, cannot go beyond this phase, and he dies, in order to escape from the nausea of life, in the annihilating whiteness of the Alps.

In contrast, his friend Birkin seeks a new organic principle for the next "world-cycle" in a new type of sexual love, which eschews the power struggle and the "horrible merging, mingling self-abnegation" characteristic of Gerald and Gudrun's relationship, and which instead creates "an equilibrium, a pure balance of two single beings: – as the stars balance each other." Instead of following "the Dionysic ecstatic way," each is "not to insist – be glad and sure and indifferent."[125] This high ideal of Birkin's and his author's (the self-appointed "prophet of love") has no precedent in Nietzsche. Instead, Frieda had introduced Lawrence to another strong German source for his cult of eroticism, her German anarchist friends Otto Gross and Ernest Frick and their circle in Ascona. However, his image for perfect love alludes to Nietzsche's image for friendship in the entry "Sternen-Freundschaft" (star friendship), in the *Fröhliche Wissenschaft*.[126]

Like Schopenhauer, Nietzsche denounced conventional sexual morality as hypocrisy, but he did not break with the philosophical-religious tradition of misogyny, even though his pronouncements are more playful than Schopenhauer's, as in Zarathustra's *kleine Wahrheit* (little truth): "Du gehst zu Frauen? Vergiss die Peitsche nicht! [You are going to women? Do not forget the whip!]." Zarathustra's authority is *ein altes Weiblein* (a little old woman), a joke alluding to Socrates's authority on love, the prophetess Diotima in the *Symposium*, perhaps with a smile in the direction of Mozart's old-young *Weiblein* Papagena. Zarathustra's reasoning starts from Schopenhauer: woman uses man as a means for her natural purpose, motherhood. For woman to be to man the necessary *Erholung des Kriegers* (recreation of the warrior) so that in him she may "den Übermenschen gebären [give birth to the overman]," woman must obey man: "Das Glück des Mannes heisst: ich will. Das Glück des Weibes heisst: er will [The happiness of man is: I will. The happiness of woman is: he wills]."[127]

Birkin's lover, Ursula, suspects that his utopian ideal of love disguises these Nietzschean attitudes: "You are just egocentric ... You want yourself, really, and your own affairs. And you want me just to be there, to serve you."[128] Indeed, the difference between the two couples' love is by no means absolute and fixed, but overall it is a difference between pessimistic fatalism and optimistic experimentation. Lawrence marks this divergence by associating Gerald with the worlds of machinery and Alpine snow and Birkin with the vegetative world. For Birkin, the possibility of humanity's extinction if it cannot change creatively – if man is "a mistake, he must go" – is "a beautiful clean thought, a world empty of people, just uninterrupted grass, and a hare sitting up."[129] In the posthumous, seminal fragment "Über Wahrheit und Lüge im aussermoralischen Sinne" (On truth and lie in an extra-moral sense [1873]), Nietzsche told a starker fable of the extinction of a remote planet on which clever animals had invented knowledge (*Erkennen*). "Es war die hochmüthigste und verlogenste Minute der 'Weltgeschichte': aber doch nur eine Minute [That was the haughtiest and most mendacious minute of 'world history' – yet only a minute]."[130] If Lawrence did not read this essay in German, he could have extrapolated the sentiment from Nietzsche's other writings on consciousness.

In *Women in Love* the realistic conventions of the English novel establish the outward conditions of life, whose inner chaos the conventions of apocalyptic vision reveal and whose prospects are debated in the manner of the critic of culture and the prophet. These other styles strongly suggest a Nietzschean persona, especially because of the unusual presence of self-mocking irony, which is quite absent, for instance, from Conrad as well as from Carlyle's *Sartor Resartus* and Eliot's *Daniel Deronda*. Elaborating on Nietzsche's use in *Zarathustra* of such objects as the tight rope and Zarathustra's animals, the eagle and the serpent, Lawrence gives a revelatory role to animate and inanimate objects in scenes of conflict, such as Gerald's Arab horse, Winifred's rabbit, the moon and the daisies on the lake, Hermione's lapis lazuli paper weight, and the old Regency chair at the jumble market.

The critical event in the novel's background is World War I, which for Lawrence confirmed his skepticism about human reason and the rationalist ideal of progress. He adapted Nietzsche's validation of the unconscious for his own conception of "blood-consciousness." As a consequence, he builds a Nietzschean skepticism about the efficacy of literary teaching into the novel. Discussing the possibility of regeneration, Birkin and Ursula are aware "that words themselves do not convey meaning, that they are but a gesture we make … Yet it must be spoken." Ursula also fears words "because she knew that mere word-force could always make her believe what she did not believe."[131] Lawrence's self-mocking terms for Birkin are "Hamletizing," "Salvator Mundi," and "Sunday school teacher." When Birkin's bohemian London friends ridicule his letter in the Pompadour Café, their response reflects both on their decadent frivolity and on Birkin/Lawrence's role as clergyman-saviour of humanity. Finally, Lawrence even mocks his novel's title and subject when he has the sculptor Loerke declare with disgust: "Women and love, there is no greater tedium."[132]

Aaron's Rod continues the question about the possibility of regeneration, which *Women in Love* left inconclusive. The protagonist, Aaron Sisson, breaks loose from his ties to marriage, work, and England to seek a new self in Italy. Italy, where Nietzsche lived his last sane years, stands for Nietzschean values. The southern race and its male culture seem to offer an alternative to decadent England and the emasculating New Woman, while Italy's post-war political anarchy seems to promise the "clearance" of the order that has led to World War I. When a terrorist bomb breaks Aaron's flute, his would-be mentor, Lilly, reassures him that, being organic, it will grow again. Lilly preaches to Aaron a Nietzschean creed of dominion and obedience, urging him to choose between the "only two great dynamic urges in *life*: love and power!" In a demonstration of his argument, Lilly has earlier practised his instinctual authority over Aaron when his massaging restored the sick Aaron's will to life; the love urge, he argues, has been exhausted, leading in the form of democracy and socialism to murder and anarchy, while heterosexual love for Aaron has meant man's surrender of his male spirit of adventure to woman's possessiveness. Lilly distinguishes "The will-to-power – but not in Nietzsche's sense. Not intellectual power ... Not conscious will-power ... But dark, living, fructifying power."[133] Again, as in *Women in Love*, Lawrence disagrees here, through Lilly, with what is only a part of Nietzsche's conception of "der Wille zur Macht, – der unerschöpfte zeugende Lebens-Wille [the will to power – the unexhausted procreative will to life]."[134] Nietzsche himself frequently devalued consciousness as the latest and therefore weakest development of the organic, as, for instance, in the entry on consciousness in *Die fröhliche Wissenschaft*.[135] And he prized primitive humankind's unselfconscious power as a model for the overman's conscious achievement of a renewed vigour.

Like *Women in Love*, the novel is open-ended; although there is general agreement among Aaron and his friends about the crisis in European civilization, his and Lilly's ideas for renewal, respectively searching and dogmatic, continue to be contested. In *Kangaroo* (1923) Lawrence reiterates the racial theme, transposed to the old-new continent, and tests and finds wanting the two radical political ideologies through the protagonist's reluctant and abortive involvement with both a communist and a fascist revolutionary organization. *The Plumed Serpent* concludes this "ring round the world."[136] It depicts a third model for renewal through the recovery of a primitive pure race, the Mexican Natives, by means of their restored pre-Aztec religion under the "natural Aristocracy" of a poet-priest, Don Ramon, and his "*miles*," Don Cipriano. Lawrence argues the applicability of this model to European civilization by, on the one hand, having the female protagonist, Kate, finally overcome her rationalist and individualist skepticism and submit in marriage to the "Pan-power" in Don Cipriano,[137] the pure-blooded Native leader of the cult of Quetzalcoatl, and by, on the other, honouring European civilization at its best in Cipriano's partner and mentor, the Spanish descendant, Don Ramon. That is, like Nietzsche in his conception of "overcoming," Lawrence is advocating, not a return to an early primitive unconsciousness, but a recovery of its strengths for the next phase of modern consciousness.[138]

The Mexican icon of the new-old cult resembles Zarathustra's animals: the eagle encircled by the serpent. Don Ramon corresponds to Zarathustra in both his reluctance and his message, as he preaches to the Natives: "You are not yet men. And women, you are not yet women." The militarist Cipriano echoes Nietzsche when he asserts to Kate, "Peace is only the rest after war ... So it is not more natural than fighting: perhaps not so natural." But as in the "anti-political" Nietzsche, his militarism is strictly an instrument in the war of true ideas versus false idols, controlled by Don Ramon, who rejects nationalist and socialist politics: "Politics, and all this *social* religion that Montes has got is like washing the outside of the egg to make it look clean. But I, myself, I want to get inside the egg, right to the middle, to start it growing into a new bird." The new cult's vitality is in its ritual dances; Kate herself joins the wheeling dance and learns, "Erect, strong, like a staff of life, yet to loosen all the sap of her strength and let it flow down into the roots of the earth."[139] Lawrence's distinction, in *Mornings in Mexico* (1927), between the mindless quality of Native American dance and the aware, performative nature of early Greek drama is reminiscent of Nietzsche's elegiac treatment, in *Die Geburt der Tragödie*, of the change from ritual ecstasy to the self-conscious mimesis of Attic tragedy.[140]

Stylistically, *The Plumed Serpent* goes much further than *Women in Love* in its minimal regard for realistic conventions and its affinity with the speculative fantasy *Zarathustra* and that work's mixing of genres. In addition to the preaching, Ramon's hymns for the cult of Quetzalcoatl, which E.M. Forster, who admired the novel, judged to be Lawrence's finest unrhymed poetry,[141] play as central a role in the work as do Zarathustra's hymns in Nietzsche's. The animate and inanimate objects and the physical sites, whose noumenal qualities here are specifically attributed to local, immanent divine powers, function as agents in the evolution of human consciousness, in a way similar to Zarathustra's cave, the tightrope, his animals, and the sun. Lawrence reserved his playful humour about this material for the essays in *Mornings in Mexico*, but Nietzschean self-mockery is present in the novel in Kate's deflationary skepticism with respect to the two messianic men. For instance, during one of her reversals she protests against Cipriano's sacred embodiment as the Living Huitzilopochtli and her own as his wife, Malintzi: "No! ... I don't see it. Why *should* you be more than just a man?"[142]

In *Lady Chatterley's Lover* (1928) Lawrence seems to agree with her; he returns to England and to a male protagonist who is no *Übermensch* but "whole man alive." Lawrence rejects the possibility, represented in Kate's marriage to Cipriano, of a grafting of primitive Native American "blood-consciousness" onto modern European "mental consciousness," in *Mornings in Mexico*: "The consciousness of one branch of humanity is the annihilation of the consciousness of another branch ... The only thing you can do is to have a little Ghost inside you which sees both ways, or even many ways."[143] Which is what these novels enable the reader to do. Nietzsche calls such "switching of perspectives" (*Perspektiven Umstellen*), "jene Psychologie des 'Um-die Ecke-sehns' [that psychology of 'looking around the corner']."[144] In contrast with Forster's anxious attempts at reconciliation, Lawrence shares Nietzsche's "gay" pursuit of multiple perspectives. And like all the novelists under consideration here, he uses allusions to Schopenhauer and Nietzsche to signal alternatives to what he perceives as the orthodoxies of his and his readers' culture.

9 Prussianized Germany and the Second Weimar Germany

The following opinions expressed by figures in this study will give a sense of the range and change in attitudes towards the new German Reich in the period under review. "The absorption of Germany in Prussia is, I am sure, a calamity for the country and the world" – Sarah Austin, translator and author in the German circle around William Taylor of Norwich, expressed this opinion in 1867, acknowledging it as a minority but expert view.[1] In contrast, Carlyle, in a public letter in 1870, welcomed as "the hopefullest public fact" that "noble, patient, deep, pious, and solid Germany should be at length welded into a nation, and become Queen of the Continent, instead of vapouring, vain-glorious, gesticulating, quarrelsome, restless, and over-sensitive France."[2] During the Franco-Prussian War (1870–71) George Eliot, herself helping with the war relief, informed a German friend that English sympathies had turned against Germany only after the battle of Sedan (1 September 1870).[3] Observing in Bad Homburg "the success of the Fatherland … reflected … in all true German faces," Henry James quietly warned that the prominence of smartly uniformed and assertive soldiers and officers "seemed to suggest that war is somehow a better economy than peace" and to confirm people's recent sense "that they must take the German tone into account."[4] Mrs Humphry Ward, who in her novels had concentrated on German *Wissenschaft* and music (see chap. 7 above), during World War 1 wrote, at former president Theodore Roosevelt's suggestion, three books of propaganda about the British war effort against "the Huns"; she was said

OF COURSE BERLIN WILL NOW SET THE FASHIONS—
VICE PARIS.

to have influenced the decision of the United States to enter the war. Quoting Dean Stanley on German theological scholarship, Ward commented in her autobiography in 1917: "Alas! merely to quote it, nowadays, carries one back to a Germany before the Flood – a Germany of small States, a land of scholars and thinkers." Its descendants, "maddened by wealth and success," had driven a "deep and hideous abyss ... between themselves and the rest of Europe."[5]

Britain had responded to the shock of the Prussian victory over France with military reforms, militarist youth organizations that glorified war, and popular propaganda literature, such as the *Boy's Own Paper*. In 1871 *Blackwood's* published the first of many works of fiction about a German invasion, Sir George Tomkyns-Chesney's "The Battle of Dorking." The new military rivalry was compounded by the newly united Germany's industrial progress and economic competition. Moreover, in the 1880s Germany began to compete in the "scramble for Africa," when British imperialist supremacy was seen necessary as a safety valve and a distraction from domestic decline and discontent – Cecil Rhodes is reported to have said in 1895; "If you want to avoid civil war, you must become imperialists."[6] The principle of "spheres of influence" for the "civilizing missions" in Africa and the Pacific was formalized, if not always acted on, at the Berlin Conference of 1884–85 under Bismarck's chairmanship. Matching the British ideology of "the white man's burden," which Kipling eulogized in his poem of the same title (1898), the German rationalizing slogan became *Lebensraum* (living space), as in the title of Hans Grimm's internationally successful novel *Volk ohne Raum* (Nation without space [1926]). Grimm was often compared with Kipling.

Although the Boer War (1899–1902) damaged Anglo-German relations, until World War I German colonial conduct was well respected, especially for its administrative efficiency and for the officials' readiness to learn native languages and customs. However, allied propaganda about German atrocities in Belgium during the war was extended to German conduct in Africa and used as a reason for the confiscation of all German colonies under the Treaty of Versailles.[7] C.S. Forester's novel of adventure and romance *The African Queen* (1935), made famous through its film version, deals with this context in a remarkably even-handed fashion. It depicts the patriotic but futile mission of two ordinary, decent English civilians who, in order "to do their bit," attempt to explode a German gunboat in revenge for the Germans' barbarous destruction, in the course of World War I, of a missionary's life work.

Generally, Anglo-German antagonism on both sides was neither unchallenged nor irreversible until the 1890s, when the governments

THE TRIUMPH OF "CULTURE."

could no longer resist the force of public opinion represented in and goaded by the press.[8] Towards World War I and promoted by the radical right and Lord Northcliffe's press, "barbarous" and its cognates became the epithets that replaced the sense of Teuton family affinities. For a British Empire that was conceived as the successor to the Roman Empire – an idea purveyed in the newly patriotic and militarist public schools – the Germans became "the Goth and the shameless Hun," soon "at the gate."[9] The commonly held view of the "two Germanys" – the one represented by scholars, scientists, musicians, and the *gemütliche* ordinary people, the other by the military caste of the Prussian Junkers – generally gave way to a unified fear and hate of German "frightfulness." Typical verses in *Punch* at the start of the war read:

Once the land of poets, seers and sages,
Who enchant us with their deathless pages,
...
Now the Prussian *Junker*, blind with fury,
Claims to be God's counsel, judge and jury.[10]

In the "war of the professors," the manifesto of "the ninety-three" proclaimed in October 1914, one of several by German academics in support of state policy, was instrumental in discrediting the more benevolent view among one of the groups resisting British jingoism, namely, German-trained British academics, who often also had German wives. The title of a propaganda pamphlet expressed the reaction: "Kaiser, Krupp and Kultur."[11] Ford Madox Ford, in a propagandist book on the dangers of the hegemony of Prussian militarist nationalist *Kultur*, warned; "l'ennemi, c'est le professeur."[12] In Germany, Heinrich Mann satirised the hypocritical pomposity of the Prussian *Kulturträger* (bearer of culture) in his novel *Professor Unrat* (1905), which would be filmed as *Der blaue Engel* (The Blue Angel) with Marlene Dietrich.

Commenting on the renewed partition of Poland, Joseph Conrad wrote in the *Fortnightly Review* in 1919: "The Germanic Tribes had told the whole world ... in tones Hegelian, Nietzschean, war-like, pious, cynical, inspired, what they were going to do to the inferior races of the earth."[13] Thus not only was World War I characterized as the "Euro-Nietzschean War" with an appeal to an erroneous and vulgarized reading of Nietzsche (see chap. 8 above);[14] it was also conceived in terms of Nietzsche's antagonist, Hegel, as a war fought for the realization of the *Weltgeist* (world spirit), a conception that did justice to Hegel, although it was deluded about the actual politi-

cal purposes of this war.[15] Bertrand Russell, an exception as a pacifist, ridiculed the paradoxical task of British philosophers, who were
"all agreed that the wickedness or virtue of a nation depends upon
the metaphysical creed of its professors of philosophy." For British
opponents of Kant and Hegel, they were "the precursors of
Bismarck, Treitschke, Ludendorff and Co"; for the majority, who had
praised Kant and Hegel, they represented "the old Germany," their
abandonment in favour of Nietzsche having "caused the invasion of
Belgium."[16]

Throughout this period there was, of course, dissent from the antagonism I have described. In a famous instance, Oscar Wilde, in "The Critic
as Artist," names Goethe as the originator of the cosmopolitan note in
the modern world. Quoting Goethe's remark to Eckermann, that despite Napoleon's subjection of Germany, he could not hate the French
nation, to whom he owed so much of his own *Bildung*, Wilde concludes:
"If we are tempted to make war upon another nation, we shall remem-
ber that we are seeking to destroy an element of our own culture, and
possibly its most important element."[17] Sir Harry Johnston, who tried to
explain the two nations to each other in lectures and articles, wrote in
1912: "The more the Englishman travels in the Germany of today, the
more ardently he desires a complete understanding between that empire and his own land; for with Germany and Britain united on a firm
basis of policy there could be no world-war, scarcely even a conflict
between any civilized nations."[18]

The Great War failed to end all wars, just as the Treaty of Versailles
failed to create conditions for peace. The Weimar Republic, founded
with the anxious invocation of the ideals of Goethe and Schiller and
dissociating itself from the Prussian past of Berlin and Potsdam, increasingly lost the uncertain support it had at home. Ironically, the
self-appointed successor of Goethe, Thomas Mann, like many other
German intellectuals and artists, denied the republic his support. In
the spirit of an erroneous and ill-timed, and later to be revoked, imitation of Nietzsche's "anti-political" attitude in his own *Betrachtungen
eines Unpolitischen* (Reflections of an unpolitical man; [1915–17]), he
rejected the western European values of civilization and society in
favour of the special German destiny of culture and community.
Abroad, the Weimar Republic had to compete with sympathies for
German conservative and radical-right forces, sympathies that would
finally contribute to the appeasement of Hitler.

Culturally, Bismarck's new German Reich and Wilhelmine Germany
proved disappointing both to Germans[19] and to foreigners, excepting
the controversial success of Wagner's Bayreuth. "The Paralysis of
German Literature" was the title of a review of Berthold Litzmann's

Ein Beitrag zur deutschen Litteratur- und Theatergeschichte (A contribution to the history of German literature and theatre [1890–94]) in the *Bookman* in 1895. The reviewer shared the author's regret that in 1870 "Germany was quivering with martial enthusiasm, but the German muse held her peace as though struck dumb." The poets "put forth after this period nothing but empty declamation," and the novelists, of whom Gustav Freytag was the most important, failed to produce the great prose epic of the new national life. In drama "German hopes are practically all directed towards Bayreuth," but, as the reviewer remarked, "surely, no one will pretend that in the development of Wagnerism the victories won by German arms had any share even as an inspiration, for the greater works of Wagner were written before 1870." The author's "rather depressing conclusion" is that "the literature of united Germany is neither hot nor cold, but dreadfully commonplace and destitute of individuality."[20] By 1895 there was, however, one German novelist of greater account, Theodor Fontane, whose concern for history and social realism in fiction was influenced by Scott, Thackeray, and Dickens, though not to the exclusion of a morality and tone all his own. Two of his major novels about Berlin and Brandenburg society – *Unwiederbringlich* (Irretrievable [1891]) and *Effi Briest* (1894) – had been published; *Der Stechlin* was to follow in 1897.

Germany distinguished itself by rapid industrialization and commercialization, the concomitant moral and cultural philistinism being a subject of Fontane's novels, especially *Frau Jenny Treibel* (1892), a gentle satire about the *Neureichen* (nouveaux riches) in the Berlin of the *Gründerjahre* (founding years). In contrast, the Weimar Republic, with government support, produced the most prodigious cultural achievements in German history and became home to everything avant-garde in intellectual life and the arts. The post-war spirit of generational rebellion against conventions of social and moral hierarchies expressed itself in the flourishing and wide popular reception of movements originating before the war, such as Expressionism, atonal music, Bauhaus architecture, the physics of relativity, and psychoanalysis, as well as new experimental work in, for instance, the theatre of Piscator and Brecht and film.[21]

The "old Germany" of numerous principalities and their petty courts had provided picturesque material for English novelists, the immediate model usually being Goethe's Duchy of Sachsen-Weimar-Eisenach. For instance, Thackeray's version, the ducal town of Pumpernickel in *Vanity Fair*, quaintly contrasts with London, centre of an empire, which produces nabobs such as Jos Sedley, ex-collector of Boggley Wallah; while Meredith, as we have seen, combines in the Duchy of Sarkeld, in *Harry Richmond*, the comical potential with the serious associations of

Goethean *Bildung*. The new German Reich, which was working hard at catching up with industrialized, urbanized, and imperial Britain, did not offer such attractive contrasts. However, as a new rival, it plays a significant role in novels that reflect on Britain's "progress" as a capitalist-imperialist state. Even when the appearance of German allusions is minimal in a work, they have considerable persuasive authority because of the widespread public sentiments about Germany, and they provide an important angle on Britain's political orientation.

After considering the two major authors in whose novels the political milieu is prominent, Trollope and Disraeli, I shall discuss allusions to the German Reich in works of fiction by Meredith, Gissing, Conrad, and Forster and allusions to Weimar Germany in those by Ford Madox Ford, D.H. Lawrence, and Christopher Isherwood.[22] Kipling did not treat Germany in his fiction, except for the brilliant World War I story "Mary Postgate" (1915), a morally tough – and authorially ambiguous – portrayal of an ordinary Englishwoman's quasi-orgiastic revenge on a downed German airman.[23] However, the other authors were reacting to "Kiplingese," that is, jingoism and xenophobia.[24]

Anthony Trollope concentrated in his fiction on the social aspects of political life, to the near exclusion of any treatment of public issues. When Germany appears, it is as the traditional place for scenic and cultural recreation, as in Phineas Finn's visit to Dresden and its countryside, the Saxon Switzerland, in *Phineas Redux* (1874). A typically short and faint political note is sounded in *The Prime Minister* (1876) when the duchess remarks to Mrs Finn on the Duke of Omnium's new office as prime minister and his likely consequent loss of simplicity: "I don't want him to sell his country to Germany, or to turn it into an American republic in order that he may be president."[25]

Vivian Grey (1826–27), the first novel by Benjamin Disraeli, who was arguably the founder of the genre of the political novel in England, owes, among its several debts, one to *Wilhelm Meister*. In part 2 the hero travels in post-Napoleonic Germany and becomes involved in the jealous intrigues of the petty courts of patriotic Little Lilliput and Napoleonic Reisenberg, whose domains have been inequitably affected by the Congress of Vienna. The prime minister of Reisenberg, Beckendorff, is Disraeli's first portrait of a "crafty" and pragmatic German statesman. Disraeli's successful last novel, *Endymion* (1880), was written before and during his second term as prime minister, when he first established British imperial foreign policy at the Berlin Conference of 1878. But he backdated the novel to the period of his youth, dealing with the

domestic effects of the first Reform Bill and with Britain's diplo-
matic and military interventions to control the European balance
of power.

In portraying the growth of a political leader, the novel has some
affinity with the *Bildungsroman*; it is also a *roman à clef*. The novel's action covers the period from the 1820s to the 1850s in the life of a rising
young statesman. Although this was a period in British politics when
domestic issues, including Irish Home Rule, far outweighed interest
in foreign policy, Disraeli imports the concerns of the period of writing by making his hero responsible for external affairs and by giving
him two expert Continental mentors, successors to the role of Beckendorff in *Vivian Grey*. Baron Sergius is modelled on Metternich and the
Count of Ferroll on Bismarck, Prussian ambassador, later minister
president, and then the "Iron Chancellor."[26] Disraeli characterizes the
count according to Bismarck's own self-representation as a man
"who has an intelligence superior to all passion, [one] might say all
feeling."[27] Both mentors are shrewd patriots, in sharp contrast to
Endymion's friend Bertie Tremain, leader of the Utilitarian camp,
who declares that he cannot understand patriotism.[28]

By antedating and contracting Bismarck's career and by attaching his
fictional counterpart to the court of St James instead of St Petersburg,
Disraeli shares with his contemporary readers a sense of urgency
through anticipation of the changed balance of European power. Prefer-
ring his mission in London to residence in "his second-rate capital" –
that is, Berlin – the Count of Ferroll is a great favourite in English society because of his urbanity and Junker attributes, as well as being
respected by men of influence as "one of the men who sooner or later
will make a noise in the world." Several conversations of his make clear
what the noise will be about. For Britain's concern over troubled Europe, that is, the repeated subversion, always originating in France, of
monarchic rule – "There is not a throne in Europe worth a year's purchase" – the count proposes as remedy a strong German state instead of
the present merely geographic entity, moulded by the Congress of
Vienna, of districts allied with various foreign powers. The count criticizes his king's request that he return home to fashion a constitution;
"Instead ... he should make a country, and convert his heterogeneous
domains into a patriotic domain." The means? "There is only one way;
by blood and iron."[29] Instead of relying on *Blut und Eisen*, Bismarck actually used the constitution written and ratified under his guidance in
its original form for the creation of the North German Confederation
and modified for the German Empire.[30] Like the slogan, the credence
given here to Bismarck's expansionism is of a much later date. Even in

1862, when at a party Disraeli heard Bismarck predict German unification, he underrated his resolve and overrated France's power.[31] After reading the novel, Bismarck remarked that Disraeli, "in spite of his fantastic novel-writing ... is a capable statesman."[32] Disraeli's sympathetic portrait of Bismarck and of his ambitions for Germany represents Disraeli's own and the majority view on British political interest in Germany's role as a useful check to France and Russia in the 1860s and even after the Franco-Prussian War.[33]

The Franco-Prussian War divided George Meredith's political sympathies between respect for the Prussians and pity for the French. He "bitterly regretted" that he could not be "out on a post of observation," as he had during the Austro-Italian War, and he wrote an ode, "France, December 1870," for the *Fortnightly Review* in 1871:

> We look for her that sunlike stood
>
> ...
>
> We see a vacant place;
> We hear an iron heel.

However, he distanced himself from British denunciations of German aggression – "I would not mind our language if it came from an unselfish people" – and protested against partisanship: "I am neither German nor French, nor, unless the nation is attacked, English. I am European and Cosmopolitan – for humanity!" But when German imperialism seemed to threaten Britain, he sounded a patriotic alarm to "slumbering England" in private and public letters as well as in poetry and fiction.[34]

In *Vittoria* (1867) Meredith had portrayed in a sympathetic light the Risorgimento in Italy, which influenced British perception of Germany's consolidation. Prussia and the new German state as rival and potential threat appear in Meredith's *Beauchamp's Career* (1876) and *One of Our Conquerors* (1891). The country of the idyllic Rhine and Black Forest and of fashionable watering places in the early *Ordeal of Richard Feverel* and the late *Amazing Marriage* here serves as a goad for British regeneration – not, as in *The Adventures of Harry Richmond*, of ideal *Bildung* (see chap. 4 above) but of military "efficiency."

Like Disraeli in *Endymion*, Meredith backdates the action in *Beauchamp's Career*, in this case to the Crimean War, yet refers to Prussia in the light of its recent supremacy. The young hero, by vocation a naval officer and later a Radical candidate and by conviction "humanity's curate," in his "baronial" uncle's words, has no enthusiasm for the war in which he has distinguished himself or for the cant of the "vivifying virtues of war," since it is paid for by the poor in England. However, he wishes for "peace at home and strength for a really national war, the only war we can even call necessary."[35] The narrator shares Nevil Beauchamp's complaint that "while the other Europeans go marching and drilling, [England bestows too large] a portion of her intelligence upon her recreations," the aristocracy shooting birds rather than attending Prussian and Austrian cavalry manoeuvres.[36] Meredith's plot suggests that the solutions for England's internal and external crises have to start with a reform of the aristocracy at the individual level. His examples are, first, the hero's success in making his stiff-necked uncle, Lord Romfrey, apologize to the champion of the poor, Dr Shrapnel, for an act of brutal and rough justice and, second, his rescue, at the cost of his own life, of a labourer's child from drowning.[37]

In the later novel, *One of Our Conquerors*, the theme of England's crisis becomes more prominent. The hero, Victor Radnor, a wealthy investment trader in the City and successful speculator in the colonies, one of the "New Aristocrats," epitomizes the material success of imperial Britain. However, his emblematic optimism is attacked by several men in his entourage, the satirist Colney Durance, the soldier Captain Dartrey Fenellan, and the German Dr Schlesien. They all deplore the fact that "Old England has taken to the arm-chair for good, ... and that, in the face of an armed Europe, this great nation is living on sufferance. Oh!" Captain Dartrey, returned from colonial service in Africa, prophesies for England: "She bleats for a lesson, and will get her lesson." In the end, Radnor himself laments "this infernal wealth of ours! ... Paradise lost for a sugar plum! ... it appears to me, Esau's the Englishman, Jacob the German, of these times ... the nation's half made-up of the idle and the servants of the idle."[38]

Meredith interweaves the action with the entertainment of Colney Durance's "Satiric serial tale, that hit accidentally the follies of the countries of Europe, and intentionally ... those of Old England." It describes an "expedition of European Emissaries to plead the cause of their several languages at the Court of Japan." Allegorically, the "Teutonic Professor" Dr Gannius, in dispute with his "Saxon cousin" Dr Bouthoin, has "the habit of pushing past politeness to carry his argumentative war into the enemy's country: and he presents on all sides a solid rampart of recent great deeds done, and mailed readiness for the doing of more."[39]

To answer this Teutonic challenge, Meredith proposes conscription, and so as to make conscription efficient, he suggests boxing as a means of physical and social redemption. Victor Radnor's man, Skepsey, practises and preaches this gospel. While directing, together with his hero, Captain Dartrey, the games at Victor Radnor's opening of his grand new country house, he is dismayed by the local "lumpish" boys: "it concerned Great Britain for them to learn how to use their legs ... while foreign nations are drilling their youth, teaching them to be ready to move in squads or masses, like the fist of a pugilist."[40] Throughout, Meredith presents the German rivalry, not in a hostile light, but as a welcome warning to Britain to regenerate itself.

George Gissing, who admired Meredith as "the strongest literary man," read *One of Our Conquerors*.[41] However, his perspective on the German Reich was less sanguine than Meredith's. When he finally visited his German friend Eduard Bertz in 1898, he stayed only four days in Berlin and Potsdam, the cities of the *Gründerjahre* and of the Prussian soldiery. He noted in his diary only "the sheer *commonness* of it all, after Italy."[42] In *The Whirlpool* (1897) Gissing had included imperialism among the negative modern trends (see chap. 8 above), but Germany appears only as the stereotypical place for classical music: Alma goes to Leipzig and then to Munich to study the violin.

In *The Crown of Life* (1899) Gissing uses Bismarck and Germany as models of the worst British developments, in contrast with older socialist and pacifist ideals; moreover, this perspective is joined to Russophilia. The action runs from 1886 to 1894. Piers Otway, the illegitimate but loved son of an English socialist writer and conspirator, is one of Gissing's "unclassed," searching for his place and vocation in English society. The novel's opposing camps of pacifist cosmopolitanism and militarist nationalism are represented, on the one side, by the memories and works of Piers's father, who dies early in the novel, having outlived his role as one of the "liberators of mankind" (an allusion to Heine's self-description; see chaps. 5 and 6 above); by an old friend of Father Otway, the Liberal MP John Jacks; and by Piers himself; on the opposite side are Piers's jingoist half-brother; Jacks's son Arnold, a colonial businessman and aspiring politician, "a high-bred bulldog endorsed with speech" whose "religion was the British Empire";[43] and the obsessive "patriot" Lee Hannaford, inventor of ever more destructive guns and explosives. All these and other members of the two camps are closely related through ties of family and old friendship, thus representing the division within English society. The novel's romance plot is integrated into the political debate: [44] the heroine, Irene Derwent, faces a hard choice between her two suitors, Arnold Jacks and Piers Otway, and finally makes it in terms of their ideologies, deciding for Otway, the champion of her name, which means "peace," as well as of cosmopolitanism, poetry, and love, rather than Jacks's jingoism, commercialism, and selfishness.

In a shared complaint about the degenerating English national character, Piers and old John Jacks point as a warning to Germany:

"Once the peaceful home of pure intellect, the land of Goethe ... My fear is that our brute, blustering Bismarck may be coming."[45] As one of the countervailing "civilizers," Piers Otway has transformed an uncongenial business career in Russia and Little Russia (Ukraine) into a vocation as "a sort of interpreter of the two nations [British and Russsian] to each other," in Irene's enthusiastic words, on the occasion of two periodical articles of his in the *Nineteenth Century* and the *Vyestnik Evropy* respectively. This positive reinterpretation of the English "bugbear of the East"[46] was novel and typical of the younger generation influenced by admiration for Russian writers – foremost among them, Tolstoy, the pacifist, and Turgenev – whereas the prevailing view of Russia since the Crimean War had been as a non-Western, semi-civilized autocracy, in contrast to Germany as the Teuton cousin.[47] However, the rejection of Germany in favour of liberal France was occasionally argued as a rejection of Bismarck's autocratic "semi-Russian Government."[48] Joseph Conrad, in his bitter personal resentment of the Polish partitions, found little to choose between Germany and Russia, as we shall see.

Conrad's comparison of Russia and Germany, as well as appearing in the essay "The Crime of Partition" (1919), cited above, is presented in the essay "Autocracy and War" (1905), where he describes Russia as contemptible, quoting Bismarck's legendary verdict "La Russie, c'est le néant," but "Prince Bismarck's Empire" as dangerously "powerful and voracious." He concludes, "Le Prussianisme – voilà l'ennemi!"[49] Conrad's contemptuous hatred of autocratic Russia shapes his portrayal of the unnamed "Foreign Power" and its formal representatives and spies in London in the *Secret Agent* (see chap. 8 above). The vagueness permits association with other police states, pre-eminently Prussia. The "harlequin" – the young Russian adventurer and Kurtz's besotted disciple – a minor figure in *Heart of Darkness*, shares the contempt. In his novels Conrad transferred his sentiments about expansionism in Europe to colonial rivalries, only recently a topic of wider British interest, promoted by Joseph Chamberlain's tenure as colonial secretary in the new conservative government. During the Boer War, he supported British attempts to contain German influence in South Africa.[50]

In *Heart of Darkness* Conrad refrains from naming the African colony and its metropolis, although the story is partly based on his own brief employment in the private territory of King Leopold II of Belgium.[51] The vagueness, in addition to permitting the extension of the imperial theme to general questions of human progress, implicates all other European colonial empires in "the horror." Although the narrative situation, in a boat on the Thames, implicates Britain in the criticism, the narrator, Marlow, exempts British imperialism from censure. He remarks on the map in the company head office: "There was a vast amount of red – good to see at any time, because one knows that some real work is done in there, [blue, green, orange, yellow] and, on the East coast, a purple patch, to show where the jolly pioneers of progress drink the jolly lager beer."[52] Red represents British territories, purple German.

The double standard, which we have also observed in *The Secret Agent* (see chap. 8 above), no doubt reflects Conrad's own ambivalence, which may partly derive from his double allegiance as a Pole resenting the expansionism of Germany and Russia and as a grateful British subject. He rationalized his partiality in terms of the arch-Victorian criterion of "real work," as in his first description of the theme of *Heart of Darkness*: "The criminality of inefficiency and pure selfishness when tackling the civilizing work in Africa is a justifiable idea."[53] And to achieve his purpose, he omitted from his African portrait all signs of the actual settlements and civilizing achievements, showing instead only destruction and waste.

As we have seen, Conrad's fictional characters with a German connection are usually paired as positive/negative, such as Heyst and his antagonist, Schomberg, in *Victory*, or they are ambivalent, such as Kurtz in *Heart of Darkness*. That is, they match the topical stereotype of the "two Germanys." They all participate and compete in the imperialist enterprise in Africa and the Pacific, motivated by humanitarian ideals, selfish pursuit of profit, or a mixture of the two. Because of the backdating of the novels, German imperialism here is of the "informal" kind, pursued by buccaneering traders and explorers without benefit of the flag and its military; but for the contemporary reader, it merged with the current "formal" claims of 1884. Heyst, as well as Stein in *Lord Jim* and Kurtz before his corruption, represents the imperialist as scholar-explorer, a type for which Germany was generally respected and which was epitomized by Gustav Nachtigal, an African explorer in the 1870s and from 1882 German consul-general in Tunis, in which capacity he brought about the annexation to Germany of Togoland and Cameroon.

In *Lord Jim* (1900) Jim's joint benefactor with Marlow, the merchant Stein, besides being an explorer, naturalist, and philosopher, is marked as a "good" German by his youthful participation in the 1848 revolution in Germany. The negative type is here a minor figure, the grossly fat captain of the *Patna*, who both jumps ship and runs away from the inquiry. He is "a sort of renegade New South Wales German, very anxious to curse publicly his native country, but who, apparently on the strength of Bismarck's victorious policy, brutalized all those he was not afraid of, and wore a 'blood-and-iron' air."[54]

In *Victory*, published in the second year of World War I, the main characters are German, and they are more sharply contrasted. As we have seen, Conrad revised his portrayal to accommodate British sentiments by blurring the nationality of the positive character, Heyst/ Berg, while leaving no doubt about the nationality of his antagonist, the hotelier Schomberg and his accomplice, the exploitative German band leader, alias Ziangiacomo. Schomberg is worked up from a minor and innocuous character in *Lord Jim* and in the short story "Falk." Demobilized after the Franco-Prussian War and claiming officer rank, he is emblematic of the German state in his financial and sexual greed and vindictiveness. The narrator sarcastically urges the reader: "Observe the Teutonic sense of proportion and nice forgiving temper."[55] Conrad's weak equivocation in his "Note to the First Edition" (1915) only emphasizes the impression: "I don't pretend that this is the entire Teutonic psychology; but it is indubitably the psychology of a Teuton."[56] For the novel's original readers, Schomberg's military status as a "time-expired" Prussian soldier would have evoked the scare – answered with internment and repatriation during World War I – that thousands of such men living in Britain were ready to join a German invasion.[57] (His conflict with Heyst is of course not to be read allegorically as an intra-German conflict; at the plot level, Heyst is a Swedish baron.)

Unlike Conrad, E.M. Forster was a reluctant partisan, even on behalf of democracy in World War II, and no militant patriot; instead in 1939 he wrote that "if I had to choose between betraying my country and betraying my friend, I hope I should have the guts to betray my country."[58] He had co-founded the *Independent Review* in 1934 to combat Chamberlain's aggressive imperialism. Apparently in reaction to Le Queux's propagandistic novel *The Invasion of 1910* (1906), he conceived of a fictional exploration of Englishness and Germanness, which resulted in *Howards End*.[59] In this novel he goes beyond Gissing in the equating of German and British imperialism. He also combines in the standards of his criticism English traditional values with those of the "other," older Germany. He dramatizes the attraction of imperialism and its ultimate rejection through Margaret Schlegel's romance with Mr Wilcox (see chap. 8 above). The alternatives are the Wilcox "fetishes" of business, imperialism, and social Darwinism versus the Schlegel "fetishes" of culture, cosmopolitanism, and philanthropy. Forster gives ironic emphasis to his critique of the Wilcox ethos by employing the German anti-philistine topos associated with Goethe and Heine and used by Matthew Arnold and George Eliot (see chaps. 5 and 6 above), but with the difference that here it derives from a German who has sought refuge in England from "Germany a commercial Power, Germany a naval Power, Germany with colonies here and a Forward Policy there." Consequently, the Schlegels, whose name alludes to German Romanticism – in an earlier draft Forster had made them direct descendants of the brothers Schlegel – are "'not Germans of the dreadful sort."[60]

A similar distinction, although in a more private and gendered context, is made by Dorothy Richardson's heroine and narrator in *Pointed Roofs*, part 1 of *Pilgrimage*. The novel is based on Richardson's six-month stay in Germany in 1890 as a teacher in a boarding school for girls, an *Internat*. She started writing the novel in 1913 and published it two years later, that is, during the war. The young heroine's "strange love of Germany" is mixed with contempt, disgust, and fear. A main object of the latter are German men and their un-English contempt for women: "[b]lind and impudent." "And yet ... German music, a line of German poetry, a sudden light on Clara's [a student's] face."[61]

In her childhood, Forster's heroine Margaret Schlegel has been puzzled by the rival imperialist claims of her English and German relatives, a situation that Forster had been able to observe as tutor of the von Arnim daughters in Pomerania.[62] For a while Margaret decides in favour of imperialism in general and its British destiny in particular. She first accepts the lease of Mr Wilcox's house, with its dining room decorated with imperialist fetishes, such as parrots and a Dutch Bible "looted" during the Boer War; then, admiring the energy and practicality of the colonial spirit, she accepts Mr Wilcox, director of the Imperial and West African Rubber Company, as her husband.[63] By the end of the novel, the Wilcox ethos has had to give way to the Schlegel ethos: "[Margaret], who had never expected to conquer anyone, had charged straight through these Wilcoxes and broken up their lives."[64] However, this "triumph" is equivocal (see chap. 8 above) and certainly restricted to the private sphere, while the outer world continues to be transformed by the Wilcox ethos.[65] In the final vision of Leonard Bast, the domestic victim of this ethos, "the Imperialist is not what he thinks or seems. He is a destroyer. He prepares the way for cosmopolitanism, and though his ambitions may be fulfilled, the earth that he inherits will be gray."[66]

Ford Madox Ford (born Hueffer) had a closer familiarity with Germany than either Forster or his own friend and collaborator Conrad. His father was German and a pupil and popularizer of Schopenhauer, his education was multilingual and cosmopolitan, and from childhood he frequently stayed in Germany. Unlike Conrad, he was against the Boer War and against imperialism in general. During World War I he suffered some harassment for his

German name, which, however, he would not change until after the war. Despite his age and poor health, he joined the army and went to the front, out of a sense of patriotic duty as well as to escape from private problems. He also wrote two propaganda books, the first one commissioned to counter G.B. Shaw's pamphlet *Common Sense about the War*.[67] In *When Blood Is Their Argument: An Analysis of Prussian Culture* (1915), he distinguishes between Prussia and the rest of Germany and, following Nietzsche,[68] between Prussian *Kultur*, which means industrious and obedient service to the state, and Anglo-French "culture," which equals the German ideal of *Bildung*. Considering the all-powerful Prussian instruments of education, bureaucratic administration, and the army, he blames the kaiser alone for the war and exonerates the German people.

In his two best works of fiction, *The Good Soldier* (1915) and the best-selling tetralogy *Parade's End*, which consists of *Some Do Not ...* (1924), *No More Parades* (1925), *A Man Could Stand Up –* (1926), and *Last Post* (1928), Germany is represented indirectly from the point of view, respectively, of a wealthy Philadelphian and of an English Tory squire. Neither work uses Germany as a polemical token. While writing *The Good Soldier*, Ford also wrote a British propaganda book on Prussianism; but of fiction he said in his account of his and Conrad's joint aesthetics, "The one thing you can not do is to propagandise, as author, for any cause"[69] – a principle that he practised more nearly than Conrad did.

The Good Soldier is set in the pre-war years; however, the significant events connected with the narrator's wife all occur on the 4th of August, the date of the British declaration of war in 1914. The narrative strategy mirrors in the private sphere a public revisionist history which showed the war as the catastrophic result of the disintegrating forces in pre-war society.[70] The Germany of the novel is the country of spas – Ford uses actual places in the Taunus: Bad Nauheim, Homburg, and Wiesbaden – where "good people" form a cosmopolitan society based on "taking everything for granted" without true knowledge of one another.[71] As he would make explicit in *Parade's End*, private delusion and hypocrisy about the actual conditions of personal relations are interrelated with public prejudice and propaganda about international relations. Ford also insists on the elusiveness of just evaluations; that is the "saddest story": "Yet, if one doesn't know [how to judge] at this hour and day, at this pitch of civilisation to which we have attained, after all the preachings of all the moralists ... what does one know and why is one here?"[72] The assessment, though not the tone, is similar to Robert Musil's novel *Der Mann ohne Eigenschaften* (The man without qualities [1930–32]), a portrait of European society in dissolution on the eve of World War I.

Rather than contrasting Germany with England, Ford connects the two as Protestant countries. During the four main characters' excursion to the castle of Marburg, with its mementos of Luther and the Protest, Florence flirts with Captain Ashburnham: "It's because of that piece of paper that you're honest, sober, industrious, provident, and clean-lived. If it weren't for that piece of paper you'd be like the Irish or the Italians or the Poles, but particularly the Irish."[73] Although her remark is a self-interested, "schismatic" attack on his Irish Catholic wife, Leonore, and in the literal sense a misrepresentation of him, it coincides with the narrator's ultimate view on the relative morality of Ashburnham, "a sort of Lohengrin," and his wife, "the perfectly normal type."[74]

Whereas the narrator of *The Good Soldier* fails to resist the war era's threat of nihilism and the narrator's hero, Ashburnham, can only escape from the clash of values through suicide, the hero–cum–anti-hero of the post-war work *Parade's End* keeps faith with an obsolete idealist code and succeeds in finding a mode of surviving. Ford's portrait of Christopher Tietjens, the work's central consciousness, as a "sentimental Tory" is arguably more indebted to German Romantic models of the noble, and therefore alienated, champion of the good, the true, and the beautiful than to an actual English type, which is well represented in his elder brother, Mark.[75] In this work Ford makes his analogy between private and public morality explicit, both being ruled by greed and hypocrisy, when the protagonist predicts at the start that "war is as inevitable as divorce."[76]

Though a war novel – possibly the best English novel about World War I – the tetralogy *Parade's End* exhibits diverse facets of and attitudes to Germany. The first correspond to the stereotype of the "two Germanys," which Ford also employed in his first propaganda book. The good aspects are varied and particularized in terms of characterization. Tietjens is haunted by Heine's poetry, the dominant note of which is an abrupt shift from sentimentalism to irony. He resents the fact that he should recall it even under German shelling in the trenches and tries to make an exception of Heine: "Damn the German language! But that fellow was a Jew."[77] In his propaganda work Ford wrote of the German language and of Heine that, because of the language's simplicity and masculinity, "the poems of Heine, which are written in *colloquial* German and with absolute directness of phrase, are the most exquisite things in the world."[78] Tietjens's lover, Valentine, who is singled out for her sound and original mind, eclectically admires "the Fatherland of Goethe and Rosa Luxemburg," as well as the late Prince Albert, with whose goodness she compares Tietjens's.[79]

Aspects of demonic Prussia are largely implicit in the fact of the war. They include the bombing of hospital huts, which results in Tietjens's brain injury. He speaks of it sarcastically to his estranged wife, Sylvia, who has German prisoner friends: "The poor bloody Huns, ... it was, no doubt, just carelessness."[80] While in the trenches, he is more bored and exasperated with the Germans and their propaganda than hostile: "they were like continual caricatures of themselves and they were continually hysterical."[81]

Ford again uses a German resort in the Taunus, here the imaginary Lobscheid, for a scene dealing with brazen adultery – the ruthless ne-gotiations between Sylvia, her mother, and her truly saintly priest about Sylvia's return to her husband after her adulterous affair. But here Ford invests the German spa with a German evil. At night Father Consett hears "the claws of evil things scratching on the shutters. This was the last place in Europe to be Christianized. Perhaps it wasn't ever even Christianized and they're here yet."[82]

Besides giving his hero complex attitudes to Germany, Ford distrib-utes diverse views in the novel. Jingoism is represented in the popular song, sung at Valentine's school: "Hang Kaiser Bill from the hoar apple tree / And Glory Glory Glory till it's tea-time!" Extreme attitudes re-side in minor characters, whereas Tietjens and Valentine try to make sense of contradictory motivations, Tietjens as a pacifist soldier and Valentine by being involved in "War-work for a b——y pro-German. Or pacifist."[83] The divisions go through families: Valentine's mother and brother "both seemed to be filled with a desire for blood and to torture," their hatred being directed at opposite targets, the kaiser and the British soldier respectively.[84] Passionately fair, Tietjens rejects the request of Valentine's mother that he should help her with statistics for a spurious propaganda article on German atrocities. More strikingly, the francophile Ford, who wrote the first novel of the series in France, argues against the notion of war guilt when Tietjens predicts that, for the same economic necessity which caused Germany to go to war this time, bankrupt Britain would have to attack prosperous France in the near future: "Towards 1930 we shall have to do what Prussia did in 1914." Then "we should be decently loyal to our Prussian allies and brothers."[85]

An even more thoroughly sympathetic representation of the German "point of view" during the war is pursued by the hero, a respected culture critic and *Times* leader writer, in H.G. Wells's war novel *Mr. Britling Sees It Through* (1916). The book portrays the pro-tagonist's conversion, through personal experience, from welcom-ing the war as "the greatest opportunity" for British renewal to deploring it as evil waste, suffered equally by "England bereaved [and] Germany bereaved," and to resigning himself to doing his best in the fight for a pacifist World Republic.

In anticipation of the armistice, Ford's heroine, Valentine, suddenly recognizes and rejoices at the impending crisis of authority: "If ... at this crack across the table of History, the School – the World, the future mothers of Europe – got out of hand, would they ever come back? ... Authority all over the world – was afraid of that ... Wasn't it a possibility that there was to be no more Respect? None for constituted Authority and consecrated Experience?"[86] She expresses her generation's common post-war rejection of the older generation and its values, combined with solidarity with youth across national, even enemy, borders. The best-selling German war novel, Erich Maria Remarque's *Im Westen nichts Neues* (1928; trans., *All Quiet on the Western Front* [1929]), shares this generational attitude. Because of its situation resulting from the war, German society experienced in an extreme way both the rebelliousness and the fear of it, as well as the anxious grasping for new sources of authority. D.H. Lawrence, in *Women in Love* (1921), and Christopher Isherwood, in his *Berlin Stories* (1935–39), show aspects of this chaotic world in both its exhilarating creativity and its appalling destructiveness.

In his novel *Kangaroo* Lawrence described the persecution he had suffered from neighbours and the government during the war on account of his unfitness for service, his critical attitude to the war, and his German wife.[87] He wrote *Women in Love* during the war, planning to title it "Day of Wrath." He associates the war with the novel's negative, mechanical forces of dissolution, as, for instance, in the figure of Gerald, who, unlike Birkin, has fought in the war and is a "Napoleon" and a "Bismarck" of industry (see chap. 8 above).[88] Gerald takes exception to an assertion by Hermione, who here speaks for the author, that the patriotic appeal is "an appeal to the proprietory instinct, the *commercial* instinct."[89]

Birkin shares the positive sense of revolutionary change expressed by Valentine in Ford's *Parade's End*, but he desires a more profound and total transformation and despairs of it coming about in post-war England: "absolutely smash up the old idols of ourselves, that we sh'll never do."[90] Hoping to break with their old life, the two couples go abroad together, where in the inhuman winter landscape of the Tyrolean Alps they encounter an apostle of a radically new morality, the German sculptor Loerke. His literary forebears are Mephistopheles and artist figures in German Romantic novellas, such as E.T.A. Hoffmann's; his contemporary milieu is the iconoclastic German avant-garde. His aesthetics is anti-humanistic formalism, and it prescribes that art should interpret industry, the new religion. In this he follows the new Berlin style of the Neue Sachlichkeit, which gave priority to material facts. Morally, he is a nihilistic sensualist. Birkin acknowledges that Loerke is even more radical than himself: "Stages further in social hatred ... we want to take a quick jump downwards, in a sort of ecstasy – and he ebbs with the stream, the sewer stream [rat-like]." Gudrun sees him as fulfilling promises that she has perceived and been attracted to in Gerald: "Loerke ... dispensed with all illusion ... He existed a pure, unconnected will, stoical and momentaneous. There was only his work."[91] Gerald ends his life when Gudrun chooses Loerke over himself; she accompanies Loerke to work in his studio in Dresden, which was, with Berlin and Munich, a centre of modernist art, the home, for instance, of the expressionist painters' group Die Brücke (The bridge [1905–13]) and of the dancer Mary Wigman. But Birkin and Ursula, the characters on the side of organic life in Lawrence's terms, reject this "German" option, which is shown to be not a true departure but a climax of tendencies in English life.[92] In subsequent novels Lawrence tests Italy, Australia, and Mexico in turn for their capacities for renewal of European life (see chap. 8 above).

In the "golden twenties," Berlin, now the largest German city and the capital of the Weimar Republic, also became the centre of German intellectual and artistic life, ahead of older cultural centres such as Munich and Dresden, and a magnet for Germans and foreigners alike.[93] To Stephen Spender, Berlin in 1930 seemed "'realer' ... the *reductio ad absurdum* of the contemporary situation, ... Berlin was a town ... where action was conceived entirely in terms of power – enormous power for good or for evil."[94] One of the many Wahlberliner (Berliners of choice) was Christopher Isherwood, who followed W.H. Auden to the city in 1929, that is, at the end of the mythical "golden" period, and was in turn joined by Stephen Spender. Hailed by Cyril Connolly as "a hope of English fiction," Isherwood himself admired E.M. Forster as "the only living writer whom he would have described as his master ... A Forster novel taught Christopher the mental attitude with which he must pick up the pen."[95]

In his novels *The Last of Mr. Norris* (1935; in England, *Mr. Norris Changes Trains*) and *Goodbye to Berlin* (1939) – the latter popularized through the film *Cabaret* – Isherwood portrayed the last phase of the "new Berlin." As an impecunious English tutor, the semi-autobiographical narrator, whom for narrative purposes Isherwood made a mere asexual "demi-character,"[96] moves in several social milieus: the world of his working-class and petit-bourgeois landladies, the demi-monde and world of petty crime where his fellow boarders and friends seek a living "in those bankrupt days,"[97] and the upper-class homes of his employers, including a patrician Jewish family threatened by anti-Semitism. Across these social strata cut the political allegiances, notably to the two radical movements, the Communists and the Nazis. They also divide members of the same social group, including families, as in the case of the Nowaks, whose neighbourhood is "daubed with hammers and sickles and Nazi crosses and plastered with tattered bills which advertised auctions or crimes." One son is hard-working and a Nazi, another is unemployed and a Communist, and their mother wishes, "Why can't we have the Kaiser back?"[98]

Isherwood shows in his characters the nexus between economic, political, and moral life, portraying both bankruptcy and heroism in these aspects. The characters divide into those whose conduct is determined by real need and those who are motivated by gratuitous desires. Typical of the first is Olga, who earns her living in numerous occupations as "a procuress, a cocaine seller and a receiver of stolen goods; she also let lodgings, took in washing and, when in the mood, did exquisite fancy needlework." The second group includes Sally Bowles, the Baron von Pregnitz, and foremost, Mr Norris, who exploits the general chaos of these "stirring times," first through commercial swindles and then through political double-dealing. While the narrator accepts unconventional sexual conduct and forgives crimes of property – "[n]early every member of my generation is a crime-snob"[99] – he will not compromise his political faith, which originates in Cambridge left-wing anarchism. He will not forgive the second group's political opportunism and betrayal, although he forgives them in the first, who are "doomed to live in this town."[100] Consequently, Isherwood distinguished the two groups' stories as "serious" and "trivial" respectively.[101]

In his later autobiography, *Christopher and His Kind, 1929–1939*, Isherwood "condemn[ed] Christopher the novelist for not having taken a psychological interest, long before [1933], in the members of the Nazi command." Having neglected to interview them, "[h]e missed what would surely have been one of the most memorable experiences of his Berlin life."[102] He writes in his preface of 1954 that he first planned a "melodramatic novel" with the title "The Lost." Instead, he gave an exuberant and humorous portrait of Berlin only possible, as he says, for a "very young and frivolous foreigner," such as "Herr Issyvoo." He links his original plan to

Balzac, but curiously not to Alfred Döblin, the author of the great modernist novel of Berlin – in particular, lower-class Berlin – *Berlin Alexanderplatz*, which was published in the year of Isherwood's arrival. To Isherwood as a homosexual with left-wing and pacifist convictions, Berlin meant a contrast to and a refuge from the social and moral respectability of England and a new, true life without lies and inhibition. According to Stephen Spender, Isherwood's "hatred ... was for English middle-class life. He spoke of Germany as the country where all the obstructions and complexities of this life were cut through." Isherwood's consequent enthusiasm for Berlin's social and sexual anarchy made him ignore the fatal direction of its political anarchy as it staggered via emergency decrees towards its *Gleichschaltung* as Hitler's capital, what Spender calls the "sensation of doom in the Berlin streets ... the *Weimardaemmerung*."[103]

In one of the *Xenien* (1795–96) Goethe and Schiller ask, "Deutschland? Aber wo liegt es? Ich weiss das Land nicht zu finden. / Wo das gelehrte beginnt, hört das politische auf" [Germany? I don't know how to find the country. Where the learned one begins, the political one ends]."[104] Political Germany in the years of the *Xenien* meant such internal divisions as those over the French Revolution and French occupation. Only by anachronistically injecting the later power politics of Bismarck into his novel about the period from the 1820s to the 1850s, *Endymion*, could Disraeli make the political Germany of those decades interesting to English readers. However, from the time of the Prussian defeat of France and the unification of Germany, political Germany, in the commonplace of the "two Germanys," acquired an increasingly negative connotation of "blood and iron," which for some even contaminated "learned" Germany.

Of the novelists under discussion, only Meredith uses political Germany as a positive model of "efficiency" for Britain to emulate. Gissing represents the two Germanys elegiacally as historically successive – that is, the Germany of Goethe, Heine, and Schopenhauer versus Bismarck's "Potsdam" Germany – whereas Conrad portrays them in contrasted characters synchronically. Ford alone creates his major characters as themselves aware of the dichotomy and torn by ambivalence. Consequently, his novels eschew any propagandizing, as he theorized fiction should, while the other novels have strong strains of the *Tendenzroman* in their grouping of characters, plot, and authorial voice.

The Germany of the Weimar Republic appears in the fiction of Lawrence and Isherwood, not for its political significance, but, in a variant of the "good" Germany, for its avant-garde artistic and sexual freedom. While Lawrence tests and rejects it as a potential model for English communal regeneration, Isherwood limits himself to a private therapeutic prescription for his rebellion against English life. He later came to regret his disregard, in his fiction, for German political reality.

Conclusion

Evelyn Waugh satirized Isherwood and Auden's joint departure to the United States at the start of World War II in the inseparable pair of Parsnip-Pimpernell in his novel *Put Out More Flags* (1942). Another character accuses them of "sheer escapism,"[1] a charge to which the character who is modelled on the pacifist E.M. Forster, Ambrose Silk, fails to find an answer. Waugh developed a portrait of a reluctant, skeptical fighting spirit in the hero of his World War II trilogy *Sword of Honour*: *Men at Arms*, *Officers and Gentlemen*, and *The End of the Battle* (1952–62). Considered the best English novel inspired by the war by Auden, among others,[2] the work strongly alludes to Ford's World War II tetralogy, *Parade's End* (see chap. 9 above), in its panoramic and episodic conception, the characters of the hero and heroine and their marriage, and the authorial ethos. Waugh's novel is more conventional in not using the stream-of-consciousness technique to the degree that Ford does. The attitude of the hero, Guy Crouchback, to the war and to his own soldiering changes radically in the course of the trilogy. As soon as he learns of the Hitler-Stalin pact (1939), he welcomes the opportunity to heal his private psychological "wounds" in a just war: "The enemy at last was plain in view, huge and hateful, all disguise cast off. It was the Modern Age in arms. Whatever its outcome there was a place for him in that battle."[3] However, when he learns of the German invasion of Russia two years later, as he recovers from his escape during the British capitulation on Crete, he calls his original conviction a "hallucination" – "and he was back ... in the old ambiguous world, where priests were spies and gallant friends proved traitors and his country was led blunderingly into dishonour,"[4] and where, by implication, not every German is an enemy.

Hitler's dictatorship and the Holocaust have largely dominated the treatment of Germany in English post-war fiction. D.M. Thomas's novel *The White Hotel* (1981) is typical. The protagonist, a young wife and singer in Vienna between the wars, is debilitated by psychosomatic symptoms, such as pains, breathlessness, and hallucinations, which her psychoanalyst, Professor Freud, traces back to repressed childhood traumas. Her own insistence that she senses a qualitative difference between her dreams and free associations, on the one hand, and her hallucinations of falling from a great height and of mourners being buried by a landslide, on the other, is tragically validated when she becomes one of the victims of the Nazi mass murder at Babi Yar. The connection that the author makes between these two spheres, the private "family romance" and the public political evil, is ambiguous. While the plot seems to put in question Professor Freud's assimilation of the public to the private, the style makes the two spheres continuous, as does the suggestion that they can be understood in terms of his theory of the balancing instincts of eros and thanatos. This ambiguity results in the uneasy impression that Thomas uses the Nazi Holocaust frivolously as a means of giving his story of sexual repression and obsession more pathos.

Anthony Burgess, in his last work, *Byrne* (1996), a comic novel in verse, uses Nazi Germany to satirize the opportunism and corruption of artists. Byrne, an Irishman, second-rate musician and painter, and first-rate womanizer, spends the Nazi period in Germany, where as "Börn" he eagerly replaces the "undesirable" Jewish musicians and composes, among other things, an opera for a libretto of Goebbels's and a choral work on a passage from Hitler's *Mein Kampf*.

For an example of the typical fictional post-war German, David Lodge's academic comedy *Small World* (1984) represents German academe solely with a menacing German scholar of literature and proponent of *Rezeptionsästhetik* (reception theory), Professor Siegfried von Turpitz. Like the cinematic Dr Strangelove, he always wears a black kid-leather glove on one hand, which is rumoured to be artificial and to replace the hand that was "crushed and mangled in the machinery of the Panzer tank which Siegfried von Turpitz commanded in the later stages of World War II."[5] Fact in this case has come to confirm fiction: the recent death, in 1997, of Hans Robert Jauss, co-founder with Wolfgang Iser of the influential Konstanz school of reception theory, has occasioned the public revelation and discussion of what at the time of Lodge's novel was merely academic rumour, of Jauss's war service in the Waffen-SS and his conviction and imprisonment by the Americans after the war. (For the present study and its use of Jauss's methodology, Gustav Seibt's essay "Kann eine Biografie ein Werk zerstören? Bemerkungen zu de Man, Jauss, Schwerte und Hermlin [Can a biography destroy a work? Notes on …]" [1998] is of special interest.)[6] Another fictional example is the former assistant of the unnamed Dr Mengele in Martin Amis's unsuccessfully contrived "backwards" novel, *Time's Arrow* (1991). The novel's experimental structure and its philosophical premise group it with the earlier "German" novels in this study.[7] In John Le Carré's *A Small Town* (1968) the West German capital, Bonn, shares a main feature with the London of Conrad's *Secret Agent* (see chap. 8 above). Both physically and morally, the town is enveloped in fog, as the German government and its uneasy British ally are abandoning justice for Nazi crimes and secretly and separately negotiating with a new crypto-Nazi movement.

A critical view of British collusion with Nazism is introduced in *The Remains of the Day* (1989) by Kazuo Ishiguro. The novel won the Booker Prize and has been filmed. It portrays with sympathy but without equivocation the error and waste of a life spent in the service of politically naive notions of duty, both as it applies to the narrator, the butler Stevens at Darlington Hall, and to his employer, Lord Darlington. In his first longer sojourn away from the hall and his work, the narrator recalls and for the first time judges the now-deceased Lord Darlington's service to his country and his own "historic" service to Lord Darlington. Lord Darlington had first attempted through informal diplomacy, especially country house politics, to soften the conditions of the Treaty of Versailles, the vindictive character of which offended his sense of honour; later, in his efforts to preserve the peace, he unwittingly became "the single most useful pawn Herr Hitler has had in this country for his propaganda tricks."[8] That is, Lord Darlington was instrumental in Chamberlain's policy of appeasement. In the end an early warning by an American participant at Lord Darlington's unofficial international conference about the treaty is confirmed: Lord Darlington is a "classic English gentleman. Decent, honest, well-meaning. But his lordship here is *an amateur* … and international affairs today are no longer for gentlemen amateurs." That in this new "sort of place the world is becoming all around"[9] the Nazis were fitter, for a fatal spell, than English gentlemen is a sadly ironic reversal of the balance of worldliness between England and Germany at the beginning of the period under study in the present work.

The Germany which originally suggested positive images in English fiction, that of Goethe's Weimar and the Romantics, has found a recent sympathetic reinterpretation in Penelope Fitzgerald's novel *The Blue Flower* (1995). Based on the early love of Friedrich von Hardenberg, who would become the major Romantic poet and aesthetic philosopher Novalis, it portrays with fine humour and sympathy the discrepancy, so remarkable to English visitors at the time, between material frugality and intellectual and imaginative aspiration and achievement. The other recent examples cited above show a tendency to allude to Germany for the sake of the anomalous, monstrous, and sensational aspects of the Nazi terror, which is in sharp contrast to the use of Germany in the fiction of earlier periods for its comparable, intelligible, and instructive affinity as the Teuton cousin.

The novels in this study all use German allusions to reflect on English life, and most of them also use them to authorize an alternative practice of fiction. The main topics for the first type of criticism are *Bildung*, the anti-philistinism of Goethe and Heine, the Tübingen higher criticism, Schopenhauer's and Nietzsche's pessimistic and optimistic philosophies of the Will to Life and the Will to Power respectively, Prussian militarism, and finally the artistic and sexual freedom of the Weimar Republic. Over the period studied, of the "two Germanys," the model of Goethean *Bildung* was first "imported" by Thomas Carlyle, to counter utilitarianism and materialism, and combined with Schiller's idealism by Edward Bulwer-Lytton and with Goethe's anti-philistinism by George Eliot, who also used Heine as a figure of anti-philistinism as well as of music and Jewry. Allusions to the religious and philosophical teachings of the higher criticism, Schopenhauer, and Nietzsche are more ambivalent, the authors portraying both the common horror of them and their truth and consequent challenge to English intellectual compromise and complacency. In the most important crisis-of-faith novel, Mrs Humphry Ward depicts the higher criticism as a necessary agent in the loss of an uncritical faith and the gain of true religiosity. George Gissing is the most complete disciple of Schopenhauer, making his protagonists and his narrators equally so. While D.H. Lawrence quarrels with Nietzsche's teachings, he adopts for himself the role of the Nietzschean prophet. The monster of Prussian militarism is generally alluded to in aid of rejecting British jingoism – for instance, by Gissing and E.M. Forster; Joseph Conrad, however, contrasts it, in conjunction with Russian despotism and imperialism, with English ethical conduct. Only George Meredith represents Prussian "efficiency" as a model for English emulation. Life in the Weimar Republic functions as a model for free individual development in Christopher Isherwood's Berlin novels, an idea that Lawrence also tests but rejects as a dead end for communal regeneration.

For the authors' rhetorical purposes, fidelity to the original is less important than the evocative power of an allusion. Thus Carlyle's adaptation of Goethean *Bildung* and Lawrence's engagement with popular misconceptions of Nietzsche's philosophy deliver as persuasive a criticism of English life as do the more faithful allusions of Eliot and Gissing.

In their strong allusiveness to foreign intertexts, the novels in this study distinguish themselves from what was considered the mainstream of English realist fiction. Both the critics' reservations and the authors' justifications attribute the intellectual and speculative tone, the "brainstuff," to Continental and especially German models. Of these the *Bildungsroman* is the pre-eminent genre, together with its derivative, the *Entsagungsroman* (novel of renunciation). The *Bildungsroman* strategy of effecting the implied reader's *Bildung* in the course of his or her reading about that of the protagonist is most evident in the novels of Meredith, George Eliot, and Lawrence. The *Tendenzroman* (novel with a purpose) is another genre that some of the novels participate in, usually together with the *Bildungsroman*. Among the heteroglossia of discourses in these novels, the learned, the speculative, and the visionary allude especially strongly to the German Romantic conception of the novel as the modern world-inclusive genre.

From the high status that the serious English novel achieved and maintained during the period under discussion, it has now been demoted to a marginal role, in competition with mass cultural forms and technologies. For this reason and the following ones, the enterprise of this study could not be profitably extended to contemporary English fiction. Despite occasional flare-ups of the old national stereotypes in the course of soccer matches or European Union conflicts, the German cousin is no longer the obvious figure of comparison for the English in their multi-ethnic society and the global community. Even the traditional three-nation jokes – "An Englishman, a Frenchman, and a German ..." – have lost currency.

The immediate post-war period in English fiction has generally been defined as provincial, neo-realist, and anti-modernist. In his introduction to the 1976 reissue of *Eating People Is Wrong* (1959), Malcolm Bradbury describes his novel as "very much *about* its time. It is, like many 'fifties novels, about provincial life, the virtues and limitations of uncosmopolitan and ordinary existence," its style a "straight-forward, local commonsense realism." In a recapitulation of Podsnappery, Emma, a post-graduate student, pities the anti-hero's efforts on behalf of a foreign post-graduate student, Herr Schumann: "Poor man, he has tried to show us all that foreigners aren't funny; but they are. After all, there was one thing that every Englishman knew from his very soul, and that was that, for all experiences and manners, in England lay the norm."[10]

During the 1960s and 1970s English fiction again became more cosmopolitan, not however, by looking to Germany but by "stepping westward," to borrow Bradbury's title for his 1965 novel, for North and South American influences, as well as that of the French *nouveau roman*. The expatriate trend begun by James Joyce and Samuel Beckett was resumed, Anthony Burgess and Muriel Spark, for instance, living in Italy and writing about cosmopolitan characters and plots, as in Spark's *The Takeover* (1976), and for an international market.[11] In addition, returning exiles and "reverse colonists" such as Doris Lessing and Salman Rushdie have brought an eccentric perspective to "Englishness."[12] Together with Commonwealth and post-colonial authors, these novelists write not for England but for the English-speaking world.

Neither multicultural England nor the international market provide the conditions for the culturally defined implied reader I have studied, who can self-consciously disengage himself or herself from his or her culture in order to critique it in terms of another. Ian Buruma and other critics have observed a recent international trend in both serious and popular fiction towards "cultural minimalism, entirely lacking literary or cultural allusions."[13] This new cosmopolitanism crucially differs from Goethe's ideals, and those of his English disciples, of *Weltliteratur* (world literature), the *Weltbürger* (citizen of the world), and *Bildung*. Following Herder's philosophy of culture, Goethean cosmopolitanism and *Bildung* are achieved through knowledge of the particular and distinct characteristics of one's own and other cultures and through respect for their equal value.[14] In a draft for an introduction to Carlyle's *Life of Schiller*, Goethe wrote: "Denn daraus nur kann endlich die allgemeine Weltliteratur entspringen, dass die Nationen die Verhältnisse aller gegen alle kennen lernen, und so wird es nicht fehlen, dass jede in der andern etwas Annehmliches und etwas Widerwärtiges, etwas Nachahmenswertes und etwas zu Meidendes antreffen wird."[15] In translation this observation provides a fitting conclusion to this study: "For universal world literature can only arise when the nations come to know the reciprocal relations of all with all; and then they will each be sure to encounter in the other something pleasing and something disgusting, something worth imitating and something to avoid."

Notes

INTRODUCTION

1 Chesterton, *Victorian Age in Literature*, 11; James, "*Daniel Deronda*," 111.

2 Dickens, *Our Mutual Friend*, 128 (chap. 11).

3 James, "*Daniel Deronda*," 102.

4 See Lawrence Price's study, *The Reception of English Literature in Germany*, part 3.

5 For instance, the Penn State Project on Anglo-German and American-German Literary and Cultural Relations.

6 On Arnold's confusing approach to the relation between race, or nation, and culture, see Herbert, *Culture and Anomie*, and Pecora, "Arnoldian Ethnology."

7 Stephen, "Importation of German," 36.

8 See Klieneberger, *Novel in England and Germany*, 87 and elsewhere.

9 See, for instance, Buruma, *Anglomania*.

10 Carlyle, "State of German Literature" (*Works*, 26:31).

11 Letter to William Allingham, 4 September 1850, in Carlyle, *Collected Letters*, 25:194.

12 Eliot, "German Wit: Heinrich Heine" (*Essays*, 222–3).

13 Mayhew's repeated comparison of provincial Germany with Ireland is doubly prejudiced (*German Life and Manners*, 22 and elsewhere).

14 Anderson, *Imagined Communities*, 4–6.

15 See Brooker and Widdowson, "Literature for England."

16 Hamburger, *From Prophecy to Exorcism*, 9.

17 See, for instance, Walter Schirmer's study of literary influence, *Der Ein-fluss der deutschen Literatur auf die Englische*; H.R. Klieneberger's study in comparative sociology of literature, *The Novel in England and Germany*; and Robert Colls and Philip Dodd on "Englishness" in *Englishness: Politics and Culture, 1880–1920*.

18 Barthes, *S/Z*, 19, 5.

19 Hinds, *Allusion and Intertext*, 17, 47.

20 Genette, *Palimpsests*, 9. For another instance of classical studies besides Hinds, see Conte, *Rhetoric of Imitation*.

21 Pasco, *Allusion and Intertext*, 6, 18, 12. Ben-Porat similarly defines "literary allusion" as "the activation of indirectly evoked elements from an independent text for the formation of intertextual patterns" ("Poetics," 109).

22 Wheeler, *Art of Allusion*, 8. Wheeler cites Hermann Meyer, whose study deals mostly with German novels and only with biblical and classical quotations, Harold Bloom, who analyzes "misreading" and the "anxiety of influence," and Ziva Ben-Porat, who theorizes on intertextuality. For a review of the distinction between influence, reception, and "false" influence and their frequent methodological confusion, see Balakian, "Influence and Literary Fortune."

23 Wheeler, *Art of Allusion*, 3, 18, 2.

24 McMaster, *Thackeray's Cultural Frame of Reference*, 2, 1.

25 Jauss, "Literary History," 18–19, 41, 32, 19.

26 Panayi, *Enemy in Our Midst*, 11.

27 Sir Harry Johnston, *Views and Reviews*, 103–4.

28 On the misleading restriction to the canonical "major" novels, see Sutherland, *Victorian Fiction*, 151.

CHAPTER ONE

1 Susanne Howe, in her thorough survey *Wilhelm Meister and His English Kinsmen* (1930), used this term derived from Carlyle's translation, *Wilhelm Meister's Apprenticeship*.

2 Buckley, *Season of Youth*, 13, 18. Buckley's cursory evaluation of Goethe's *Wilhelm Meister* as a "curious medley" with "irrelevant interpolated tales" and his criticism of Goethe's ambivalence towards Wilhelm (10) are inadequate.

3 See Enright's witty essay on "English attitudes of non-liking towards German literature," "Aimez-vous Goethe?" 209.

4 Tennyson, "Bildungsroman," 143.

5 *Werther* was first translated into English from a French translation in 1929. For a summary of the novel, see chapter 7 below.

6 Norbert Elias discusses the German valuation of "culture" over "civilization" as arising from the new intelligentsia's polemic against the francophile courts. See also Moretti's comparative study of the changing relative
priority of freedom over happiness in the *Bildungsroman* genre in *The Woy
of the World*.

7 For a fuller critical account, see Boyle, *Goethe*, 2:422–4.

8 The Weimar classicists demanded for their secular fiction a close reading
borrowed from pietist habits and in contrast to the reading of popular
fiction (Kontje, *Private Lives in the Public Sphere*, 4).

9 Schlegel, *Fragmente* ([1797–98] reprinted in *Goethes Werke*, 7:661); Novalis,
Fragmente und Studien ([1799–1800] reprinted in *Goethes Werke*, 7:685).
Translations are my own, unless otherwise indicated.

10 This summary is indebted to Schirmer, *Einfluss der deutschen Literatur*,
29–30, and Morgan, *German Literature in British Magazines*, 86–7.

11 Coleridge, *Table Talk*, 20 October 1811 (*Collected Works*, 14.2:340); Ashton,
Life of S.T. Coleridge, 86, 367; *Table Talk*, 16 February 1833, (*Collected Works*,
14.1:341–2).

12 Quoted in S. Howe, *Whilhelm Meister* 80.

13 Abrams, *Natural Supernaturalism*, 74.

14 *London Magazine* 10 (August 1824): 190; quoted in Ashton, *German Idea*, 84.

15 Bruford, *Culture and Society*, 291.

16 Herder, *Briefe zur Beförderung der Humanität* (*Sämtliche Werke*, 17:138).

17 The non-sexist "Mensch" (human) was translated as "man," in contemporary English sources. In 1789 Humboldt had an actual experience of female *Bildung* in the Berlin circles – the "Aesthetic Tea" in *Sartor Resartus* –
that of Henriette Herz and her friends Dorothea Veit (who left her husband to marry Friedrich Schlegel) and Rahel Levin (who later married
Varnhagen von Ense, an important source for Lewes's biography of
Goethe). See Bruford, *Culture and Society*, 413.

18 Lessing, *Briefe über die Erziehung der Menschheit* (Letters on the education
of mankind [1770]); Schiller, *Briefe über die ästethische Erziehung der Menschen* (Letters on the aesthetic education of mankind [1794–95]).

19 Humboldt, "Theorie der Bildung des Menschen" (Theory of the *Bildung* of humankind [1793]; in *Gesammelte Schriften*, 1:283); Mill, *On Liberty*, 74; Humboldt, *Ideen zu einem Versuch die Gränzen der Wirksamkeit
des Staates zu bestimmen* (Ideas for an essay to determine the limits of
the effect of the State [1793]; in *Gesammelte Schriften*, 1:106–7). Houghton, in *The Victorian Frame of Mind*, finds a radical difference between
Mill's idea of self-development and that of Goethe and Arnold in
Mill's stress on the unique to the exclusion of the harmonious (290–1).
While supported by a diary entry, this assertion is not borne out by
Mill's translation of the quotation from Humboldt in *On Liberty*: "the

highest and most harmonious development of his powers to a complete and consistent whole" (74). Collini (*Public Moralists*, 102) follows Houghton despite his express purpose of examining the "*public* moralists" (emphasis added) in their relation to their audience (2–4). In Humboldt's discussion there is no contradiction between the two ideas. For a more detailed examination of Humboldt's idea of *Bildung*, although without reference to this issue, see Bruford's chapter on Humboldt in *The German Tradition of Self-Cultivation*.

20 *Goethes Briefe*, 1:324; Bruford, *Culture and Society*, 236.

21 Goethe, *Lehrjahre*, bk 8, chap. 5.

22 Schiller acknowledged his debt to Kant in a footnote to the title.

23 Letters 21 and 23, in Schiller, *Sämtliche Werke*, 5:635, 641.

24 *Goethes Werke*, 7:290–1 (bk 5, chap. 3).

25 Schiller, Goethe's best critic, praised the figure of Werner as the right foil for the realism that Wilhelm finally achieves as a beautiful human mean between the fantastic and the philistine (*Goethes Werke*, 7:636).

26 *Goethes Werke*, 7:498 (bk 8, chap. 1).

27 Ibid., 7:520 (bk 8, chap. 3).

28 Ibid., 8:282–3 (bk 2, chap. 10).

29 Ibid., 13:64, no. 61.

30 Wilde, *Intentions*, 187.

31 10 November 1829, quoted in Carlyle's *Life of John Sterling* ([1851]; *Works*, 11:50).

32 Carlyle, *Works*, 26:19.

33 Bruford, *Culture and Society*, 3–6, 8; Williams, *Culture and Society*, 13, 17.

34 Two later examples of the *Bildungsroman*, Adalbert Stifter's *Der Nachsommer* (1857) and Thomas Mann's *Der Zauberberg* (1929), respond to industrialism and democracy respectively.

35 See, for instance, letter 6 in Schiller, *Sämtliche Werke*, 5:582.

36 Kant, *Werke*, 8:36.

37 Knights, *Idea of the Clerisy*, 18–19.

38 Carlyle, *Works*, 1:3 (bk 1, chap. 1), and 1:219 (bk 3, chap. 10).

39 Collini, *Public Moralists*, 62–3. Walter E. Houghton shows that enthusiasm and the ethic of earnestness worked both in opposition to and in conjunction with each other (*Victorian Frame of Mind*, chap. 11).

40 Carlyle introduced the word "Philistine" into English in 1827 in "The State of German Literature," repeating Goethe's and Schiller's nickname for the old-fashioned rationalists Nicolai and his friends, who had no feeling for contemporary poetry (*Works*, 26:68). Goethe and Schiller had adapted the meaning of the word, from its original use by the students of Jena for the distinction between town and gown, in the epigraph of the *Zahme Xenien*. In a letter to Eckermann, Carlyle explained that in England

Philistines were called Utilitarians (*Correspondence*, 173), and he used the word to denote a utilitarian judgment of art.

41 See Haines, *Essays on German Influence*, 4.

42 Mill quotes from an English translation, *Sphere and Duties of Government* (1854).

43 Mill, *On Liberty*, 74; Mill, *Autobiography*, 190, 103, 118, 131. For Mill's rejection, in his private diary, of Goethe's ideal of harmonious *Bildung*, see note 19 above.

44 Arnold, *Complete Prose Works*, 5:94.

45 Arnold, *Lectures and Essays in Criticism*, in *Complete Prose Works*, 3:380.

46 Smiles, *Self-Help*, 22, 203–4, 231.

47 Arnold is referring to the separate publication of chapter 2 (see above). He here called Humboldt "one of the most beautiful souls that have ever existed" (*Complete Prose Works*, 5:161). For a discussion of this term see chapter 2 below.

48 Arnold, *Complete Prose Works*, 5:161.

49 Fichte, *Von den Pflichten der Gelehrten*, 37, 40, 112.

50 Arnold, *Schools and Universities on the Continent* (1868); 2d, abr. ed., *Higher Schools and Universities in Germany* (1874).

51 The reform of Oxford and Cambridge, as well as the foundation of the new city colleges in the 1870s, was driven by a different attitude to Germany: admiration for its systematic, "scientific" (*wissenschaftlich*), professional approach to learning and fear of its industrial competition based on the success of this approach (Haines, *Essays*, 47, 53–7). For the earlier period, see also Haines, *German Influence upon English Education and Science, 1800–1866* (1957).

52 See Kennedy, *Rise of the Anglo-German Antagonism*, 110–14; Schirmer, *Einfluss der deutschen Literatur*, 65.

53 Quoted in Mander, *Our German Cousins*, 62–3.

54 Kaplan, *Thomas Carlyle*, 136.

55 Ashton, *German Idea*, 19.

56 *Goethes Werke*, 7:291–2 (bk 5, chap. 3).

57 Quoted in Martini, "Bildungsroman," 57. I am indebted for this source to Randolph P. Shaffner, who surveys the history of the term in *The Apprenticeship Novel*, 3.

58 *Goethes Werke*, 7:653.

59 Quoted in *Reallexikon der deutschen Literaturgeschichte*, 1:175.

60 For a critical historical survey of *Bildungsroman* criticism, see Kontje, *German Bildungsroman*.

61 Tennyson, "Bildungsroman," 135.

62 In his essay "The *Bildungsroman* and Its Significance in the History of Realism (Toward a Historical Typology of the Novel)," M.M. Bakhtin, whose

book-length manuscript on this genre was lost, defines what he calls interchangeably the *Erziehungsroman* and the *Bildungsroman* as dealing with "man in the process of becoming" and assimilating both historical time and historical man, in contrast to the "ready-made" hero of epic and tragedy; it is the "novel of human *emergence*" (*Speech Genres*, 19, 21).

63 Dilthey, *Erlebnis und die Dichtung*, 327–9.
64 Sammons, "Mystery of the Missing *Bildungsroman*," 237–41.
65 Jacobs, *Wilhelm Meister und seine Brüder*, 271.
66 Swales, *German Bildungsroman*, 12. Swales also notes several innovative studies of structural and narrative features, rather than thematic ones – for instance, Gerhart von Graevenitz's *Die Setzung des Subjekts: Untersuchungen zur Romantheorie* (1973) and Monika Schrader's *Mimesis und Poiesis: Poetologische Studien zum Bildungsroman* (1975) – but he does not find adequate their account of the *Bildungsroman* as "a highly self-reflective novel, one in which the problem of *Bildung*, of personal growth, is enacted in the narrator's discursive self-understanding rather than in the events which the hero experiences" (4).

CHAPTER TWO

1 Carlyle, *Works*, 5:157.
2 Kaplan, *Thomas Carlyle*, 55, 66.
3 Carlyle, *Works*, 26:66.
4 Kaplan, *Thomas Carlyle*, 137. Until then, the *Edinburgh Review* had not approved of the German influence, and its editor, Francis Jeffrey, had in fact condemned *Wilhelm Meister's Apprenticeship* in Carlyle's translation as "almost from beginning to end, one flagrant offence against every principle of taste, and every just rule of composition" (quoted in Ashton, *German Idea*, 67).
5 Goethe wrote a short review of the book and an introduction to the translation of 1830 (*Goethes Werke* [Sophien-Ausgabe], 1:41.2:302–3; 1:42.1:186–91).
6 Kaplan, *Thomas Carlyle*, 101.
7 For instance, Ashton, *German Idea*, 85. In contrast, Carr lists many errors in the *Apprenticeship*, attributing omissions and some mistranslations to Carlyle's concern for British taste, some additions to his "tendency to stress the sinfulness and joylessness of this world" ("Carlyle's Translations," 227), and unintentional errors to his imperfect command of German, which Carr finds improved in the *Travels*.
8 Carlyle acknowledged this failure, making a virtue of his own lack of talent by arguing that "in this 'iron age' prose was a more suitable vehicle for ... feelings and ideas" (Kaplan, *Thomas Carlyle*, 256).
9 Ashton, *German Idea*, 21.

10 "Parodistisch": "wo man sich in die Zustände des Auslandes zwar zu versetzen, aber eigentlich nur fremden Sinn sich anzueignen und mit eignem Sinne wieder darzustellen bemüht ist [when one attempts to enter into the foreign conditions, but really only in order to appropriate the foreign meaning and to render it by one's own meaning]"; "dem Original identisch": "der Übersetzer, der sich fest an sein Original an- schliesst, gibt mehr oder weniger die Originalität seiner Nation auf, und so entsteht ein Drittes [the translator, who stays close to his original, more or less surrenders the originality of his nation, and thus a third entity is created]; see "Noten und Abhandlungen: Übersetzungen," *West-östlicher Divan* (*Goethes Werke*, 2:255–6).

11 *Goethes Werke*, 7:120, 276, 290, 422; Carlyle, *Works*, 23:151 (bk 2, chap. 9), 313 (bk 4, chap. 19), 327 (bk 5, chap. 3); 24:2 (bk 7, chap. 1).

12 In Rousseau's *Julie, ou La nouvelle Héloïse* (1761), Julie desires a lasting at- tachment, not to a charming man, but to a man who has "une belle âme" (part I, letter 13).

13 Book 6 is based on the autobiographical writings of the Pietist friend (not a relative, as is sometimes maintained) of Goethe and his mother, Susanna Katharina von Klettenberg.

14 *Goethes Werke*, 7:608; Carlyle, *Works*, 24:187 (bk 8, chap. 10).

15 Schiller's letter to Goethe, 3 July 1796, in *Goethes Werke*, 7:634; Goethe's letter to Schiller, 7 July 1796, ibid., 7:639; also, 9 July 1796, ibid., 7:644.

16 *Goethes Werke*, 7:180; Carlyle, *Works*, 23:213 (bk 3, chap. 8).

17 Carlyle, *Works*, 23:10, 26:232.

18 For instance, Ashton, *German Idea*, 88. This version is not included in the collected works of the Sophien-Ausgabe and the Hamburger Ausgabe. Carr footnotes the circumstantial evidence of the publication dates, but has no further comment on the two versions and Carlyle's work ("Carlyle's Translations").

19 Carlyle, *Works*, 23:2.

20 Ibid., 27:39, 1:149 (bk 2, chap. 9). See also Vida's discussion (*Romantic Affinities*, 114–22). Ben Knights traces in this concept "the thread to the ideal of purity (conceived as the renunciation of the sensible world) that was one of the great secularisations achieved on behalf of culture by [British] nineteenth-century theorists" (*Idea of the Clerisy*, 3).

21 Novalis, *Poeticismen*, no. 134 (*Schriften*, 1:56).

22 Goethe, *Wilhelm Meisters Wanderjahre* (1821), 12 (chap. 1); Carlyle, *Works*, 24:200.

23 Goethe, *Wilhelm Meisters Wanderjahre*, 150 (chap. 14); Carlyle, *Works*, 24:346.

24 Goethe, *Wilhelm Meisters Wanderjahre*, 33 (chap. 5); Carlyle, *Works*, 24:223.

25 *Goethes Werke*, 7:431, 491 (bk 7, chaps. 3, 8); Carlyle, *Works*, 24:11, 71.

26 See Kontje, *German Bildungsroman*, 105.

27 11 October 1828, in Eckermann, *Gespräche mit Goethe*, 233.

28 8 and 9 July 1796, in *Goethes Werke*, 7:643, 644–5.

29 James, *Literary Reviews and Essays*, 270–1.

30 Carlyle, *Works*, 23:10.

31 Ibid., 23:6.

32 Ibid., 23:7–8.

33 Besides occurring repeatedly in *Dichtung und Wahrheit*, the maxim informs the country parson's treatment of the harpist in the *Lehrjahre* (*Goethes Werke*, 7:34; Carlyle, *Works*, 23:386 [bk 5, chap. 16]).

34 All quotation from the introductory essay to the *Travels* are from Carlyle, *Works*, 23:12–33.

35 Carlyle, *Works*, 26:208, 210.

36 Ibid., 1:153 (bk 2, chap. 9).

37 Ibid., 26:224–6.

38 Ibid., 23:2.

39 Letter to W. Lattimer, 3 March 1858, in Carlyle, *New Letters*, 1:189.

40 Carlyle, *Works*, 26:233.

41 Bk 2, chaps. 1 and 2, in the final version.

42 Carlyle, *Works*, 26:234.

43 Ibid., 26:238.

44 Letter of 10 June 1831, in Carlyle, *Collected Letters*, 5:286.

45 This is to make an exception to Auerbach's observation that, until toward the end of the nineteenth century, German novels "portray the economic, the social, and the political as in a state of quiescence" (*Mimesis*, 399).

46 Letter of 28 July 1819, in *Goethes Briefe*, 4:339. Emil Staiger observes that Goethe presents every proposed dogma, such as the one on reverence, as conditional, relative to a character or situation; that is, as always less than just to the whole of life. Staiger concludes that the overarching moral seems to be the reciprocal value of the individual person and the general ideal, where the value of the one depends on recognition of the value of the other (*Goethe*, 3:160–8).

47 Letter of 2 January 1827, in Carlyle, *Collected Letters*, 4:180.

48 See Harrold, *Carlyle*; Ashton, *German Idea*; and Vida, *Romantic Affinities*. Harrold concludes that "without the shaping influence of German doctrines, Carlyle would hardly have attained that prophetic stature which made him so great a force in Victorian life" (237).

49 "Mein Vermächtniss, wie herrlich weit und breit! / Die Zeit ist mein Vermächtniss, mein Acker ist die Zeit." This is a slight misquotation of the original: "Mein Erbteil wie herrlich, weit und breit! / Die Zeit ist mein Besitz, mein Acker ist die Zeit [My inheritance, how wide and large! Time is my inheritance, my acre is time]"; see "Buch der Sprüche," *West-östlicher Divan* (*Goethes Werke*, 2:52).

50 Carlyle, *Works*, 1:209 (bk 3, chap. 8).
51 Ibid., 1:235–6 (bk 1, chaps. 7–8); cf. I/not-I, in "Carlyle, Novalis" (*Works*, 27:25).
52 Carlyle, *Works*, 1:158–9 (bk 2, chap. 10).
53 Ibid., 1:149 (bk 2, chap. 9); cf. Carlyle, "Novalis" (*Works*, 27:39).
54 Carlyle, *Works*, 1:190 (bk 3, chap. 6); cf. Carlyle, "Novalis" (*Works*, 27:39).
55 Carlyle, "Novalis"(*Works*, 27:29).
56 Carlyle, *Works*, 1:43 (bk 1, chap. 8).
57 *Tag- und Jahreshefte 1811* [1830] *Goethes Werke*, 10:511). For Goethe, *Anschauung* was not Kantian intuition but observation, a literal gazing. As he said in the poem "Epirrhema" about nature's "sacred public secret" (*heilig öffentlich Geheimnis*), "Nichts ist drinnen, nichts ist draussen; / Denn was innen, das ist aussen [Nothing is inside, nothing is outside; / For what is within is without]." Schiller initially deplored the Weimar circle's study of plants and minerals and their trust in the five senses, instead of metaphysical speculation, and he disputed with Goethe whether the latter's *Urpflanze* was an idea or a visual experience.
58 Carlyle, *Works*, 26:5.
59 Carlyle, "Goethe" (*Works*, 26:245).
60 Carlyle, *Works*, 1:63 (bk 1, chap. 11).
61 Carlyle, *Travels* (*Works*, 24:300 [chap. 12]. For Goethe's final version of the *Wanderjahre*, the job of selection fell in fact partly to his secretary, Eckermann.
62 Carlyle, "Jean Paul Friedrich Richter" (*Works*, 26:12). For instance, in the *Leben des Quintus Fixlein*, the author-editor is "extracting [the biography of the hero] from fifteen boxes of notes," according to the subtitle.
63 Carlyle, *Works*, 1:123 (bk 2, chap. 6).
64 In her chapter on Weimar, de Staël praises it for being more "un grand château" than "une petite ville."
65 Goethe's journal of 1819–20, retrospectively for the period from 1780 to 1786 (*Goethes Werke*, 7:618).
66 Carlyle, *Works*, 24:189 (bk 8, chap. 10).
67 Kaplan, *Thomas Carlyle*, 130.
68 Letter to Goethe, 31 August 1830, in Carlyle, *Collected Letters*, 5:155; cf. *Sartor* (*Works*, 1:201–2 [bk 3, chap. 7]) – literature as religion, Goethe its prophet.
69 Carlyle, *Works*, 1:110 (bk 1, chap. 5).
70 Letter of 10 June 1831, in Carlyle, *Collected Letters*, 5:289.
71 See De Laura ("Heroic Egotism," 47–9), who also reads Tennyson's "glorious devil" of "The Palace of Art" as an allusion to Goethe and as representative of English suspicion of Goethe's *Bildungs* ideal.
72 *Goethes Werke*, 7:570 (bk 8, chap. 7); Carlyle, *Works*, 24:150.
73 Carlyle, *Works*, 1:78 (bk 1, chap. 2).

74 *Goethes Werke*, 9:478 (part 3, bk 11).

75 Second scene in the study. In *Faust, Part Two*, act 5, Sorge appears as a character before Faust. The phrase "encircled with Necessity" also echoes Novalis (Harrold, *Carlyle*, 65).

76 Carlyle, *Works*, 1:105 (bk 1, chap. 4).

77 Ibid., 1:127 (bk 2, chap. 6).

78 Ibid., 1:132 (bk 2, chap. 7).

79 *Goethes Werke*, 8:283 (bk 2).

80 Carlyle, *Works*, 1:156 (bk 2, chap. 9).

81 Ibid., 1:91 (bk 2, chap. 3).

82 "Israel in der Wüste" (*Goethes Werke*, 2:208).

83 10 October 1831, Carlyle, *Carlyle Reader*, 21.

84 Carlyle, *New Letters*, 2:189.

85 For instance, in *Dichtung und Wahrheit* Goethe defended *Werther* from criticism of its lack of didactic purpose by arguing that, although a good work of art will have moral consequences, it is wrong to expect a moral purpose from the artist (*Goethes Werke*, 9:590 [part 3, bk 13]; cf. 9:539 [part 3, bk 12]).

CHAPTER THREE

1 See Stevenson, *English Novel*, 226, 234; and Christensen, *Edward Bulwer-Lytton*, x. While Kathleen Tillotson ranked Bulwer as a minor novelist who followed the market in successive grooves (*Novels of the Eighteen-Forties*, 585), Stang gave him credit as a serious critic (*Theory of the Novel*), and Christensen reclaimed him as a dedicated and innovative artist (*Edward Bulwer-Lytton*).

2 Letter to Bulwer, 22 February 1868, in V.A. Lytton, *Life*, 2:446.

3 Carlyle, *Sartor*, bk 3, chap. 10.

4 23 February 1842, in Carlyle, *Collected Letters*, 14:48.

5 Bulwer-Lytton, *Pilgrims of the Rhine*, 89.

6 See Zipser, *Edward Bulwer-Lytton*, chap. 1. I can find no evidence for Susanne Howe's claim that Goethe told Müller (presumably Kanzler Friedrich von Müller) that Bulwer and Carlyle seemed to him the two most promising English authors (*Wilhelm Meister*, 177).

7 Lewald, *Meine Lebensgeschichte*, 195. "*Vormärz*" designates authors associated with the ideas leading up to the 1848 revolutions.

8 Possibly based on Mme de Staël's phrase *la patrie de la pensée* (the country of thought) for Prussia and its northern neighbours, in her preface to *De l'Allemagne* (Staël, *Germany*, xiv).

9 Bulwer-Lytton's preface to the 1845 edition of his *Night and Morning*, ix.

10 Jauss, "Literary History," 25.

11 E.R.B. Lytton, *Life*, 1:506.

12 Stang, *Theory of the Novel*, 11. Kathleen Tillotson puts the beginnings of serious novel criticism in the 1840s, without mention of Bulwer (*Novels of the Eighteen-Forties*, 16).

13 Bulwer-Lytton, "On Art in Fiction," 70, 66, 58.

14 Goethe's notebook of 1793, in *Goethes Werke*, 7:616.

15 Kathleen Tillotson makes no reference to Bulwer or the apprenticeship plot when she comments on the connection between the three-volume format prevalent from about 1830 and the three-part structure of many novels, "as clear as the three acts of a play" (*Novels of the Eighteen-Forties*, 222–3). John Sutherland, who considers Bulwer unfairly neglected, only treats his publishing innovation – novels in half-volume parts – which G.H. Lewes borrowed for *Middlemarch* (*Victorian Fiction*, chap. 5).

16 See King and Engel ("Emerging Carlylean Hero," 280) on Bulwer's transformation, in the course of his novels, of the "Romantic alien" into the Carlylean Romantic hero.

17 Masson, *British Novelists*, 231.

18 While expressing great admiration for other aspects of the novel, Bulwer wrote: "I put the merits of the construction out of the question – for here he seems to entertain a wilful contempt for the art" (undated letter to Forster, quoted in Flower, "Charles Dickens," 82).

19 Lettis, *Dickens on Literature*, 129.

20 See Sucksmith, *Narrative Art of Charles Dickens*, chap. 4. Sucksmith speculates that their discussions may even have prompted Bulwer's essays on the aesthetics of fiction (118).

21 Braun, *Disraeli the Novelist*, 76.

22 See, for instance, his diary entry for 6 May 1832, in Thackeray, *Selected Letters*, 21.

23 V.A. Lytton, *Life*, 1:528.

24 Bulwer-Lytton, *Alice* (Boston, 1893), vii–viii. All subsequent references are to the 1877 edition.

25 Bulwer-Lytton, *Ernest Maltravers*, 31 (bk 1, chap. 4).

26 Bulwer-Lytton, *Poems and Ballads of Schiller*, 13.

27 J.S. Mill praised *England and the English* in his *Autobiography* as "at that time greatly in advance of the public mind" (154).

28 Bulwer-Lytton, *Ernest Maltravers*, bk 8, chap. 2. The epigraph alludes to Florence Lascelles as the author of the secret tutelary letters to Ernest.

29 1840 preface (reprinted in Bulwer-Lytton, *Ernest Maltravers*, viii).

30 Bulwer-Lytton, *Ernest Maltravers*, 194 (bk 5, chap. 1).

31 For inventories of parallels see Zipser and Susanne Howe; Howe limits herself to the *Lehrjahre*.

32 Bulwer-Lytton, *Ernest Maltravers*, 96 (bk 2, chap. 3).

33 Ibid., 65 (bk 1, chap. 12), 71 (bk 1, chap. 14), and 101 (bk 2, chap. 4).

34 Ibid., 142 (bk 3, chap. 4), 201 (bk 5, chap. 4), 210 (bk 5, chap. 6).

35 An early version of *Wilhelm Meister* was *Wilhelm Meisters theatralische Sendung* (Wilhelm Meister's theatrical mission [1785]).

36 In the enthusiastic opinion of the publisher's reader, the poet and historian Henry Hart Milman, the novel, subtitled "A Psychological Auto-Biography" (Disraeli's own original title), was "very wild, very extravagant, very German, very powerful, very poetical" (introductory note to Disraeli, *Contarini Fleming*, vii).

37 Heine, *Deutschland: Ein Wintermärchen*, Kaput VII.

38 On this anomaly, see Craig, *Politik der Unpolitischen*, 144.

39 The addition of the political context was probably suggested to Bulwer by his two previous historical novels, *The Last Days of Pompeii* and *Rienzi* (King and Engel, "Emerging Carlylean Hero," 291).

40 After a rapid political career in England, which ends in an accidentally fatal duel, the hero, a "political Don Juan," escapes from his guilt and despair to the spas and petty principalities of Germany for the larger part of the novel.

41 Bulwer-Lytton, *Ernest Maltravers*, 199 (bk 5, chap. 3).

42 Bulwer-Lytton, *Alice*, 145–6 (bk 4, chap. 2).

43 King and Engel, in contrast, judge Bulwer's "[transformation of] his earlier prototypes of the [Byronic] romantic alien into the Carlylean romantic hero" as completely achieved by the end of the Regency period ("Emerging Carlylean Hero," 280).

44 Bulwer-Lytton, *Ernest Maltravers*, 34 (bk 1, chap. 5).

45 The difference between Bulwer and Goethe in this respect may partly be attributed to the difference between their own respective social rank. In both *Werther* and *Torquato Tasso* the socially inferior genius, true to the Sturm und Drang credo, is in conflict with the less gifted nobility.

46 *Goethes Werke*, 7:291 (bk 5, chap. 3). *Great Expectations*, which Dickens wrote during a period of sustained aesthetic debate with Bulwer, deals with a very different ambition, namely, for upper-class gentility, which is exposed as consisting of external attributes, in contrast to the education of the heart.

47 See, for instance, Bulwer-Lytton, *England and the English*.

48 Bulwer-Lytton, *Alice*, 268 (bk 6, chap. 5).

49 Ibid., 269 (bk 6, chap. 5).

50 *Goethes Werke*, 7:291 (bk 5, chap. 3).

51 Bulwer-Lytton, *Alice*, 353–4 (bk 9, chap. 3), 388 (bk 10, chap. 5).

52 Goethe, *Lehrjahre*, bk 7.

53 Goethe, "At the Well," *Faust, Part One*.

54 Bulwer-Lytton, *Ernest Maltravers*, 46 (bk 1, chap. 7).

55 Stang, *Theory of the Novel*, 153.

56 Bulwer-Lytton, "On Art in Fiction," 53.

57 Bulwer-Lytton, *Zanoni*, xiv.

58 Schiller, *Sämtliche Werke*, 5:755, 712.

59 Schiller's poem originated in the same year and context as the essay and the letter to Goethe cited above.

60 Carlyle thanked Bulwer on receiving a copy in his "own name and that of a multitude of others" for this rare "glowing, hearty and altogether vivid, sympathetic and poetic" biography (12 April 1844, in Carlyle, *Collected Letters*, 18:9).

61 Bulwer-Lytton, *Poems and Ballads of Schiller*, 70, 310.

62 See Morgan, *German Literature*, 101, and Schirmer, *Einfluss der deutschen Literatur*, 30–2.

63 King and Engel note the two English sources ("Emerging Carlylean Hero," 239).

64 Schiller, *Sämtliche Werke*, 5:694, 695, 702, 718.

65 Bulwer-Lytton, *Ernest Maltravers*, 181 (bk 4, chap. 8).

66 Bulwer-Lytton, *Alice*, 84 (bk 1, chap. 6).

67 Ibid., 436 (last chapter).

68 Ibid., bk 6, chap. 5.

69 15 April 1862, in V.A. Lytton, *Life*, 2:347–8.

70 Edwin M. Eigner argues that Bulwer did not understand the relevance of Goethe's interpolations to Wilhelm's *Bildung* ("*Pilgrims of the Rhine*," 20–1).

71 Bulwer-Lytton, *Alice*, 231 (bk 6, chap. 1).

72 Bulwer-Lytton, *Zanoni*, 210 (bk 3, chap. 18), 283 (bk 5, chap. 1).

73 Bulwer allegedly became a member of the Rosicrucian Lodge in Frankfurt/Main in 1840. See Zipser on the controversy (*Edward Bulwer-Lytton and Germany*, 22, 128).

74 I have not seen any critical mention of the Makarie story in connection with Bulwer. Zipser limits his discussion of Bulwer's occult novels to the question of his German Rosicrucian sources (*Edward Bulwer-Lytton and Germany*, chap. 4).

75 *Goethes Werke*, 8:126 (bk 1, chap. 10).

76 Bulwer-Lytton *Zanoni*, 408 (bk 7, chap. 14).

77 Letter to Forster, 3 October 1838, in V.A. Lytton, *Life*, 1:542.

78 Trollope, *Autobiography*, 250.

CHAPTER FOUR

1 Forster, *Aspects of the Novel*, 89. Woolf, "Novels of George Meredith," 231–2. On his changing reputation see, for instance, Horsman, *Victorian Novel*, chap. 10.

2 5 April 1906 and ? May 1905, in Meredith, *Letters*, 3:1556, 1523.

3 ? June 1904, in Meredith, *Letters*, 3:1503. For a more comprehensive
account of his familiarity with and response to German matters and his
use of German allusions in his fiction, see my study *German Elements*
(chaps. 7 and 8).

4 Petter, *George Meredith*, 18–20.

5 See Wilt, *Readable People of George Meredith*, 19.

6 Kafka's "Letter to His Father" (written in 1919) is one of the most affecting literary documents dealing with this conflict, and it can be read as a
quasi-*Bildungsroman*.

7 This theme has strong auto-biographical roots: like Harry Richmond,
Meredith grew up under the pressure of his father's spurious social
aspirations, and like Sir Austin with Richard but self-critically, he was an
anxious, dogmatic father to his son, Arthur, and an unforgiving betrayed
husband.

8 See Bakhtin, *Speech Genres*, 389.

9 Meredith, *Works*, 2:557–8 (chap. 45).

10 Sir Austin may partly be modelled on John Austin, the self-centred,
melancholic father of Meredith's friend Lucie Duff Gordon.

11 Meredith, *Works*, 2:321–2 (chap. 32).

12 Mitchell, "*Ordeal of Richard Feverel*," 88.

13 Unpublished letter of 1859, in the Yale University Library, quoted in
Kelvin, *Troubled Eden*, 8–9.

14 *Goethes Werke*, 7:520 (bk 8, chap. 3).

15 Meredith, *Works*, 2:345 (chap. 33).

16 Ibid., 2:35 (chap. 4), 228 (chap. 25), 102 (chap. 12), and 121–2 (chap. 15).

17 Nikki Lee Manos believes that "Meredith intended to write in *Richard
Feverel* ... a *Bildungsroman* counteracting the anti-*Bildung* tenets found in
Sartor Resartus" ("*Ordeal of Richard Feverel*," 19).

18 Sassoon, *Meredith*, 25.

19 Meredith, *Works*, 2:153 (chap. 19).

20 Ibid., 2:554 (chap. 45), 536 (chap. 44).

21 *Lehrjahre*, bk 8, chap. 5 (*Goethes Werke*, 7:547).

22 *Lehrjahre*, bk 8, chap. 5 (*Goethes Werke*, 7:550).

23 Meredith, *Works*, 2:523 (chap. 42).

24 James Stone argues Goethe's influence on Meredith's conception of
nature, but only with reference to the latter's poetry ("Meredith and
Goethe").

25 30 August 1883, in Meredith, *Letters*, 2:709.

26 Eckermann, *Gespräche mit Goethe*, 239.

27 Nikki Manos is mistaken when he relates Richard's return to nature and,
as he sees it, through that to true *Bildung* to the Abbé's valediction of
Wilhelm Meister after Wilhelm's receipt of his *Lehrbrief*, which Manos
renders, "nature has absolved you" ("*Ordeal of Richard Feverel*," 22). The

Abbé's words "die Natur hat dich losgesprochen" (*Lehrjahre*, bk 7, chap. 9 [*Goethes Werke*, 7:497]) mean "Nature has released you" – Carlyle has, correctly, "Nature has pronounced thee free" (*Works*, 24:77) – that is, from the indenture.

28 *Lehrjahre*, bk 7, chap. 2 (*Goethes Werke*, 7:427).

29 *Lehrjahre*, bk 8, chap. 1 (*Goethes Werke*, 7:498).

30 Disraeli, *Vivian Grey*, bk 8, chap. 1.

31 Meredith, *Works*, 10:350 (chap. 33).

32 Ibid., 2:1 (chap. 1), 10:517 (chap. 44).

33 Meredith, *Essay on Comedy*, 101–2.

34 *Lehrjahre*, bk 7, chap. 9 (*Goethes Werke*, 7:496); Meredith, *Works*, 10:576 (chap. 50), 9:298 (chap. 27), 10:385 (chap. 35). Göttingen was the university where Meredith's first literary mentor, Charnock, had earned a doctorate in philosophy.

35 Meredith, *Works*, 10:394 (chap. 36), 10:575 (chap. 50), 10:578 (chap. 50).

36 Disraeli, *Vivian Grey*, 325 (bk 6, chap. 3).

37 Meredith, *Works*, 9:312 (chap. 29).

38 25 October 1870 and 28 January 1868, in Meredith, *Letters*, 2:429–30, 368.

39 Beer, *Meredith*, 49.

40 *Lehrjahre*, bk 3, chap. 8 (*Goethes Werke*, 7:175).

41 Goethe, *Lehrjahre*, bk 1, chap. 8.

42 Carlyle, *Sartor*, bk 2, chap. 7.

43 This interpretation is to contradict Norman Kelvin (*Troubled Eden*, 82), for instance. Margaret Tarratt disagrees with Barbara Hardy's description of the novel as a typical *Bildungsroman*, and instead, she analyzes it as a more ambivalent interpretation of the "state of British society and the dilemma of the young Englishman looking for a field of relevant action" ("*Adventures of Harry Richmond*," 165–6).

44 18 June 1874, in Meredith, *Letters*, 1:485; Meredith, *Works*, 11:38–9 (chap. 4), 12:631 (chap. 56); Kettle, "Beauchamp's Career," 199. Norman Kelvin attributes Meredith's "gratuitous contempt" here to his wishing to protest against the insistence of his radical friends, particularly Maxse and Morley, that he write politically engaged fiction in advocacy of "the people" (*Troubled Eden*, 95).

45 Darwin, *On the Origin of Species*, 489–90. Kelvin distinguishes between Meredith's views on nature and on society: the first remained constant, namely, faith in a benevolent principle, which assimilated a spiritualized version of Darwin's theory of evolution; the second changed from enthusiasm for the 1848–49 revolutions to belief in liberal reform (*Troubled Eden*, 3–4). With respect to the first, Stone maintains, on the basis of Meredith's poetry, that because of his "[Goethean] faith in the goodness of the law of change" including death, "Malthusian and Darwinian proofs of waste in nature could have no effect on him" ("Meredith and Goethe," 160).

46 See Kettle on Meredith's relevant personal experiences, namely, his help with his friend Maxse's unsuccessful candidacy as a Radical eight years before the novel, in 1867, and his sympathy with the Paris Communards four years before it ("Beauchamp's Career," 188–9).

47 *Goethes Werke*, 8:459 (bk 3, chap. 18).

48 The hero of Somerset Maugham's *Bildungsroman*, *Of Human Bondage* (1915), also concludes his search for a vocation, which has taken him, like Wilhelm, to business and art, with the decision to settle down as a country doctor. He comments on his resolve with the unacknowledged quotation of Lothario in the *Lehrjahre*, repeated in *Sartor*, "America was here and now" (606 [chap. 122]).

49 20 September 1862, in Meredith, *Letters*, 1:160.

50 Beer, *Meredith*, 16.

51 Mitchell, "*Ordeal of Richard Feverel*," 69.

52 Smirlock sees this critique of the System as extended, as a major theme, to language itself, "its unavoidable tendency, and man's inescapable fate in using it, to construct self-referential systems with no explanatory power" ("Models of *Richard Feverel*," 100).

53 See Beer, *Meredith*, 59, and Kelvin, *Troubled Eden*, 74.

54 Meredith, *Works*, 10:346 (chap. 33). Gillian Beer observes that, in matching the style to the development of consciousness, Meredith is a precursor of Joyce in *A Portrait of the Artist as a Young Man* (*Meredith*, 53).

55 Beer, *Meredith*, 61.

56 Meredith, *Works*, 10:672 (chap. 56).

57 Ibid., 10:526 (chap. 45).

58 Sassoon, *Meredith*, 22–3.

59 Quoted by Tarratt in, "*Adventures of Harry Richmond*," 167; see also *Catalogue of the Altschul Collection of George Meredith in the Yale University Library*, compiled by Bertha Coolidge (New Haven, 1931), 90.

60 James, "*Daniel Deronda*," 111.

CHAPTER FIVE

1 *Goethes Werke*, 7:290–1; see chap. 1 above.

2 Eliot, *Middlemarch*, 112 (chap. 10).

3 Eliot, *Essays*, 213.

4 See, for instance, Haight, *George Eliot*, 342.

5 Its new motto, from Goethe's *Wanderjahre*, on the title page was her choice (Haight, *George Eliot*, 98): "Wahrheitsliebe zeigt sich darin, dass man überall das Gute zu finden und zu schätzen weiss [Love of truth is shown in finding and treasuring the good everywhere]." See "Betrachtungen im Sinne der Wanderer" (*Goethes Werke*, 8:292; bk 2).

6 Eliot, *Essays*, 222–3. For an overview of her familiarity with German letters, see Argyle, *German Elements*, chap. 2.

7 "Middlemarch," *Academy* 4 (1 January 1873), reprinted in Haight, ed., *Century of George Eliot Criticism*, 74.

8 See George Eliot's reference to Mill on this ideal in "The Modern Hep! Hep! Hep!" 164.

9 Eliot, *Middlemarch*, 894 (Finale).

10 See also Hans Ulrich Seeber's study of "cultural synthesis" in *Middlemarch*.

11 See, for instance, Roazen, "*Middlemarch* and the Wordsworthian Imagination."

12 George Eliot's change of sentiment was typical at the time. She informed her Munich friend Frau Siebold in 1871, when she was helping with the war relief: "I think you misconceive the state of English minds generally at the opening of the War. So far as our observation went, English sympathy was mainly on the German side. It was not till after the battle of Sedan, that there was any widely-spread feeling on behalf of the French" (? June 1871, in *George Eliot Letters*, 5:159).

13 On this topic see particularly Barrett, *Vocation and Desire*; Beer, *George Eliot*; and Edwards, *Psyche as Hero*. Alan Mintz, in his study of vocation based on Weber (*George Eliot*), does not consider the German context, the concept of *Bildung*, or the genre of the *Bildungsroman*.

14 Brontë, *Jane Eyre*, 141 (chap. 12).

15 Eliot, *Middlemarch*, 25 (Prelude), 173 (chap. 15).

16 *George Eliot Letters*, 4:458 n. See also McCobb, "Of Women and Doctors." For a synopsis of von Hillern's novel, see chapter 7 below.

17 For von Hillern, see Walshe, "Life and Works"; for von Hahn-Hahn, see Morgan, *German Literature*, 91, and Schirmer, *Einfluss der deutschen Literatur*, 136, 154.

18 Eliot, *Essays*, 146–7.

19 The name alludes to the purely intellectual immortalist in Bulwer-Lytton's novel *Zanoni*.

20 Lewes, *Life and Works of Goethe*, 2:212. This work (1855), which he dedicated to his mentor in German matters, Carlyle, was the first complete biography of Goethe in any language; it was an immediate success at home and abroad, the German translation of 1857 going through many editions, and it is still considered useful.

21 Carlyle, *Works*, 23:6.

22 Lewes, *Life of Goethe*, 2:212.

23 Eliot, *Middlemarch*, 25 (Prelude).

24 Ibid., 896 (Finale).

25 The major female characters in *Wilhelm Meister*, while functioning in the conventional female spheres, enjoy a scope for their individual talents

which is defined only by their own dispositions, whether it is in love and pleasure, as for the actress Philine, in estate management, as for Therese, or in mystical knowledge, as for Makarie.

26 Eliot, *Essays*, 205.

27 Eliot, *Middlemarch*, 89 (chap. 7), 112 (chap. 10).

28 Ibid., 30 (chap. 1).

29 I disagree with critics who read the narrator as unambiguously undercutting Dorothea's longing (see, for instance, Edwards, *Psyche as Hero*, 93). In these instances the narrator speaks partly with a Middlemarch voice, as it were in indirect style; that is, with implied authorial criticism of the Middlemarch mentality.

30 Eliot, *Mill on the Floss*, 379 (bk 4, chap. 3). See also *Middlemarch*, 51 (chap. 3).

31 David Carroll reads all her novels as thematizing hermeneutics, growing out of her German work: "life at all levels is envisaged as a never-ending interpretative quest to fit together idea and experience, part and whole, into ever-larger units" (*George Eliot*, 35).

32 Eliot, *Middlemarch*, 846 (chap. 80).

33 Ibid., 849 (chap. 81). *Faust, Part Two*, act 1 (*Goethes Werke*, 3:148).

34 Eliot, *Middlemarch*, 594 (chap. 55). See Faust's project in *Faust, Part Two*, act 5. Note also Ernest Maltravers's resorting, when brighter ideals fail, to the improvement of his estate (chap. 3 above).

35 Eliot, *Middlemarch*, 896 (Finale).

36 Starting with Henry James, who found his character "insubstantial," the author's "eminent failure," in an 1873 review ("George Eliot's *Middlemarch*," 83), to Barbara Hardy, who found him more sensitive than sensual and therefore an "inadequate rescuer" (*Particularities*, 31), to Richard Ellmann's biographical explanation: middle-aged "johnnycrossism" ("Dorothea's Husbands," 80). In contrast, Dorothea Barrett argues that his inadequacy is intended (*Vocation and Desire*, 130). Hans Ulrich Seeber judges him positively from the German Romantic context ("Cultural Synthesis," 29–31).

37 Seeber, "Cultural Synthesis," 29.

38 Eliot, *Middlemarch*, 427 (chap. 39).

39 Ibid., chaps. 51, 71.

40 Ibid., 241, 237 (chap. 21).

41 *Culture and Anarchy* was published serially in the *Cornhill* in 1867 and 1868 and as a book under the new title in 1869. On its reception and influence, see Collini, *Arnold*, chap. 1. Barbara Hardy cautiously "suspects" in a note that "George Eliot's use of art to express social value owes much … to *Culture and Anarchy*" (*Particularities*, 33n).

42 Arnold, *Complete Prose Works*, 5:94.

43 See Baldick, "Matthew Arnold's Innocent Language," 33.

44 Arnold, *Complete Prose Works*, 3:380.

45 "The State of German Literature" (*Carlyle, Works*, 26:68). See also the introductory essay on Goethe for *Wilhelm Meister's Travels*, initially in *German Romance* ([1827] *Works*, 23:22n1). In a letter to Goethe, Carlyle explained that in England Philistines were called Utilitarians (Carlyle, *Correspondence between Goethe and Carlyle*, 173).

46 Goethe, *Leiden des jungen Werthers* (1774), bk 1, 26 May).

47 *Goethes Werke* (Sophien-Ausgabe), 5.1:235, 240.

48 Arnold, *Complete Prose Works*, 5:146.

49 See Habermas, "Heinrich Heine."

50 On Meredith's admiration for Heine's journalism and poetry, see Argyle, *German Elements*, 154–9.

51 See "Reise von München nach Genua," *Reisebilder III: Italien* (Heine, *Sämtliche Werke*, 7.1:74 [chap. 31]). In this instance, writing in 1828–29, Heine was actually speaking of political liberation and the fight for democracy.

52 Arnold, *Complete Prose Works*, 3:108, 11.

53 *Fortnightly Review* 8 (November 1867): 603.

54 *George Eliot Letters*, 4:395.

55 Arnold, *Complete Prose Works*, 5:140.

56 Eliot, *Middlemarch*, 730 (chap. 67).

57 Knoepflmacher, *Religious Humanism*, 79.

58 See Riehl, *Bürgerliche Gesellschaft*, 218 (bk I.i, chap. 2).

59 Eliot, *Essays*, 296–7.

60 *Sprüche*, no. 112 (*Goethes Werke*, 1:322); slightly misquoted.

61 Eliot, *Middlemarch*, chap. 16.

62 Carroll sees Ladislaw as George Eliot's self-conscious experiment in a new kind of character who "represents a significant response to a decentered world – open-minded, receptive, *ad hoc*, ungrounded, … He is the anomaly which tests all the accepted Middlemarch paradigms" (*George Eliot*, 247–8).

63 Eliot, *Middlemarch*, 474 (chap. 43), 106 (chap. 9), 393 (chap. 37), 414 (chap. 38).

64 Ibid., 106–8 (chap. 9).

65 Ibid., 109–10 (chap. 10), 501 (chap. 46).

66 Ibid., 51 (chap. 3).

67 Painting is also the vocation of Bulwer's apprentice in *Zanoni*, who pursues it in Italy (see chap. 3 above), and of the heroes of the German Romantic *Künstlerromane* (see note 68). The *Bildungsroman* hero of Somerset Maugham's novel *Of Human Bondage* tries it in Paris as one of several attempted vocations.

68 Tieck's *Franz Sternbalds Wanderungen* (1798) and Wackenroder's *Herzensergiessungen eines kunstliebenden Klosterbruders* (1796; edited by Tieck).

69 Heine, *Sämtliche Werke*, 8.1:139 (bk 1).

70 Eliot, *Middlemarch*, 219 (chap. 19). One of the painters was Ford Madox Brown, who on his return to England was connected with the English Pre-Raphaelites.

71 Bell, *Victorian Artists*, 15–16, Andrews, *Nazarenes*, 34.

72 Hugh Witemeyer (*George Eliot and the Visual Arts*) stresses the negative aspects, relating Naumann's practice of an "outmoded convention" to Casaubon's obsolete scholarship. However, the return to pre-Raphaelite models gave an important new impulse of naturalism to nineteenth-century painting.

73 Eliot, *Middlemarch*, 247 (chap. 22).

74 Ibid., 252 (chap. 22).

75 Ibid., 25.

76 Ibid., 221 (chap. 19).

77 However, Heine later reversed his judgment, giving the Jews – "powerful, unbending men" – precedence over the Greeks – "beautiful youths only" (*Geständnisse* [1853–54], *Sämtliche Werke*, 15:41).

78 Arnold, *Complete Prose Works*, 5:165.

79 Coleridge had caricatured Fichte's "crude *Egoismus*" in the *Biographia Literaria*: "I, you and he, and he, you and I, / All souls and all bodies are I itself I!" (86n [chap. 9]).

80 Eliot, *Middlemarch*, 221 (chap. 19).

81 Ibid., 220 (chap. 19). The play is Schiller's translation, for the Weimar theatre, from Picard. Most collected works do not include the play, but it is in *Schillers sämtliche Werke*, 12 vols. (Stuttgart: Cotta, 1838), vol. 7.

82 Eliot, *Middlemarch*, 501 (chap. 46).

83 Ibid., 394 (chap. 37).

84 See Espinasse, *Literary Recollections*, 282. In a letter George Eliot introduced Lewes as "a person of the readiest, most facile intercourse, … a very airy, bright, versatile creature – not at all a formidable personage" (quoted in Haight, *George Eliot*, 332).

85 Eliot, *Essays*, 233.

86 Ibid., 234.

87 Ibid., 294, 297. Riehl, *Bürgerliche Gesellschaft*, 291. George Eliot used and annotated the third edition, that of 1856 (McCobb, *George Eliot's Knowledge*, 139).

88 Riehl, *Bürgerliche Gesellschaft*, 305–7, 329. It is interesting to note, with respect to *Daniel Deronda* and George Eliot's sentiments, that in his animus Riehl goes on to define this type of the "negating" writer as "Jewish par excellence," in mentality if not in religion or even lineage (329). Bernard Semmel discusses George Eliot's selective use of Riehl and his changed reputation in Germany (*George Eliot*, 50–3).

89 T.W. Heyck finds this moderation typical of English Victorian intellectuals (*Transformation of Intellectual Life*, 19).

90 Eliot, *Essays*, 298. Riehl, *Bürgerliche Gesellschaft*, 296–7.

91 Eliot, *Middlemarch*, 406 (chap. 37), 877 (chap. 84), 502 (chap. 46).

92 Ibid., 427 (chap. 39).

93 Ibid., 894 (Finale).

94 Ibid., 240 (chap. 21).

95 Eliot, *Essays*, 36.

96 Eliot, *Middlemarch*, 254 (chap. 22).

97 Eliot, *Essays*, 39. See also her story of the scholar Merman in *Impressions
of Theophrastus Such*, chap. 3.

98 Eliot, *Middlemarch*, 297 (chap. 27).

99 George, *Eliot Letters*, 2:226.

100 Eliot, *Essays*, 389.

101 Goethe, *Wilhelm Meisters Wanderjahre*, bk 3, chaps. 3, 18.

102 Lewes, *Life of Goethe*, 351, 341–2. In the 1850s and 1860s Lewes found, for
his own scientific studies, helpful demonstrations in the newest developments in physiology and neurology at the universities of Berlin, Munich,
Bonn, and Heidelberg (*George Eliot Letters*, 4:416). For a modern account
of Goethe's science and the course of its reputation, see Amrine,
"Goethe's Science."

103 Eliot, *Middlemarch*, 382 (chap. 36).

104 Matthias Jakob Schleiden and Theodor Schwann are generally considered the founders of the cell theory, which they first published in 1833
(Weisz, *Science of Biology*, 82).

105 Eliot, *Middlemarch*, 383 (chap. 36).

106 Ibid., 179 (chap. 15).

107 Eliot, *Essays*, 93. For a modern response, see Walter Benjamin, "Weimar III,"
Denkbilder, 354–5.

108 Eliot, *Middlemarch*, 892 (Finale).

109 Ibid., 203–4 (chap. 17).

CHAPTER SIX

1 James, *Literary Reviews*, 190.

2 James, "Homburg Reformed," 354–7.

3 4 October 1872, *George Eliot Letters*, 5:314.

4 G.H. Lewes's diary (McCobb, *George Eliot's Knowledge*, 213). George Eliot
read the second edition of 1850.

5 Reynolds, *Victorian Painting*, 58.

6 See Argyle, "George Eliot's *Daniel Deronda*." Witemeyer, in *George Eliot
and the Visual Arts*, does not mention Frith's painting. It is now owned by

the Rhode Island School of Design; for a colour reproduction, see Reynolds, *Victorian Painting*, 49.

7 Eliot, *Daniel Deronda*, 298 (chap. 23).

8 Ibid., 36 (chap. 1).

9 *Goethes Werke*, 3:17–18.

10 End of the "Prelude in the Theatre," *Faust, Part One* (*Goethes Werke*, 3:15).

11 Eliot, *Daniel Deronda*, 38 (chap. 1). For a study of parallels with *Faust* and also with *Wilhelm Meister*, see also Röder-Bolton, *George Eliot and Goethe*.

12 Ibid., 75 (chap. 5); *Goethes Werke*, 3:71.

13 Eliot, *Daniel Deronda*, 658 (chap. 148).

14 "Outside the City Gate," *Faust, Part One* (*Goethes Werke*, 3:41).

15 Eliot, *Daniel Deronda*, 831 (chap. 64).

16 For instance, Heller, "Jews and Women in George Eliot's *Daniel Deronda*," 88–95.

17 Eliot, *Essays*, 103.

18 *Neue Zeitschrift für Musik*, 16 June 1854. George Eliot possibly read Liszt's article in Adolf Stahr's book *Weimar und Jena* ([1852]; see McCobb, *George Eliot's Knowledge*, 213).

19 Eliot, *Essays*, 103.

20 Lewes's Journal, 2 October 1854, quoted in Eliot, *Essays*, 102n.

21 29 March 1870, in *George Eliot Letters*, 5:85.

22 Eliot, *Essays*, 97.

23 See McCobb, "Morality of Musical Genius," 323–5.

24 Eliot, *Daniel Deronda*, 79 (chap. 5).

25 Ibid., 77 (chap. 5).

26 Rubinstein, who like Klesmer was born "on the outskirts of Bohemia," had been introduced to the Leweses by Liszt in Weimar, and they met him again in London (Haight, *George Eliot*, 156, 490). Delia da Sousa Correa adds E.T.A. Hoffmann's fictional Kapellmeister Johann Kreisler to Klesmer's "pedigree" ("George Eliot," 105).

27 Eliot, *Daniel Deronda*, 284 (chap. 22).

28 Ibid., 401 (chap. 37). According to Rosemary Ashton, of the German exile community in London after 1848, "those who were not language teachers were invariably teachers of music or art" (*Little Germany*, 21). Wagner had found refuge in Zürich.

29 Eliot, *Daniel Deronda*, 78 (chap. 5).

30 Ibid., 307 (chap. 23).

31 Sheppard, *Charles Auchester*, 1:134 (chap. 17).

32 Ibid., 1:304 (chap. 31). There are additional parallels with *Daniel Deronda*, such as between the Auchester family and the Meyricks, between Laura's exploitative father and Mirah's father, and between Clara's vocation and marriage and Mirah's vocation and marriage.

33 George Eliot had herself mesmerized in 1844 (letter by Mrs Bray, 28 July 1844, in *George Eliot Letters*, 1:180).

34 Eliot, *Daniel Deronda*, 76 (chap. 5).

35 Ibid., 541 (chap. 39).

36 Ibid., 542 (chap. 39). "Vor den Wissenden sich stellen, / Sicher ist's in allen Fällen! [To present oneself to the expert, brings certainty in all cases!]"; from the *West-östlicher Divan* (*Goethes Werke*, 2:39–40).

37 Eliot, *Daniel Deronda*, 284 (chap. 22).

38 Ibid., 812 (chap. 63); Heine, "Geständnisse" ([1854] *Sämtliche Werke*, 15:41). George Eliot read the work in Berlin in 1854.

39 Eliot, *Essays*, 289.

40 5 August [1849], in *George Eliot Letters*, 1:293.

41 Eliot, *Impressions of Theophrastus Such*, 172–3.

42 Eliot, *Daniel Deronda*, 462 (chap. 35).

43 Disraeli, *Sybil*, bk 2, chap. 4.

44 Eliot, *Impressions of Theophrastus Such*, 173, 187, 190.

45 Eliot, *Daniel Deronda*, 284 (chap. 22).

46 Eliot, *Essays*, 288.

47 On George Eliot's selective use of Riehl, see chap. 5 above.

48 Eliot, *Daniel Deronda*, 213, 220 (chap. 16), 413 (chap. 32).

49 There is some resemblance with Bulwer's Alice (see chap. 3 above).

50 Goethe, *Lehrjahre*, bk 8, chap. 2.

51 *Goethes Werke*, 8:81–3 (bk 1, chap. 7).

52 Eliot, *Daniel Deronda*, 214 (chap. 16).

53 Ibid., 413 (chap. 32).

54 Eliot, *Essays*, 298; Riehl, *Bürgerliche Gesellschaft*, 297.

55 See also Bernard Semmel's study of George Eliot's quasi-Burkean politics and its German sources, including Riehl and Herder, in *George Eliot*.

56 Eliot, *Daniel Deronda*, 724 (chap. 53), 592 (chap. 42), 570–1 (chap. 41).

57 See Shaffer's chapter on *Daniel Deronda* in "*Kubla Khan*," which focuses on the joining of East and West and on the originary character of Judaism. See also Knoepflmacher, *Religious Humanism*, and McCobb, *George Eliot's Knowledge*, for Eliot's German reading.

58 See Dockhorn, *Deutsche Historismus in England*, chap. 4.

59 Preface by Strauss to the first German edition (Eliot, trans., *Life of Jesus*, xxix).

60 *Macmillan's* 10 (October 1846): 433.

61 *Fortnightly* 8 (July 1867): 96.

62 Eliot, trans., *Essence of Christianity*, 271; Feuerbach, *Wesen des Christentums*, 444.

63 18 January 1854, in *George Eliot Letters*, 2:137.

64 5 August 1854, quoted in *George Eliot Letters*, 2:173n.

65 Eliot, *Essays*, 188.
66 Eliot, *Daniel Deronda*, 628 (chap. 46), 553 (chap. 40).
67 Ibid., 383 (chap. 29).
68 Ibid., 878 (chap. 69).
69 Goethe, *Lehrjahre*, bk 6; *Wanderjahre*, bk 1, chap. 10.
70 Eliot, *Daniel Deronda*, 705 (chap. 52). For studies of the specifically Jewish context of *Daniel Deronda*, see Rosenberg, *From Shylock to Svengali*, and Baker, *George Eliot and Judaisn*.
71 Eliot, *Daniel Deronda*, 549 (chap. 40), 792 (chap. 60).
72 Disraeli, *Coningsby*, chap. 2. In 1848 George Eliot dismissed Disraeli's claims, on behalf of Sidonia, for the superiority of the Jews on account of their "unmixed race" (chap. 10): "everything specifically Jewish is of a low grade" (11 February 1848, in *George Eliot Letters*, 1:247).
73 Haight, *George Eliot*, 470. On proto-Zionism in *Daniel Deronda*, see Meyer, " 'Safely to Their Own Borders,' " 747–50.
74 Eliot, *Essays*, 190–2. William Baker argues that Mordecai's proto-Zionist proposals were by no means fantastic, since they were related to actual plans and measures of the Jewish Diaspora, the British government, and the Palestine Jewish community (*George Eliot and Judaism*, 134).
75 Eliot, *Daniel Deronda*, 557 (chap. 40), 529–30 (chap. 38).
76 Ibid., chap. 32.
77 Part 1, bk 4 (*Goethes Werke*, 9:149–50).
78 Lewes, *Life of Goethe*, 1:30.
79 Baker, *George Eliot and Judaism*, 145.
80 Eliot, *Daniel Deronda*, 790 (chap. 60).
81 Ibid., 575 (chap. 42).
82 Brod, *Heinrich Heine*, 133.
83 Sammons, *Heinrich Heine*, 91.
84 Haight, *George Eliot*, 193. Haight misquotes Heine's title.
85 Jacobs, "Mordecai," 36.
86 Brod, *Heinrich Heine*, 120. See also Kuschel, "Critical Spirit."
87 Heine, "Hebräische Melodien," *Romanzero*, bk 3 (*Sämtliche Werke*, 3.1:125–9).
88 Eliot, *Daniel Deronda*, 447 (chap. 34).
89 Heine, "Italien," II, "Die Bäder von Lukka," chap. 9, *Reisebilder III* (*Sämtliche Werke*, 7.1:117).
90 Arnold, *Complete Prose Works*, 3:127–8.
91 Heine, "Lamentazionen," *Romanzero*, bk 2 (*Sämtliche Werke*, 3.1:78).
92 Eliot, *Daniel Deronda*, 555 (chap. 40).
93 Ibid., 746 (chap. 54).
94 Eliot, *Essays*, 105.
95 Eliot, *Daniel Deronda*, 286 (chap. 22); from Heine, *Buch der Lieder*, XLIV (*Sämtliche Werke*, 1.1:177).

96 Eliot, *Daniel Deronda*, 76 (chap. 5).

97 Ibid., 289–90 (chap. 22).

98 *Torquato Tasso* 5.5.3430–1 (*Goethes Werke*, 5:166).

99 Eliot, *Daniel Deronda*, 669 (chap. 48).

100 David Carroll reads the rivalry between Deronda and Grandcourt for Gwendolen as a struggle for the soul of England (*George Eliot*, 297).

101 See Feltes, *Modes of Production*, 36–56.

10 Most famously, Henry James and Leslie Stephen.

103 See, for instance, Beer, *George Eliot*; Barrett, *Vocation and Desire*; and Pritchett, "Poetics and Narrative."

104 Eliot, *Daniel Deronda*, 567–8 (chap. 41).

105 James, "*Daniel Deronda*," 101.

106 Eliot, *Essays*, 296–7.

107 Shaffer, "*Kubla Khan*," 250.

108 See George Eliot's journal, 2 December 1870, in *George Eliot Letters*, 5:124. Shaffer calls the neglect of *Wilhelm Meister* and of its influence on the English novel a scandal ("*Kubla Khan*," 12, 248). For the complex *Romantik/Roman* (Romanticism/the novel), see, for instance, Novalis, "Aus dem 'Allgemeinen Brouillon,'"no. 24.

CHAPTER SEVEN

1 The title of this chapter was suggested by a phrase of Henry P. Liddon, vice-principal of St Edmund's Hall, Oxford, where he lectured on the New Testament, and later canon of St Paul's, who used to refer to "German infidel" knowledge (quoted in Ward, *Writer's Recollections*, 220).

2 Eliot, *Essays*, 310.

3 Eliot, *Adam Bede*, 226 (chap. 17).

4 Eliot, *Middlemarch*, 50 (chap. 3).

5 Arnold, *Complete Prose Works*, 6:175.

6 For the case of personal development, see Turner, "Victorian Crisis of Faith," 11; for legitimation and professionalization see Moore, "Theodicy and Society," 153, and von Arx, "Victorian Crisis of Faith," 265.

7 Gosse, *Father and Son*, 34 (preface), 35 (chap. 1).

8 Ibid., 103.

9 See Haines, *Essays on German Influence*, 55–67.

10 Chadwick, *Secularization of the European Mind*, 165–70.

11 Quoted ibid., 166.

12 Turgenev, *Fathers and Sons*, chap. 10.

13 Chadwick, *Secularization of the European Mind*, 168. Most notorious was Feuerbach's pun that man is what he eats: "Der Mensch ist was er isst" (quoted in Reardon, *Religious Thought*, 82).

14 Maison, *Victorian Vision*, 215; the author is named as C——, MA.

15 This early historicism is not to be confused with the relativistic historicism originating with Dilthey in the late nineteenth century.

16 For a source of this summary, see Dockhorn, *Deutsche Historismus in England*, 11, 15, 26.

17 Letter to J.L. Hoskyns, 22 September 1839, in Stanley, *Life and Correspondence*, 2:153.

18 See W.R. Ward, "Faith and Fallacy," 48–53. On the irreligiosity of the Romantics, see Schenk, *Mind of the European Romantics*, 66–77.

19 Meredith, *Works*, 2:30 (chap. 34).

20 Trollope, *Barchester Towers*, 90 (vol. 1, chap. 11).

21 Quoted in Mander, *Our German Cousins*, 64.

22 Verheyden, introduction to *Life of Jesus*, xxix.

23 Mackay, *Tübingen School*, 16, 196. A review of Mackay's *Progress of the Intellect* was George Eliot's first contribution to the *Westminster Review*, in 1851.

24 Horton Harris emphatically characterizes the Tübingen school as "the most important theological event in the whole history of theology from the Reformation to the present day" (*Tübingen School*, v).

25 For an overview, see Reardon, *Religious Thought*.

26 Kingsley, *Alton Locke*, 348 (chap. 38), 278 (chap. 30).

27 Butler, *Way of All Flesh*, 15 (chap. 47).

28 Jowett, "On the Interpretation of Scripture," 377.

29 Rowland Williams on Bunsen in "Bunsen's Biblical Researches," 93.

30 Jowett, "On the Interpretation of Scripture," 372.

31 Arnold, *Complete Prose Works*, 6:157–8.

32 Renan, *Life of Jesus*, 28 (author's introduction).

33 Ibid., 388, 392 (chap. 28).

34 Taine, *Notes on England*, 192.

35 Note, in *Wilhelm Meisters Lehrjahre*, the philosophical conversations on geology connected with Jarno/Montan and on astronomy connected with Makarie.

36 For more general studies of crisis-of-faith novels, see Maison, *Victorian Vision*, and Wolff, *Gains and Losses*.

37 Ward, *Robert Elsmere*, 37–8 (bk 1, chap. 3).

38 Ashton, "Doubting Clerics," 75.

39 Cockshut, *Unbelievers*, 117. Cockshut considers the novel unjustly neglected.

40 Froude, *Nemesis of Faith*, 18–19, 51.

41 Ward, *Writer's Recollections*, 107.

42 Newman, *Newman: Prose and Poetry*, 123 (chap. 3).

43 Froude, *Nemesis of Faith*, 144, 35, 156, and 96.

44 11 March 1832, in Eckermann, *Gespräche mit Goethe*, 614.

45 Froude, *Nemesis of Faith*, iii.

46 First English translation, from the French, in 1779; from the original, in 1786.

47 *Werther* I, 18 August (*Goethes Werke*, 6:52–3).

48 Froude, *Nemesis of Faith*, 37, 81, 3.

49 Ibid., 98.

50 Ibid., 180.

51 Ashton, introduction to Froude, *Nemesis of Faith*, 29. Carlyle had ignored this novel of Goethe's.

52 Goethe, *Wahlverwandtschaften*, part 1, chap. 12.

53 Ibid., part 2, chap. 13.

54 Quoted in Ashton, Introduction to Froude, *Nemesis of Faith*, 31.

55 *Wahlverwandtschaften*, part 2, chap. 18.

56 Froude, *Nemesis of Faith*, 181.

57 "Am Brunnen" (Part 1, "At the Well"), *Faust, Erster Teil* (*Goethes Werke*, 3:114).

58 Rutherford, *Autobiography*, v.

59 Rutherford, *Deliverance*, 224–5 (chap. 5).

60 Rutherford, *Autobiography*, 12–13, 17, 19 (chap. 2).

61 Ibid., 79 (chap. 6).

62 Ibid., 124 (chap. 9).

63 The friend's name, M'Kay, is reminiscent of Alton Locke's mentor, the bookseller Sandy Mackaye.

64 Rutherford, *Deliverance*, 27–8 (chap. 6), 269 (chap. 9).

65 Ibid., 231 (chap. 6), 253 (chap. 8).

66 Ward, *Writer's Recollections*, 183.

67 Morley, *On Compromise*, 169, 177 (chap. 4). *On Compromise* was first serialized in the *Fortnightly Review*.

68 See Jay, "Doubt and the Victorian Woman," 88.

69 Yonge, *Clever Woman*, 2:151 (vol. 2, chap. 9).

70 Ibid., 2:160 (vol. 2, chap. 9).

71 Ibid., 2:268 (vol. 2, chap. 14).

72 Ibid., 2:191 (vol. 2, chap. 10).

73 Ward, *Writer's Recollections*, 232.

74 Von Hillern, *Arzt der Seele*, 2:168 (vol. 4, chap. 5). The original puns on "Weib," which means both "woman" and "wife."

75 E.A. McCobb, in "Of Women and Doctors," stresses the contrast between von Hillern's endorsement and Eliot's ironic questioning of gender roles.

76 See Collie, *Alien Art*, 26.

77 8 June 1880, in Gissing, *Collected Letters*, 1:281–2.

78 Morley, *On Compromise*, 165.

79 Gissing, *Workers in the Dawn*, 1:52 (vol. 1, chap. 3).

80 Gissing specifies "the popular edition," that is, Strauss's popularizing version of 1864.

81 Gissing, *Workers in the Dawn*, 1:301–2 (vol. 1, chap. 13).
82 See Collie, *George Gissing*, 41. For a discussion of their friendship in a German context, see Argyle, *German Elements*, 90–9.
83 Gissing, *Workers in the Dawn*, 1:327 (vol. 1, chap. 14).
84 See Willey, *Nineteenth-Century Studies*, 221.
85 Gissing, *Workers in the Dawn*, 3:413 (vol. 3, chap. 15).
86 Ward, *Writer's Recollections*, 168.
87 Lightman stresses the fact that this is only one of several types of nineteenth-century religious crises ("*Robert Elsmere* and Agnostic Crises of Faith," 292).
88 Ward, *Writer's Recollections*, 232. See also Melnyk, ed., *Women's Theology*.
89 Wilde, "The Decay of Lying," in *Intentions*, 16.
90 Sutherland, *Mrs. Humphry Ward*, 126.
91 *Nineteenth Century*, May 1888.
92 Elizabeth Gaskell, in *North and South* (1854–55), also treats sympathetically the familial dislocation, moral and social as well as physical, typically caused by a clergyman's doubts about the authority of the church. For a general discussion of the gender issue, see Turner, "Victorian Crisis of Faith," 32.
93 Ward, *Robert Elsmere*, 196 (bk 2, chap. 14).
94 John Updike, in his recent novel *In the Beauty of the Lilies* (1996), attributes the loss of faith of the first protagonist, a Presbyterian minister in Paterson, New Jersey, in 1910 to largely the same canon of German books, similarly shown in the minister's library.
95 Ward, *Writer's Recollections*, 111, 105.
96 Ward, *Robert Elsmere*, 254 (bk 3, chap. 19).
97 However, politically on the bourgeois left, Mommsen was an opponent of Bismarck's politics.
98 "Studierzimmer" (Part 1, "Study"), *Faust, Erster Teil* (*Goethes Werke*, 3:47).
99 Ward, *Robert Elsmere*, 364 (bk 4, chap. 28); "Marthas Garten" (Part 1, "Martha's Garden"), *Faust, Erster Teil* (*Goethes Werke*, 3:109).
100 Ward, *Robert Elsmere*, 380 (bk 4, chap. 30).
101 Ibid., 507 (bk 6, chap. 41).
102 Ward, *Writer's Recollections*, 163.
103 Ward, *Robert Elsmere*, 342 (bk 4, chap. 26).
104 See Ashton, "Doubting Clerics," 79.
105 Ward, *Robert Elsmere*, bk 6, chap. 43.
106 Arnold, *Complete Prose Works*, 6:175. Later in her life Ward relaxed her opposition to the established church, and she thought, like Arnold, that theological reform should occur from within it (*Writer's Recollections*, 236).
107 Arnold, *Complete Prose Works*, 6:407.
108 Ward, *Robert Elsmere*, 72 (bk 1, chap. 6).
109 Ibid., 89 (bk 1, chap. 7), 83 (bk 1, chap. 6).

110 Ibid., 54 (bk 1, chap. 5), 52 (bk 1, chap. 5).
111 Ward, preface to the sixth edition of *The History of David Grieve*, reprinted in the ninth, xiv.

CHAPTER EIGHT

1 Hardy's notebooks show no familiarity with Schopenhauer at this date (Millgate, *Thomas Hardy*, 199).
2 For a reproduction of this caricature, see Riewald, *Beerbohm's Literary Caricatures*, no. 24.
3 Michael Hamburger defines Nietzsche as a critic of culture in the tradition of Arnold's *Culture and Anarchy* (*Reason and Energy*, 228). For fuller accounts of the reception of Schopenhauer, see Argyle, *German Elements*, chap. 4; on the reception of Nietzsche, see Thatcher, *Nietzsche in England*.
4 Schopenhauer, "Ueber die Universitäts-Philosophie" (On philosophy at the universities), in *Parerga*, 1:166 (Payne, *Parerga*, 1:154).
5 *Westminster Review* 59 (April 1853): 388–407.
6 Darwin quotes Schopenhauer on women's selection of a mate from an article on "Schopenhauer and Darwinism" in the *Journal of Anthropology* of 1871 (*Descent of Man*, 669 [chap. 20]).
7 Gosse, "The Limits of Realism in Fiction," 149. Gosse is discussing the naturalist novel and its narrator, who is an anatomist rather than a moralist. The epigraph, in German, is "Der Glaube ist wie die Liebe; er laesst sich nicht erzwingen [Faith is like love; it won't be compelled]"; from Schopenhauer, "Ueber Religion," in *Parerga*, 2:420 (Payne, *Parerga*, 2:391).
8 Laing, *Modern Science and Modern Thought*, 228–30. Nietzsche answered his own question as to whether Schopenhauer's pessimism was necessarily a German philosophy in the negative, given the Hegelian "delay" of atheism. See *Fröhliche Wissenschaft*, no. 357 (*Nietzsche Werke*, 5.2:281).
9 "Streifzüge eines Unzeitgemässen," no. 5, *Götzendämmerung* (*Nietzsche Werke*, 6.3:108); and *Jenseits von Gut und Böse*, part 8, no. 252 (*Nietzsche Werke*, 6.2:203.) The term *Umwerthung aller Werthe* appears, for instance, in the *Genealogie der Moral* and in the subtitle of *Wille zur Macht*.
10 Nordau, *Degeneration*, 47. Nietzsche's recent translator and biographer, Walter Kaufmann, finds all previous translations replete with "travesties" (*Portable Nietzsche*, 110).
11 "Der Fall Wagner" (The Wagner case) and "Nietzsche contra Wagner" (Nietzsche contra Wagner), both 1888, trans. 1896. Deploring the disagreement about the direction that progress should take, Chesterton described one of the polarizations as "whether we should love everybody with Tolstoy, or spare nobody with Nietzsche" (*Heretics*, 29).
12 Notoriously, a London bookshop displayed an advertisement to this effect (quoted in Bruford, *German Tradition of Self-Culture*, 185).

13 The Nazi connection was promoted by the misleading edition of Nietzsche's published and unpublished writings produced by his fascist sister, Elisabeth Förster-Nietzsche.

14 Auden continues

But tell us, O tell us, is

This tenement gangster with a submachine gun in one hand

Really the superman your jealous eyes imagined

("Nietzsche;" and "Notes to Part 1," in *New Year Letter*, 96).

15 "Von der schenkenden Tugend," *Zarathustra* 1:3 (*Nietzsche Werke*, 6.1:97; Kaufmann, *Portable Nietzsche*, 190).

16 Nietzsche gave up his Prussian citizenship in 1869 in order to be released from further military service. He remained stateless.

17 Payne's translation, "the will-to-live," is common, but the form of the original is analogous to Schopenhauer's synonym "Drang zum Dasein" and to Nietzsche's "Wille zur Macht" (Will to Power). I shall capitalize "will" when it refers to Schopenhauer's concept.

18 Schopenhauer, *Welt als Wille*, 1:220 (bk 3, no. 36).

19 For a full treatment of Schopenhauer's philosophy and his place in nine-teenth-century German philosophy, see Safranski, *Schopenhauer*.

20 "Schopenhauer als Erzieher," *Unzeitgemässe Betrachtungen* (*Nietzsche Werke*, 3.1:337, 342); "Der Wahrsager," *Zarathustra* 2, (*Nietzsche Werke*, 6.1:168; Kaufmann, *Portable Nietzsche*, 245); "Über den höheren Menschen," no. 16, *Zarathustra* 4. See also *Die fröhliche Wissenschaft*, no. 129.

21 See the chapter of that title in *Zarathustra* 2.

22 *Genealogie der Moral*, part 1, no. 11 (*Nietzsche Werke*, 6.2:289–91).

23 "Über den höheren Menschen," nos. 2 and 20, *Zarathustra* 4 (*Nietzsche Werke*, 6.1:353, 363; Kaufmann, *Portable Nietzsche*, 399, 407). In his essay on David Strauss's revised *Leben Jesu*, Nietzsche attacked Strauss as the "Philister als Gründer der Religion der Zukunft [philistine as founder of the religion of the future]," that is, the religion of scientism (*Unzeitgemässe Betrachtungen*, 1873).

24 *George Eliot Letters*, 2:95.

25 E.A. McCobb makes a larger claim in "*Daniel Deronda* as Will and Represen-tation."

26 Ward, *Marcella*, 555 (bk 4, chap. 4).

27 Ward, *Marriage of William Ashe*, 438 (chap. 22).

28 Ward, *Writer's Recollections*, 317; Meredith, quoted in Field, *Works and Days*, 93–4; Chesterton, *Victorian Age in Literature*, 92 (chap. 2).

29 For a thorough analysis of the latter, see Firebaugh, "Schopenhauerian Novel."

30 James, *Princess Casamassima*, 275 (chap. 24), 406 (chap. 30), 309–10 (chap. 28); *Bostonians*, 32 (chap. 3).

31 Wells, *Island of Doctor Moreau*, 94 (chap. 14).

32 See Thatcher, *Nietzsche in England*, 82–3.

33 "Der hässlichste Mensch," *Zarathustra* 4 (*Nietzsche Werke*, 6.1:328; Kaufmann, *Portable Nietzsche*, 379); Wells, *Island of Doctor Moreau*, 99 (chap. 14), 127 (chap. 16). For a study of the "Beast People" as representative of English anxiety about blacks, Jews, and New Women, see DeVere, *Impossible Purities*.

34 Wells, *Island of Doctor Moreau*, 127 (chap. 16).

35 Hardy, *Tess of the D'Urbervilles*, 218 (chap. 25); Chesterton, *Victorian Age in Literature*, 89 (chap. 2).

36 Mary Ann Kelly ("Schopenhauer's Influence") discusses his influence, in *Jude*, on Hardy's insistence on the irrational will and the need for human pity. See also William J. Scheick's discussion of the Schopenhauerian plot structure in *Fictional Structure & Ethics*.

37 Quoted in Millgate, *Thomas Hardy*, 199.

38 See the entry for 31 May 1891, in Hardy, *Literary Notebooks*, 2:28–31.

39 See Barbara De Mille on Hardy's "nominalism" in "Cruel Illusions."

40 Hartmann, *Philosophie des Unbewussten*, 2:390–2. Hardy read this work in translation (Southerington, *Hardy's Vision of Man*, 227).

41 In what follows I make some use of my work in *German Elements* and "Gissing's *The Whirlpool* and Schopenhauer."

42 Gissing, *Letters ... to Eduard Bertz*, 283.

43 Gissing, "Hope of Pessimism," 88, 95. In his *Commonplace Book* Gissing asked himself, "might one define *Art* as a satisfying and abiding expression of the zest for life?"(69) In *The Private Papers of Henry Ryecroft* he answered in the affirmative (59).

44 Gissing, *Letters ... to Members of His Family*, 168.

45 "Notes on Social Democracy," *Pall Mall Gazette*, September 1880.

46 Gissing, *Unclassed*, 211 (chap. 25). Scheick links the "rise-and-fall rhythm" within a cyclical narrative structure to Schopenhauer's philosophy of life (*Fictional Structure & Ethics*, 61).

47 Gissing, "Hope of Pessimism," 94–5; Schopenhauer, *Welt als Wille*, 1:416–17 (bk 4, no. 63). William Greenslade traces Gissing's image to Nordau's phrase "the vertigo and whirl of our frenzied life" (*Degeneration*, 137; see also Nordau, *Degeneration*, 42). Rachel Bowlby includes in the application of the image Gissing's authorial ambivalence about literary success and artistic authenticity (Review of Gissing's *Whirlpool*, 29).

48 Gissing, *Whirlpool*, 44 (part 1, chap. 5).

49 Ibid., 9 (part 1, chap. 2).

50 He wrote of Harvey to H.G. Wells in 1897, shortly after publication of the novel, "later he is ripe in that experience which kills the cruder egoism" (Gissing, *George Gissing and H.G. Wells*, 48). Daniel Born finds Gissing's attitude more compromised (*Birth of Liberal Guilt*, 86–99).

51 Gissing, *Whirlpool*, 12–13 (part 1, chap. 2), 42 (part 1, chap. 5).

52 Ibid., 420–1 (part 3, chap. 13).

53 Ibid., 305 (part 3, chap. 1).

54 Schopenhauer, *Welt als Wille*, 1:442 (bk 4, no. 66), 1:473 (bk 4, no. 69).

55 Schopenhauer, *Parerga*, 2:649–62.

56 Gissing, *George Gissing's Commonplace Book*, 63; *Whirlpool*, 251–2 (part 2, chap. 11).

57 Schopenhauer, *Welt als Wille*, 1:371 (bk 4, no. 57).

58 Gissing, *Whirlpool*, 146 (part 2, chap. 2).

59 Ibid., 402 (part 3, chap. 10), 212 (part 2, chap. 8).

60 Schopenhauer, *Welt als Wille*, 1:301 (bk 3, no. 52); Gissing, "Hope of Pessimism," 95.

61 Patrick Bridgwater stretches his claim for indebtedness to Nietzsche, especially in *The Unclassed* (1884), leaving unresolved the question of influence and independent similarity, and finding even *ante litteram* parallels (*Gissing and Germany*, 59–67).

62 Gissing, *Our Friend the Charlatan*, 235–6 (chap. 16).

63 As a typical example, the hero of Somerset Maugham's *Bildungsroman*, *Of Human Bondage* (1915), goes through phases of indoctrination in Schopenhauer's and Nietzsche's philosophy (chaps. 31, 45).

64 Trilling, *E.M. Forster*, 8; Forster, *Two Cheers*, 80–1.

65 "Was den Deutschen abgeht," no. 4, *Götzendämmerung* (*Nietzsche Werke*, 6.3:100), and "Grosse Politik und ihre Einbussen," no. 481, *Menschliches, Allzumenschliches* 1 (*Nietzsche Werke*, 4.2:324–6). See also his rejection of the Hegelian state, in "Vom neuen Götzen" (On the new idol), *Zarathustra* 1. For a discussion of Nietzsche's anti-political position, see Bergmann, *Nietzsche*, chap. 1.

66 Forster, *Maurice*, 155, 62, and 132.

67 This dichotomy is a variation on Schiller's distinction between the naive and the sentimental, which Bulwer introduced in his novels (see chap. 3 above). Forster says of Stephen: "he lived too near the things he loved to seem poetical" (*Longest Journey*, 275).

68 Forster, *Longest Journey*, 66, 89, and 63. For instance, in the entry "Anti-Darwin," in *Götzendämmerung* (Twilight of the idols), no. 14, Nietzsche argues: "Die Gattungen wachsen *nicht* in der Vollkommenheit: die Schwachen werden immer wieder über die Starken Herr, – das macht, sie sind die grosse Zahl, sie sind auch *klüger* … Darwin hat den Geist vergessen (– das ist englisch!), *die Schwachen haben mehr Geist* … Man muss Geist nöthig haben, um Geist zu bekommen [The species do *not* grow in perfection: the weak prevail over the strong again and again, for they are the great majority – and they are also more *intelligent*. Darwin forgot the spirit (that is English!); *the weak have more spirit*. One must need spirit to acquire spirit]" (*Nietzsche Werke*, 6.3:114–15; Kaufmann, *Portable Nietzsche*, 523).

69 Forster, *Longest Journey*, 318, 327.

70 Critical assessments of Forster's novels have generally been polarized as optimistic versus pessimistic. Brian May follows Forster in reading the novel as fiction in the " 'junction' of mind and heart' " and sees its "instability of modes and movements" as distinctive of its rank "as one of the most purely transitional documents of its time" ("Modernism and Other Modes," 236).

71 Forster, *Longest Journey*, 27.

72 Ibid., 318.

73 Sharing the name of the Romantic brothers Schlegel, the Schlegels are not "Germans of the dreadful sort"; their father is classed as "the countryman of Hegel and Kant, as the idealist ... whose Imperialism was the Imperialism of the air" (Forster, *Howards End*, 23). Their origins in pre-Bismarck Germany are conceived in the tradition discussed above with respect to George Eliot and Matthew Arnold. For the imperial theme, see chap. 9 below. Peter Firchow stresses the novel's "mythological layer" related to Wagner's *Ring*, but he ignores Schopenhauer and Nietzsche (*Death of the German Cousin*, 70–6).

74 Forster, *Howards End*, 280 (chap. 43), 211 (chap. 28).

75 Ibid., 206 (chap. 27).

76 Forster, *Longest Journey*, 197. See also Margaret in *Howards End*: "Nothing has been done wrong" (291 [chap. 44]); and Professor Godbole in *Passage to India*: "Whatever had happened had happened" (310 [chap. 36]).

77 Forster, *Howards End*, 281 (chap. 43).

78 For a close analysis, see Rosecrance, *"Howards End."*

79 Letter of 13 December 1914, in Forster, *Selected Letters*, 1:216.

80 Forster, *Howards End*, 45 (chap. 5); *Passage to India*, 160.

81 Forster, *Longest Journey*, 201; *Two Cheers*, 100–1.

82 Forster, "Not Listening to Music" and "The Raison d'Être of Criticism in the Arts," in *Two Cheers*, 138, 117.

83 Forster, "Joseph Conrad: A Note," 160.

84 Schopenhauer, *Welt als Wille*, 1:230 (bk 3, no. 37); Conrad, preface to *The Nigger of the "Narcissus,"* xl. See Magee, *The Philosophy of Schopenhauer*, 385. On Conrad's Schopenhauerian aesthetics, see also Wollaeger, *Joseph Conrad*, and Scheick, *Fictional Structure & Ethics*.

85 Letter of 2 November 1895, in Conrad, *Collected Letters*, 1:253.

86 See also Firchow's chapter "Conrad's Diabolic and Angelic Germans" in *Death of the German Cousin*. He ignores Schopenhauer and Nietzsche; in *Lord Jim* he stresses allusions to both parts of Goethe's *Faust*.

87 Conrad, *Lord Jim*, 129 (chap. 20), 56 (chap. 8).

88 "Er heisst" means "his name is." Conrad also deleted an explanation of the German origin of Heyst's pet name for the heroine, Lena.

89 Conrad, *Victory*, 196, 198 (part 3, chap. 3), 175 (part 3, chap. 1). The image of "shipwreck with spectator" on the shore has of course a long tradition as a "metaphor of existence"; see Blumenberg's essay of this title.

90 Letters of 22 July 1899 and 30 March 1913, in Conrad, *Collected Letters*, 2:188, 5:203.

91 Conrad, *Notes on Life and Letters*, 190–1.

92 Conrad, *Heart of Darkness*, 116–18.

93 Ibid., 81.

94 Ibid., 65, 116. Ursula Lord (*Solitude versus Solidarity*) discusses the tension between solitude and solidarity in Conrad's fiction, but in terms of social and political theories.

95 Conrad, *Heart of Darkness*, 94, 85.

96 See, for instance, Nietzsche, *Genealogie*, 1.10–13. For a discussion of Conrad's avoidance of the social implications in Marlow's ethic of work, see Wilding, *Social Visions*, 62–6.

97 Conrad, *Secret Agent*, 58 (chap. 4).

98 Ibid., 116 (chap. 8).

99 *Geburt der Tragödie*, no. 4 (*Nietzsche Werke*, 3.1:35–7). See Butte for a thorough analysis of the allusions to Nietzsche's Dionysian and Apollonian concepts. Butte sees Conrad's response to Nietzsche as contradictory: "unwilling sympathy and hostility, imitation and parody, as Conrad seems to argue with Nietzsche about the best human response to knowing the worst of our condition" ("What Silenus Knew," 155).

100 Conrad, *Secret Agent*, 226 (chap. 13), 61 (chap. 4), 225 (chap. 13).

101 See also Fogel, "Fragmentation of Sympathy."

102 Conrad, *Secret Agent*, 217 (chap. 12).

103 Ibid., 40 (chap. 3).

104 Conrad, *Nigger of the "Narcissus"*, xxxviii. Conrad published the originally suppressed preface in the editon of 1914. For diverse views on his irony and the absence or presence of a moral positive, see the essays by Irving Howe, Albert J. Guérard, and J. Hillis Miller in Watt, ed., *Conrad*.

105 Thomas Mann, in his preface to the German translation of 1926, remarked on Conrad's anti-Russian, "tendentious Western bias" (Watt, ed., *Conrad*, 104). Alan Sandison (*Wheel of Empire*) gives a positive, Carlylean cast to Conrad's portrayal of work as the process of securing identity and integrity.

106 Conrad, *Secret Agent*, 159 (chap. 90).

107 Edward Said places Conrad's narrative style more completely in a common tradition with Nietzsche's "radical attitude towards language" ("Conrad and Nietzsche," 66). See also Barbara De Mille on Conrad's Nietzschean "nominalism" in *Lord Jim* ("Cruel Illusions").

108 Letter to Edward Garnett, 30 October 1912, in Lawrence, Letters, 1:465.

109 Schneider, *Consciousness of D.H. Lawrence*, 57. Schneider gives a full account of Lawrence's reading. Of Nietzsche's works, *Zarathustra, Die*

fröhliche Wissenschaft, and *Der Wille zur Macht* are certain. See Brunsdale, *German Effect*, for a detailed account of parallels in Lawrence's early work.

110 See also Schneider, "Schopenhauer and the Development of D.H. Lawrence's Psychology," and Zoll on Schopenhauer and *The Rainbow* and *Women in Love* in "Vitalism and the Metaphysics of Love."

111 "Vorspiel," *fröhliche Wissenschaft* (Prelude, *Gay science*), no. 7 (*Nietzsche Werke*, 5.2:26). See also Zarathustra's advice to his disciples, cited above.

112 Letter of 2 November 1915, in Lawrence, *Letters*, 2:424. Lawrence added, "We have had enough of the disintegrating process."

113 T.S. Eliot, *After Strange Gods*, 39–41.

114 "Philosophy interests me most now – not novels or stories ... I am weary of humanity and human things. One is happy in the thoughts only that transcend humanity" (letter of 23 May 1917, in Lawrence *Letters*, 3:127).

115 Lawrence, *Phoenix*, 537, and *Kangaroo*, 328 (chap. 14).

116 See Margot Norris's Lacanian discussion of the instinctual epistemology in the "biocentric" tradition, in which she includes Lawrence (*Beasts of the Modern Imagination*, introduction and chapter on Lawrence's *St. Mawr*).

117 *Fröhliche Wissenschaft*, no. 319 (*Nietzsche Werke*, 5.2:231; Kaufmann, *Portable Nietzsche*, 101).

118 Lawrence, *Selected Poetry*, 197.

119 Schneider judges it, against many detractors, "Lawrence's fullest attempt to depict the wholeness and balance that are both destructive *and* constructive" (*Consciousness of D.H. Lawrence*, 170).

120 Lawrence, *Women in Love*, 491 (Prologue).

121 Ibid., 150 (chap. 13).

122 John B. Humma cautiously interprets Lawrence's "apparent" misunderstanding of Nietzsche's concept as a refusal to acknowledge him and finds that "Nietzsche's ethic completely anticipates that of Lawrence" ("D.H. Lawrence as Friedrich Nietzsche," 120).

123 Nietzsche, *Genealogie*, Part 1, no. 10.

124 Lawrence, *Women in Love*, 223–31 (chap. 17).

125 Ibid., 148 (chap. 13), 251 (chap. 19).

126 Nietzsche speculates that he and his friend are like ships whose courses and goals may be "included" in an "ungeheure unsichtbare Curve und Sternenbahn" (immense and invisible curve and star track) (*Fröhliche Wissenschaft*, no. 279 [*Nietzsche Werke*, 5.2:203–4)].

127 "Von alten und jungen Weiblein," *Zarathustra* 1, (*Nietzsche Werke*, 6.1:80–2; Kaufmann, *Portable Nietzsche*, 177–9). On women, see also *Fröhliche Wissenschaft*, nos. 60–75.

128 Lawrence, *Women in Love*, 250 (chap. 19).

129 Ibid., 127 (chap. 11).

130 *Nachgelassene Schriften, 1870–73* (*Nietzsche Werke*, 3.2:369; Kaufmann, *Portable Nietzsche*, 42).

131 Lawrence, *Women in Love*, 186 (chap. 14), 437 (chap. 30).

132 Ibid., 458 (chap. 31).

133 Lawrence, *Aaron's Rod*, 293, 297 (chap. 21).

134 "Von der Selbst-Überwindung," *Zarathustra* 2, (*Nietzsche Werke*, 6.1:143; Kaufmann, *Portable Nietzsche*, 226).

135 *Fröhliche Wissenschaft*, book 1, no. 11 (*Nietzsche Werke*, 5.2:56).

136 Lawrence, *Kangaroo*, 408 (chap. 18).

137 Later, in *Lady Chatterley's Lover* (1928), Lawrence rejected this model of sexual relations in favour of tender mutuality.

138 Lawrence wrote about Melville's *Typee*: "We can't go back to the savages … We can take a great curve in their direction, onwards … But we cannot turn the current of our life backwards, back to their soft warm twilight and uncreate mud" (*Selected Literary Criticism*, 369–70).

139 Lawrence, *Plumed Serpent*, 199 (chap. 13), 185 (chap. 12), 191 (chap. 13), 132 (chap. 8).

140 *Geburt*, no. 4 (*Nietzsche Werke*, 3.1:36–7).

141 Obituary in the *Listener* 3 (30 April 1930): 753–4.

142 Lawrence, *Plumed Serpent*, 371 (chap. 22).

143 Lawrence, *Mornings in Mexico*, 46.

144 "Warum ich so weise bin" (Why I am so wise), no. 1, *Ecce homo* (*Nietzsche Werke*, 6.3:264).

CHAPTER NINE

1 Letter of 1 January 1867, quoted in Ross, *Three Generations*, 2:167.

2 Quoted in Kennedy, *Rise of the Anglo-German Antagonism*, 119. Bismarck congratulated Carlyle on his eightieth birthday in 1875 and expressed his gratitude for Carlyle's lives of Schiller and Frederick the Great (Ashton, *German Idea*, 79).

3 Letter of [June 1871], in *George Eliot Letters*, 5:159.

4 James, "Homburg Reformed" (1873), 360–3.

5 Ward, *Writer's Recollections*, 107.

6 Quoted in Strachey, *End of Empire*, 146. See also Thornton, *Imperial Idea*, 67.

7 See Kiernan, *Lords of Human Kind*, 227.

8 See Kennedy, *Rise of the Anglo-German Antagonism*, 366. For this introduction see also Craig, *Germany, 1866–1945*; Schmitt, *England and Germany*; Wallace, *War and the Image of Germany*; Panayi, *Enemy in Our Midst*; and Kiernan, *Lords of Human Kind*.

9 Kipling, "The Rovers" (1902) and "For All We Have and Are" (1914), both in *Years Between*, 5, 20.

10 Quoted in Kennedy, *Rise of the Anglo-German Antagonism*, 463.

11 See Wallace, *War and the Image of Germany*, 26–33; also Hynes, *War Imagined*, 67–74.

12 Ford, *When Blood Is Their Argument*, 289.

13 Conrad, *Notes on Life and Letters*, 124.

14 See also Stern, *Politics of Cultural Despair*, 345–50.

15 See, for instance; "Der Staat ist die göttliche Idee, wie sie auf Erden vorhanden ist. Er ist so der näher bestimmte Gegenstand der Weltgeschichte überhaupt, worin die Freiheit ihre Objectivität erhält und in dem Genusse dieser Objectivität lebt (The state is the divine idea as it exists on earth. The state is therefore the object of world-history in a more definite shape, in which freedom achieves its objectivity and lives in the enjoyment of this objectivity]" (Hegel, *Vorlesungen über die Philosophie der Geschichte*, 71).

16 Russell, "Philosophy and Virtue," *Athenaeum*, 1 May 1919, quoted in Wallace, *War and the Image of Germany*, 43.

17 Wilde, *Intentions and The Soul of Man*, 219; Goethe quoted in Eckermann, *Gespräche mit Goethe*, 583 (14 March 1830).

18 Johnston, *Views and Reviews*, 147.

19 See Stern (*Politics of Cultural Despair*), on the "mood of cultural despair" and the "conservative revolution."

20 *Bookman* 2 (November 1895): 198.

21 On Weimar culture, see Craig, *Germany, 1866–1945*, and Gay, *Weimar Culture*.

22 Peter Firchow's "imagological" study, *Death of the German Cousin*, in parts parallels and complements my discussion of Conrad, Forster, Ford, Lawrence, and Wells. His argument, that British chauvinism from 1890 through World War I completely and permanently "killed" the "German cousin," substituting for this conception of affinity and even admiration or envy the stereotype of the subhuman Hun, results in a different focus, different allusions, and different observations from mine here.

23 See also Firchow's discussion of the story and its critical reception (*Death of the German Cousin*, 102–13).

24 See Born, *Birth of Liberal Guilt*, 6.

25 Trollope, *Prime Minister*, 53 (chap. 6).

26 For a key to the historical personages, see Blake, *Disraeli*, 737.

27 Disraeli, *Endymion*, 271 (chap. 60).

28 Ibid., 160 (chap. 37).

29 Ibid., 239 (chap. 53), 266 (chap. 59), 392 (chap. 85).

30 See Craig, *Politik der Unpolitischen*, 38–45. Wilhelm I recalled Bismarck from the Paris embassy in 1862 to solve the Prussian constitutional conflict. Bismarck spoke of "Blut und Eisen" in a speech in the Prussian House of Deputies, 28 January 1886.

31 See Blake, *Disraeli*, 430.

32 Quoted ibid., 679.

33 See Kennedy, *Rise of the Anglo-German Antagonism*, 18–29.

34 Letters of 25 July 1870 and 27 February 1871, in Meredith, *Letters*, 1:425 and 441; Meredith, *Poetical Works*, 497.

35 Meredith, *Works*, 11:35, 38 (chaps. 3, 4).

36 Ibid., 12:369, 430 (chaps. 33, 38).

37 For a debate on this self-sacrifice as an equivocal sign of both hope and waste, see Speare, *Political Novel*, 249–54, and Howard, "George Meredith," 164–70.

38 Meredith, *Works*, 17:105 (chap. 10), 17:350 (chap. 29), 17:466–7 (chap. 39).

39 Ibid., 17:216, 219–20 (chap. 19).

40 Ibid., 17:238 (chap. 21).

41 Letter of 2 December 1897, in Gissing, *Letters ... to Eduard Bertz*, 164.

42 Quoted in Collie, *George Gissing*, 152.

43 Gissing, *Crown of Life*, 83, 11 (chaps. 10, 1).

44 Daniel Born sees them as disjointed (*Birth of Liberal Guilt*, 86).

45 Gissing, *Crown of Life*, 194 (chap. 21).

46 Ibid., 296, 104 (chaps. 32, 12).

47 See Briggs, *Age of Improvement*, 379, and Wallace, *War and the Image of Germany*, 25. Gissing judged Turgenev, whom he read in French, "the greatest living writer of fiction," in a letter to Bertz, 14 October 1883 (*Collected Letters*, 2:170). E.M. Forster argued, in *Aspects of the Novel* (1927), that despite the fact that "our writers have never been much influenced by the continentals," the critic of the novel cannot "quite ignore fiction written in other languages, particularly French and Russian" (26).

48 Gissing's friend Frederick Harrison, quoted in Kennedy, *Rise of the Anglo-German Antagonism*, 82.

49 *Fortnightly Review* (Conrad, *Notes on Life and Letters*, 95, 114). The radical republican French statesman Léon Michel Gambetta had said, "L'ennemi, c'est le Prussien."

50 See Watt, *Conrad in the Nineteenth Century*, 157–8.

51 See Batchelor, *Life of Joseph Conrad*, 44; Watt, *Conrad in the Nineteenth Century*, 139. The possession was ratified at the Berlin Conference in 1885.

52 Conrad, *Heart of Darkness*, 55.

53 Letter to Blackwood, 31 December 1898, in Conrad, *Collected Letters*, 2:139–40. Edward Said discusses Conrad's "two visions" in terms of a pessimistic view of European civilizing efforts and a Eurocentric skepticism about African autonomy (*Culture and Imperialism*, xviii, 19–30).

54 Conrad, *Lord Jim*, 13 (chap. 2).

55 Conrad, *Victory*, 27 (part 1, chap. 2).

56 Ibid., xxxii.

57 For the scare and the policy, see Panayi, *Enemy in Our Midst*, 283.

58 Forster, "What I Believe," in *Two Cheers*, 78; see chap. 8 above.

59 See Beauman, *E.M. Forster*, 213.

60 Forster, *Howards End*, 41–2 (chap. 4).

61 Richardson, *Pointed Roofs*, 118, 167, 82.

62 Their Australian-born and anglophile mother, Elizabeth, née Beauchamp, was a cousin of Katherine Mansfield and well known in England through her popular fictionalized account of her life as a Pomeranian lady of the manor, *Elizabeth and Her German Garden* (1898). The name von Arnim belongs to the Heidelberg Romantics, namely, to Achim von Arnim, compiler with Clemens Brentano of the collection of folksongs *Des Knaben Wunderhorn*. His sister, and Brentano's wife, Bettina was famous as the author of her largely fictive childhood correspondence with Goethe. Peter Firchow suggests that Forster found for his characters another Romantic name in lieu of their actual models' name (*Death of the German Cousin*, 68).

63 Together with ivory, rubber was a major tropical product gained through exploitation of the natives in the Congo and in the Amazon (Hobsbawm, *Age of Empire*, 63).

64 Forster, *Howards End*, 290 (chap. 44).

65 Peter Brooker and Peter Widdowson single out, in the "literature for England," Forster's contradictory affirmation here as the best "instance of myth being substituted for history; of a preferred pastoral 'civilization' at rest being held against the acknowledged logic of change" ("Literature for England," 139).

66 Forster, *Howards End*, 276 (chap. 41).

67 Hynes, *War Imagined*, 72.

68 For instance, "Soweit Deutschland reicht, *verdirbt* es die Cultur [Wherever Germany reaches it *spoils* culture]" ("Warum ich so klug bin," no. 5, *Ecce Homo* [*Nietzsche Werke*, 6.3:287]).

69 *Joseph Conrad: A Personal Remembrance* (1924), in Ford, *Good Soldier*, 285.

70 See Hynes, *War Imagined*, 249.

71 Ford, *Good Soldier*, 29–30 (part 1, chap. 4). On German spas, see also chap. 6 above.

72 Ibid., 13–14 (part 1, chap. 1).

73 Ibid., 37 (part 1, chap. 4). Ford conflates the Protest and the doctrinal Articles of Marburg (ibid., 36n2). See also Jacobs, [The Passion for Talk], 341; In what follows I disagree with her interpretation. Ford's own German origins were Westphalian Catholic; his attitude to Roman Catholicism was ambivalent.

74 Ford, *Good Soldier*, 157 (part 3, chap. 4), 238 (part 1, chap. 5).

75 See Judd, *Ford Madox Ford*, 107.

76 Ford, *Some Do Not* (*Parade's End*, 1:26).

77 Ford, *No More Parades* (*Parade's End*, 2:313).

78 Ford, *When Blood Is Their Argument*, 295.

79 Ford, *A Man Could Stand Up* and *Some Do Not* (*Parade's End*, 2:29 and 1:25 respectively).
80 Ford, *Some Do Not* (*Parade's End*, 1:173).
81 Ford, *A Man Could Stand Up* (*Parade's End*, 2:131). This attitude is criticized as a common but inadequate literary disposition by H.G. Wells in *Mr. Britling Sees It Through*, 208. See below.
82 Ford, *Some Do Not* (*Parade's End*, 1:35).
83 Ford, *A Man Could Stand Up* (*Parade's End*, 2:18).
84 Ford, *Some Do Not* (*Parade's End*, 1:236).
85 Ibid., 1:167–8.
86 Ford, *A Man Could Stand Up* (*Parade's End*, 2:15).
87 Lawrence, *Kangaroo*, chap. 12 ("The Nightmare").
88 The vicious rabbit owned by Gerald's sister is also called Bismarck (chap. 18).
89 Lawrence, *Women in Love*, 28 (chap. 2).
90 Ibid., 54 (chap. 5).
91 Ibid., 427–8 (chap. 29).
92 Ursula's association of Birkin's remorse at Gerald's death with the kaiser's – "Ich habe [den Krieg] nicht gewollt" (*Women in Love*, 479 [chap. 32]) – seems more a topical, than a well-integrated, allusion, since Birkin's call for creative change cannot readily be compared with the kaiser's imperialist ambitions for Germany.
93 See Gay, *Weimar Culture*, 128–32.
94 Spender, *European Witness*, 236.
95 Connolly quoted in Isherwood, *Christopher and His Kind*, 271, 105.
96 Ibid., 186.
97 Isherwood, *Mr. Norris* (*Berlin Stories*, 80).
98 Isherwood, *Goodbye* (*Berlin Stories*, 100, 109).
99 Isherwood, *Mr. Norris* (*Berlin Stories*, 80, 69, 36).
100 Isherwood, *Goodbye* (*Berlin Stories*, 107).
101 Isherwood, *Christopher and His Kind*, 244.
102 Ibid., 120.
103 Spender, *World within World*, 104, 129.
104 *Goethes Werke*, Sophien-Ausgabe, 1:5.1:218.

CONCLUSION

1 Waugh, *Put Out More Flags*, 45 (chap. 1).
2 Stevenson, *British Novel*, 75.
3 Waugh, *Sword of Honour*, 14 (*Men at Arms*, chap. 1).
4 Ibid., 532 (*Officers and Gentlemen*, chap. 9).
5 Lodge, *Small World*, 97.

6 On Jauss, see Seibt, "Kann eine Biografie," 215–16. There has also been discussion on the Internet.

7 W.E. Yuill observed in 1971 a "rapprochement" between the English and the German novelistic traditions ("Tradition and Nightmare," 165).

8 Ishiguro, *Remains of the Day*, 224.

9 Ibid., 102.

10 Bradbury, *Eating People Is Wrong*, 4, 41. See also Stevenson, *British Novel*, 190.

11 Sutherland, *Fiction and the Fiction Industry*, 56–62.

12 Connor, *English Novel*, 86.

13 Buruma, "Road to Babel," 26.

14 For a positive account of contemporary philosophical cosmopolitanism as continuous with the ideal of *Bildung*, see A. Anderson, "Cosmopolitanism, Universalism," 267–9.

15 "Entwurf zur vorstehenden Einleitung. 5 April 1830" (*Goethes Werke*, 12:364).

Bibliography

Abrams, M.H. *Natural Supernaturalism: Tradition and Revolution in Romantic Literature*. New York: Norton, 1971.

Acton, Lord. "George Eliot's Life." In *A Century of George Eliot Criticism*, edited by Gordon S. Haight, 151–60. Originally published in the *Nineteenth Century*, March 1885.

Amrine, Frederick. "Goethe's Science in the Twentieth Century." In *Goethe in the Twentieth Century*, edited by Alexej Ugrinsky, 87–93. New York: Greenwood Press, 1987.

Anderson, Amanda."Cosmopolitanism, Universalism, and the Divided Legacies of Modernity." In *Cosmopolitanism: Thinking and Feeling beyond the Nation*, edited by Pheng Cheah and Bruce Robbins, 265–89. Minneapolis: University of Minnesota Press, 1998.

Anderson, Benedict. *Imagined Communities*. Rev. ed. London: Verso, 1991.

Andrews, Keith. *The Nazarenes*. Oxford: Clarendon Press, 1964.

Argyle, Gisela. "George Eliot's *Daniel Deronda* and Frith's *The Salon d'Or, Homburg*." *Victorian Studies Association Newsletter, Ontario* 40 (fall 1987): 13–16.

– *German Elements in the Fiction of George Eliot, Gissing, and Meredith*. Frankfurt: Peter Lang, 1979.

– "Gissing's *The Whirlpool* and Schopenhauer." *Gissing Newsletter* 17, no. 4 (October 1981): 3–21.

– "Meredith's 'Readable Marriage': A Polyphony of Texts." *Essays in Literature* 22, no. 2 (fall 1995): 244–52.

Arnold, Matthew. *The Complete Prose Works of Matthew Arnold*. 11 vols. Edited by R.H. Super. Ann Arbor: University of Michigan Press, 1960–77.

Arx, Jeffrey von. "The Victorian Crisis of Faith as a Crisis of Vocation." In *Victorian Faith in Crisis: Essays on Continuity and Change in Nineteenth-Century Religious Belief*, edited by Richard J. Helmstadter and Bernard Lightman, 262–82. London: Macmillan, 1990.

Ashton, Rosemary. "Doubting Clerics." In *The Critical Spirit and the Will to Believe*, edited by David Jasper and T.R. Wright, 69–87. New York: St. Martin's Press, 1989.

– *George Eliot: A Life*. London: Penguin, 1997.

– *G.H. Lewes: A Life*. Oxford: Clarendon Press, 1991.

– *The German Idea: Four English Writers and the Reception of German Thought, 1800–1860*. Cambridge: Cambridge University Press, 1980.

– Introduction to *The Nemesis of Faith*, by J.A. Froude, 7–36. Reprint of the 2nd ed., 1849. London: Libris, 1988.

– *The Life of Samuel Taylor Coleridge: A Critical Biography*. Oxford: Blackwell, 1996.

– *Little Germany: Exile and Asylum in Victorian England*. Oxford: Oxford University Press, 1986.

– ed. *Versatile Victorian: Selected Writings of George Henry Lewes*. London: Bristol Classical Press, 1992.

Auden, W.H. *New Year Letter*. London: Faber and Faber, 1941.

Auerbach, Erich. *Mimesis: The Representation of Reality in Western Literature*. 1946. Translated by Willard Trask. Princeton: Princeton University Press, 1953.

Baker, William. *George Eliot and Judaism*. Salzburg: Institut für Englische Sprache und Literatur, 1975.

Bakhtin, M.M. *Speech Genres and Other Late Essays*. Translated by Vern W. McGee. Edited by C. Emerson and M. Holquist. Austin: University of Texas Press, 1986.

Balakian, Anna. "Influence and Literary Fortune: The Equivocal Junction of Two Methods." *Yearbook of Comparative and General Literature* 11 (1962): 24–31.

Baldick, Chris. "Matthew Arnold's Innocent Language." In *The Social Mission of English Criticism, 1848–1932*, 18–58. Oxford: Clarendon Press, 1983.

Barrett, Dorothea. *Vocation and Desire: George Eliot's Heroines*. London: Routledge, 1989.

Barthes, Roland. *S/Z*. Translated by Richard Miller. New York: Hill and Wang, 1974.

Batchelor, John. *The Life of Joseph Conrad: A Critical Biography*. Oxford: Blackwell, 1994.

Beauman, Nicola. *E.M. Forster*. New York: Alfred A. Knopf, 1994.

Beer, Gillian. *George Eliot*. Brighton: Harvester Press, 1986.

– *Meredith: A Change of Masks*. London: Athlone Press, 1970.

Bell, Quentin. *Victorian Artists*. London: Routledge and Kegan Paul, 1967.

Benjamin, Walter. *Denkbilder*. In *Gesammelte Schriften*, 4.1, edited by Tillman Rexroth. Frankfurt/Main: Suhrkamp, 1972.

Ben-Porat, Ziva. "The Poetics of Literary Allusion." *PTL: A Journal for Descriptive Poetics and Theory in Literature* 1 (1976): 105–28.

Bergmann, Peter. *Nietzsche, "the Last Antipolitical German."* Bloomington: Indiana University Press, 1987.

Blake, Robert. *Disraeli*. London: Eyre and Spottiswoode, 1966.

Bloom, Harold. *The Anxiety of Influence: A Theory of Poetry*. 2nd ed. New York: Oxford University Press, 1997.

– *A Map of Misreading*. New York: Oxford University Press, 1975.

– ed. *E.M. Forster*. New York: Chelsea House, 1987.

Blumenberg, Hans. *Schiffbruch mit Zuschauer: Paradigma einer Daseinsmetapher*. Frankfurt: Suhrkamp, 1979.

Born, Daniel. *The Birth of Liberal Guilt in the English Novel: Charles Dickens to H.G. Wells*. Chapel Hill: University of North Carolina Press, 1995.

Bowlby, Rachel. Review of Gissing's *Whirlpool* (Harvester ed., 1984). *The Gissing Newsletter* 21, no. 2 (1985): 22–9.

Boyle, Nicholas. *Goethe: The Poet and the Age*. 2 vols. Oxford: Clarendon Press, 1991–2000.

Bradbury, Malcolm. *Eating People Is Wrong*. 1959. Reissue with new introduction. London: Secker & Warburg, 1976.

Braun, Thom. *Disraeli the Novelist*. London: George Allen and Unwin, 1981.

Breazeale, Daniel, trans. and ed. *Fichte: Early Philosophical Writings*. Ithaca: Cornell University Press, 1988.

Bridgwater, Patrick. *Gissing and Germany*. London: Enitharmon Press, 1981.

– *Nietzsche in Anglosaxonry: A Study of Nietzsche's Impact on English and American Literature*. Leicester: Leicester University Press, 1972.

Briggs, Asa. *The Age of Improvement, 1783–1867*. London: Longmans, 1959.

Brod, Max. *Heinrich Heine*. Translated by Joseph Witriol. New York: New York University Press, 1957.

Brontë, Charlotte. *Jane Eyre*. Edited by Q.D. Leavis. Harmondsworth: Penguin, 1966.

Brooker, Peter, and Peter Widdowson. "A Literature for England." In *Englishness: Politics and Culture, 1880–1920*, edited by Robert Colls and Philip Dodd, 116–63. London: Croom Helm, 1986.

Bruford, Walter H. *Culture and Society in Classical Weimar, 1775–1806*. Cambridge: Cambridge University Press, 1962.

– *The German Tradition of Self-Cultivation: "Bildung" from Humboldt to Thomas Mann*. Cambridge: Cambridge University Press, 1975.

Brunsdale, Mitzi M. *The German Effect on D.H. Lawrence and His Works, 1885–1912*. Utah Studies in Literature and Linguistics. Bern: Peter Lang, 1978.

Buckley, Jerome H. *Season of Youth: The Bildungsroman from Dickens to Golding*. Cambridge: Harvard University Press, 1974.

Bulwer-Lytton, Edward. *Alice, or The Mysteries*. London: George Routledge and Sons, 1877.

– *Alice, or The Mysteries*. Boston: Little, Brown and Co., 1893. Includes "Note to the 1851 edition."

– *England and the English*. Edited by Standish Meacham. Chicago: University of Chicago Press, 1970.

– *Ernest Maltravers*. London: George Routledge and Sons, 1877.

– *Night and Morning*. London: George Routledge and Sons, 1873.

– "On Art in Fiction." Vol. 1, *The Critical and Miscellaneous Writings of Sir Edward Lytton*. Philadelphia: Lea and Blanchard, 1841.

– *The Pilgrims of the Rhine*. In *Leila, or The Siege of Granada; Calderon the Courtier; and The Pilgrims of the Rhine*. London: George Routledge and Sons, 1878.

– *Zanoni*. London: George Routledge and Sons, 1878.

– trans. *The Poems and Ballads of Schiller*. London: Frederick Warne, 1887.

Burgess, Anthony. *Byrne*. New York: Carroll and Graf, 1996.

Buruma, Ian. *Anglomania: A European Love Affair*. New York: Random House, 1999.

– "The Road to Babel." *New York Review of Books* 48, no. 9 (31 May 2001): 23–6.

Butler, Samuel. *The Way of All Flesh*. Edited by Michael Mason. Oxford: Oxford University Press, 1993.

Butte, George. "What Silenus Knew: Conrad's Uneasy Debt to Nietzsche." *Comparative Literature* 41, no. 2 (spring 1989): 155–69.

Carlyle, Thomas. *A Carlyle Reader*. Edited by G.B. Tennyson. Cambridge: Cambridge University Press, 1984.

– *The Collected Letters of Thomas and Jane Welsh Carlyle*. 25 vols. Edited by Charles Richard Sanders and Kenneth J. Fielding. Durham: Duke University Press, 1970–97.

– *Correspondence between Goethe and Carlyle*. Edited by C.E. Norton. London: Macmillan, 1887.

– *New Letters of Thomas Carlyle*. 2 vols. Edited by Alexander Carlyle. London: Bodley Head, 1904.

– *The Works of Thomas Carlyle*. Centenary Edition. 30 vols. London: Chapman and Hall, 1896–99.

Carr, C.T. "Carlyle's Translations from German." *Modern Language Review* 42 (1947): 223–32.

Carroll, David. *George Eliot and the Conflict of Interpretations*. Cambridge: Cambridge University Press, 1992.

Chadwick, Owen. *The Secularization of the European Mind in the Nineteenth Century*. Cambridge: Cambridge University Press, 1975.

Chesterton, G.K. *Heretics*. 1905. London: Bodley Head, 1960.

– *The Victorian Age in Literature*. London: Oxford University Press, 1913.

Christensen, Allan Conrad. *Edward Bulwer-Lytton: The Fiction of New Regions*. Athens: University of Georgia Press, 1976.

Cockshut, A.O.J. *The Unbelievers: English Agnostic Thought, 1840–1890*. London: Collins, 1964.

Coleridge, Samuel Taylor. *Biographia Literaria, or Biographical Sketches of My Literary Life and Opinions*. Edited by George Watson. London: J.M. Dent, 1965.

– *Table Talk*. Vol. 14, *The Collected Works of Samuel Taylor Coleridge*. Edited by Carl Woodring. Princeton: Princeton University Press, 1990.

Collie, Michael. *The Alien Art: A Critical Study of George Gissing's Novels*. Folkestone: Dawson, 1979.

– *George Gissing: A Biography*. London: Dawson, 1977.

Collini, Stefan. *Arnold*. Oxford: Oxford University Press, 1988.

– *Public Moralists: Political Thought and Intellectual Life in Britain, 1850–1930*. Oxford: Clarendon Press, 1991.

Colls, Robert, and Philip Dodd, eds. *Englishness: Politics and Culture, 1880–1920*. London: Croom Helm, 1986.

Connor, Steven. *The English Novel in History, 1950–1995*. London: Routledge, 1996.

Conrad, Joseph. *The Collected Letters of Joseph Conrad*. 5 vols. Edited by Frederick R. Karl. Cambridge: Cambridge University Press, 1983–.

– *Heart of Darkness*. In *Youth, Heart of Darkness, The End of the Tether*, edited by Robert Kimbrough. Oxford: Oxford University Press, 1984.

– *Lord Jim: A Tale*. Edited by Thomas C. Moser. New York: W.W. Norton, 1996.

– *The Nigger of the "Narcissus."* New York: Harper, 1951.

– *Notes on Life and Letters*. London: Dent, 1924.

– *The Secret Agent*. Edited by Bruce Harkness and S.W. Reid. Cambridge: Cambridge University Press, 1989.

– *Victory: An Island Tale*. Edited by John Batchelor. Oxford: Oxford University Press, 1996.

Conte, Gian Biagio. *The Rhetoric of Imitation: Genre and Poetic Memory in Virgil and Other Latin Poets*. Translated by Charles Segal. Ithaca: Cornell University Press, 1986.

Correa, Delia da Sousa. "George Eliot and the Germanic 'Musical Magus.'" In *George Eliot and Europe*, edited by John Rignall, 98–112. Aldershot: Ashgate, Scolar Press, 1996.

Craig, Gordon A. *Germany, 1866–1945*. New York: Oxford University Press, 1980.

– *Die Politik der Unpolitischen: Deutsche Schriftsteller und die Macht, 1770–1871*. Translated by Karl Heinz Siber. Munich: C.H. Beck, 1993.

Darwin, Charles. *The Descent of Man, and Selection in Relation to Sex*. 2nd ed. New York: A.L. Burt, 1874.

– *On the Origin of Species*. Cambridge: Harvard University Press, 1964.

De Laura, David J. "Heroic Egotism: Goethe and the Fortunes of *Bildung* in Victorian England." In *Johann Wolfgang von Goethe: One Hundred and Fifty Years of Continuing Vitality*, edited by Ulrich Goebel et al., 41–60. Lubbock: Texas Tech Press, 1984.

De Mille, Barbara. "Cruel Illusions: Nietzsche, Conrad, Hardy, and the 'Shadowy Ideal.'" *Studies in English Literature* 30, no. 4 (autumn 1990): 697–714.

Dent, Edward J. "Early Victorian Music." In *Early Victorian England, 1830–1865*, edited by E.M. Young, 2: 249–64. London: Oxford University Press, 1934.

DeVere, Jennifer. *Impossible Purities: Blackness, Femininity, and Victorian Culture*. Durham: Duke University, 1999.

Dickens, Charles. *Our Mutual Friend*. London: Oxford University Press, 1951.

Dilthey, Wilhelm. *Das Erlebnis und die Dichtung: Lessing, Goethe, Novalis, Hölderlin*. Leipzig: B.G. Teubner, 1906.

Disraeli, Benjamin. *Contarini Fleming; A Psychological Romance*. Bradenham Edition. London: Peter Davies, 1927.

– *Endymion*. Montreal: Dawson, 1880.

– *Vivian Grey*. Bradenham Edition. London: Peter Davies, 1927.

Dockhorn, Klaus. *Der deutsche Historismus in England*. Göttingen: Vandenhoeck and Ruprecht, 1950.

Drews, Arthur. *Eduard von Hartmanns Philosophie und der Materialismus in der modernen Kultur*. Leipzig: Hermann Haacke, 1898.

Eckermann, Johann Peter. *Gespräche mit Goethe*. Leipzig: Brockhaus, 1909.

Edwards, Lee R. *Psyche as Hero: Female Heroism and Fictional Form*. Middletown: Wesleyan University Press, 1984.

Eigner, Edwin M. *"The Pilgrims of the Rhine*: The Failure of the German *Bildungsroman* in England." *Victorian Newsletter* 68 (fall 1985): 19–21.

Elias, Norbert. *The Civilizing Process*. 1939. Translated by Edmund Jephcott. Oxford: Blackwell, 1994.

Eliot, George. *Adam Bede*. Edited by Stephen Gill. Harmondsworth: Penguin, 1980.

– *Daniel Deronda*. Edited by Barbara Hardy. Harmondsworth: Penguin, 1967.

– *Essays of George Eliot*. Edited by Thomas Pinney. New York: Columbia University Press, 1963.

– *The George Eliot Letters*. Edited by Gordon S. Haight. 7 vols. New Haven: Yale University Press, 1954–55.

– *Impressions of Theophrastus Such*. Edited by Nancy Henry. Iowa City: University of Iowa Press, 1994.

– *Middlemarch*. Edited by W.H. Harvey. Harmondsworth: Penguin, 1965.

– *The Mill on the Floss*. Edited by A.S. Byatt. Harmondsworth: Penguin, 1979.

– "The Modern Hep! Hep! Hep!" In *Impressions of Theophrastus Such*, edited by Nancy Henry, 143–65. Iowa City: University of Iowa Press, 1994.

- trans. *The Essence of Christianity,* by Ludwig Feuerbach. New York: Harper, 1957.
- trans. *The Life of Jesus, Critically Examined*, by David Friedrich Strauss. 4th ed. London: Swan Sonnenschein, 1902.
Eliot, T.S. *After Strange Gods: A Primer of Modern Heresy.* New York: Harcourt, Brace, 1934.
Ellmann, Richard. "Dorothea's Husbands." In *George Eliot,* edited by Harold Bloom, 65–80. New York: Chelsea House, 1986. Originally appeared in *Golden Codgers: Bio-graphical Speculations* (1973).
Enright, J.D. "Aimez-vous Goethe?: An Enquiry into English Attitudes of Non-liking towards German Literature." In *Conspirators and Poets*, 208–18. Chester Springs: Dufone, 1966.
Espinasse, Francis. *Literary Recollections and Sketches.* London: Hodder and Stoughton, 1893.
Essays and Reviews. London: John W. Parker and Son, 1860.
Feltes, N.N. *Modes of Production of Victorian Novels.* Chicago: University of Chicago Press, 1986.
Feuerbach, Ludwig. *Das Wesen des Christentums.* Vol. 5, *Gesammelte Werke.* Edited by Werner Schuffenhauer. Berlin: Akademie Verlag, 1973.
Fichte, Johann Gottlieb. *Fichte: Early Philsophical Writings*. Translated and edited by Daniel Breazeale. Ithaca: Cornell University Press, 1988.
- *Von den Pflichten des Gelehrten: Jenaer Vorlesungen, 1794/95*. Edited by Reinhard Lauth, Hans Jacob, and Peter Schneider. Hamburg: Felix Meiner, 1971.
Field, Michael. *Works and Days: From the Journal of Michael Field.* Edited by T. and D.C. Sturge Moore. London: John Murray, 1933.
Firchow, Peter Edgerly. *The Death of the German Cousin: Variations on a Literary Stereotype, 1890–1920*. Lewisburg: Bucknell University Press, 1986.
Firebaugh, Joseph J. "A Schopenhauerian Novel: James's *The Princess Casamassima.*" *Nineteenth-Century Fiction* 13 (1958–59): 177–97.
Fitzgerald, Penelope. *The Blue Flower.* Boston: Houghton Mifflin, 1995.
Fletcher, Ian, ed. *Meredith Now: Some Critical Essays.* New York: Barnes and Noble, 1971.
Flower, Sibylla Jane. "Charles Dickens and Edward Bulwer-Lytton." *The Dickensian* 69 (1973): 79–89.
Fogel, Aaron. "The Fragmentation of Sympathy in *The Secret Agent*." In *Joseph Conrad*, edited by Elaine Jordan, 168–92. New York: St. Martin's Press, 1996.
Ford, Ford Madox. *The Good Soldier.* Edited by Martin Stannard. New York: Norton, 1995.
- *Parade's End: Some Do Not …; No More Parades; A Man Could Stand Up –; Last Post.* 2 vols. New York: New American Library, 1964.
- *When Blood Is Their Argument*. New York: Hodder and Stoughton, 1915.
Forester, C.S. *The African Queen.* New York: Random House, 1940.

Forster, E.M. *Aspects of the Novel*. Edited by Oliver Stallybrass. Harmondsworth: Penguin, 1976.

– *Howards End*. Edited by Alistair M. Duckworth. Boston: Bedford Books, 1997.

– "Joseph Conrad: A Note." In *Abinger Harvest*, 159–64. London: Edward Arnold, 1936.

– *The Longest Journey*. Garden City: Garden City Publishing, 1922.

– *Maurice*. Toronto: Macmillan, 1971.

– Obituary for D.H. Lawrence. In *D.H. Lawrence: The Critical Heritage*, edited by R.P. Draper, 343–7. London: Routledge and Kegan Paul, 1970. Originally published in the *Listener*, 30 April 1930, iii, 753–4.

– *A Passage to India*. Edited by Oliver Stallybrass. Harmondsworth: Penguin, 1979.

– *Selected Letters of E.M. Forster*. 2 vols. Edited by Mary Lago and P.N. Furbank. Cambridge: Harvard University Press, 1983–85.

– *Two Cheers for Democracy*. London: Edward Arnold, 1951.

Friedenthal, Richard. *Goethe: sein Leben und seine Zeit*. München: R. Piper, 1963.

Froude, James Anthony. *The Nemesis of Faith*. Repr. from the 2nd ed., 1849; London: Libris, 1988.

Gay, Peter. *Weimar Culture: The Outsider as Insider*. New York: Harper and Row, 1968.

Genette, Gérard. *Palimpsests: Literature in the Second Degree*. Translated by Channa Newman and Claude Doubinsky. Lincoln: University of Nebraska Press, 1997.

Gissing, George. *The Collected Letters of George Gissing*. Edited by Paul F. Mattheisen, Arthur C. Young, and Pierre Coustillas. 5 vols. Athens: Ohio University Press, 1990.

– *The Crown of Life*. 2nd ed. London: Methuen, 1927.

– *George Gissing and H.G. Wells: Their Friendship and Correspondence*. Edited by Royal A. Gettmann. Urbana: University of Illinois Press, 1961.

– *George Gissing's Commonplace Book*. Edited by Jacob Korg. New York: New York Public Library, 1962.

– "The Hope of Pessimism." In *George Gissing: Essays and Fiction*, edited by Pierre Coustillas, 75–98. Baltimore: Johns Hopkins Press, 1970.

– *The Letters of George Gissing to Eduard Bertz, 1887–1903*. Edited by Arthur C. Young. London: Constable, 1961.

– *Letters of George Gissing to Members of His Family*. Edited by Algernon and Ellen Gissing. New York: Haskell House, 1970.

– *Our Friend the Charlatan*. Edited by Pierre Coustillas. Rutherford: Fairleigh Dickinson University Press, 1976.

– *The Private Papers of Henry Ryecroft*. London: Constable, 1903.

– *The Unclassed*. Edited by Jacob Korg. Rutherford: Fairleigh Dickinson University Press, 1976.
– *The Whirlpool*. New York: AMS Press, 1969.
– *Workers in the Dawn*. 3 vols. in 1. New York: Garland, 1976.
Goethe, Johann Wolfgang von. *Briefe an Goethe*. Edited by Karl Robert Mandelkow. 2 vols. Hamburg: Christian Wegner, 1965.
– *Goethes Briefe*. Edited by Karl Robert Mandelkow and Bodo Morawe. 4 vols. Hamburg: Christian Wegner, 1962.
– *Goethes Werke*. Hamburger Ausgabe. 10th ed. 14 vols. München: C.H. Beck, 1981. This is the edition cited except where otherwise indicated.
– *Goethes Werke*. Sophien-Ausgabe. 143 vols. Weimar, 1887–1912; Tokyo: Sansyushya, 1975.
–*Wilhelm Meisters Wanderjahre, oder Die Entsagenden. Urfassung von 1821*. Repr., Bonn: Bouvier Verlag Herbert Grundmann, 1986.
Gosse, Edmund. *Father and Son*. Edited by Peter Abbs. Harmondsworth: Penguin, 1983.
– "The Limits of Realism." In *Questions at Issue*, 137–54. New York: D. Appleton, 1893.
Graham, Kenneth. *English Criticism of the Novel, 1865–1900*. Oxford: Clarendon Press, 1965.
Gray, Ronald. *The German Tradition in Literature, 1871–1945*. Cambridge: Cambridge University Press, 1965.
Greenslade, William. *Degeneration, Culture and the Novel, 1880–1940*. Cambridge: Cambridge University Press, 1994.
Guérard, Albert J. "A Version of Anarchy." In *Conrad*, The Secret Agent: *A Casebook*, edited by Ian Watt, 150–65. London: Macmillan, 1973.
Habermas, Jürgen. "Heinrich Heine und die Rolle des Intellektuellen in Deutschland." *Merkur* 50, no. 12 (December 1996): 1122–37. Originally published in *Merkur* 448 (June 1986).
Haight, Gordon S. *George Eliot: A Biography*. Oxford: Clarendon Press, 1968.
– ed. *A Century of George Eliot Criticism*. Boston: Houghton Mifflin, 1965.
Haines, George. *Essays on German Influence upon English Education and Science, 1850–1919*. Hamden: Connecticut College, 1969.
– *German Influence upon English Education and Science, 1800–1866*. New London: Connecticut College, 1957.
Hamburger, Michael. *From Prophecy to Exorcism: The Premisses of Modern German Literature*. London: Longmans, 1965.
– *Reason and Energy*. London: Weidenfeld and Nicholson, 1970.
Hardy, Barbara. *Particularities: Readings in George Eliot*. London: Peter Owen, 1982.
Hardy, Thomas. *The Literary Notebooks of Thomas Hardy*. Edited by Lennart A. Björk. 2 vols. New York: New York University Press, 1985.

– *Tess of the D'Urbervilles*. Edited by David Skilton. Harmondsworth: Penguin, 1978.

Harris, Horton. *The Tübingen School*. Oxford: Clarendon Press, 1975.

Harrold, Charles F. *Carlyle and German Thought: 1819–1834*. 1934; London: Archon Books, 1963.

Hartmann, Eduard von. *Die Philosophie des Unbewussten*. 2 vols. in 1. Berlin: Carl Duncker, 1882.

Hegel, Georg Wilhelm Friedrich. *Vorlesungen über die Philosophie der Geschichte*. Stuttgart: Fr. Frommann, 1961.

Heine, Heinrich. *Heinrich Heine: Sämtliche Werke*. Düsseldorfer Ausgabe. Edited by Manfred Windfuhr. 15 vols. Hamburg: Hoffmann und Campe, 1975–82.

Heller, Deborah. "Jews and Women in George Eliot's *Daniel Deronda*." In *Jewish Presences in English Literature*, edited by Derek Cohen and Deborah Heller, 76–95. Montreal: McGill-Queen's University Press, 1990.

Helmstadter, Richard J., and Bernard Lightman, ed. *Victorian Faith in Crisis: Essays on Continuity and Change in Nineteenth-Century Religious Belief*. London: Macmillan, 1990.

Herbert, Christopher. *Culture and Anomie: Ethnographic Imagination in the Nineteenth Century*. Chicago: University of Chicago Press, 1991.

Herder, Johann Gottfried. *Sämtliche Werke*. Edited by Bernhard Suphan. 33 vols. 1881; Hildesheim: Georg Olms, 1967–69.

Heyck, T.W. *The Transformation of Intellectual Life in Victorian England*. London: Croom Helm, 1982.

Hillern, Wilhelmine von. *Ein Arzt der Seele*. 4 vols. in 2. Berlin: Otto Janke, 1886.

Hinds, Stephen. *Allusion and Intertext: Dynamics of Appropriation in Roman Poetry*. Cambridge: Cambridge University Press, 1998.

Hobsbawm, E.J. *The Age of Empire, 1875–1914*. London: Weidenfeld and Nicolson, 1987.

Horsman, Alan. *The Victorian Novel*. The Oxford History of English Literature, vol. 8. Oxford: Clarendon Press, 1990.

Houghton, Walter E. *The Victorian Frame of Mind, 1830–1870*. New Haven: Yale University Press, 1957.

Howard, David. "George Meredith: 'Delicate' and 'Epical' Fiction." In *Literature and Politics in the Nineteenth Century*, edited by John Lucas, 131–72. London: Methuen, 1971.

Howe, Irving. "Conrad: Order and Anarchy." In *Conrad*, The Secret Agent: *A Casebook*, edited by Ian Watt, 140–9. London: Macmillan, 1973.

Howe, Susanne. *Wilhelm Meister and His English Kinsmen*. New York: Columbia University Press, 1930.

Humboldt, Wilhelm von. *Wilhelm von Humboldts Gesammelte Schriften*. Vol. 1. Edited by Albert Leitzmann. Berlin: Walter de Gruyter, 1968.

Humma, John B. "D.H. Lawrence as Friedrich Nietzsche." *Philological Quarterly* 53, no. 1 (January 1974): 110–19.

Hynes, Samuel. *A War Imagined: The First World War and English Culture*. London: The Bodley Head, 1990.

Isherwood, Christopher. *The Berlin Stories: The Last of Mr. Norris, Goodbye to Berlin*. New York: New Directions, 1963.

– *Christopher and His Kind, 1929–1939*. New York: Farrar, Straus, Giroux, 1976.

– "From Down There on a Visit." In *Critical Essays on E.M. Forster*, edited by Alan Wilde, 29–30. Boston: G.K. Hall, 1985.

Ishiguro, Kazuo. *The Remains of the Day*. London: Faber and Faber, 1989.

Jacobs, Carol. [The Passion for Talk]. In *The Good Soldier*, by Ford Madox Ford, edited by Martin Stannard, 337–44. New York: Norton, 1995.

Jacobs, Joseph. "Mordecai: A Protest against the Critics by a Jew." In *Critics on George Eliot*, edited by William Baker, 34–42. London: George Allen and Unwin, 1973. Originally published in *Macmillan's Magazine* 34 (June 1877).

Jacobs, Jürgen. *Wilhelm Meister und seine Brüder: Untersuchungen zum deutschen Bildungsroman*. München: Wilhelm Fink, 1972.

James, Henry. *The Bostonians*. The Bodley Head Henry James, vol. 3. London: The Bodley Head, 1967.

– "*Daniel Deronda*: A Conversation." In *A Century of George Eliot Criticism*, edited by Gordon S. Haight, 97–112. Boston: Houghton Mifflin, 1965. Originally published in *Atlantic Monthly* 38 (December 1876): 684–94.

– "George Eliot's *Middlemarch*." 1873. In *A Century of George Eliot Criticism*, edited by Gordon S. Haight, 80–7. Boston: Houghton Mifflin, 1965.

– "Homburg Reformed." In *Transatlantic Sketches*, 354–66. Boston: James R. Osgood, 1875.

– *Literary Reviews and Essays by Henry James, on American, English, and French Literature*. Edited by Albert Mordell. New York: Twayne, 1957.

– *The Princess Casamassima*. The Bodley Head Henry James, vol. 10. London: The Bodley Head, 1972.

Jasper, David, and T.R. Wright, ed. *The Critical Spirit and the Will to Believe*. New York: St. Martin's Press, 1989.

Jauss, Hans Robert. "Literary History as a Challenge to Literary Theory." In *Toward an Aesthetic of Reception*, 3–45. Translated by Timothy Bahti. Minneapolis: University of Minneapolis Press, 1982.

Jay, Elizabeth. "Doubt and the Victorian Woman." In *The Critical Spirit and the Will to Believe*, edited by David Jasper and T.R. Wright, 88–103. New York: St. Martin's Press, 1989.

Johnston, Sir Harry. *Views and Reviews, from the Outlook of an Anthropologist*. London: Williams & Norgate, 1912.

Jowett, Benjamin. "On the Interpretation of Scripture." In *Essays and Reviews*, 330–433. London: John W. Parker and Son, 1860.

Judd, Alan. *Ford Madox Ford*. Cambridge: Harvard University Press, 1990.

Kant, Immanuel. *Kants Werke*. Akademie-Textausgabe. Vol. 8. Berlin: Walter de Gruyter, 1968.

Kaplan, Fred. *Thomas Carlyle: A Biography*. Ithaca: Cornell University Press, 1983.

Kaufmann, Walter, ed. and trans. *The Portable Nietzsche*. New York: Viking Penguin, 1954.

Kelly, Mary Ann. "Schopenhauer's Influence on Hardy's *Jude the Obscure*." In *Schopenhauer: New Essays in Honour of His 200th Birthday*, edited by Eric von der Luft, 232–46. Lewiston: E. Mellen Press, 1988.

Kelvin, Norman. *A Troubled Eden: Nature and Society in the Works of George Meredith*. Stanford: Stanford University Press, 1961.

Kennedy, Paul M. *The Rise of the Anglo-German Antagonism, 1860–1914*. London: G. Allen and Unwin, 1980.

Kettle, Arnold. "Beauchamp's Career." In *Meredith Now: Some Critical Essays*, edited by Ian Fletcher, 188–204. New York: Barnes and Noble, 1971.

Kiernan, V.G. *The Lords of Human Kind: European Attitudes towards the Outside World in the Imperial Age*. London: Weidenfeld and Nicolson, 1969.

King, Margaret F., and Elliot Engel. "The Emerging Carlylean Hero in Bulwer's Novels of the 1830s." *Nineteenth-Century Literature* 36, no. 3 (1981): 277–95.

Kingsley, Charles. *Alton Locke: Tailor and Poet*. London: Dent, 1970.

Kipling, Rudyard. *The Years Between*. Garden City, NY: Doubleday, Page, 1919.

Klieneberger, H.R. *The Novel in England and Germany*. London: Oswald Wolff, 1981.

Knights, Ben. *The Idea of the Clerisy in the Nineteenth Century*. Cambridge: Cambridge University Press, 1978.

Knoepflmacher, U.C. *Religious Humanism and the Victorian Novel: George Eliot, Walter Pater, and Samuel Butler*. Princeton: Princeton University Press, 1965.

Kontje, Todd. *The German Bildungsroman: History of a National Genre*. Columbia: Camden House, 1993.

– *Private Lives in the Public Sphere: The German* Bildungsroman *as Metafiction*. University Park: Pennsylvania State University, 1992.

Kuschel, Karl-Josef. "The Critical Spirit and the Will to Believe: Heinrich Heine: A Test Case." In *The Critical Spirit and the Will to Believe*, edited by David Jasper and T.R. Wright, 158–90. New York: St. Martin's Press, 1989.

Laing, S. *Modern Science and Modern Thought*. 1885. 6th ed. London: Chapman and Hall, 1902.

Lawrence, D.H. *Aaron's Rod*. Edited by Mara Kalnins. Cambridge: Cambridge University Press, 1988.

– *Kangaroo*. New York: Thomas Seltzer, 1923.

– *The Letters of D.H. Lawrence*. Edited by James T. Boulton. 7 vols. Cambridge: Cambridge University Press, 1979–93.

– *Mornings in Mexico and Etruscan Places*. Melbourne: William Heinemann, 1956.
– *Phoenix: The Posthumous Papers of D.H. Lawrence*. Edited by Edward D. McDonald. New York: Viking Press, 1936.
– *The Plumed Serpent*. Edited by L.D. Clark. Cambridge: Cambridge University Press, 1987.
– *Selected Literary Criticism*. Edited by Anthony Beal. New York: Viking Press, 1956.
– *Selected Poetry and Non-Fictional Prose*. Edited by John Lucas. London: Routledge, 1990.
– *Women in Love*. Edited by David Farmer, Lindeth Vasey, and John Worthen. Cambridge: Cambridge University Press, 1987.

Lettis, Richard. *Dickens on Literature: A Continuing Study of His Aesthetic*. New York: AMS Press, 1990.

Levine, George. "Scientific Discourse as an Alternative to Faith." In *Victorian Faith in Crisis: Essays on Continuity and Change in Nineteenth-Century Religious Belief*, edited by Richard J. Helmstadter and Bernard Lightman, 225–61. London: Macmillan, 1990.

Lewald, Fanny. *Meine Lebensgeschichte*. Edited by Gisela Brinker-Gabler. Frankfurt/Main: Fischer, 1980.

Lewes, George Henry. *The Life and Works of Goethe*. 2 vols. London: David Nutt, 1855.

– *The Life of Goethe*. 2nd ed. London: Smith, Elder, 1864.

Lightman, Bernard. "*Robert Elsmere* and the Agnostic Crises of Faith." In *Victorian Faith in Crisis: Essays on Continuity and Change in Nineteenth-Century Religious Belief*, edited by Richard J. Helmstadter and Bernard Lightman, 283–311. London: Macmillan, 1990.

Lodge, David. *Small World: An Academic Romance*. London: Secker and Warburg, 1984.

Lord, Ursula. *Solitude versus Solidarity in the Novels of Joseph Conrad: Political and Epistemological Implications of Narrative Innovation*. Montreal: McGill-Queen's University Press, 1998.

Lucas, John. Introduction to *Literature and Politics in the Nineteenth Century*. London: Methuen, 1971.

– ed. *Literature and Politics in the Nineteenth Century*. London: Methuen, 1971.

Lytton, Edward Robert Bulwer. *The Life, Letters, and Literary Remains of Bulwer, Lord Lytton, by His Son*. 2 vols. London: Kegan Paul, 1883.

Lytton, Victor Alexander. *The Life of Edward Bulwer, First Lord of Lytton, by His Grandson*. 2 vols. London: Macmillan, 1913.

McCobb, Anthony. *George Eliot's Knowledge of German Life and Letters*. Salzburg: Institut für Anglistik und Amerikanistik, University of Salzburg, 1982.

McCobb, E.A. "*Daniel Deronda* as Will and Representation: George Eliot and Schopenhauer." *Modern Language Review* 80, no. 3 (July 1985): 533–49.

– "The Morality of Musical Genius: Schopenhauerian Views in *Daniel Deronda*." *Forum for Modern Language Studies* 19, no. 4 (October 1983): 321–30.

– "Of Women and Doctors: *Middlemarch* and Wilhelmine von Hillern's *Ein Arzt der Seele*." *Neophilologus* 68, no. 4 (October 1984): 571–86.

McGill, Vivian J. *Schopenhauer: Pessimist and Pagan*. New York: Haskell House, 1971.

Mackay, R.W. *The Tübingen School and Its Antecedents: A Review of the History and Present Condition of Modern Theology*. London: Williams and Norgate, 1863.

McMaster, R.D. *Thackeray's Cultural Frame of Reference: Allusion in* The Newcomes. Montreal: McGill-Queen's University Press, 1991.

MacShane, Frank. Introduction to *Ford Madox Ford: The Critical Heritage*. London: Routledge and Kegan Paul, 1972.

– ed. *Ford Madox Ford: The Critical Heritage*. London: Routledge and Kegan Paul, 1972.

Magee, Bryan. *The Philosophy of Schopenhauer*. Oxford: Clarendon Press, 1983.

Maison, Margaret M. *The Victorian Vision: Studies in the Religious Novel*. New York: Sheed and Ward, 1962.

Mander, John. *Our German Cousins: Anglo-German Relations in the 19th and 20th Centuries*. London: J. Murray, 1974.

Mann, Thomas. Preface to German translation of *The Secret Agent* (1926). In *Conrad,* The Secret Agent: *A Casebook*, edited by Ian Watt, 99–112. London: Macmillan, 1973.

Manos, Nikki Lee. "*The Ordeal of Richard Feverel*: *Bildungsroman* or anti-*Bildungsroman*?" *Victorian Newsletter* 70 (fall 1986): 18–24.

Marcuse, Ludwig. *Heine*. Rothenburg: Verlag J.P. Peter, Gebr. Holstein, 1970.

Martini, Fritz. "Der Bildungsroman: Zur Geschichte des Wortes und der Theorie." *Deutsche Vierteljahrsschrift für Literaturwissenschaft und Geistesgeschichte* 35 (1961): 44–63.

Masson, David. *British Novelists and Their Styles: Being a Critical Sketch of the History of British Prose Fiction*. Boston: Willard Small, 1892.

Maugham, W. Somerset. *Of Human Bondage*. 1915; New York: Penguin, 1992.

May, Brian. "Modernism and Other Modes in Forster's *The Longest Journey*." *Twentieth Century Literature* 42, no. 2 (summer 1996): 234–57.

Mayhew, Henry. *German Life and Manners, as Seen in Saxony at the Present Day*. London: Wm.H. Allen, 1865.

Melnyk, Julie, ed. *Women's Theology in Britain: Transfiguring the Faith of Their Fathers*. New York: Garland Press, 1998.

Meredith, George. *An Essay on Comedy and the Uses of the Comic Spirit*. London: Constable, 1897.

– *The Letters of George Meredith*. 3 vols. Edited by C.L. Cline. Oxford: Clarendon Press, 1970.

- *The Poetical Works of George Meredith*. London: Constable, 1912.
- *The Works of George Meredith*. Memorial Edition. 27 vols. London: Constable, 1909–11.

Meyer, Hermann. *The Poetics of Quotation in the European Novel*. 1961. Translated by Theodore and Yetta Ziolkowski. Princeton: Princeton University Press, 1968.

Meyer, Susan. "'Safely to Their Own Borders': Proto-Zionism, Feminism, and Nationalism in *Daniel Deronda*." *English Literary History* 60, no. 3 (1993): 733–58.

Mill, John Stuart. *Autobiography*. Edited by John M. Robson. London: Penguin, 1989.

- *On Liberty*. In *John Stuart Mill: A Selection of His Works*, edited by John M. Robson. Indianapolis: Odyssey Press, 1966.

Miller, J. Hillis. "On *The Secret Agent*." In *Conrad*, The Secret Agent: *A Casebook*, edited by Ian Watt, 179–201. London: Macmillan, 1973.

Millgate, Michael. *Thomas Hardy: A Biography*. New York: Random House, 1982.

Mintz, Alan. *George Eliot and the Novel of Vocation*. Cambridge: Harvard University Press, 1978.

Mitchell, Juliet. "*The Ordeal of Richard Feverel*: A Sentimental Education." In *Meredith Now: Some Critical Essays*, edited by Ian Fletcher, 69–94. New York: Barnes and Noble, 1971.

Moore, James R. "Theodicy and Society: The Crisis of the Intelligentsia." In *Victorian Faith in Crisis: Essays on Continuity and Change in Nineteenth-Century Religious Belief*, edited by Richard J. Helmstadter and Bernard Lightman, 153–86. London: Macmillan, 1990.

Moretti, Franco. *The Way of the World: The* Bildungsroman *in European Culture*. London: Verso, 1987.

Morgan, Bayard Quincy, ed. *German Literature in British Magazines, 1750–1860*. Madison: University of Wisconsin Press, 1949.

Morley, John. *On Compromise*. London: Macmillan, 1886.

Newman, John Henry. *Newman: Prose and Poetry*. Edited by Geoffrey Tillotson. London: Rupert Hart-Davis, 1957.

Nietzsche, Friedrich. *Nietzsche Werke*. Kritische Gesamtausgabe. Edited by Giorgio Colli and Mazzino Montinari. 30 vols. Berlin: Walter de Gruyter, 1967–.

Nordau, Max. *Degeneration*. Translated from the 2nd ed. London: William Heinemann, 1898.

Norris, Margot. *Beasts of the Modern Imagination*. Baltimore: Johns Hopkins University Press, 1985.

Novalis [Friedrich von Hardenberg]. *Schriften*. Edited by Richard Samuel, Hans-Joachim Mähl, and Gerhard Schulz. 6 vols. Stuttgart: W. Kohlhammer, 1960–.

Panayi, Panikos. *The Enemy in Our Midst: Germans in Britain during the First World War*. New York: Berg, 1991.

Pasco, Allan H. *Allusion: A Literary Graft*. Toronto: University of Toronto Press, 1994.

Payne, E.F.J., trans. *Parerga and Paralipomena: Short Philosophical Essays by Arthur Schopenhauer*. 2 vols. Oxford: Clarendon Press, 1974.

Pecora, Vincent P. "Arnoldian Ethnology." *Victorian Studies* 41, no. 3 (spring 1998): 355–80.

Petter, Guy B. *George Meredith and His German Critics*. London: H.F. and G. Witherby, 1939.

Pimlott, J.A.R. *The Englishman's Holiday: A Social History*. London: Faber and Faber, 1947.

Pinney, Thomas, ed. *Essays of George Eliot*. New York: Columbia University Press, 1963.

Price, Lawrence Marsden. *The Reception of English Literature in Germany*. 1932. Repr., New York: Benjamin Blom, 1968.

Pritchett, Stephen. "Poetics and Narrative: Biblical Criticism and the Nineteenth-Century Novel." In *The Critical Spirit and the Will to Believe*, edited by David Jasper and T.R. Wright, 1–22. New York: St. Martin's Press, 1989.

Reallexikon der deutschen Literaturgeschichte. 2nd ed. Edited by Werner Kohlschmidt and W. Mohr. 5 vols. Berlin: Walter de Gruyter, 1958–84.

Reardon, Bernard M.G. *Religious Thought in the Nineteenth Century, Illustrated from Writers in the Period*. Cambridge: Cambridge University Press, 1966.

Renan, Ernest. *The Life of Jesus*. Introduction by John Haynes Holmes. New York: Random House, 1955.

Reynolds, Graham. *Victorian Painting*. London: Studio Vista, 1966.

Richardson, Dorothy M. *Pointed Roofs*. In *Pilgrimage*, 1:13–186. London: Virago, 1979.

Riehl, Wilhelm Heinrich. *Die bürgerliche Gesellschaft*. Vol. 2, *Die Naturgeschichte des Volkes als Grundlage einer deutschen Social-Politik*. 2nd ed. Stuttgart: Cotta, 1854–55.

Riewald, J.G. *Beerbohm's Literary Caricatures: From Homer to Huxley*. Hamden: Archon Books, 1977.

Rignall, John, ed. *George Eliot and Europe*. Aldershot: Ashgate, Scolar Press, 1996.

Roazen, Deborah Heller. "*Middlemarch* and the Wordsworthian Imagination." *English Studies* 58, no. 5 (October 1977): 411–25.

Robinson, Henry Crabb. *Diary, Reminiscences, and Correspondence of Henry Crabb Robinson*. Edited by Thomas Sadler. London: Macmillan, 1869.

Röder-Bolton, Gerlinde. *George Eliot and Goethe: An Elective Affinity*. Amsterdam: Rodopi, 1998.

Rosecrance, Barbara. "*Howards End*." In *E.M. Forster*, edited by Harold Bloom, 107–34. New York: Chelsea House, 1987.

Rosenberg, Edgar. *From Shylock to Svengali: Jewish Stereotypes in English Fiction*. Stanford: Stanford University Press, 1960.

Ross, Janet. *Three Generations of Englishwomen*. 2 vols. London: John Murray, 1888.

Rutherford, Mark [William Hale White]. *Autobiography* and *Deliverance*. Repr. from the 2nd ed., 1888. New York: Humanities Press, 1969.

Safranski, Rüdiger. *Schopenhauer and the Wild Years of Philosophy*. 1987. Translated by Ewald Osers. London: Weidenfeld and Nicolson, 1989.

Said, Edward W. "Conrad and Nietzsche." In *Joseph Conrad: A Commemoration*, edited by Norman Sherry, 65–76. London: Macmillan, 1976.

– *Culture and Imperialism*. New York: Alfred A. Knopf, 1993.

Sammons, Jeffrey L. *Heinrich Heine: A Modern Biography*. Princeton: Princeton University Press, 1979.

– "The Mystery of the Missing *Bildungsroman*, or: What Happened to Wilhelm Meister's Legacy?" *Genre* 14 (summer 1981): 229–46.

Sandison, Alan. *The Wheel of Empire: A Study of the Imperial Idea in Some Late Nineteenth and Early Twentieth-Century Fiction*. New York: St. Martin's Press, 1967.

Sassoon, Siegfried. *Meredith*. London: Constable, 1948.

Scheick, William. *Fictional Structure & Ethics: The Turn-of-the-Century English Novel*. Athens: University of Georgia Press, 1990.

Schenk, H.G. *The Mind of the European Romantics: An Essay in Cultural History*. Garden City: Doubleday, 1969.

Schiller, Friedrich. *Sämtliche Werke*. Edited by Gerhard Fricke and H.G. Göpfert. 5 vols. München: Carl Hanser, 1967.

Schirmer, Walter Franz. *Der Einfluss der deutschen Literatur auf die Englische im 19. Jahrhundert*. Halle/Saale: M. Niemeyer, 1947.

Schmitt, Bernadotte Everly. *England and Germany, 1740–1914*. 1916; New York: Howard Fertig, 1967.

Schneider, Daniel J. *The Consciousness of D.H. Lawrence: An Intellectual Biography*. Kansas: University Press of Kansas, 1986.

– "Schopenhauer and the Development of D.H. Lawrence's Psychology." *South Atlantic Review* 48, no. 1 (January 1983): 1–19.

Schopenhauer, Arthur. *Parerga und Paralipomena*. 3rd ed. 2 vols. Leipzig: F.A. Brockhaus, 1874.

– *Parerga and Paralipomena: Short Philosophical Essays by Arthur Schopenhauer*. Translated by E.F.J. Payne. 2 vols. Oxford: Clarendon Press, 1974.

– *Die Welt als Wille und Vorstellung*. Edited by J. Frauenstädt. 2 vols. Leipzig: F.A. Brockhaus, 1873.

Seeber, Hans Ulrich. "Cultural Synthesis in George Eliot's *Middlemarch*." In *George Eliot and Europe*, edited by John Rignall, 17–32. Aldershot: Ashgate, Scolar Press, 1996.

Seibt, Gustav. "Kann eine Biographie ein Werk zerstören? Bemerkungen zu de Man, Jauss, Schwerte und Hermlin." *Merkur* 52, no. 3 (March 1998): 215–26.

Semmel, Bernard. *George Eliot and the Politics of National Inheritance*. Oxford: Oxford University Press, 1994.

Shaffer, E.S. *"Kubla Khan" and* The Fall of Jerusalem: *The Mythological School in Biblical Criticism and Secular Literature, 1770–1880*. Cambridge: Cambridge University Press, 1975.

Shaffner, Randolph P. *The Apprenticeship Novel*. New York: Peter Lang, 1984.

Sheppard, Elizabeth. *Charles Auchester*. 1853. 2 vols. Chicago: A.C. McClurg, 1894.

Skilton, David, ed. *The Early and Mid-Victorian Novel*. London: Routledge, 1993.

Smiles, Samuel. *Self-Help*. 1859; Harmondsworth: Penguin, 1986.

Smirlock, Daniel. "The Models of *Richard Feverel*." *Journal of Narrative Technique* 11, no. 2 (1981): 91–109.

Southerington, F.R. *Hardy's Vision of Man*. London: Chatto and Windus, 1971.

Speare, Morris Edmund. *The Political Novel: Its Development in England and America*. 1924; New York: Russell and Russell, 1966.

Spender, Stephen. *European Witness*. Cornwall, USA: Cornwall Press, 1946.

– *World within World: The Autobiography of Stephen Spender*. [N.p.]: Hamish Hamilton and the Book Society, 1951.

Staël, Mme de (Anne Louise Germaine). *Germany*. Translation of the 2nd ed. 3 vols. London: John Murray, 1814.

Staiger, Emil. *Goethe*. 3 vols. Zürich: Atlantis Verlag, 1959.

Stang, Richard. *The Theory of the Novel in England, 1850–1870*. New York: Columbia University Press, 1959.

Stanley, Arthur Penrhyn. *The Life and Correspondence of Thomas Arnold, D.D.* 2 vols. in 1. Boston: Fields, Osgood, 1870.

Stephen, Sir Lesley. "George Eliot." In *A Century of George Eliot Criticism*, edited by Gordon S. Haight, 136–49. Originally published in *Cornhill Magazine* 43 (February 1881): 152–68.

– "The Importation of German." In *Studies of a Biographer*, 2:35–70. London: Smith, Elder, 1907.

Stern, Fritz. *The Politics of Cultural Despair*. Garden City: Doubleday, 1965.

Stevenson, Lionel. *The English Novel: A Panorama*. Cambridge, Mass.: Riverside, 1960.

Stevenson, Randall. *The British Novel since the Thirties: An Introduction*. Athens: University of Georgia Press, 1986.

Stone, James. "Meredith and Goethe." *University of Toronto Quarterly* 21, no. 2 (1952): 157–66.

Strachey, John. *The End of Empire*. London: Gollancz, 1959.

Sucksmith, Harvey Peter. *The Narrative Art of Charles Dickens*. Oxford: Clarendon Press, 1970.

Sutherland, J.A. *Fiction and the Fiction Industry*. London: Athlone Press, 1978.

Sutherland, John. *Mrs Humphry Ward: Eminent Victorian, Pre-eminent Edwardian*. Oxford: Clarendon Press, 1982.
– *Victorian Fiction: Writers, Publishers, Readers*. New York: St. Martin's Press, 1995.
Swales, Martin. *The German Bildungsroman from Wieland to Hesse*. Princeton: Princeton University Press, 1978.
Taine, Hippolyte. *Notes on England, 1860–1870*. Translated by Edward Hyans. Fair Lawn: Essential Books, 1958.
Tarratt, Margaret. "*The Adventures of Harry Richmond – Bildungsroman* and Historical Novel." In *Meredith Now: Some Critical Essays*, edited by Ian Fletcher, 165–87. New York: Barnes and Noble, 1971.
Tennyson, Alfred Lord. *In Memoriam*. Edited by Susan Shatta and Marion Shaw. Oxford: Clarendon Press, 1982.
Tennyson, G.B. "The Bildungsroman in Nineteenth-Century English Literature." In *Medieval Epic to the "Epic Theater" of Brecht*, edited by Rosario P. Armato and John M. Spalek, 135–46. Los Angeles: University of Southern California Press, 1968.
Thackeray, William Makepeace. *Selected Letters of William Makepeace Thackeray*. Edited by Edgar F. Harden. New York: New York University Press, 1996.
Thatcher, David S. *Nietzsche in England, 1890–1914*. Toronto: University of Toronto Press, 1970.
Thomas, D.M. *The White Hotel: A Novel*. Toronto: Clarke, Irwin, 1981.
Thornton, A.P. *The Imperial Idea and Its Enemies: A Study in British Power*. New York: St. Martin's Press, 1966.
Tillotson, Kathleen. *Novels of the Eighteen-Forties*. Oxford: Clarendon Press, 1956.
Trilling, Lionel. *E.M. Forster*. 1943. Oxford: Oxford University Press, 1982.
Trollope, Anthony. *An Autobiography*. London: Oxford University Press, 1950.
– *Barchester Towers*. Edited by Robin Gilmour. Harmondsworth: Penguin, 1983.
– *The Prime Minister*. Oxford: Oxford University Press, 1973.
Trübners Deutsches Wörterbuch. Edited by Alfred Götze. 8 vols. Berlin: Walter de Gruyter, 1939–57.
Turner, Frank M. "The Victorian Crisis of Faith and the Faith That Was Lost." In *Victorian Faith in Crisis: Essays on Continuity and Change in Nineteenth-Century Religious Belief*, edited by Richard J. Helmstadter and Bernard Lightman, 9–38. London: Macmillan, 1990.
Verheyden, Jack C. Introduction to *The Life of Jesus*, by Schleiermacher. Philadelphia: Fortress Press, 1975.
Vida, E.M. *Romantic Affinities: German Authors and Carlyle: A Study in the History of Ideas*. Toronto: University of Toronto Press, 1993.
Wallace, Stuart. *War and the Image of Germany: British Academics, 1914–1918*. Edinburgh: John Donald, 1988.

Walshe, Maire Josephine. "The Life and Works of Wilhelmine von Hillern, 1836–1916." PhD dissertation, State University of New York at Buffalo, 1988.

Ward, Mrs Humphry (Mary Augusta). *The History of David Grieve*. 9th ed. London: Smith, Elder, 1893.

– *Marcella*. London: Smith, Elder, 1894.

– *The Marriage of William Ashe*. London: Smith, Elder, 1905.

– *Robert Elsmere*. Edited by Clyde de L. Ryals. Lincoln: University of Nebraska Press, 1967.

– *A Writer's Recollections*. London: W. Collins Sons, 1918.

Ward, W.R. "Faith and Fallacy: English and German Perspectives in the Nineteenth Century." In *Victorian Faith in Crisis: Essays on Continuity and Change in Nineteenth-Century Religious Belief*, edited by Richard J. Helmstadter and Bernard Lightman, 39–67. London: Macmillan, 1990.

Watt, Ian. *Conrad in the Nineteenth Century*. Berkeley: University of California Press, 1979.

– "The Political and Social Background of *The Secret Agent*." In *Conrad, The Secret Agent: A Casebook*, edited by Ian Watt, 229–51. London: Macmillan, 1973.

– ed. *Conrad, The Secret Agent: A Casebook*. London: Macmillan, 1973.

Waugh, Evelyn. *Put Out More Flags*. London: Chapman and Hall, 1948.

– *Sword of Honour: Men at Arms (1952); Officers and Gentlemen (1955); The End of the Battle (1962)*. Boston: Little, Brown, 1962.

Weisz, Paul B. *The Science of Biology*. 2nd ed. New York: McGraw Hill, 1963.

Wellek, René. "Carlyle and German Romanticism." In *Confrontations: Studies in the Intellectual Relations between Germany, England, and the United States in the Nineteenth Century*, 34–81. Princeton: Princeton University Press, 1965.

Wells, H.G. *The Island of Doctor Moreau*. London: Heinemann, 1960.

– *Mr. Britling Sees It Through*. New York: Macmillan, 1916.

Wheeler, Michael. *The Art of Allusion in Victorian Fiction*. London: Macmillan, 1979.

Wilde, Alan, ed. *Critical Essays on E.M. Forster*. Boston: G.K. Hall, 1985.

Wilde, Oscar. *Intentions* and *The Soul of Man*. Vol. 8, *The First Collected Edition of the Works of Oscar Wilde, 1908–1922*. Edited by Robert Ross. London: Dawsons of Pall Mall, 1969.

Wilding, Michael. *Social Visions*. Sydney: Sydney Association for Studies in Society and Culture, 1993.

Willey, Basil. *Nineteenth-Century Studies*. New York: Columbia University Press, 1949.

Williams, Raymond. *Culture and Society, 1780–1950*. Harmondsworth: Penguin, 1961.

Williams, Rowland. "Bunsen's Biblical Researches." In *Essays and Reviews*, 50–93. London: John W. Parker and Son, 1860.

Wilt, Judith. *The Readable People of George Meredith*. New Jersey: Princeton University Press, 1975.

Witemeyer, Hugh. *George Eliot and the Visual Arts*. New Haven: Yale University Press, 1979.

– "George Eliot, Naumann, and the Nazarenes." *Victorian Studies* 18 (December 1974): 149–58.

Wollaeger, Mark A. *Joseph Conrad and the Fictions of Skepticism*. Stanford: Stanford University Press, 1990.

Wolff, Robert Lee. *Gains and Losses: Novels of Faith and Doubt in Victorian England*. New York: Garland, 1977.

Woolf, Virginia. "The Novels of George Meredith." 1928. In *Collected Essays*, 1: 224–32. New York: Harcourt, Brace, 1967.

Yonge, Charlotte M. *The Clever Woman of the Family*. New York: Garland, 1975.

Yuill, W.E. "Tradition and Nightmare: Some Reflections on the Postwar Novel in England and Germany." In *Affinities: Essays in German and English Literature*, edited by R.W. Last, 154–67. London: Oswald Wolff, 1971.

Zipser, Richard A. *Edward Bulwer-Lytton and Germany*. Berne: Herbert Lang, 1974.

Zoll, Allan R. "Vitalism and the Metaphysics of Love: D.H. Lawrence and Schopenhauer." *D.H. Lawrence Review* 11, no. 1 (spring 1978): 1–20.

Illustration Credits

"The Water Cure" and "Schlafen Sie Wohl." William Makepeace Thackeray, "The Kickleburys on the Rhine," *The Christmas Books of Mr. M.A. Titmarsh*, The Works of William Makepeace Thackeray (New York: AMS Press, 1968), 13: oppos. 222 and 238.

"Things One Would Rather Have Left Unsaid." *Punch* 91 (2 October 1886): 166.

"Advantages of a Foreign Education." *Punch* 92 (16 April 1887): 186.

"Music at Home." *Punch* 88 (9 December 1884): n.p. [start of vol.].

Georg Brandes and G.B. Shaw. Max Beerbohm, *Beerbohm's Literary Caricatures.*

"Why We Have No Supermen like the Germans?" *Punch* 147 (21 October 1914): 337.

"Of Course Berlin Will Now Set the Fashions – *vice* Paris." *Punch* 60 (11 February 1871): 62.

"The Triumph of 'Culture.'" *Punch* 147 (26 August 1914): 185.

Index

Eliot, 69; Nietzsche on, 216n23. *See also* Tübingen higher criticism
Sturm und Drang (Storm and Stress), 6, 15, 46, 52

Tendenzroman (*roman à thèse*), 7, 178, 184; and crisis-of-faith novel, 104, 109–10, 121, 125
Tennyson, Alfred, 1st Baron Tennyson, 61, 107, 109–10, 112, 122; and *Bildung*, 195n71
Thackeray, William Makepeace, 3, 6, 43–4, 46, 85, 162; *Vanity Fair*, 3, 64, 102, 162
Thomas, D.M., 181
Tieck, Ludwig, 14, 25, 28, 78
Trollope, Anthony, 55, 105, 107, 163
Tübingen higher criticism, 11, 104–25, 183. *See also* crisis-of-faith novel, Strauss
Turgenev, Ivan, 57, 65, 85, 90, 106, 168
"two Germanys," the, 160–1, 169–71, 173, 178–9, 183

University College London, 24

Varnhagen von Ense, Karl August, 99
"Volk der Dichter und Denker" (nation of poets and thinkers), 44, 46, 158
Vormärz (pre-1848), 44, 125

Wagner, Richard, 162, 173, 219n73. *See also* Eliot, Nietzsche, Schopenhauer
Ward, Mrs Humphry, 9, 11, 117, 125, 183; and Arnold, 121, 123–4; and *Bildung, Bildungsroman*, 121, 124; and higher criticism, 110–11, 117–18, 121–5, 183; and Nietzsche, 132; and Prussia, 156, 158; and Schopenhauer, 132; and *Tendenzroman*, 121, 125. *See also* crisis-of-faith novel
watering place, spa, 4, 84–7, 172, 174
Waugh, Evelyn, 180–1

Weimar, 64, 124; Goethe's, 6, 12, 39, 41, 77, 162, 182–3. *See also* Eliot
Weimar Republic, 11, 161–3, 175–9, 183
Wells, H.G., 133–4, 174–5
Westminster Review, 9, 69, 89, 116, 128
Wilde, Oscar, 121, 161
Wilhelmine, 25, 27, 161–2. *See also* kaiser, Reich
Wissenschaft (science, scholarship), 23–4, 81–4, 99, 106–7. *See also* *Historismus*, Tübingen higher criticism
Wordsworth, William, 15, 52, 59, 110, 116; and Eliot, 70, 102
World War I, 56, 158–61, 163, 170–5; as "Euro-Nietzschean War," 160. *See also* Conrad, Ford, Lawrence
World War II, 11, 170, 180–2

Yonge, Charlotte, 117–18